Nissequott

A New Directions Book

Grateful acknowledgment is made to the following for permission to reprint song lyrics: "As Time Goes By," by Herman Hupfeld, © 1931 (Renewed), Warner Bros. Inc.; all rights reserved; used by permission. "Little Child," words and music by John Lennon and Paul McCartney, © Copyright 1963, 1964 by Northern Songs; all rights controlled and administered by MCA Music Publishing, a division of MCA Inc., New York, New York 10019, under license from Northern Songs; used by permission; international copyright secured; all rights reserved. "Till There Was You" from "The Music Man" by Meredith Willson, © 1950, 1957 (Renewed) Frank Music Corp. and Meredith Willson Music; all rights reserved; used by permission. "To Sir, with Love" by Don Black and Marc London, © 1967 by Screen Gems-EMI Music Inc.; all rights reserved; international copyright secured; used by permission. The McDonald's advertising jingle is used by permission of McDonald's Corporation.

Author's Note: This book was written with support from the Virginia Center for Creative arts, for which I am grateful.

Book design by Sylvia Frezzolini
Manufactured in the United States of America
New Directions Books are printed on acid-free paper
First published clothbound in 1992
Published simultaneously in Canada by Penguin Books Canada Limited

Library of Congress Cataloging-in-Publication Data
Dawe, Margaret, 1957–
Nissequott / Margaret Dawe.
p.   cm.
ISBN 0-8112-1202-5 (alk. paper)
I. Title.
PS3554.A942N57   1992
813'.54—dc20   91-44444
                                                                              CIP

New Directions Books are published for James Laughlin
by New Directions Publishing Corporation,
80 Eighth Avenue, New York 10011

Nissequott

(NISS-a-kwat)

from the Massachusetts pissaqua,
means "the clay or mud country"
where the Indians went to obtain
material to make their pottery.

*The Indian Place-Names on Long Island
and Islands Adjacent*
BY WILLIAM WALLACE TOOKER

for my Mother and my Father,
with love

_____

The Long Island Railroad ran through our backyard crossed into my window over my black oval rug ran into my mirror crossing back out again circling round my black oval rug out through my window, in and out like the E train as Ma would say, waking me up in time to see the cows milked. It was on Channel 11 at six o'clock. Either that or cutting the wheat. The wheat falls, the wheat falls. You wonder why you're so interested. The blade, the blade, the blade. I loved the Lucy where she's working in the chocolate factory, stuffing bonbons in her mouth, trying to keep up with that black conveyor belt. SPEED IT UP, the very mean boss lady says, like my lady every Sunday at the bakery wrap wrapping knot tight string around our box of buns.

This is the story of my face.

First thing was the train whistle at a distance off then the train engine, closer and closer, jittering us more and more so that little by little everything in our house began to shake, clothes hanging without bodies, our six toothbrushes and our plants—real in sun and dirt and water and fake in dry dark—all thwapping in their containers, and the textbooks Ma stole from Andrew Jackson High in Queens covered in geometric material to match the curtains, and all of Ma's colognes she got every Christmas and June from her kids tip tapped alive on shelves, like in a certain favorite cartoon about a lady wristwatch come alive, and all our utensils lay shaking separated in their drawer, the knives from the forks from the spoons, shaking stainlessly on their backs and all

1

the five human rest of them asleep in their white sheets went on breathing in and out, their lungs slightly blowing back and forth and me I jumped out fast, trying not to flatten too much the uplifted nap on my black oval rug that Ma had just vacuumed beautifully for me, fast jumping while the train went by to watch in my wall mirror, who's the fairest?, to see was there a difference with a blurry shaking movement face. Was it better?

Doesn't that bother you? people said about the train. We don't even hear it, we said. Or better yet was sitting outside with someone innocent, watching the facial confusion grow as the roaring grew closer and you sat calmly with your legs lightly crossed, one leg swinging, an actress say in a tight 1940s secretarial skirt, or say it is December 7, 1941, and you are Ma throwing a football and midair it disappears, caught by Pop, just back from Mass, The Japs just bombed us, and the invisible planes went on through. Ever since I was born we had the Vietnam War. And the train was gone. Silence. The mirror picture of my face again held still, too bad.

I leapt over our little deformed black kitten, waiting for me every morning.

—Uuuuuuowwww.

That little black kitten's paddy footsteps came desperate behind. Down the stairs, split level (something one day I hoped to learn the true meaning of) to Colonial, as they put it at Newmark and Lewis, with an eagle over the fireplace and couch illustrations of the Revolutionary War, where often I looked near John Hancock's for one of the smaller ones supposedly a relative of Joyce's. When we first moved to Nissequott we had no couch. We were sitting on green and white webbed beach chairs watching President Kennedy loaded in the ambulance. It was day in Texas then night. We were sitting on laps. He got shot in the afternoon. Was this a regular part of history or not? Was it regular for the President to get shot? Pop called from Queens. Mother of God, Mother of God, for the sake of all the Irish. Then Ma and I were hanging out the wash, that long long white rope looping between us. Aunt Rita flew over sobbing into her turned up hands, just a distant lady then, Mrs. Hanrahan, like a neighbor in a Tide commercial.

—Jack is dead, Jack is dead.

And Jack had four letters and dead had four letters and Dad was named Jack but Dad was alive walking up and down those long empty haunted speckled Nissequott School hall floors, dismissing early for tragedy.

—Uuuuuuowwww, our deformed kitten went.

Mrs. Hanrahan sobbed. Stop with the hysterics, Rita, would you, Ma said. Christ. I was pulling out a long white sheet twisted and twisted into a funnel from their double bed.

—How can you be so cold? Don't you feel anything, Mary?

—Uh, I said, pulling it.

I pulled the on-off out for the usual empty hum. Back! I pushed that deformed cat away. I heard the Hanrahans' color one came on right away.

Then Ma and I were alone. It was a beautiful day, November 22, 1963, Ma and I alone because I got dismissed early and the white wash whap flapped on the long long white rope, green cross to green cross, whap: sun, blue. Possibly I was prettier then.

—Back! I pushed, avoiding that disgusting tail wound. I sat on our Colonial rag rug. The center white dot, then off, and, like a lady behind a sexy bendable wall throwing underwear pieces over the top, in its dark privacy our television got dressed. My face gray greenish bulged worried in the off screen and heavier and heavier its bad parts grew until thanks be to God the cows came. Cows were mainly anyway black and white and the milk bottles clear and the milk white and their tools stainless steel and black conveyor belt.

—Kitty! Okay, okay, already, but I'm only doing this

during the agriculture. I rubbed and rubbed the kitty's skull, strategy to keep the tail wound away. I just didn't want her dried blood to smear across me. Her tail, if it was a her, her tail fell off yesterday but it'd been hanging on by threads for days.

—He's still alive, one announcer said. But the other said no, President John Fitzgerald Kennedy got shot in the head. You can see the bloodstains on Mrs. Kennedy's dress.

The milk ran separated into bottles. I loved the pouring always to the same level. The bottles (pet pet pet) came down lined on their black conveyor belt. Pull down your pants, Ma said. She slammed a window. Oh. The neighbors and the screams. Then she went along the three older of us, just with her hand and it's smartest to act hurt because then they stop sooner. (Pet pet pet.) When that little black kitten first came to our back door she was a stray with a tail, mewing for milk. Little by little that tail got chopped from her standing undecided as our storm door closed, heavier now with the winter window in.

I held the storm door open for Dad, finally going to the bakery. All the trees were brown, some with slight buds, and our purple crocus bloomed since Ma's birthday near our back stoop.

—Is that a new jacket, babe?
—Yup. I just ordered it from Sears.
—That's nice, Dad said.
We passed the wall he built out of slates.
Dad said, What's it made out of, babe?
—I think canvas.
—That's nice. Let me see that.
Dad touched the grain of my sleeve.
—I got to get a jacket like that.
—I don't think they would make white for men, Dad. I dropped my arm and walked. Unfortunately, I said, it only has one pocket, but otherwise I would recommend it. They have any good food last night?

4

We passed our pile of loose rocks and floating down our driveway was Dad's first rock wall, falling at the bottom because of rain, because Dad built first with mud and after, when he built useless rock walls like pyramids Ma ordered for decoration in the middle of grass, then Dad used cement and they would never fall.

—They had some sweet and sour meatballs, Dad said.

—Sweet and sour. Not Swedish!

Dad released our emergency brake and we slid, loosened, backwards, down. Once Joyce had a birthday party at the Chinese restaurant in Port Sands and we had sweet and sour pork and it was so good.

—To reform the world monetary program, the radio said. Prosperity.

Our rock wall slid straight up into the air. Last night I went rushing awake, all the sound coming from everywhere, driving up, and your heart's in a total state, the headlights rushing at my closet, off. Slam, slam, their doors. Our big tree at the driveway top had no leaves, the lilac, no leaves, and in the moonlight those rocks looked like bare toes. Below me their dark man and woman figures moved and the click clacking of Ma's high heels past Dad's loosely made slate. Tap tap tap. I heard those heels above me during Superman, that tap tap high heeled cocktail party sound, of Ma crossing back and forth to get ready.

—Nail polish? I said.

Ma had on her black cocktail party dress and her gold bird pin and gold bird earrings, screw ons, sitting near our red brick kitchen wall that Dad put up with black mortar and our yellow kitchen light, sitting at her end with the emery boards, nail polish remover, her box of Red Cross cotton and her polish, tomato red. Ma sat thinking very hard, making herself more and more beautiful, stopping now and then to carefully lift her white cigarette with her glistening red wet ends. When I was little I had an operation that I couldn't remember but I still had the dangling red scar. Then my second cousin had a nose job. Ooo, Rosie, you look fab, Ma said. Dad swung us out backwards leveling us, sliding backwards, braking, moving forward on our asphalt blue road. When Lucy's in that factory she has to swirl each wet brown bonbon exactly the same. I knew from the first ten seconds what the whole plot would be, every show getting closer to the end in Connecticut and you can just feel the tension in their living room rock wall fireplace, pow, the whole show ends, and they switch it back to the beginning again in New York before Little Ricky is born, then California, Florida, Italy, Connecticut and it all starts black and white over again, never telling you the truth: Lucy and Ricky in real life got a divorce.

—Arsonists using Molotov cocktails, the radio said, interrupted shopping at Bloomingdale's and S. Klein department stores on one of—

—Yellow crocuses, Dad.

—In Saigon a second swing-wing F-111A fighter bomber crashed yesterday.

Dad braked.

—Nine marines were reported killed, the radio said.

—Well, babe, what should I make for your birthday?

And across those two vicious german shepherds came tearing with their fangs toward that very low fence.

—Chicken, I said.

(—Jesus, Ma said, you're white as a ghost. I'll take care of those dogs, and Ma marched down throwing rocks left and right.)

—What kind? Dad said.

—About a mile from the demilitarized zone.

—Oh, I don't care.

—What else?

—Mashed patooties and string beans almondine.

—String beans almondine! Dad yelled.

Dad stopped at the light. Our town Indian was not

standing near his telephone pole. Probably he did not go to church either.

—President Johnson will address the nation tonight at 9 p.m. eastern standard time.

—Dad, you know the dead, the wounded, and the missing in action?

—Yeah. Dad swung us left past possibly the Methodist Church, this distant sense of Protestants.

—What if you're wounded one day and you die the next?

Past Esso, past our two town billboards, Arrow Termite, a bull's eye, and Centreville Rug Works, rolled carpets in that same circling design.

—I don't know, babe.

Blinka blinka, waiting to go left into Hills. I remembered Nissequott even before we had Hills, and across unfortunately they were all emptying out of Mass. St. Joseph R.C. and R.C. was also a soda, medium priced compared to C&C, cheapo, Pepsi-Coke the best, that rich people drank. I had no idea what R.C. stood for because I only went to catechism once. They said, You don't know how Jesus Christ is related to God?

(—Dominus dominus dominus, said the priest who was also the father but not the main Father, Our Father Who Art in Heaven.

—What, babe? Dad leaned toward me in the pew. Dad and I were not allowed to talk.

—My foot feels funny.

—Shake it, Dad said. It's asleep.

—Asleep!

I was swinging it under the pew, sitting near my father while the father passed under the red and blue sainted windows swinging his ball and chain puffing holy smoke, like clearing out an Etch-a-Sketch, lead beads inside your skin.)

—Two quarters today, Dad. Don't forget.

Dad parked illegally in the fire zone and shut our engine off. TOW AWAY. I ran. They're standing, jingling, in good clothes and derbies from church, jingling, watching you in your sneakers and pants on Sunday, jingling, and hand to hand to hand passed the collection basket, jingling, which you did not today throw money in. And they all furthermore since they went to confession got to buy the Daily News with Dick Tracy, his skin extremely hard black-edged carrying always some wristwatch mystery which one day I really hoped to solve, getting also all the great Daily News headlines like once that giant black headline all day lying on the hassock at Grandma and Grandpa's in Queens, circling around and around it, all day eating sweet miniature gherkins with all your relatives in good clothes, circling around, around, with the three younger ones, around and around the block in Queens in your eight good shoes, centipede, meanwhile lying there all day in giant black you're dying for five minutes alone in the bathroom with: TWO TOTS SLAIN, MOM HELD.

—Chop chop, Ma said. I want you guys to finish those buns and get your sneaks on.

—What for? I said.

The four of us stopped in our jellies mid-chew.

Ma tossed her breakfast chicken leg in the garbage. We're going to get rocks, she said.

—No way, Annie screamed.

I said, You said only Saturday.

—Done and done. I don't want to hear it. Ma left with her Comet headed down the hall.

—Dad, Annie said.

—Your ma-ma wants to get that wall done, guys. Robert, give me a little bite of that crumb bun, huh, bud?

—Little. He held it cautiously near Dad's mouth.

I had this immediate nightmare instead of rocks we would find that little black kitten's tail, like a sin. They had catechism in the basement of the Nissequott Fire Department with those basement windows above to let in the light and workbooks with supposedly God's picture at the top of one page, His head coming out of the clouds and light rays beaming out.

Ma had the beaters on, circling the blurry silver around and around inside her giant brown bowl, Elsie the Cow brown like I remembered earlier before we moved to Nissequott the milkman, bam, shutting your silver box. It was Saturday morning, fifteen before catechism using our red Scotch plaid clock, our first clock for Goldwater, Bomb 'em back to the Stone Age, who our neighbor the pediatrician was for.

—Ma!

Ma shut the beaters off. Excuse me. She got the vanilla and fast I handed her the measuring spoons on their little chain. For babies they gave you the oversized plastic keys on a chain that you could bang bang bang on your feeding tray.

—Could I measure it?

—Thank you but no. I have to get this done. Ma took the measuring spoons from my hand, four in size order like the four of us.

—Ma, you don't have to drive me to catechism this week or anymore.

—Okay. She dashed the liquid in her bowl.

I said, Don't you want to know why?

—Excuse me.

—Oh, I said, I forgot pound cake uses lemon extract too.

And she measured again in her silver spoon, dashing in, while I sniffed until she took the bottle away from me. I jumped, holding up on the counter by my shaking straightened elbows: brown liquid lying up and down upon the batter, not mixing, and the lemon extract colorless, the batter yellow gold with smooths and folds and dips which

9

you could always keep changing the shape of. I dropped back down to the floor.

—Could I get the eggs? I yelled.

Ma circled the beaters through the yellow wet. Her orange dot preheat oven light clicked off.

—Ma, could I get the eggs?

—I'll get them. That's all I need is broken eggs on the floor. She set the beaters and slowly, gathering its force, the yellow batter dripped. Ma smashed a knife into the shell.

I said, I'm not going because I know it's a pain for you to drive and second because then I miss Rocky and Bullwinkle's Fractured Fairy Tales.

Ma threw the shells on top of their cigarettes and coffee grinds and smashed the knife through the second one. The Fractured Fairy Tale's moral wasn't real but it was the best I could get for trying to learn the difference between good and bad. Ma hated the Catholic Church with a pash. Who's the Son of God? they said. I said, I don't know, who? I was interested. Like I knew about the angels. The angels were in the air, don't ask me how. I did not know exactly who Jesus was. They're all staring: You don't know who's the Son of God? They all looked at me because I made one mistake. Plop. Then the two eggs are out of their shells whole, waiting to be destroyed. I figured Ma would like me a lot more for not going to catechism.

—Ma, could you save me the bowl?

—Yes. Ma went on smoothly turning in the raw.

All those little brown bakery buns lay sleeping, resting after their formation trauma, inside their glass. I was never in an incubator because I was normal when I was born, but my second cousin got put in one with too much oxygen and for the rest of her life she was blind. What a goddamn shame, Ma said. I thought, imagine that, never seeing your face. Every Sunday at the bakery ordering was your deformed little face staring back all around the cash register mirror.

Every Sunday at the bakery was my same blue dressed Nazi bakery lady. Four jelly, four crumb, four cheese, four twisters (You mean crullers. Yeah, twisters.) and a large loaf of rye sliced with seeds, and she pulled the long white string from that gold ceiling ball, wrapping, snap, with her bare flesh breaking it, and slid the box across the glass. Yes?, talking over me, like suddenly I did not exist any more.

I got the Fractured Fairy Tale's moral and shut it off. I rose up our stairs like in a dream: our white counter empty with no brown bowl. I pulled up to my waist. You keep your shaking elbows straight. The bowl was in the sink filled with white soapy water. Pop, a bubble burst. I dropped back down to the floor. The first thing in my life I remembered was standing in a crib with a white guardrail holding on in the hospital above the floor. The second thing was drinking shampoo. I said, Ma, can I have some apple juice? and I drank from the cup left on the counter edge, convenient where a kid could reach, Breck's actually very similar in color, golden brown, tilting toward your mouth, thickerish, with a just washed smell.

—Move it, people. Ma came behind us down the stairs.
We six slid backwards down, our rock wall made with mud rising, meanwhile at the driveway top, atop that wall made with cement, our little black kitten paced, her behind held up, strung, like she still had a puppet tail.
—Annie, do you still have your shoebox from the beginning of the school year?
—You can't have it.
Dad stopped, all of us hanging pointed up in the air. Anything coming? he said.
—No, Annie said, always trying to talk to Dad.
—Only a cement truck, Michael said.
Dad raised one eyebrow and swung us out backwards, then leveling the six of us with our mailbox.

—You don't even know what it's for, Annie. It's for a good cause.

The shoebox was to bury the tail.

—King planning a Poor People's Campaign in Washington next month. Meanwhile in Memphis striking sanitationmen are awaiting Reverend King's arrival.

—Must you, Michael said, because Ma had changed it to music singing in her sexy saxophone voice as Dad braked us and those two german shepherds tore out. What the world needs now is love sweet love. Ma had a terrible voice, but she tried hard. And Dad stepped on it because that was a bad curve, and we all flung six around inside the station wagon, whoa whoa, flinging extra flesh and bones rolling into each other and Robert's bones rolled all alone in the flat back and I fast turned keeping my eye on those yellow crocuses until, under the train trestle, the yellow dots disappeared.

I said, You know the kitten's tail fell off, you guys.

—I don't want to hear it, Ma said.

I put my head against the glass, cold, the end of March. I had this really bad pain in my throat and under all my face, the whole facial structure hurt. I kept my head against the glass and you can feel vibrating through you the exact bumping of the road, rolling along in your family's powder blue station wagon. Actually we really weren't the kind of family that would take our pet to the vet's anyway.

—Okay, guys. Ma slammed her door and threw her cigarette down and twisted it with her sneaker into the mud.

—How many each? I said.

—Ten.

—Ten! we said. Ma walked off. She had on her ridiculous bermudas in the way too cold. I looked at Dad. I said, She is such a slave driver. Dad smiled. He ping flicked his cigarette off and strode out across the land.

Tanglewood Section 2 Coming Soon, it said across the road in front of gray unbloomed trees, those woods still standing, and through the wintry bare gray branch net was the mass solid outlines below of a giant granite rock next to a house.

I turned and walked up onto the vast brown land, amazingly no other families out on a Sunday looking for rocks. All the trees were gone. Dirt as far as the eye could see until the woods at the end where the bulldozers left piles of broken knocked trees. I was sinking a little in the mud. I remembered so many cartoons of quicksand.

—Hello, Ma. I clapped my drier dirt off with energy.

—Uh. Ma heaved a giant one and it crashed, that depth depth crashing of stone upon stone, crashing inches from Robert who flinched and went on rolling Matchbox cars up up and down the seat back cushion bumps and in a low voice, one car bobbing like a head: Let's drive to the store and park.

—Fancy meeting you here, I said to Ma.

—Christ, this is a lot of work.

—I know, but we're almost done. I patted her, everything dirty anyway, and went cheerily off looking for Five. They can't be too big or otherwise you could not carry it alone, forget it Annie and me trying to cooperate, though sometimes Dad got big ones for the bottom row, totally bent, ugh ugh, man alive, heaving it, phew, up went dust, really shaking Robert and the station wagon. And the best, getting near the top, Okay guys, Dad said, we need some flats. You got to specialize. Dad, Dad, is this flat enough? Very rarely, one in fifteen, grayish possibly igneous with what you pretend are glittering jewels inside, very rarely would one be the perfect flat, make the best of it.

I bent and dug. My sneaks were totally in mud. Then it was fun to let them dry and sitting on the back stoop near your friendly crocus scrape them with a knife. This looked like a normal brown rock but you could never tell. I clawed up the ground. Luckily today the ground was wet and luckily today I did not have a manicure. I wanted to bury that tail so we could have a Catholic religious ceremony. I could steal some of Ma's black thread and tie two sticks making a pathetic homemade cross like living on the frontier, make the best of it. Joyce and I buried a shoebox of mementos before she moved, but I had this feeling the bulldozer that dug our pool might have demolished it.

—Sheila!

I threw Eight close enough to terrify Robert.

—Sheila!

Seagulls dipped above us in the robin's egg sky. Joyce actually found robin's eggs once which meant their mother would never come back.

—Sheila!

Annie was at the top flapping her arms, her striped bellbottoms flapping below. Why she wore her good pants to get rocks was beyond me.

—We found a really big one, Annie said and Michael knelt clawing at mud. Joyce and I buried mementos for the bloodsister ceremony. I heard the Indians slit their wrist with a knife and pressed together to mix their blood, but since I did not want to get fooled into committing suicide I took Aunt Rita's suggestion and simply mixed through fingertip holes, sterilizing the silver needle to charred black first with a match. Annie, Michael, and I were digging, loosening that rock with our hands, outlining the edge, bigger and bigger, meanwhile those black moons of dirt really growing under our nails.

—Kids! Ma's voice came broken chopped in the almost April wind. Kids! Come on! We're going! Ma waved way below across the empty brown standing near that strangely dropped baby blue puff of car, Ma waving her brown hands and below, holding her up, were her bare flesh legs. So we had to leave it there, still covered.

Chapter 2

*A*unt Rita stood on her patio ironing, connected by an extension cord slipped out the bottom of her dining room window. We just got off prison duty washing rocks, Dad with the hose and the thrill of turning it on its back, he sprays. Washing rocks in March is like teeth breaking off it's so cold.

The Hanrahans built all their walls out of railroad ties and their steps ended in uniform white gravel they ordered delivered. I stepped down and held out my new sleeve. I said, It's machine washable. Aunt Rita touched it. She had clear nail polish today, stones in a pond. I said, Thank God since it's white.

Aunt Rita picked up her brown quart bottle of Rheingold and tilted her glass to pour, her glass part clear strips, part frost white with autumn leaves cut in, changing as you drank. I sat on her stoop, concrete. We had slate covering ours to match our patio, not the shiny blue black slate like at Joyce's or what used to be Joyce's, but ours a dull no shine granite and without white mortar but fit tightly like a puzzle by Dad, meanwhile the Hanrahans had simple poured concrete, kidney shaped that the workers had shaped with outer molding three days, and drew scalloping in with a stick when still partly wet, a process I wished and I did not wish I could have seen. For my operation they broke my cartilage and re-formed it, basically re-molding me from a hunchback.

—It's very becoming, Aunt Rita said.

I blushed. She lifted her beer and drank. Once last year Aunt Rita told me I looked good in yellow. I was like jumping up and down, swinging from the trees. I said, Ma, Aunt Rita says I look good in yellow. My heart was pounding, my breath was rasping. Ma just snorted and went on raking around the juniper roots with her little metal claw. Either she was snorting because I could not ever look good or snorting because Aunt Rita's colors were so bad, a redhead should not wear green, and if it was just the color's bad then I could still have a chance, just don't wear yellow. Maybe it was because Ma thought yellow was exactly wrong.

—Well, Happy April Fool's Day eve, Aunt Rita.

—Thank you. And it's almost your birthday. Eleven. She smiled.

When she smiled it felt like swimming inside something wonderful that was always going to last.

She said, Too young for boys and too old for dolls.

—Well, I said. The white gravel was spread like a fan. I never really thought of myself with boys since my face was so bad. She still smiled at me. Well, I said again, it's not a big one anyway. I'm used to the double digits though it will be nice having the digits the same.

Aunt Rita pulled a cigarette out of her snap-top case and picked her silver lighter up. Ma would never use a snap case and she just used matches from Hills. Flick flick. Aunt Rita turned that little silver wheel. I had this terrible feeling he had a matching one and they got them for a wedding present and they were engraved. She leaned in with her mouth, aiming at the flame. She snapped it shut and wedged her cigarette inside the opened beak of her poor silver stork ashtray and through the March light blue that butane smell sifted, like angels.

—Aunt Rita, do you happen to have an extra shoebox?

The storm door shot open behind me and I jumped.

—Noivous Nellie, he said.

I laughed the minimum. Once he called me Madge like the Palmolive dishwashing liquid (you mean my hands have been soaking in dishwashing liquid the whole time) which I really did not know was that real or a joke since he went to a psychiatrist. He had his gun stuck in his belt and he stood over me pouring Rheingold, like I was supposed to be getting it on the head.

Aunt Rita picked the iron up and it flashed silver, clump. She ironed the inside collar flat. Clouds were creeping over us toward the railroad tracks. She moved the iron up his sleeve, down, the liquid pouring over me.

—Honey, do you still have that box from your oxfords? She flipped the shirt, ran up the sleeve, down, her wedding and engagement rings glittering.

—How the hell should I know?

—I thought Oxford was in England, I said.

She flipped and ran wrongside up the buttonholes. It's also a kind of men's shoe, she said. Flip. Up rightside.

—Ach, he said. I could sense him pouring more.

Up wrongside the buttonbacks bump bump bump bump.

—Sheila, I'll run in and find that shoebox. Flip.

—Oh, don't worry.

Down rightside, the buttons, running the iron in and out. I also made you some lime Jell-O, she said.

I smiled. Ever since I told Aunt Rita lime Jell-O was my worst flavor it was the only kind she made for me.

She ran it up and down his front and all over his back. She hung it on a hanger and he burped. I sat facing forward, that feeling behind me of the two of them exchanging things. Next door Ma dumped a bucket of Miracle Gro.

—Bring me another, he said. The storm door hissed. What's the old man up to, building that rock wall?

I had to twist around backwards, looking up. No, I said. You could see the comb marks still in his hair. He's resting and fertilizing the bushes with my mother.

—Ho ho. He raised his eyebrows. I glanced off, like looking inside her.

Their storm door was more glass than ours, glass on the top and the bottom and aluminum scrollwork across the waist and you really had to bend over to knock. I knocked one time. Is Aunt Rita home? Yes. He's standing smiling smiling. He's standing at the door looking at me. I said, Can I see her? Oh, he says, you want to see her. I thought you just wanted to know if she was home. I thought well, I would never try a stupid joke like that so at least I'll never have to go to a psychiatrist.

—Fertilizing the bushes, huh? He came around stepping on the concrete in his black extremely pointed shoes next to my behind. Anyone else would just wear sneakers on Sunday. He set his beer glass next to me and pulled his gun out. He cracked it open in half and looked in. He had on tan pants, black shoes, a white T-shirt, a V-neck sweater, the Vitalis smelling a mile away. I'm just sitting there, la la la.

—I never knew the guy who played Spanky got the electric chair. I said, Maybe he only kidnapped someone.

—Does this look like a rose? Aunt Rita had pink painted fingernails holding a cut up red and white radish which looked like a stubbed toe to me. It was Thursday, two days after my birthday, peacefully sucking Kool-aid through a flexible red and white striped straw, about three hours before Martin Luther King Junior got shot.

—How about slices, I said. Slices are nice.

—I need it to look like his eyes. Aunt Rita leaned back over her Better Homes and Gardens Cookbook. I had this distinct feeling Aunt Rita never went to college. She said, Maybe I'm starting at the wrong end. By the way you know who else got the electric chair? Superman.

—George Reeves?

—George Reeves is right.

I said, George Reeves killed someone? I said, God Aunt Rita, do you remember that one where Superman saves the guy from the electric chair? They do a close-up on his arm stuck inside the switch that the warden just pulled? I said, He killed someone? I wonder why he killed someone.

—Who?

—Well, both. Spanky and Superman.

—Who can understand passion, Sheila?

I blushed. Ma would never mention passion out loud. I gripped my feet around the barstool rungs. Ma said once, Don't you think Mr. Hanrahan is handsome? Her ironing board groaned, squeaking. Don't you think he looks like Montgomery Clift? Clump, clump, back and forth. I said, Montgomery who? Ma yelled, YOU DON'T KNOW MONTGOMERY CLIFT? She's leaning over the ironing board like this is a crime.

—It's a lot of pressure being in front of the camera all the time, Aunt Rita said. You pay a price for fame.

—How much?

—I mean you pay a toll.

Toll, toll, my blood tolled. Dad worked on the toll bridge to Fire Island once. Come on, come on. He waved our car through free.

I said, Do not ask for whom the bell tolls. It tolls for you. I bent and sucked again.

—You know who else paid a price for fame? Aunt Rita tilted her glass pouring more. Marilyn Monroe.

—What price?

—She died.

—She died? I stared at her. I said, Marilyn Monroe died? Are you kidding?

—She's been dead four or five years now. She died of a drug overdose.

I said, I didn't know Marilyn Monroe was dead.

Aunt Rita peeled a carrot into the sink. I felt like bursting out in tears. It felt like it was going out of control. Marilyn Monroe was one of my favorite people. She was so beautiful. I had no idea she was dead. I remembered her on a Saturday night movie riding a train to Florida. I was just walking down Two Mile Hollow and a field there reminded me of her. I thought we were both alive together, her in Holly-

wood and me thinking about her now and then in Nissequott.

—More Kool-aid?

I held up my hand. Aunt Rita scraped another carrot into
the sink. You might as well do it straight into the garbage and
save some work.

I said, How did she die?

—A drug overdose. Aunt Rita looked at me.

I sucked and let it drop. I felt like climbing down off my
stool and lying on the linoleum. Outside, the train came
from the dining room end of Port Sands, the beginning.
Through the storm door was their red and white striped
swingset Mr. Hanrahan built for his daughter Irene. Adults
meant well by the red and white candy cane but to me it
looked like bandages. It was supposed to rain tonight. Aunt
Rita scraped along making carrot curls for the hair.

—Well, I said, you don't even have to be famous to get
killed. Remember those eight nurses in Chicago?

—Oh. Aunt Rita gasped. That was awful.

—Yeah, I'll never forget that. Remember it was summer.
They were all in their rooms reading and this jerk comes in.

—Richard Speck.

—Richard Speck. I spit the name out. You know Aunt
Rita how the one survived? What would you do if you were
tied up and left in a room and he went to the other room to
kill them first?

Aunt Rita laughed, putting her cigarette in her mouth.

—What one nurse did.

I stopped.

—I'm sorry to laugh. She came forward, the smoke
trailing off. You are the most serious girl. Her hands were
out to fit my skull. She leaned in, kissing. She smelled like
Kents, Rheingold, and Pond's Seven Day.

It did not really feel comfortable to have someone kissing
me. I said, But, Aunt Rita, you know what you should do?
And she let go, turning her back. She picked up her beer and

drank. I looked out the storm window and one of those spring flowers had opened yellow a bit. I said, Aunt Rita, what you should do to survive is one nurse rolled under the bed and hid there. Then Richard Speck came back to kill them all and he didn't even notice the one missing. The next morning she rolled out.

I jumped off the barstool with my hands and feet pretend tied.

—She jump jumped out to the balcony and it was early in the morning, right? There was all this fog and she saw this guy walking his dog down below her balcony. I think it was a poodle. And she yells to him, Help! Help!

Aunt Rita had her jaw dropped. I knew she would be interested. She said, Is that how that nurse survived?

—You better believe it, I said.

The only thing wrong with that nurse story was my bed was too low to roll under.

—Voila. Aunt Rita turned with the platter.

—Oh, Aunt Rita, that's beautiful. Those curls look like Harpo Marx's.

—Then the dip goes in the stomach. She set it back on the counter, Aunt Rita's stovelight on. We had a stovelight but it didn't work and her white counter was dashed with gold stars unlike ours, plain, the gold stars with the longer up and down line like the Star of Bethlehem, and they had barstools and a counter in the kitchen, which we would never have, built by him so he got to constantly walk around with his level in his back pocket. He probably brought that level to his psychiatrist's. Aunt Rita reached above her oven and I slid his shoebox further away, Thom McAn's, Men's Black Size 8½, like I really wanted to know his size.

I said, Everyone always says voila. What is voila anyway?

—That's French. It means, here it is.

She was bent inside her avocado-colored refrigerator. Everyone else on the block at the most had brown and Ma daring white. And I liked inside Aunt Rita's refrigerator too,

Kraft Miracle Whip, not just Hills mayo, and maraschino cherries, cocktail onions, Reddi-Whip, great to take shots right in the mouth during commercials babysitting, and tubs of soft margarine with plastic flowers in a chain which reminded me of something really really horrible I did once to a kid when I was babysitting which I did not like to think about.

—What, honey? She plopped the sour cream, glug.

—I said did you think Alice Crimmins deserved the electric chair?

—Sheila, I'm not so sure she did it.

—You're not sure she did it? I said. I had never heard anyone say that, especially with a name like Crimmins.

—What did they have for evidence?

—That neighbor! I said. That neighbor who got up in the middle of the night and she was drinking iced tea sitting near the window and she looked down and who does she see but Alice Crimmins walking under the street light with two really heavy suitcases.

—We don't know, Sheila. Aunt Rita ripped the Lipton envelope opened and poured. That neighbor might have been lying. I just don't believe a mother would kill her own children. Taste.

I opened my mouth. I didn't see why a mother wouldn't kill her own children. I said, Very good.

I hated onions. They tasted like tapeworms existing in the dark.

—It's raining, I sang.

Big plops fell on the concrete.

When I came back from Aunt Rita's Sunday Ma was sitting at our red picnic table in her purplish work sweater reading the Sunday magazine. I said, Where's Dad?

Ma said, Daddy went to the dump.

I said, He went to the dump without me?

Ma said, Oh, cripes, don't sweat the small stuff. She looked back at her magazine.

Going to the dump was one of my best things because the ride was so long and all back roads, riding along down the middle of a very long thin gray spring road, riding on and on past empty trees, and Dad's got his arms all around the steering wheel and you can feel every bump of the road and from far off the sound of the dogs in the pound. Then coming back over the tracks going down our road I would remind Dad of when we first moved to Nissequott how he dumped our beach chairs there and our farmer neighbor corrected him NO LITTERING $50 FINE actually dumping the beach chairs we watched the assassination on.

Ma slid the two pineapple upside downs on the top rack and the orange preheat light clicked back on since she took so long. Dad was at the garbage trying to clean out pepper seeds, our storm windows slightly opened in beginning April and way far in back the train was parked for some reason, idling. It was Thursday, like four hours before Martin Luther King Junior got shot. Ma came back with the third raw one crossing the garbage so Dad backed off holding his green pepper and knife, making a face.

—Sanneefranneetime, Ma sang. She shut the oven and picked up her drink. Once Ma made me into a pumpkin with orange burlap over bent curtain rods and she pinned a little green felt pepper stem hat. Dad was bent over trickling white seeds down the brown garbage bag.

—Well. I banged my arithmetic shut, trying to make him jump. We're going into remainders with three digits now, Dad.

Dad leaned back, lifting his eyebrows, gulping from his Black Label with the knife still in his hand.

—Really getting up there, Ma said.

I blinked. Dad bent back down with another pepper

plopping its green hat off, then trickling the white small pepper seeds down. I set my hand lightly on Dad's back, Dad scraping around with his knife. You can feel the muscle and bone movements running through him. I said, Are you guys glad LBJ isn't running?

Dad stood and I took my hand off.

I said, Ma?

—What?

—Are you glad LBJ isn't running?

—I really don't care. Ma sat down in her chair and lit a cigarette.

—Dad, do you care?

—I care. Dad smiled at me.

—You would want him to run again?

—Well, you know, Sheila, his Vietnam position is so bad. I mean, he is bad news. But on other things, like civil rights, hey, for a Southerner, for a guy from Texas, LBJ was not that bad. Dad lifted his can and drank.

Ma sat smoking. I said, Ma, I thought you liked Eugene McCarthy.

—I love Eugene McCarthy! Ma yelled. Love him! He is aces up with me, man. Aces up, I'm telling you.

Dad nodded his head twice in Ma's direction, smiling.

—Why?

—Why? Ma yelled. You're asking me why?

—Yes.

—I can tell you in one word, Ma said. Uno. She raised one finger, staring at me.

Dad bent and cleaned another pepper out, a pearl necklace cut.

—What word?

—What word? Ma said. Are you mad?

—No.

—Vietnam, man, Veee-et-nam. Pull out! Pull out! What a lot of horseshit and gunsmoke that is, Christ.

Dad nodded at Ma, smiling. He set the pepper up and took his last one and bent, letting the seeds trickle out.

—Sheila, Ma said, Vietnam yes or no?

—No, I said. I'm going to Aunt Rita's. Bye.

I turned back and pressed my face in where Dad had the window slightly opened. I said, Dad, I know you don't agree with me but can I please put more milk out for the cat? You never know, it might work.

—Sure, Dad said.

Then I washed the bowl because it had ants and I filled it with milk and Dad had the hamburger meat on low and I looked at him, balancing that milk through our kitchen. I set the milk on the stoop, this white circle, just this white circle, and inside Dad went on making supper.

—Hello, crocus, I said. Purple thing.

One thing I really wished was I could see The Wizard of Oz on a color TV. When Aunt Rita told me about the middle color switch I dropped my jaw. I could not believe grown-ups would allow that. That really gave me hope. Then if only that night he could be gone at his psychiatrist's that would be perfect to see The Wizard of Oz switch from black and white to color and not have him around. I had Lucy in black and white seven o'clock weeknights saying for our audience imaginations how her hair came out of a red bottle but in real life I had neighbors in rainbow red hair shades: Aunt Rita's highly held ponytail tomato soup, his V-8 juice rusted around the stainless steel can cut, and finally their product daughter, Irene, the simple orange in the twelve-crayon box with the scalp scar parts of white drawn through. One good thing about babysitting for the Hanrahans was secretly reading his Playboy magazines from eight to eight-thirty, between Truth or Consequences and Ironside, such a good babysitter I was.

What happened before was I let the baby smash off his changing table on to the floor. Way to go, Sheila. He had crap all up inside his crack. I just wanted to clean him off. Would you wrap up a baby with doo doo smeared in his skin? I would never ever wrap a baby like that. I said, Baby, you stay against the wall. It had the plastic mat to wipe off shit and pee pee and many little blue teddy bears lying on their backs too. I never saw a washcloth so far away. I went running to the bathroom. Whump. Michael fell out of his top bunk once. Whump. That's the sound of flesh and bones and heart on wood. He's lying there in the light blue of Joe, Robert's nightlight, lying with the guardrail on top, now suddenly the guardrail acting like it could help and keep him warm. Ma said, The baby will be all right. I said, What if that baby comes out retarded because of me? Ma said, You do not worry. The baby will be all right. I'll tell Mrs. Mahoney. I never in a million years thought Ma would do that much for me.

Irene still slept with a guardrail and Mother Gooses over her body, her bedroom pink fogged from her nightlight, like inside I Dream of Jeannie's bottle, such a shocking sexy show to be on TV. Yes, Master, no, Master. Irene slept with her mouth opened. You know you drool when you sleep? Ma said to me. Irene had on plastic green and pink barettes shaped like tied ribbons, like in 1968 pretending it was way earlier in time, when girls really did wear material string bows. I remembered before we moved to Nissequott when Mother Goose things hung on my wall and the outline of Mary Had a Little Lamb where the paint was lighter lasted long after they took the baby symbols down. Now my wall had my black silhouette like some president, JFK on fifty cents, drawn by Ma in our back room using her desk lamp and a silver lead pencil tracing my shadow. Your mother's across the room drawing and erasing, making distant lines and scratches on your head, like being worked on with Novocain, and how Ma lied really curling out my eyelashes and smoothing out the bad.

I went out and got his Playboy, skip right to the pictures.

R and R time! as Ma would sing. I reached under LIFE's usual heart transplant with Dr. Christian Barnard, extremely reddish pulp close-ups, which I often wondered how close to that body part they came when they opened me. All the fathers on the block had Playboy hidden in a different place, except Dad with none. Under LIFE, master bedroom left night table, master bedroom closet above the shirts, master bedroom under the bed. I still had it on black and white, 5, Hazel, the maid, either that or The Flying Nun. I would not like to be either, thank you. A girl sat ramrod straight, her legs curled under and with like a tablecloth around her bottom but her nipples showing fully, like a wet spread brown, spreading larger circles, her eyes staring straight out, that heavy brown dripping like when running along the stream after it has rained, the road is overflowed. On TV Rosie was raising and lowering a coffee cup on a wet paper towel. Running rainwater a mix of brown, running along with your floating stick bouncing down the stream and the water flowing brown, actually like a fish moving between my legs.

—Bounty, the quicker picker upper. Then, SPECIAL BULLETIN, the television said.

I'm sitting in this living room with fake guitars on the wall across from me, empty armchairs, pictures of people on the mantel, mirror showing the back of my head, and the dinette with behind glass shelves holding stopped ceramic elephants and the tick tick tick from the kitchen of her diamond shaped Roman numeral clock. You try to judge how bad it's going to be for our country by how much they interrupt. JFK they stopped regular programming for nights and days. Astronauts burned up in a rocket lying on the ground at Cape Canaveral they just sent white letters with the bad news streaming across the bottom of the screen, Time Tunnel continuing.

—We interrupt our regularly scheduled programming to bring you the following special news bulletin.

27

Then you're sitting there. SPECIAL BULLETIN, the screen says. It's like they came in the room. They said, We have some bad news, and then they left. It's like everyone needs some time to calm down and get prepared. They come back in:

They said, The Reverend Martin Luther King Junior was shot tonight in Memphis, Tennessee. We repeat, the Reverend Martin Luther King Junior was shot tonight in Memphis, Tennessee.

Hazel came back on. I felt very alone with those kelly green armchairs.

Hazel went off. SPECIAL BULLETIN, it said again.

I said, Now what? I said this out loud. I thought someone else got shot somewhere else in the country and they were doing all separate bulletins. They said Martin Luther King Junior was at the hospital. When they said hospital I almost burst out in tears. I remembered taking JFK to the hospital. Hospital was my worst word in life. When I heard that word I felt like folding over and lying down and never getting up.

I felt this deep sad sickness for our country and civil rights. I realized I had Playboy magazine open on my lap and Martin Luther King Junior just got shot. The TV said: cordoned off, believed to be a white male in a late model white Mustang and they put out an A.P.B. A.P.B. I knew already from Adam-12, but they had to explain it to other people. I put the Playboy under LIFE. The back storm door clicked open. The inside knob of the wooden slowly turned, like a close-up. Slowly the inside wooden swung in, the outer storm hissing, shut. He set his shoe on the linoleum, soft give. The feet stopped, listening. Slowly walked across. He rolled the utensil drawer out, my fate rolling toward disaster. He slid out a knife. Now because this country was prejudiced and the prejudiced South let him through the roadblock, he had driven all the way up through the eastern seaboard, right at the city, out on the LIE, turn at Nissequott, turn at Two Mile Hollow, turn at Meeting House, second cedar shingle on the left, the one house in the whole United States of America where I was babysitting alone.

I stood. Some babysitters like to sit around and get attacked but not me. I picked up a dinette chair with autumn multicolored flowers on the seat. I proceeded forward lion-tamer style. I had this plan he should have glasses and I could smash each lens. I rounded the corner, for part of a second fainting because a human being might really be there.

The kitchen was empty, stovelight on, click clock a ticking. I could never tell what time it was on that damned Roman numeral thing.

—Sheila. Aunt Rita was bending over. It's like when Dorothy wakes at the end. I looked at the TV and Johnny Carson was on.

—Martin Luther King Junior got shot, I said.

—Isn't it awful, awful. Aunt Rita was smiling at me. It's like those really extreme close-ups when her face blurs. She said, Were you scared?

I said no. She picked up one of the dinette chairs moving like in a dream. I had three chairs around me and all the throw pillows across my legs and chest. I figured he would trip over the chair and the knife would stab my pillow, thus saving me. I stretched, yawning, like that was my normal mattress way with pillows on top. I helped return the last chair.

—It was a white guy, I said.

—Isn't it so sad? Isn't it the saddest thing? Sheila, I feel so terrible inside. He was such a good man. He gave us so much hope.

Aunt Rita opened her change purse. Underneath the garage, roaring, closed. I was trying to grab the money quick before he came up the basement steps and tried to walk me home.

I ran out alone into the spring, exiting left as he entered right. Martin Luther King Junior got shot leaning over a balcony railing just as at eight-thirty Ironside came on. How

29

the whole Ironside began was Raymond Burr leaning on a porch railing is shot. The people who ran TV did not understand all their meanings. I was running in the spring dark the night of another assassination. Ma said the worst thing about babysitting was later hitting the cold air and sometimes I merged it so Ma running home long ago in Queens and me running now in Nissequott happened together so neither running girl was alone. I was running holding that Men's Black Oxford shoebox and in the faint far clouded moonlight the little black cat's bowl full of milk shone up. I locked our outside storm and inside wooden and I put the shoebox at the head of the stairs to be burned. Dad brought the little black kitten to the dump and left her because of her deformed tail. I jumped under the covers with my closet door closed to keep out hanger shadows like the shapes of men. I had my two stuffed bunnies balanced on top. The train roared by very fast and giant in the dark and in the kitchen on Ma's pineapple upside down the knife gleamed.

Chapter 3

*M*a turned, startled, in the midst of pouring through that plastic top to control the flow, her cigarette smoke rising in her face, one eye closed gangsterish.

I held Ma's original Tom Sawyer which she stole from Andrew Jackson High but unfortunately written in the river scenes in front was some other girl's name. Ma looked back and finished pouring.

—Sure, she said and got ice. Sometimes she threw ice in first but if second watch out, splash, do not put your homework on the white counter because that liquid was invisible. Once in first I left my red arithmetic workbook at the head of the stairs. Next scene I'm looking through the black iron curlicues of our banister at Ma poking it in flames, unfortunately January so I had to do over half the year. I thought it was garbage, Ma said. My favorite fairy tale the Wolf gets in wearing a kerchief Mother Goat disguise and eats all the goats except the littlest, a-trembling in the grandfather clock, until the Mother Goat comes home and grabs a knife. Follow me, she says and marches the Little Goat to the riverside where the full Wolf lies asleep. She slits the Wolf, no anesthesia, the Little Goat watching, slitting him that same central path as on me, popping out the rest of the family who are fine. Get rocks, the Mother Goat says, and she loads his center and sews, pulling the silver needle and black thread through and through his flesh. They hide. He wakes. He yawns. He bends, bulged stomached, to drink and splash. The end. The Wolf is drowned. I remembered once before we moved to Nissequott Ma had on a red and white striped maternity shirt, her stomach way loaded out, and fast I bent and picked up something near that white concrete curb, helping Ma like that Little Goat.

Our lilacs bloomed above our original mud rock wall. In back out the open kitchen window between the white curtains the crabapple Dad won in a poker game was entirely flutter white like a bride standing on her head in front of their newest rock wall made with cement. Ma was on our black kitchen telephone telling the nineteenth person in a row how fab her field trip to the potato chip factory was. I went in their bedroom. Walking room to room all our storm windows were lifted, our screens dropped, and the bottoms of curtains swung. The main thing different if I took a shower was I wouldn't have to scream for someone to come in with a pot and rinse my lather, which used to be Dad, then suddenly one Sunday in walks Ma. I said, What are you doing here? She said, Daddy thinks you're getting too old. Then she dumps me off with a pot of freezing ice cold.

Dad had his money drawer open and a toilet paper tad stuck with central blood just under his jaw where the skin got loose. Dad was playing poker tonight. Ma was always afraid Dad would bring us to rack and ruin through gambling because Grandma lost an arm and a leg at the track but if they were so ruined why were they living in Fort Lauderdale with a banana tree and a canal in their backyard? Dad scraped metal across the drawer, too high for me to see.

—Dad, did you hear Mr. Callahan is getting a gun in case Mr. Hanrahan goes off his lum-lum?

Dad cleared his throat. He said, I did.

I knew this by lying underneath our living room couch to read.

—But he's keeping it taken apart in his bedroom closet so the boys don't shoot each other. Dad scraped the metal again. Dad had a gun one summer when he was a cop at the beach, his only arrest someone for firecrackers on the Fourth. I wished Dad would move in Martin Luther King

Junior style and calm all these neighbors down. Hold on now, Mr. Callahan says, and Mr. Hanrahan stands on the back stoop frothing at the mouth while Mr. Callahan has the instructions: Attach A to S. Whirl W in. I crossed in their wide bedroom mirror and sat on their bed. Ma was screaming laughing on our black kitchen phone. Mmmm. Mmmm. I'm telling you, everybody loved it. You know what the bus driver said? He said, Ooo, Mrs. Gray, can we come back next year?

—Dad, Kennedy won Nebraska. Does that matter?

—Doesn't hurt. Dad made a face and got his yellow shirt.

—What helps?

—New York, California, Illinois. Those are some of the biggies. Dad turned back to face his closet and undid his fly to tuck his shirt in and turned forward again, buckling his belt, Dad was so polite.

I said, Guess what's happening to me today. Ma's teaching me how to take a shower.

Dad smiled and sat on the bed nearly knocking me off with his weight. He put on a sock.

—Dad, what's whitewash? Not a white wash but like whitewash for a fence.

—White paint with some water added I would say.

—Oh. What did the Warren Commission do?

—The Warren Commission? Basically they determined Oswald acted alone when he shot Kennedy. Dad walked to his bureau wearing socks.

—So Ma thinks it was more than Oswald? Do you think it was more than Oswald?

Dad smiled. He picked up his Black Label and drank. He went to his closet and got his shoes. He said, Well, babe, I don't know.

I said, I think it was just Oswald. What do you think?

—Well, I don't know. Dad set his beer and walked to his closet.

I said, Do poorer people use whitewash to stretch it out?

—I think so. Dad sat back down and tied his shoes.

Our family really believed in unions and people should not be poor.

I said, Dad, who paid for my operation?

—Who paid for your operation? Dad crossed back toward his tall bureau, the other father crossing in the silvery mirror room.

They did not like to talk about my operation too much. Ma said once, You would have never been able to play volleyball. So then I knew play volleyball. You're always looking for advice. Dad opened his second drawer down again.

—Pop said he paid for it.

—Pop! Dad smiled. He is some piece of work, that guy.

—Well, did he?

—Kind of. I tell you what happened. Dad turned. He looked like a stand up comedian. At the time we didn't have too much money, Dad said.

—Did you have Blue Cross Blue Shield?

—No.

—God.

—Or we had something but it didn't cover it. So I remember I went in to see the doctor. I said how much will this operation cost? So the doctor says, That depends.

—Depends on what? I yelled.

—That's what I said, depends on what? He said that depends on how much you can afford. Dad raised his eyebrows.

I smiled.

—I think I gave the guy about four hundred bucks, and if I remember Pop loaned me part of that.

—Ma, I said, who paid for my operation?

—That's a lot of towels, Ma said.

We were in the yellow bathroom, Dad gone to play poker in his rotten raincoat, Dad always saving his good for a better day.

I said, One for the floor, one for my head, and one for the rest of me. I'll hang them up.

—You got some shampoo?

I raised my cup. Ma set her cigarettes, ashtray, and drink down on our vanity. She said, You see this? She shook the shower curtain. This is my good curtain. Do not get this wet.

—How do you take a shower then?

—This. See this? You keep this on the inside.

—Oh. I never even noticed there are two.

Ma looked at me, like suspicious. She said, Now this, this controls which direction the water comes from. Down is for a bath and up for a shower.

—I always wondered what that faucet was for.

—Look. Are you looking? See it's got an arrow. You turn the arrow up.

I bent in squinting, luckily daylight savings but unluckily Ma only put one lightbulb in the two-bulb over the mirror socket, Ma liking our areas dark. It felt like ancient hiero-glyphics on a wall.

—Oh, yeah, I lied.

—You want me to adjust the water temp for you?

—Thank you.

I stood back and Ma worked the controls. She looked like she was flying a plane. She was spinning this, adjusting that, testing, going back to the drawing board, holding her hand out in the spray, like how she once showed me testing the milk drop on your inner white and blue veins.

—So, Ma, you going to tell me?

—Tell you what?

—Who paid for my operation?

—Oh, Christ, I don't remember all that crap. Ma stood. I tell you what I do remember.

I waited. You never know what's next.

—I remember the day the doctor called about it. Christ, that was bad. I remember I was on the phone holding Annie and the doctor said I'm sorry, the baby has to have the operation. I thought oh, Jesus! I thought he was talking about Annie! Christ, she was just a little baby! Ma's eyes were wide, very upset, the fine spray hitting down our brown tile wall.

That would have been bad for someone littler than me to have to be cut open and operated on. I could see why that would get Ma upset. I said, How old was she?

—She was just born! Cripes, I just got her home from the hospital. I said Jesus, we have to turn right around and bring this poor kid back.

I shut the bathroom door and took off my clothes. Lucky it was me that needed the operation in the family. I held my hand in the spray. It was a good temperature. Ma did a good job. I stepped inside the spray and the train went by. I had this pain in my throat. I looked up where the water comes from. We had a black and white picture of Annie and me, Annie sitting in the kitchen sink sucking her thumb and I'm on a wash-up step-up thing with all these pincurls in my hair, like someone went over my head every inch with bobby pins, and my face actually looked good, like normal, and there's a white radio perched above the water so Annie always emphasized how they didn't even care if she got electrocuted.

I poured the Breck's into my palm. Ma's mother also used Breck's down in Florida. One mistake was when I drank Breck's. Another mistake was asking for shampoo help when I shouldn't have. I had on my white winter undershirt with white polar ice cap sleeves. In the bathtub the water thundered down and struggling I moved Ma's giant glass gallon of Breck's onto our cold winter tile floor, Ma buying the biggest heaviest Breck's for Normal possible to save money, buying a glass gallon I could not possibly open and tip without smashing (and swarming from all over the house would come the rest of them, and the four of us whipping off our shoes to walk on the glass, GET BACK GET BACK, which was how

36

retarded Ma thought we were, throwing out her arms, like when Michael smashed the glass gallon of milk on the banister and flowing white Niagara Falls, Ma screaming at him like he did it deliberately and Michael's standing there, white, holding the cracked off glass throat not talking).

What happened was I opened their bedroom door. You try to judge by where the locks are but the lock control was on my side and I needed help. Ma sat on her bed edge facing Dad, facing away from me. I stood in the bathroom holding my empty cup. Dad was bending. The top of Ma was all tan like the guy who drew the cartoon forgot to draw in the top. She had underpants on but nothing else. Dad was all in his clothes, reaching his hand, touching Ma almost like a scientist. Oh, he is giving Ma a medical exam for cancer. That was nice of him. They were turned, looking at me. I was short, standing in a doorway in white underpants and a white winter undershirt, holding an orange cup in my hand.

—I need shampoo.

Then Dad was rushing toward me, filling up the entire room, filling up between Ma and me so I had this urge, in that moment before she completely disappeared, to crane my neck and wave to Ma, alone now on her bed.

I rubbed our orange washcloth around the Ivory soap 99.9 per cent pure. I never made my First Communion. I never got to one spring Sunday wear a dress of white. One thing, I would never wipe this red scar off. I wasn't really sure what order to go in taking a shower, my body first or my head? It felt very strange to stand up naked in the rain. One summer we went upstate and we went to Niagara Falls on the Canadian side and we had on black raincoats looking out of our caves and way way far down below was the chugging Maid of the Mist. When babies had little plastic tugboats the ugly ups and downs of the little toy boat top always reminded me of my face. Ma took me to a doctor for my face, about second grade, and it was a white house with white

37

wooden stairs and a white banister going up and we each slammed our door and walked toward the doctor in the rain.

—I'll tell you the biggest shock, Ma was saying into our black phone. I had come out in my turban with a tail of steam. I smelled burning. Ma said, Did you know all those potato chips, "Ripplies, Ruffles," sanneefrannee, they all come from the same vat?

Supper wasn't too good when Dad was gone. I said, Ma, these grilled cheeses are totally black.

Ma lifted and crashed her ice cubes around her mouth, looking at me. Fast she slid them back shouting, I said that to the guy!

I got out the potholders Annie and I wove for Dad on a loom and turned it off from Bake.

—I said I am shocked! You know what he said? He said oh, you teachers are so naive.

I started scraping them in the garbage onto the white cigarette butts. If Dad was there he would have by now switched the radio from the flying weather in Saigon is excellent to that old movie song he loved.

> You must remember this
> A kiss is still a kiss.

I had another bathtub experience when David Weitzen, Michael's friend, was eating supper over in December, probably since he was Jewish his worst time of year, with strings of lights everywhere, even a lifesize Santa and reindeer set up tilting on our Indian's roof. I was nine-tenths underwater. When the train passed while I was in the bathtub I liked to dunk and hear its deep central earth core rumbling a new and different way. I sat up and worked myself into a lather. Rabbit ears, devil horns, a crown. A halo I could not do. I started yelling for Dad, the dear dead days beyond recall. David Weitzen and I could never be together because he was Michael's grade, a year younger, though he was always in the driveway asking me to play two on two and always in the kitchen kept his eyes following me like soft ropes. Is this guy blind or what? Supper for him would be probably another Jewish trauma of loin of pork. Annie and Dad have the meat grease running down their chins, breaking off pieces of the skin, and the red cabbage like shocking arteries passed back and forth around, everyone chomping madly within our red brick walls, chomping in that yellow hanging light as the clock hits five after six, tearing off bits of lumpish dead pork flesh with our incisors while David, in the extra chair between Michael and me, gaped, white as a ghost.

Dad said, David, come on, buddy, have some meat.

—Uh, no thanks, Mr. Gray.

—What!

—Calm down, Dad, Annie said.

—You're not eating my pork!

Everyone grew quiet.

—Are you allowed to eat pork? Ma said.

—Oh, yeah, David said. I mean I guess so. I just never have.

—Did you ever eat bacon? I said.

—I can't remember. Probably.

—You don't remember if you ever ate bacon? I said. I could name the dates and times I loved bacon so much.

—Make the guy a PB and J, Ma said. Done and done.

I was yelling and yelling in that bathtub for Dad. I yelled opera, Swiss yodel chalet, megaphone like when the Marx Brothers play football in college. I yelled for Dad until I thought I would faint. I rose, all my water streams thundering, I dried off so as not to drip on Ma's precious wall to wall. I dropped the towel on our bathroom floor and proceeded into the kitchen with my hair in a crown. Michael and David Weitzen were making sandwiches in case of pork, their backs to me, and Dad with his back turned and Ma, leaning holding her plastic cup, looked at me. She said, Uh oh. Dad turned. His face looked like if his hands were full of cards or flowers he would have thrown them all up in the air at once.

I said, I'm getting a pot because no one will rinse me off. And I walked, not looking at Michael or David Weitzen but veering I went off my long course plan for a pot and veering bent instead closer for Tupperware. Which color? Aqua, white or pink. Also, what shape? Then I realized, just grab a big one and I turned, everyone watching me sailing in my lather, gone, though part of me stayed behind to watch my behind disappear.

I had out the applesauce, raisins, walnuts, and cinnamon, trying to get people's dessert orders. Four oval rye bread char black food pieces iced our garbage now. Ma ate hers. Ma had one of our striped dish towels, winding it into a whip chasing Michael around. She said, You think you're tough, buddy. Ma whapped the towel at him. Ma whapped the towel again and Michael backed into a chair that dragged along with him a bit. Ma started chasing Michael with the towel because Michael attacked Robert with one first. Actually Michael learned that towel whip trick from the lifeguards at Lake Ontario upstate and he was the one who taught it to Ma.

—You think you're tough, buddy boy?

Annie and Robert were on the other side of the kitchen table watching Ma back Michael out the door past the telephone whapping the towel.

Ma said, Come on, buddy.

I said, Who wants applesauce with raisins, walnuts and cinnamon, raise your hand.

The towel snapped Michael's flesh and he screamed, jumping out the kitchen door.

I said, Annie, don't throw that salad out. She was paused over the garbage.

—You save it. I'm not saving it.

I said, I'm not saving it. You save it. It's your job.

Ma made it all with rusted lettuce and the strange part a beautiful net of orange carrot curls on top. Ma wound her towel and whapped, Michael backing up.

I said, I'm garbage. It's your job to clear. How many want applesauce for dessert?

Ma whapped the towel again. The trouble was Ma was bigger and had better towel control. I only just invented that applesauce dessert and I liked it for taste but also because all the shades of brown from applesauce to the raisins near black. Annie was looking at me. They were in the dining room, Ma whapping Michael in a circle around our chairs. What I remembered in the hospital was standing in my crib, leaning on the guardrail, and my crib was white, and against the wall was a white cot with an apricot-colored nightgown laid there which I had this hope was for Ma, and the speckled hall floor stretched off and far away was the opening and closing of an elevator door, but no one got off.

Michael was backed into the corner sitting crying on the floor where the drapes Ma made got thick.

—Enough. Ma threw her towel over her shoulder and walked out. She walked by us and picked up a cookie sheet to dry.

Chapter 4

Misty Nixon bent toward the water loop sucking, her blond hairs curtaining across her perfect face, like the face on a doll I had before Nissequott when Ma still used a washing machine with a wringer, flattening each of our shirts and pants through separately by hand. Misty came to school late today because her mother took her to court to change her name, Ann Melissa to Melissa Ann or the other way, something we would never do but they were richer, probably Protestant, and they were used to having the President, but for us having a President even only that short time was a heightened special thing.

—Misty, are you voting for Nixon?

She looked up, blinking, the two of us standing in the long speckled floor hall, her eyelids like on a doll's long lashes, blinking very slowly. I lost that doll somewhere.

—We're not related. She blinked and walked away.

REPUBLICANS DEMOCRATS, Mrs. Hope wrote on our green blackboard. It was June 5, the day of the California and New Jersey primaries. All the girls were lined up under the I LOVE TO READ BOOKWORM with the author, title, and kid reader on each worm part, all the girls lined up to see Edith Eisenlau's older brother's Playboy in our classroom bathroom for your milk money. You would have thought Mrs. Hope would notice all the girls had to go at once.

—Ronald Reagan? she said.

The bathroom door opened and flushing flooded invisible water over the classroom tiles, washing over everything.

Zero, Mrs. Hope wrote. Governor Rockefeller? Joseph Rakov raised his hand.

I remember Ma said, Sheila, I found your doll behind the washing machine. How did it get there? Oh, I said and I took her back with the arms pulled out, like really I wanted to pull the head out. I said, I don't know. The Playboy line moved forward. Under Rockefeller Mrs. Hope wrote two.

—Richard Nixon? She said, Twelve, thirteen counting Mark Rogers' hand. Mark Rogers was also blond haired, the boy blond perfect version of a doll, and tight black pants, black shirt, black belt with gold buckle like Man from U.N.C.L.E. I just switched this year from a half hour every night of pretend dreams with those two Time Tunnel guys (brown hairs) to Mark Rogers instead. We lived in Alaska in an igloo like my sugar cube model built in third for Peoples of the World. We had yellow cafe curtains to give the effect of sunshine in our house and every night we heated baked beans like that commercial of the couple eating beans singing, Life's simple pleasures are the best. But now alas morally I could never have that pretend dream again because Mark Rogers was a Republican for Tricky Dick for the war for that black and white picture in LIFE of the Vietnamese girl running naked screaming burning in invisible napalm flames.

Sixteen for Nixon, Mrs. Hope wrote. That was bad news for our country.

I said, Misty, that was just for Nixon. Who are you voting for?

—I don't know. She blinked.

Our line shuffled again, the flushing rolling out. I was shocked she had not voted for her family. When we had the red Scotch plaid clock in our kitchen that was the time of Goldwater vs. LBJ and that was the time Ma told me I needed to go to a doctor for my face and I said why and Ma said, Those bags under your eyes are not normal at all. I just felt kind of this shock. I just felt stunned. I had a really good time once before Joyce moved her family invited me to the beach for a picnic supper and we were sitting on this beautiful red plaid blanket with fringe on top of rocks and sand looking across to Connecticut and the water and earth were so beautiful.

I had this semi-hope maybe Edith Eisenlau and I could be friends since she lived pretty close. Edith was very tall, that Jolly Green Giant effect especially in her Girl Scout uniform.

—Hubert Humphrey? Mrs. Hope said. Eight, she wrote.

—Robert Kennedy?

Only Stephen Gephardt raised his hand.

—Eugene McCarthy?

I raised my hand. That was very sad that everyone was voting for war and the Tet Offensive and F-111s, every week the count of the dead and the wounded, every week the P.O.W.s and M.I.A.s, the DMZ, Saigon, Hanoi, Ho Chi Minh, and meanwhile in Paris they're fighting about the shape of the table for peace talks. I felt bad not voting for Kennedy because he was for peace and civil rights, but Eugene McCarthy went in the race first and Ma and Dad were for him. Stephen Gephardt stared at me. In May we were developing black and white film for our science project and I bent taking a close up of a dandelion, which you would have to color yellow in your mind, when Stephen came up and said, You want to go steady? By a miracle Pop had sent me Reader's Digest for my birthday and by a miracle Ways to Increase Your Word Power had platonic so I passed it on, increasing Stephen's word power too. Sadly, fatly, Stephen lumbered away.

Edith Eisenlau took my nickel. She was like a giant inside that small pale green room. Her hair looked like the wild dirty blond thatchings of a cottage too tall to comb. She was stepping through the valley holding vegetable cans, while next to her I looked like a brunette dwarf. Edith held the Playboy high, really craning up my neck.

—What month?

—June. But I also have May.

—June is fine. My neighbor has May. I said, That was smart to bring two. I smiled at her.

It was a blond girl with her nails ovals, filed, lying on her stomach and up on one elbow with her nipples very huge and she was smiling and under it said her height and ambition to be an airline stewardess.

—Go, I said watching Edith's hands turn.

She was sitting with her legs apart, a cloth roped up between her legs, her back very straight and they hung like weights, the dark brown circles at the center. In February doing the record of Hiawatha Guicheeguimee with earphones Edith also set up a service to keep moving the record arm back to bosom bosom. I said, Go, watching Edith's hands move. And of course there was also the excitement of any second Mrs. Hope could bang madly on our door, demanding to get in. I said, Go. She stood with a string down her crack and turned so the side showed round and the nipple hard, her face laughing, the brown a spreading beat. Go, I said.

Bird tweeties came through my June opened window the next morning and my window in my mirror contained all gianting green. Since such a bee-you-tee-full day I put on my hot pink, red, green A-line miniskirt Ma made with back zipper and two front pockets, giving the effect on my bottom of a jungle and, more all American on top, my red shirt with white collar from Sears. It was very strange Dad had not come yelling down the hall, Rise and shine, boobalas. The three of them still lay twisting in their sheets, Annie's a tornado wreck and her room smell too strong to go near, and both boys with mouths opened, Michael's face pale, who you would always want to cheer up, and Robert's shocked in his dream.

Our kitchen was empty. Dad was not bent into the sink

45

with a towel and Breck's for Oily on the counter. The window was open, a silver spoon lay on its back, the oven off, no Pillsbury on 350 to bake, no four fluoride pills and no four raisin piles left by Ma, no sound of Neal Busch in the CBS traffic helicopter shouting FDR, BQE, Lincoln and Holland Tunnels, but only Ma's beautiful blue bowl of ivy growing for our centerpiece.

—Dad? Both hands were near the eight on our orange clock. Usually Dad woke us at quarter after and seven-twenty-five we ate. Vaguely came sounds from another room. I moved on through the kitchen, like moving in a dream, and I walked into their bedroom. Ma and Dad stood in front of their TV, their stomachs at the level of the picture, and behind their bed was already made.

—Dad?

Dad looked at me. His collar ends stood up.

—What happened?

Dad said, Bobby Kennedy was shot.

They were looking at the TV. I thought, I must have made this up. This couldn't have happened. I was trying to think if I was having a dream and if John Kennedy got shot before and I was making this up a few years later that Bobby Kennedy got shot. I thought someone is making this up. Ma and Dad were looking at the TV. It had a room in black and white with all the tops of people's heads jostling around. In a pool of blood, the TV said. I thought just let him be shot in the leg, please just let him be shot in the leg, that would be enough of a punishment and he can't run for President but he can be alive.

Ma pulled out her desk chair and sat.

—Is he dead? I said.

—It doesn't look good, Dad said.

—A Roman Catholic priest administered Last Rites in the emergency room at Good Samaritan Hospital, the TV said.

—He was shot in the head. Dad looked at me. He had his collar ends up and toilet paper stuck on his face. Dad turned to the closet and pulled out a tie. It went back to Bobby Kennedy speaking on the podium in black and white. He said, On to Chicago and let's win there, and waved and walked off and it went darker, moving around, and it went to shaking hands then screaming and the guy said, Number of shots.

Dad walked into the bathroom. Ma sat in her soft green V-neck jumper that she got the summer we went upstate. I remembered it on the dummy in the window, then we went in and Ma tried it on. It was soft pale green that reminded me of spring and above the TV was that black and white picture of the four of us in size order and Ma had dropped her two gold bird earrings on the desk, sitting in her lovely pale green V-neck jumper and short sleeved white blouse and I was standing very close and I put my hand behind, holding onto the back of her chair.

Bam, bam. Ma and I each slammed our car door and we walked in the rain toward that distant white house with the white wooden railing and white, outside steps. I was seven. HIGHLIGHTS FOR CHILDREN, the magazine covers said with different color browns in squares and inside stories about talking squirrels, which reminded me of sitting on Joyce's little green blue bench playing stagecoach ladies on the frontier, all over the lawn squirrels the color of Brownies were run stop run stop looking around with beady detective eyes. I remembered that time when Dad left, possibly the fight where Ma threw a sneaker at him. He had all his shirts on hangers over his back flowing down our stairs. I climbed back on my top bunk to read a mystery which an entire Brownie troop was trying to solve, and Ma came in and reached, petting over my guard rail, and I started to cry. Ma said, I know you're upset about Daddy, but everything will work out.

The nurse said, Sheila Gray? And Ma and I walked into the examining room. Does she sneeze? Does she cough?

Does she have a runny nose? Do her eyes tear? No no no, you're getting warm. He had white Venetian blinds to cover his windows like I remembered once on TV watching the Invisible Man with white bandages wrapped around and around. I was sat up on his special black table with that forever unrolling white paper sheet so you do not contaminate the next one. When Joyce and I were friends some mothers were suddenly buying paper dresses in mod geometric go go fashions, then throwing them away.

—What's this? he said.

Ma did not say anything. I would have liked some help with this scar once in awhile. Every year, every September they looked inside your undershirt. What's this? What's this? They're always in a panic someone touched your heart. I said, I had an operation when I was two and a half.

—For what?

Ma didn't say anything.

—My chest was bent in too far and they had to pull it out.

—Oh. Then he leaned in, listening. Turn around. Cough. Cough. Get dressed. Does she have any rashes?

—No. Ma cleared her throat, holding onto her pocketbook like a thief might sweep through the door.

—She doesn't have any symptoms of an allergy. Why did you bring her here?

Ma cleared her throat and shifted. This doctor had the same hairdo as Bozo the Clown though now he seemed more respectable to me because I did not think I had an allergy.

—Look at the bags under her eyes, Ma said. That's not normal.

I was buttoning my shirt, performing well. Always wear a skirt to the doctor's not a jumper so he can examine your chest. We were all born into these containers with a certain outside shape, then inside us we had what you would call your soul which would be like a Casper the Ghost shape floating inside you perhaps with tentacles to attach lightly to your skin, like the tabs to line up material Ma cut when she cut out Simplicity patterns to sew, and possibly our souls could receive messages through these tentacles, You're deformed, like through the Morse code, three long three short three long, S.O.S., my only message I knew.

The Saturday after school ended Ma wanted to talk to me.

—How about we sit at the picnic table?

I liked the picnic table. In the morning it had water bubbles that the sun slowly dried and it was deep red and strong enough for all four of us to stand on in summertime to see the train over the trees. I figured this was going to be about my face. Ma led out the back. I had this feeling Ma was going to ask me to leave because it was much too depressing to day after day see my face and I thought I could make it all right walking up the railroad tracks then doing work for people and sleeping in their barns.

Ma faced outward, one elbow back, crossing her legs. I was scared. I was trying to get ready inside myself. One blessing I had was in our bathroom mirror only my forehead showed unless I sat up on the vanity. I never got to see my whole face while standing but I had the interesting fun of jump the nose, jump the cheek, jump the mouth, and then back down on our bathroom floor putting all my face pieces together, forgetting and remembering in blurs.

Ma had on her matching bermudas and top she made of medium blue with thicker red threaded strawberries like the old fashioned days of embroidery. She had her dark curled hair and her lipstick and bermudas and no sleeve top, her arms sticking out showing down their length her scattered constellation combinations of freckles and darker velvetier moles, and on my arms not quite so many, still developing.

—Here. Why don't you sit here.

Ma meant same red bench as her.

It was clear, no humidity, everything abounding green, the green grass shining like a thousand mirror blades, then diamond repeating green chain link fence, then their latest model rock wall held together with cement beside our crabapple marked over and over with green young dots. Ma was seated on that red wide strong slatted picnic table bench, red in every backyard I ever saw in my life, and way in the distance glinted the rails.

—I wanted to talk to you about how babies are born.

Ma looked at me. I felt like laughing, jumping up and shaking Ma's hand that we could be normal, have a normal difficult birds and bees time. I wanted to tell her Ma, don't worry, I saw this on Andy Griffith and rest assured I know this is hard. I wanted to say Ma, I went through it already, Andy Griffith is sitting on the porch after supper feeling low and Aunt Bee comes out drying her hands and gives Andy the courage to bring it up with his son. The children had to help. All the girls already saw Growing Up and Liking It about menstruation anyway, sitting in the dark auditorium while Joseph Rakov rattled those locked double doors, desperate to get in.

—Do you know anything about how babies are born?

I shook my head. It was such a pretty day and now that I had Ma sitting next to me on the same backyard bench I wanted as full a facts of life treatment as possible. Ma looked kind of pale.

—Well, I said, just what you gave me in that book from the library about the swimming.

—Swimming?

—Doesn't something swim and it looks like a tadpole?

—Well, I don't know about that. Ma shifted her legs and cleared her throat. Ma said, You know that men and women are built differently?

I nodded.

—You know that men have something called a penis and women have something called a vagina?

I nodded.

—And when a man and a woman love each other a man puts his penis inside the woman's vagina.

I stared at her. I had no idea what she was talking about.

—And the man secretes a type of fluid which contains sperm and when this unites with what is called a woman's ovary the two together form the beginning of a baby. The baby begins to grow in a woman's uterus. Do you know what a uterus is?

—The planet?

—The planet? Ma stared at me.

I was trying for a joke.

—The uterus is the womb, Ma said. It's where the baby grows.

—Oh. So what's the belly button then?

—The belly button is where the umbilical cord was once attached. When a baby is still inside its mother, how shall I put this? Well, to eat and breathe it gets food through the umbilical cord.

—Like paste?

—What do you mean paste?

—I don't know, I was just thinking the astronauts have to eat paste.

Ma cleared her throat and switched her legs. She didn't have her cigarettes and matches so this was going to be a short one. I was thinking of when the astronauts walk in space and how they are attached by a rope, trying to make a semi-joke with the paste.

Ma said, Do you understand?

—Yes. Except then why do boys have belly buttons?

—Everyone has a belly button, Ma partly yelled.

—Oh.

—The belly button is where the umbilical cord was cut.

I said, Cut?

A nurse wheeled in with a cart and many little brown bottles with black stoppers, like we once used to keep a baby bird alive in the garage with milk.

—I'll wait outside, Ma said.

—We're going to test your arms for reactions, Sheila, the nurse said. You want to lay your arms out? The other way.

I turned them over, the whiter side up. Now suddenly I had this hope I could be allergic since the doctor said, well, they would try to test me anyway, and I hoped I could be allergic to shrimp so then I could get a lot of attention when the relatives came over and Dad put out cold shrimp on lettuce with toothpicks to dip inside ketchup and horseradish and they would all be wild devouring pigs and I would have to sit sadly left out in my little chair, maybe only eating a Saltine, and I could get all this attention that I was allergic to shrimp, which was an outside thing that you could not be blamed for.

—This is alcohol. She swabbed up and down my arm. It always felt good to be cleaned. She took out a silver machine like a hole puncher teachers had.

—Now, this will pinch a little.

She moved along my arm punching a row of holes like planting for the crops, making a juicy mechanical sound. I was hoping and praying she would not puncture all the way down where the veins rise up near your wrist. Tears were in my eyes, a sign of you know what.

—Does that hurt?

I shook my head. They do not mean to hurt you but they have to to do their job.

She pulled the feeding cart closer and moved along down my holes just like on agriculture six a.m., that over and over fascination of dropping solutions in, having to go back each time for a different drop. She said, moving along, this is dust, this is cotton, this is wool.

This is the dust in the arrow of sunlight through your window in the afternoon.

This is the cotton in your underwear one hundred per cent.

This is the wool on the sheep who lived in another time on Upper Sheep Pasture Road.

This is the dog who came once during the football play-offs who you would never name Lassie because that was too obvious.

This is the cat that's gone.

—Okie dokie. She wheeled the cart away. I really liked her. She said, I'll be back in a few minutes to see if you have a reaction. She shut the door.

—Would you like to have a reaction? I said to my arms.

Ma slammed her car door, walking fast on a mission from the allergist. Ahead it said GRANT'S in giant orange, all capitals. I was chasing behind. Ma swung in the ENTRANCE, passing by blue baskets FOR YOUR SHOPPING CONVENIENCE, heading up the underwear aisle with ladies' legs kicking upside down and ladies' tops in white brassieres without heads or legs or arms. A Grant's lady with cat eye glasses on a chain stared at us. I felt like turning off to the Pet Department to watch the fish changing direction behind the glass.

—The allergist said you're slightly allergic to feathers, Ma said moving fast.

—I am? I felt like I just won a prize. I said, When am I near feathers?

I was thinking of one little bird very far away in the sky and how could housewares connect?

—Here. Ma grabbed and up we walked together to the cash registers, where when I was shorter on another trip with her to Grant's I was swinging from those aluminum bars to guide the people through, and I was thinking feathers must be a real allergic problem or otherwise why would Grant's sell plastic pillowcases for real?

Genovese had a pizza wheel silver cutter for a dollar twenty-nine, which would make Dad's 1968 birthday dream come true. I wrapped it and hid it in my room. The main thing that changed after the allergist was I always had this constant crackling when I went to bed, like someone was trying to talk and only static came through.

—Dad? I clawed my hands on our green chain link, basically to be dramatic. It was the end of July and next door Mr. Hanrahan was shooting at his target near the swingset. Dad had our big aluminum pan out on the grill making spareribs with onions and lemon peel. I said, Did they really put a metal bar inside my chest after they operated on me?

(Pop said, Haven't you noticed how you lean a little funny near magnets?)

Dad said, Who told you that?

—Pop.

Dad poured a tiny amount of water from his orange plastic cup, putting out a flame, and holding his Black Label can in the other. Dad said, I think they did, babe.

—Why?

—Well. Dad set the cup down. I think they had to kind of reshape the bone.

—How long did they leave it in?

—Oh, a couple of days.

—Pop said it was ten days.

—Maybe it was. Dad picked up the big fork and turned the meat around behind his fence.

—Then they took it out?

—Yup. Dad smiled at me.

—Did I have a tricycle when I was in the hospital?

—I think you did, babe. I think I brought it up for you. Dad drank his beer and the shooting next door stopped.

—Was it red?

—I think it was. He smiled.

—I think I remember it. I remember that hallway in the hospital. It had speckles on the floor.

(—I'll never forget it. There I come running all the way up

to Roosevelt Hospital on my lunch hour thinking my darling granddaughter would need a little cheering up and what do I see but you're peddling that little red tricycle up and down the hospital hall with your chest open and a metal bar in there. Thanks be to God, I says, the kid's going to be all right.)

I said, It had speckles on the floor and it had an elevator at the other end.

Dad picked up his potholder which Annie or I made. He held the pan and delicately spooned the barbecue sauce on each bone. One strange thing in second grade, the same year I got taken to the allergist, we had the California test and the only one I got wrong was about an elevator.

—So you came to visit me in the hospital?

—I did, Dad said.

—And that's true about the metal bar?

—Truth, Dad said. Why don't you do me a favor and bring this charcoal and lighter fluid back down to the garage?

Aunt Rita told me a mystery about eleven-year-old twins and the clue was the trail cut in their red clay driveway by the bicycle wheels when the thief made off. The clue was the bits of red left in the treads but the main idea was how great it would be to have a twin to talk over all your clues. We were sitting on her back stoop watching the beginning fireflies, that puzzling time when the ground is growing darker and the sky is growing light. I said, Aunt Rita, you know my first bicycle was stolen from our driveway when we first moved to Nissequott. Aunt Rita said, And here I am telling you this same story! I said, Too bad our driveway had blacktop. Aunt Rita said, There's the first star, Sheila. Make a wish. She said, No, honey, don't tell me.

You try to look for advance warning of father trouble ahead. Dad and I seemed like we were getting along pretty good, though I noticed he never used that pizza wheel cutter, understandable, since it was not sharp enough but I just wished he would fake it a little then switch to a knife.

I was clearing the picnic table in July when one night Ma stood up and lifted a plate. I said, What are you doing?

Ma said, Sheila, Daddy wants to talk to you.

I had this sudden realization no one else was around. It was just me and Ma on the patio with the picnic table. I said, I'm clearing.

Ma picked up the potato bowl. She said, I'll clear.

I didn't know she knew how.

Ma said, I think Daddy's out back by the pool.

Ma headed toward the door. She had a paper plate in one hand and the potato bowl in the other.

When I cleared I stacked all the cups, clutched all the utensils, balanced the coleslaw container in the potato bowl, brought out the garbage to do six paper plates in one three-second sweep, meanwhile telling Ma for the sixteenth or seventeenth time yes do not worry, I am getting your coffee, the water is boiling, Ma. I thought, how is she going to get coffee? How is she going to find the saccharine?

I stepped through the gate. Dad sat holding his white cup facing where the pool filter streamed. I felt this shock he had already got set up with his coffee.

—Hiyah, babe. Sit down. How you doing?

—Okay.

There was a redwood chair set up next to him like seats in a movie theater facing the same way. We had one rose in our family and our chairs faced that. It was pink, called Bahamian Sunset, and behind that a real life, more orange Nissequott sunset leaked through our maple tree. Then I looked at the ground. Dad had his delicate ankles crossed, barefoot on the patio, and his two big toenails were long and yellowy, like a piece of monster's body had strangely landed on him. Dad set his coffee cup on the table and clearing his throat swept a book of Playboy Party Jokes out of thin air.

For a second I was shocked that Dad was reading the same book as me.

—Your mother found this under your mattress.

I had this sudden sense they should have a search warrant.

—Is this yours?

I shook my head.

—This isn't yours?

—No.

Dad cleared his throat. I let him suffer a little. Well, Dad said, your mother found it under your mattress.

I said, It's not my book. It's Edith Eisenlau's older brother's. I said that because Dad taught that older brother social studies and social studies to me should include Play-boy behavior.

Dad said, Oh.

I said, She loaned it to me.

I said loan, like not borrow, you go to the library and pick it out, but what someone semi-forces on you.

Dad said, Do you understand any of these jokes?

—No.

I was looking at the filter stream pushing out.

—Okay, babe. Why don't you bring this back to Edith and tell her not to loan you this kind of book again.

I went out the gate and came around our juniper. I thought, if she would tell me the facts of life and she found the book why would she tell Dad to talk to me about this? I thought, why would the mother have the father talk about this? My face hurt and it hurt all up inside my throat. I had this skull pain like I would like a bullet in there please. I walked around the juniper and there were Annie and Robert. They always looked like part of a small circus act together. They were sitting on the red picnic bench and when they saw me they stood, both walking toward me and Robert holding out a new package of Hydrox which you could see they just opened and ate a few, waiting. The reason we had Hydrox was Dad liked them better than Oreo.

Robert said, Sheila, you want a cookie? I could hear in Ma's room she had Merv Griffin on.

I got on my blue bike. That was my replacement for the stolen. I should have wished for peace with Dad and not wasted it on a stupid long lost twin. I rode straight down without looking for cars. A cement truck would have felt nice. Tomorrow at nine I was going to ride straight over to Edith Eisenlau's and throw that book in her face and tell her my father said she was never allowed in our house anymore.

I rode to the Nissequott Harbor around to that giant rock where no one can get you. The harbor was a circle with green trees all around and in the center the soft relief of water with boats bouncing like thirty hearts. I was looking across for God in the trees.

Chapter 5

Ma said, I view organized religion as a complete waste of time, the hats and all that crap. She said, Give me a break. I am so happy NOT to go to church.

—Good. Don't go, I said. But can I borrow your lace handkerchief or not?

I fluttered the lace white when I came back and two bobby pins. I felt holy just with the future of that lace on my head. Ma leaned back in faint winter light that fell on our red floor. She had her smeary little hand mirror leaned against the kitchen window, checking out her face.

Ma said, You know, your bangs could really use a number.

—You tell me this now when I have my good dress on?

Ma said, One two three, let me shape you up. She said, Christ, you look like a goddamn sheepdog.

Actually that was part of my strategy to hide my face which I thought Ma would like, but when she put it that way next thing I'm rushing for a towel to wrap around my neck. Ma went to our cabinet with the hot and cold cereal and sometimes a trapped mouse and she pulled out her white styrofoam box of barber's equipment. I really did not want to be ruined today, but I also did not want to look like a goddamn sheepdog. I sat up on our kitchen table with Ma's blue bowl of ivy and Ma moved in holding silver blades. I immediately threw up my arm to block.

—Not too short, get it?

—Would you please?

She could ruin me for about three months with just one

cut. Or she could deliberately cut crooked and then use the legitimate reason, I had to cut it short to get it straight. I came back in the kitchen from my mirror. I put a kind hand on Ma's bending back, Ma crawling around our floor like Cinderella sweeping up my hairs. I said, Congratulations, Ma, you cut my bangs perfectly. Thank you very much.

It was quite a day. I passed Dad back his coffee now that we made it safely under the train trestle. It was ground hog's, they were having an oil spill in Santa Barbara, and I was going to church with a friend. Dad, I said, she lives where we used to go get rocks. Dad was making no comment neither here nor there about me going to church, but as usual was being just, with the even hand. Dad and I had on CBS, riding together as usual on a Sunday, though in a different direction and to pick me up a friend.

—Continue to extricate birds caught in last week's massive oil spill.

I had this vibrating fluttery hummingbird wing feeling in my stomach, laughing to myself that all these birds with feathers were being sopped with oil and drowned in California but yes, if it were in my town I would rescue such a bird and risk worsening my face. I would do the cross chest carry through the water, fireman's carry through the sand, all techniques Ma practiced on me last summer, and heaving, throw that bird down with even worsened deep bags hanging off my face.

I didn't know if Dad felt bad about having to go to the bakery alone. I said, Dad, did the ground hog see his shadow?, bringing up the light subject of spring. We passed the big rock on Two Mile Hollow and turned into now all lawns and houses the colors parents wanted in children's rooms. Marianne Gilhooley lived on Lynx Lane in section one of Tanglewood. I was giving Dad directions, right on Peacock left on Partridge right on Bunny, Possum, Horsie,

Lynx. I said, There, Dad, there. Marianne Gilhooley's driveway was the two strip kind just for wheels. Her household number was written across the garage in spelled out black one thousand beginning script, which looked like once upon a time to me.

Marianne had on her mainly green plaid kilt and green tights and a green coat with black piping, as they say. Marianne had tights in every color to match every outfit and about four different plaids for skirts. In the fall when I met her she was wearing knee socks with little plaid flags like bookmarks that somehow attached to the fold.

—Excuse me, I said, my first sentence when I met her.

—Oh, she said and bounced back like shocked.

Actually I bumped into her on purpose and actually excuse me was a little fancier than our family would really be. We would just say, Sorry Charlie.

—Marianne?

Marianne Gilhooley and I collided in the cafeteria and that was a cafeteria lady calling her. She had black roots and a hair net leaning down trying to see out the tray deposit window made of ghostly reflections from that unclear aluminum. Fix your goddamn slip, the lady said.

I quick threw my lunch bag, S marked in black Magic Marker by Ma and turned pretending I didn't hear a thing. Once I said to Ma, Shouldn't I wear a slip? Ma said, Forget about it. Slips are a complete waste of time. And I always meant to bring up, then why do you always wear one? It was interesting that Marianne Gilhooley's mother made Marianne wear a slip, but was losing the battle, however, because Marianne was on the verge of becoming a hoodlum. On the other hand, I was on the verge of goody goody two shoes. At recess I was forever walking on that concrete curb between the clattering excited squealings of hopscotch being played in anklets and in the distance, as close to that steel link fence where garbage was blown up as they could, that group of hoodlums wearing black fishnets, black eyeliner, white London Fog mod lipstick, and white go go boots listening to one girl's transistor radio,

> If you wanted the sky
> I would write across the sky in letters,
> To sir, with love.

I kept having this hope someone would ask me why are you walking back and forth balancing on that curb? I could explain, Well, it's because my favorite cartoon is the one with the lady wristwatch balancing on a tightrope in the circus who falls and then how they have to cut her open and operate.

The phone rang just as I came in from Mass still with Ma's lace handkerchief on my head. I said, Guess what, Ma, you don't have to wear a hat anymore and there are ladies in pantsuits now.

—You're kidding me. Ma had rushed to our wooden banister for Catholic Church news. So, how was it?

Then the phone rang.

I said, Good. I received communion.

Ma gasped. She said, You can't do that, then answered the phone. Ma said, Oh. Tommy. She said, What's up? Ma pulled out Dad's chair, then stopped. Ma said, When?

The reason I couldn't get communion was that unlike Marianne Gilhooley who was perfect Catholic all the way, I never made my First Communion, never mind confirmation further along down the road. Every time I went to church with my cousin I had to sit there all alone in the pew with the old people and the ones with cerebral palsy who couldn't walk up to the altar to get the food. But at St. Joseph's R.C. today Marianne Gilhooley just said, Come on! It doesn't matter!, like the voice of a great, glorious dinner bell holding more than enough for all. I was waiting on line in church with all the normal people looking at those stained glass windows where birds and angels swooped in holy blue and red. We were shuffling to Jesus, who I totally loved. Jesus was up there in all His sinews with both arms spread and one foot crossed over the other, that dangerous diaper thong about to slip and shuffling closer and closer to Him than I had ever been before, I had this horrible realization the nails He had were not like the shelf bracket Dad used simply to hold underneath, but they were hammered right through His flesh. Body of Christ, the father said, slipping that white food on each faint red tongue. Amen, I said like Marianne Gilhooley told me, and I got mine.

I figured if I was going to get hit by lightning it would be right outside the church on 37A. Our two town billboards that looked like bull's eyes were right there and that was the same dirt scarred path where once Ma and I driving to Hills saw a hunchback old lady so short she could hardly reach the handle on her shopping cart. Total silence in the car. In November I'd had another distancing attack. Everything in the world gets further and further. Those arithmetic fours begin to look like broken arms or wings. My hands are waving goodbye like my own flesh is lengthening. Sweat is forming. In my stomach acid drips. In my mouth it tastes like loosened blood. I had this bad association with November. It was when Annie was born and Ma got the phone call about which daughter had to have an operation and it was when JFK got shot. I said, Ma. Ma was bent down in the tub. Ma turned and looked at me. Ma was way way at the other end of the bathroom with Comet in her hand. I said, I don't feel so good. Ma said, What's the matter? I said, it feels like everything is getting far away. I thought Ma would say, Cut the crap, would you? Ma said, Get your jacket. Let's go for a walk. We both got our jackets. We went down the stairs and up the road. Those black long telephone lines stretched on and on. Our feet were far away, our four feet marching far away along that distant blue road, their sounds like miles behind, and gradually the distance of the black telephone lines shrunk, moving in more normal, and I could hear that the sound of our footsteps matched the touching of the ground. The gray November trees were bending and our giant big solid rock appeared. I said, I feel better now, Ma. Ma said, Good, let's turn around.

I stood on our slate landing, watching Ma through the kitchen door. Ma wasn't saying anything, just holding the phone. Downstairs, they had Wonderama on.

—How's Dad? Ma said. You better get him on tran-quilizers.

I walked up the steps and stood outside the door arch watching.

Ma said, Hold on a minute, Tommy, I want to switch phones. Ma took it off her ear and held it to her heart. Ma said, Sheila?

I said, Yes?

Ma said, Could you please hang this up for me?

—Yes. I reached and Ma handed. I covered the bottom, the black phone curl shaking. Ma's door shut, in, all the way and I put the phone to my ear. Once right before we moved to Nissequott I got the greatest telephone call of my life. It was the black office-type telephone in Grandma and Pop's hallway on a circle of lace. Pop said, It's your dad, Sheila. He wants to talk to you. It was Dad calling from Nissequott to Queens to tell me there's a girl your age living on our block and she said she wants to be friends with you.

Uncle Tommy was breathing on the line. Dad had left me a jelly, a crumb, a snake, and a twister on a plate. Their normal rooster coffee pot was on the stove. They used to have one all glass that you could watch pumping clear to brown and Ma loved to death how that coffee tasted but one day in the middle of the kitchen the whole pot shattered, only the glass handle left in her hand, and Ma would never get a glass one again. Uncle Tommy breathed. It's like in aquariums when the fish rest behind the glass barely fluttering their gills. The phone clicked up and we were all connected from Nissequott to Uncle Tommy closer to the city to Ma on the extension to me on the black.

Dad heaved the Sakrete bag up on the table and looked at me as I rushed directly in my outfit from church. It was a pink and white small flowered Little House on the Prairie style dress with empire waist elastic smocking on the chest to add some interest since no bra. Dad was about to wet the Sakrete with water, mix it with a branch, then pour in molds like ice cube trays, making bricks to cover our bathroom wall. In the garage the air was cold white. Behind Dad was that line of windows showing our hemlocks planted in a line atop our rock wall to stop the soil from washing away. I said, Dad, Uncle Tommy just called. I think Grandma died.

Ticka ticka went the part inside the storm door to keep it from slamming too fast. I thought I should have got some credit or a thank you for sending Dad right away up to Ma. That garage air was like someone just sprayed white paint when we made winter wreaths out of Glad bags tied on a reshaped wire hanger, then did the final step.

On the garage floor was the box of Indian River grapefruit Grandma sent us for Christmas before she died. Between each fruit was plastic grass we could save and use for Easter. In February only the extremely sour grapefruits were left that you had to dump half of Ma's Sugarcal on. In January Ma had passed me the phone. I said, Hello? Ma was smiling, lifting out the vodka, getting ice smiling because of the daughter mother link. Grandma said, Didn't your mother teach you any goddamn manners? I fast pulled the phone out of the kitchen and said, Yes. Grandma said, Your cousin Patsy sent me a thank you note for the citrus right away.

I wanted to show Marianne Gilhooley the sandpit. I thought since it was a hole dug in the ground it was maybe a good thing to do on the day my grandmother died.

—You'll probably feel depressed, Marianne said. When my grandmother died I was really depressed for like a week.

—I feel depressed all right, I said. My voice was soft. I gave Marianne Gilhooley one of Dad's empty beer boxes and roared our garage door down.

The trees were gray, bowing over our blue humped road, no kids out on banana seat bicycles February the second, two two sixty nine. I said, I wonder why my grandmother died on ground hog's day.

Marianne Gilhooley looked at me. She had a very round white face, like a kitten's bowl of milk. She looked like the only brown haired model in the Sears catalog, this year inching out of Junior Bazaar into Young Miss, who I suspected I would look like if I didn't have bags under my eyes.

I said, You know someone got killed on our road once. I said, This was back in first. Marianne, did you go to first in Queens? I said, Yeah, I went to every grade in Nissequott. I said, So anyway one day my brother Michael and I were walking to the Nissequott School. You know the one with the spies on the roof? Once, Marianne, that was the only school in town. Michael and I were walking and suddenly there's all these ambulances and fire trucks coming up the road. We had to step up on the grass so we wouldn't get run over. You could feel the whole ground shake. So we're watching them and they turn right up our road! I didn't want to say anything to Michael but I figured our house was burned to the ground and we were the only ones left. Then when we got to school, when we got to school this teacher calls us aside. She says, Do you guys live on Cumsewauke? I said yes. Then she said the garbageman's son was crossing the railroad tracks on our road in a convertible and he got hit by a train. So that was that.

—Jesus, Marianne said.

—See that house? That guy goes to a psychiatrist.

—Really?

—That guy, he used to be an air traffic controller. Marianne, you know radar screens? He left his once I think to go to the bathroom and he let a plane crash. I think it crashed right in your development before they built the houses because I think I remember I was riding my bike by that day.

—What a great street, Marianne said.

—It looked like that scene in The Wizard of Oz, you know the skywriting? It looked like that with the smoke. There was this lady with purple curlers standing there.

—He was probably beating off.

—Oh, yeah, I said.

We walked past a few more neighbors. I said, Speaking of which, you know what's a nice thing to do? When you walk along hit your box against your legs.

We went beating along our road. That's our big rock, I said. We came out under the winter trees to wet cement color sky with crossing black telephone lines and Lilco wires and above the warning RR painted in white on the road. In the fall Dad's father died of cancer. We were all in the kitchen polishing our shoes in the light that fell through our window. Use transparent if there's no more brown, I said to the three of them. We had to use that old black and brown marked rag, that was polishing things probably before I was born. Dad came in and opened our little kitchen closet and cleared his throat. He looked down at his glasses for driving and used a dish towel to clean them off. It was the morning of his father's funeral and Dad was still thinking of us, wanting to drive us safely. Ma came in in her black cocktail party dress with her two gold bird earrings and gold bird pin and she honked her nose into one of Dad's handkerchiefs. My nose keeps running, Ma said and Dad walked to our hall closet and got his good raincoat out.

The path to the sandpit was straight up through Scottish type scenery like the opening scene of one of Dad's favorite movies, The 39 Steps, which ended with poor Mr. Memory up on a stage unable to stop his mouth from spouting off. I led Marianne Gilhooley up the sand scar path, the ground frozen hard. We were paused at the level landing of the railroad tracks made of gravel and timber ties painted in creosote to last longer, our silver rails stretching two ways, Port Sands or Stony Point, running right behind Ma's bedroom where she still was with the door closed when I left.

I didn't have much of a reaction really about Grandma. Grandma was okay but she picked on Ma a lot. Ma accidentally let their old dog Blackie into traffic and the dog got killed and Pop walked in and said, What's this, a funeral? and Grandma said Mary killed Blackie and Uncle Tommy walked across the living room and slapped Ma across the face. Pop said, You know your mother did not cry one tear for that dog. Not a one.

—You ever flatten pennies? Marianne Gilhooley said.

I said, No. I heard it's illegal. I turned and kept walking. We had further to climb. The sun was gone in white. No shadows left for us. Both the ground hog and Jesus had a story about coming out of a cave. At Easter Grandma always gave us a chocolate egg with almond paste the weight and shape of a loin of pork. Dad said Grandma got up this morning, went into the bathroom, had a heart attack and died. I remembered that bathroom had a purple throw rug. Once Grandma walked in on me in that bathroom when I was reading Look, an article about the American family. She said, Hello, sugar pie, and just started putting her silver clips in, getting ready for the trotters like I wasn't even there.

It was cold. The train's coming, I said. I can feel the ground shake. You feel that?

Marianne looked around and said no.

I said, You develop your instincts living here. I said, Well, are you ready? The wind blew hollowly over the great giant sunken tan hole. I said, When I stand here I always think of Judge Crater.

—Who's Judge Crater? Marianne Gilhooley said.

I said, Look! It was the train. I never got used to it. It was deep blue, painted with white whisker stripes, like a wave. The oncoming headlight made you think about God. There was such a roaring. The engineer waved in his tiny window and Marianne Gilhooley and I waved back. Then car car car went by, some with dark heads in the windows looking at us, outside, standing on frozen sand in the winter with jackets and mittens on.

I said, Judge Crater was this guy like in his forties who walked off from his family once and they've never seen him since. I said, We're almost there. This is the part where I start to think about Brazil '66. Do your parents have that album? I said, Oh, it's unbelievable. It has this album cover, Marianne, it looks like a sand desert that the group is standing on and you open the album and it's not a sandhill at all, know what it is? I said, A bosom. It rises up and you can see the nipple inside.

—Shit, Marianne said. Can we look at it?

—Sure. I just have to be careful with the timing. You got any good albums like that?

—That bitch locks everything up.

I said oh.

A few dark strands lifted behind Marianne Gilhooley's head, twisting, still attached. Marianne had on real Irish knit mittens. The closest we had were Ma's plain white which she always let me borrow, no questions asked. We were at the top. I said, You get a really outer space feeling here, don't you, Marianne? I could have talked about sandpit comparisons from here to kingdom come. I said, Voila, let's ride.

Marianne stood alone on the brown rim with her box while I stood in the pit, encouraging. Marianne looked like a Wheaties flake about to pour into a bowl. The trees on the rim looked like hairs caught in a filmstrip. The movies alone was where I had my first distancing attack. This guy got thrown onto Mars, walking alone on red sandhill formations. It looked like being inside a stomach for an Alka-Seltzer commercial. In the Port Sands theater the black aisles tipped up, all the black lumped chairs ahead while on the screen this man walked alone on red Martian forms. I started getting my distancing. I was clinging struggling up the movie aisle climbing finally to the white porcelain and bending for water—at the bottom was a wildly chawed piece of pink gum.

At the funeral Grandpa had his eyes closed, his skin very white, lying on his back with every inch around him flowers. One of his last things he said to me was, You're putting on weight there, Sheila, kindly meaning a compliment. Grandpa had electric windows in his car, which was dangerous going over a bridge over water to Queens. Open your windows, I had to quietly order the backseat kids near windows so the four of us could swim out and survive. Dad, I said once driving back from Queens, you ever notice how many bridges we have near us? Dad got his cigarettes from the dash. I said, How come we have so many bridges near us?

—Because we live on an island, babe.

—Oh. I laughed. I said, I never thought of that.

Dad lit his cigarette, the trees outside all gray stick blurs. Dad always took us the most beautiful route, Northern State, coming back from Queens. We went by trees and beautiful useless rock wall bridges that didn't go anywhere.

—How come all our bridges start with T? Except George Washington.

—I don't know, babe, Dad unrolling his window down an inch, why that would be, pushing the burnt match out, fast rolling it back up.

—The Triborough, Tappan Zee, Throg's Neck.

—The Whitestone, Dad said.

—Darn. I snapped my fingers. Also, the Verrazano.

—True. Dad raised his eyebrows, steering us down the white concrete road.

At the bottom of the sandpit Marianne and I plowed straight lines with our heels. We were living on Mars, six months in an ice block igloo, six months in red clay baked adobe, planting our red crops, strawberries tomatoes radishes beets, in red soil. Marianne was so sexy hoodlum when I gave her the planet choice she wanted Venus, us walking around in I Dream of Jeannie outfits, but I said, Marianne, Mars is better because you don't have to just lay around. You get to farm.

When they buried Grandpa it started raining. They lowered him in his box into the ground and Grandma threw some brown dirt on top of him. Men not from our family were waiting under a tree with shovels. Anytime, anywhere in the world I could hear that dirt hitting Grandpa's box.

I said, Marianne, so say we're here for awhile and everything is good but one day we're walking along and we come around a big rock and we see footprints that are a different size than ours, and say they're different sized from each other so we can tell it's two of them. Oh, Sandy! Yoo hoo, I see a footprint!

—A footprint, Rusty, Marianne Gilhooley said.

We quick tested our size feet and just then it was dawning on us:

—Why, they're humans, I said.

—They're coming over, said Marianne.

—I hope we speak the same language. I said, Okay, so pretend it's the two guys from Time Tunnel and they accidentally got sent to our planet and we each fall in love. I don't care which one I get, they're both the same. Hi, I said as they approached.

—Take your jacket off, Marianne said.

We were in her bedroom. I quick hung my jacket fast on the back of her white painted with gold trim chair, moving fast because my jacket was reversible and the inside really bad. I said, God, you have a canopy double bed.

Marianne went and locked her bedroom door, click. They took all our locks off because Annie locked herself in once and Marianne had that same gold button push kind I had once. You don't really know what you're supposed to do on the day your grandmother died. I looked out Marianne Gilhooley's window, the second floor. A guy down there was out in the cold with his car hood up and half disappeared, only his legs sticking out and I noticed they had white concrete curbs in Tanglewood, whatever that meant. Cold white. I turned. Marianne had wall to wall carpeting and a full length mirror and all her walls had red pink roses repeating everywhere.

—You want to play boy and girl? Marianne said.

—What nice tits you have, Marianne Gilhooley said and bent, her sideburns curtaining across, licking me.

Chapter 6

When Ma came back from Grandma's funeral her skin was off color, orangish. I was afraid she was using that new Coppertone skin dye stuff to give you a tan in New York in the middle of February. Orangish, Ma leaned half hanging upside down behind those wooden banister bars to look down at me eating tuna on rye watching Wide World of Sports. Ma used to mix caraway seeds in tuna back in Queens when she was a girl and she also ate pot cheese which was cottage cheese and sour cream.

Ma said, How about we walk to Genovese? Enough of this sitting around. A little action, man.

I automatically laughed. I said, I was just at Genovese yesterday! I smiled. Usually Ma would clap spelling A-C-T (clap clap) I-O-N (clap clap) action, action, we want action, that long gone song she remembered from cheerleading tryouts in Queens, which she failed. But she did not do that today. Ma looked at me then got up. It wasn't really that hilarious that I went to Genovese yesterday. Yesterday I went to Genovese with Marianne Gilhooley and we got Glow Juice which made your skin a greenish cheese like on one two-part Superman, certain underground creatures who are tinted by the radium they lived with in the center of the earth. Our faces floated in my dark bedroom mirror with deeply dug eye and mouth holes, both Marianne Gilhooley and I screaming at your worst nightmare identical twin standing next to you. I said, Marianne, hold my hand. Then the normal warm shape of hand penetrates to calm. I would like to go to Genovese with Ma but also I wanted to go back to the sandpit with Marianne.

—What do you need at Genovese?

Ma had our hall closet opened with on top Grandpa's hat that he left for Dad when he died, which Dad never wore. Ma said, Blue thread, and the wooden hanger tipped wildly up and down as she pulled out her camel color jacket with rope buttons like from earlier days in 1950s Queens, ciss boom bah.

I said, Ma, you have paint on your face.

—I believe it. Ma went toward our kitchen closet for her rectangle mirror.

Dad was up near the bathroom ceiling still painting the new bricks flesh colored with a sponge. They started with paint brushes and switched to sponges cut in half because the three dimensional rims were too hard to get. It felt like they were covering the bathroom with hundreds of bags under the eyes. Those bathroom bricks bulged compared to our flat red kitchen ones that they put in long ago. Either the mortar was different or the brick molds different, bulged. I asked Dad did they get new molds. I just wondered why they would do that if they had old molds already, why would they get new brick molds that bulged? But Dad said he couldn't remember, yes, maybe. To me, either you went to the store and got new molds or you did not.

I said, Dad, I'm shocked you need the ladder.

—Yup. Dad dipped his sponge and stroked.

—Ma and me are walking to Genovese.

—Good. Blow the stink off you. Dad smiled and dipped again.

—Dad, if Marianne Gilhooley calls would you please tell her I still want to go to the sandpit and I'll be back by the latest two?

—Yup. Dad painted the wavering brick top.

—Dad, did you ever see the Candid Camera where people walk under a ladder and a bucket of paint spills on them?

74

—No, I missed that one.

Actually I meant to check did the people walk under the ladder or around to see if Candid Camera was doing another level about superstition and punishment. I got my reversible winter jacket hung now on a hook too low and at the same level in the back of my closet were blue steady crayon scratches that Annie left before she moved out which looked like cave writing from a simpler time. Aunt Rita taught me all my superstitions, mirror, salt, opened umbrella in the house. It was lessons like that Ma would never give. The blue thread was for Ma to make me a muumuu for Marianne Gilhooley's birthday luau. We got the material on Friday at Sew What's New in Port Sands barrelling that usual Ma dangerous and thrilling back way over the tracks past the sandpit digging machinery which I felt like telling Ma no longer reminded me of the allergist's machine to steadily puncture holes in my skin. When I pointed out of obligation to my central scar in the middle of Marianne Gilhooley and me playing boy and girl, as she moved her wet tongue coloring and harden wetting my nipple to a matching pink red, Marianne Gilhooley said, What scar? But still it was better to immediately warn so that somewhere somehow when you least expect it the other poor person isn't suddenly shocked, did you see that long pink red disgusting flesh thing Sheila has cutting in the middle of her?

On Friday Ma and I drove over RR on the blue road and halted before the silver rails, Ma gripping her steering wheel, trying very hard to see both ways which was hard to do coming from Nissequott what with the combination of pointing your silver Dodge grill up into the air, pulling yourself a chin up by your steering wheel, and gripping looking around each way's curves so as not to get killed. Once at Pirate's World in Florida Annie and I were on a modernized ferris wheel with a capsule top and a steering wheel which if you held it with all your weight and might, totally alone because your sister was whimpering too much to help, that steering wheel could keep you from spinning around upside down and, the latch broken, falling down to Florida where Pop waited holding our sweaters over his arm.

—So you did need blue thread after all, I said to Ma, because Ma always automatically at Sew What's New refused any accessories. I zipped my jacket and out we went to Genovese.

—Woooweee, Ma said, her dark eyes very bright and beautiful when we hit the cold air, and she put her hood up right away. We ain't in Florida any more, man!

I laughed. I wondered why Ma said we since I did not go to Florida for Grandma's funeral, but stayed with Aunt Dee, staying a pale white snowbird, my little snowbirds!, as Grandma always sang to us before she died. Grandma did not exist anymore. Grandma had bottles of colored water on the counter in their Florida room. I wondered why Ma invited me to go for a walk to Genovese right after her mother died which in a way would be like going for a walk with her own younger self, both of us the oldest brown haired daughters. It felt like I must be important to her.

Pure white breath puffed out of Ma's mouth. The daylight was white and the tree trunks looked like corpses. It was a rough time for us. Ma had on her white pure mittens and I had on my disgusting off whites, a fake classy Irish knit, made with sloppy loosened yarn and dirty colored like where a dog went in the snow, and I wanted to tear those mittens, those poor little kittens right off my hands, leaving me with stumps.

—Uhhh. I shivered. We walked past the cement held rock wall where the tailless kitten used to walk back and forth crying for attention when we started the car. I said, It is cold. Then I laughed, so Ma would not suggest skipping Genovese.

—Got to move! Come on, we'll warm up. And Ma bunch stiffed her hands deep in her pockets and ran pole swaying up our road, which had two names, Indian or settler:

Cumsewauke, which Mr. Callahan said meant The Walking Place, or Meeting House which our family called it because Ma said it was easier to spell.

At the bus stop those two maniac german shepherds tore out attacking their fence, rather nice of them to bother in such cold. I reminded Ma about the time she rescued me. She said, Cripes, you were white as a ghost! That was my favorite part because she said it with such extreme eye popping exaggeration of shout and dramatic color choice. Ma said, I finally had to send Daddy over there. You know he was so scared he drove over in the car? I said Jesus Louise, if he's scared what about the goddamn kids.

I covered my face, laughing. We were crossing toward the dogs to walk against the cars. I said, Yeah, and you know who Dad brought over for protection in the car?

—Who? Ma yelled.

—Annie.

—Oh, cripes, Ma said. What a balloon.

Now Ma and I were walking where Michael and I were that time long ago when the garbageman's son got killed. What a balloon was actually Dad's expression for kids in the high school who got into fights and were good at shop so it was funny Ma used Dad's own expression to criticize him. It was a way not to criticize him. We came to our yellow sign that said STOP AHEAD. Woo, I said and turned walking backwards, a technique Ma taught us long ago for travelling in the wind, about the same time as any road we four crossed she said, Run like bunnies, and about the same time she taught us how to find a fallen log and go to the bathroom in the woods. Really it was not that cold but I could walk backwards and look at Ma and see the road lengthening behind us with faint white trace snow edges caught in the brown land, trusting Ma to take care of the traffic and me.

Once in opposite time, in the exact green growing middle of summer upstate, I was sitting in a green pale painted cement block room, paler than Ma's V-necked jumper of that time, sitting on a twin bed opposite an older brown haired girl. Twilight, when your teeth are brushed and you have your pajamas on but are still awake. From below we could hear kids playing as long as they could. One Twilight Zone an old man living alone like Pop would be now in Florida sits at twilight alone in his chair as darkness grows until he hears kids calling him, kids who are actually his childhood friends come back through time to play. He has the choice to stay outside with them and always be a kid or come back inside to his chair and one day die. Upstate those spots of growing darkness floated through the pale green room and the younger kids' voices floated and I was just thinking of an eerie moment that day when I was spinning a kid on a ride and her mother interrupted and said at that age a little kid's sockets could just pop right out when suddenly in real life this older brown haired girl said to me I just had a vision of you dying in a car accident when you are twenty-five.

Ma and I stopped and looked both ways.

> Don't cross in the middle
> in the middle
> in the middle
> in the middle of the block.

We crossed to where the safer sidewalk was and Ma took her pure white mittens off. I said, Here. I'll hold them. I really did not like to help her smoke. I didn't like to help her get cancer, but she was struggling trying to squeeze them up under her arm.

—Oh. Ma always shocked at the least sign of help.

I always figured the car accident would be on Northern State into the slamming side of one of those many useless stone bridges. Actually if I hadn't had that operation my heart, the more it grew, would have slammed into my bones and the older I got the harder it would have been for me to breathe. Ma struck a match, a quick orange lick, gone from the cold white air. Of course that Twilight Zone skipped the good parts to getting old, like for me perhaps one day Mark Rogers picks me up for a date and Dad, very nervous, rises from our Naugahyde, his newspaper slipping onto the floor, then in the lobby how I would pretend to read Coming Attractions, advice I remembered from Ann Landers on what to do so your boyfriend could pay.

Ma's second flame went out. She turned, hunching against the wind. She had her hood up but not the laces tied, Ma in a self made cave. At eight twenty-five, when Courageous Cat and Minute Mouse burst out of their cave in a convertible, that was when in first I burst out and walked to the bus stop and of course a convertible was what the garbageman's son and JFK were both in when they were killed, both the same year. On Friday Ma and I had made it over the railroad tracks alive but unfortunately at Sew What's New we had a material disagreement. Ma wedged a bolt out, displaying it. It was a really ugly floral, flowers flopping everywhere, that would make you look like something sat upon forever near a pool, or at most the redwood kind with two back wheels to let someone else slightly move you about.

—That's nice, I said. We stared at it. Sew What's New was that worst facial situation for me: overhead fluorescent lights beating down which really made the bags underneath my eyes bulge, and of course the bulging of those overly large flowers she picked. I said, But I don't think I look too good in lime green.

Ma pushed it back in. She looked pretty hurt. I knew I should have taken that material. I looked back down across the rows and saw the most beautiful deep dark purple blue, like the sky on a winter night in the front yard when there is crunching snow under your feet and the front light off. The branches are empty, moving in the wind, and someone has thrown many glowing white crescent moons across, like a person's exaggeration of a sky which people would always yell at you for even thinking of.

—This? Ma said. Get whatever you want.

(—Am I the passenger or the driver? I asked that older brown haired girl upstate.

—I just lost the vision, she said.)

Ma struck another match and the flame miraculously held, cupped inside her skin, and she leaned out of her hood cave. I had on my first beret with all my hair in except the bangs, a hat that always made me enthusiastic to go out. Okay, Ma said reaching for her mittens from me, still sucking on it hard, and throwing the dead match off. It was hard to walk along with her because the sidewalk had the upcracked bumps of large underground roots and not only the regular interval cracks because concrete would either expand or contract in the heat or cold, but all the extra cracks from roots, trying especially not to step on a crack and break my mother's back in this time right after her mother's funeral.

—Ma, do you remember that summer upstate?

—Oh, cripes, that god awful summer, please. How could I forget?

I laughed. Sometimes I wished I could tell Ma it was predicted I would die at twenty-five, but I was afraid that Ma would say, Who cares? Then I would feel like killing myself.

We passed that house that said 1700 on a plaque near the front door. I always wondered if that plaque was true. A car sped around the hill curve straight at us and Ma dropped immediately behind so we were Indian file. Last summer when she came back from driving all across the United States Grandma gave Annie and me Indian dolls and mine had a red brown suede skirt which was the most beautiful color of blood when it has stopped. I waited until Ma stepped up even with me, the two of us leaning forward diagonals walking up in the refrigerator cold air.

—You know what I remember about that summer was one time, Ma, you took just me to Howard Johnson's for an ice cream sundae.

—Christ, it is hot. What do you say we go over to Ho Jo's and get an ice cream sundae?

—What about the other kids?

—Don't worry about them.

I was sitting alone reading a book near a tree and it was a miracle Ma ever found me. Ma and I walked along. Any second another kid could pop out of a garbage can and demand equal treatment. In the blue road distance, heat mirages were wavering.

> Oh, the girls in France
> Do the hula-hula dance
> And the way they shake
> Is enough to kill a snake

AIR CONDITION, it said in melting ice block letters on the door glass. Ma's mole and freckle arm that I loved reached and opened it. I said, Ma, this is my first air conditioning.

—Booth or counter? The waitress looked like in a movie with a uniform of turquoise and white checks closely interlocked. The place was empty. I realized this was because it was two o'clock, between feedings for everyone else. It was a long row of chromium stools with turquoise centers and divided up regularly for the people to share were set gathered groups of chromium napkin holders and salt and pepper shakers and sugar, each group like a little family. Along giant windows were turquoise booths, which also I had seen in movies, with next to each an empty hook for the future hats and coats of wintertime.

—Where would you like to sit?

Both ladies looked at me.

—The counter?

—The counter, Ma said.

—Surely. The waitress went to a little rack and took some signs. Right this way.

I spun slightly testing it. It was amazing sometimes the

extremes grown ups would allow, for example, a chair in a restaurant for people to twirl. But I did not twirl all the way because being out in public with Ma I did not want to embarrass her and have them think I did not know how to behave in a restaurant.

—Do you know what you would like? It was the same waitress in the same outfit but standing now behind the counter holding a little notebook, just like in a movie.

—Do you know what you want? Ma said.

—Yes.

They looked at me.

—What? Ma said.

—A strawberry ice cream sundae with vanilla ice cream, strawberry sauce, whipped cream, and a cherry on top.

—Just give me an iced tea. Thanks. Ma handed back the signs, which I connected was a menu. Menu, I had thought, was just a word they made up in the movies that didn't mean anything. Ma crossed her legs on her stool. 32 Flavors, I saw above, the flavor words made out of movable black letters held in levels. Pistachio, pineapple nut, maple syrup. For a second I felt bad but then thought, well, strawberry is a good place to start, and I felt better again. Ma lit a cigarette with her legs crossed. It felt like Hollywood and Vine and she took me to the counter until she got discovered and the only bad thing was how huge those windows were and how any minute another kid could come along and demand a stop.

—No, Ma said.

She did not remember that Ho Jo's time. Ma and I leaned diagonally in our winter coats, walking up the hill. Halfway up was always that patch of ice and coming down, speeding, if you hit the brake at the wrong time you could spin out and slam right into that 1700 house. I never stop there, Ma told a cop once when she got pulled over, the red light on top of his car spinning around.

—We never remember the same thing, I said.

Ma just stared ahead. We rounded the top of the hill, where the Italian man sat in the summer smoking a cigar. The road stretched ahead curving at the telephone pole where the Indian usually stood.

—Danny and Rita are coming over later for a drink.

This was not such thrilling news for me. I was looking at the dead leaves, frozen on the side of the road. I thought Ma would say next we ought to get some cocktail peanuts also with our blue thread.

—Don't you think Danny Hanrahan is a handsome man?

—No, I said. I felt very bad for Dad because I knew he could not help it he had bags under his eyes.

—I think he's a very handsome man.

—He looks like Lee Harvey Oswald to me, I said and Ma said, Oh, cripes.

We walked past the house which had an area of glass for plants, a white arbor or trellis for vines to grow, now dead, and lying with her four hoofs tucked, a white beautiful statue of a mother deer, watching us.

—What color blue do we need? I said.

—Any blue.

Ma walked along with that orangish mask in front of her face, moving beside the winter killed stalks and stalks of trees. It felt like Ma had so much she knew about the world and she wasn't telling me anything. We passed the Indian's and he was not out and ahead was the all white Methodist Church with the bell down in a monument on the ground. It flew off in a hurricane the year Ma was born.

—You know, Ma said, that funeral was a complete waste of time. What a waste. A waste of time, a waste of money, Jesus. Who needs that crap?

She looked at me.

—They had the flowers, the Mass cards, the whole bit. Who needs it? When I go I want to be cremated. Done and done. Cremation, man. Forget all this crapola with the funerals. Done and done.

Ma looked at me.

The traffic light changed to green. We turned left, walking up the slight hill.

—Could we walk a little faster, I said. I want to go to the sandpit with Marianne.

Ma blinked and I sped us up, Ma moving along next to me, her face and skin color strangely separating blobs blending into the air, and floating whole were her bright red lips.

Chapter 7

—Oh, my God. I was looking at my face, Marianne Gilhooley standing with me in the mirror and I turned to her standing alone in the all pink girls room. You disappear. You can reach your arm out and tracing back connect to your shoulder and looking down find your feet and tracing up to your knee, thigh, where you go to the bathroom, up, but you can never look out and see your face. Oh, my God, I said, I actually look good. No wonder you didn't recognize me.

Marianne Gilhooley had just walked right by me backstage carrying a mattress for The Princess and the Pea who was, naturally, Misty Nixon. Misty Nixon had been being a princess since first when I was a yellow lollipop dancing in her dream with yellow cellophane around my head and white tights and white string tied around my throat by Ma. Not too tight, I said. One time they were playing tennis and the four of us were walking over the Mill Pond stone bridge with plastic bags from the dry cleaners and old people slowed and screamed where are your parents? because they thought we would suffocate. I had this total panic standing next to Marianne Gilhooley in the all pink girls room that I got accidentally shifted into someone else's body and it would be like some Twilight Zone you live it up then pay an extreme punishment for vanity like a toll.

—You look really sexy, Marianne Gilhooley said. You look like a movie star.

I said, I know. It's like a shock. I'm hitting the panic button here.

It felt like my inside and outside could not meet.

Mark Rogers was being a stagehand, doing the curtains and lights. All these ropes and pulleys and curtain folds like the cover of Ma and Dad's album The Stripper. I said, Hi, Mark. He stared. He had on his all black Man From U.N.C.L.E. and that wide gold buckle, low slung Wild Wild West black hiphugger belt. I said, It's Sheila.

—Oh. He laughed.

—You didn't recognize me?

—No. He laughed, looking away.

—Is it fun doing the lights?

—It's okay. He laughed, still looking away.

I would love to do the lights because then you could have total control. I had this immediate backstage pretend dream Mark Rogers and I could do the lady wristwatch drama. There's a man watch in love with her on the tightrope when whap she hits the floorboards and the crowd gathers in the hospital amphitheater to watch her operation. Her amplified heart (watch) ticking is life and death to him. Whap. I remembered that summer upstate I jumped off a rock wall and landed exactly on broken glass.

—Tell me break a leg. I smiled.

—What? He tossed his head back like Flicka, not really looking at me.

—That means good luck if you're going on Broadway. I laughed.

—Oh.

—Break a leg, Sheila, I said. I laughed.

It was the scene when the Emperor is mad at the little Gray Nightingale because it won't sing with gusto in a cage. Ma's favorite Candid Camera a guy walks into a pet store and there's a parakeet in a cage. The owner says wait a minute and disappears. So the guy's alone with this bird in a cage. He's looking around. Dog collars, Hartz Mountain Thirty Day, the bowls for the food and the bowls for the water. Suddenly this bird says hey, buddy, let me out of here.

—Third Imperial Lackey, the Emperor said and I stepped forward. Does the singing of the Jeweled Artificial Nightingale please you?

I had on this Oriental robe with gold and my face painted geisha white, blending in my bags, and a heavy black line drawn above and below each eye. You would not believe how great I looked. I remembered when Aunt Rita had that Maybelline party and forever after Ma wore black eyeliner above and below. I left The Emperor and the Nightingale notice on the kitchen table, so that way you give the other person time to think of an excuse.

—What notice? Ma said. I must have flung it.

I looked at our garbage. It was totally covered in ashes and cigarette butts and potato peels, coffee grinds, Black Label beer cans. I really did not want to reach my hands in there to rescue it. Ma was in her chair in her sponge curlers marking papers, C C C X. It's like you know you shouldn't say anything else. You know you should just take that level answer and leave.

I said, It's on Friday night. Do you want to come? I get two free tickets. I raised my eyebrows and smiled.

—Please, Ma said. Enough already. I need my R and R time. I need it, Sheila, believe me. I have a full time job, four kids, a house to maintain. Enough, man. R and R, rest and relaxation. Ma picked up her cup and drank.

This was a very hard time for Ma because her mother just died. I thought a play would chase the blues away but you know how boring a sixth grade school play would be. Annie sat alone downstairs watching Mr. Ed. I said, Why are you watching Mr. Ed, The Twilight Zone is on. I put my hand on the dial.

—No way, Sheila, she yelled. You're not getting your way.

I sat in my green chair. Mr. Ed's barn door was the half open half closed marked with an X for decoration which I noticed years and years later they copied onto our metal storm doors all across Long Island.

—I just invited Ma to my class play and she threw the notice in the garbage.

Annie sat across in the black Naugahyde shaking her head. What'd you expect a miracle? Annie said. They'll never go to anything. You're stupid to even try.

That really hurt when my sister called me stupid. Behind her on the mantel was that hinged together picture set of Michael and me. I looked forward at Wilbur and Mr. Ed. The black and white steady TV movement calms you down.

—Well, I get two tickets for free. You want to come? Mrs. Gilhooley could give you a ride.

—No.

I looked back at the TV. It was a commercial for Secret antiperspirant.

—You always have to be the star of everything, Sheila. Forget it. I'm sick of it.

That was true. I was way more the star. I always got a hundred and E for excellent and all the pictures in the album of babies were me because by the time of Annie they didn't care and at Christmas when every year Annie counted presents the boys and I always got more than her. Annie had a way worse life. With me from a distance people thought I was normal but Annie was fat so even from a distance she had it bad. The commercial switched. It's six o'clock. Do you know where your children are? Poor Ma. Ma got so sick of it that summer upstate she threw us in the car and drove home ten hours on the thruway without Dad and Robert threw up on her lap and she had to walk up and down the aisles of the only supermarket open on Sunday looking for Velveeta, bread, and milk, and Ma got back in the car and she said Jesus you would not believe the looks people gave me in there, disgust, Ma said and I'm like the wife sitting in the passenger seat. Then we got home and our driveway rock wall made of mud was fallen in and Dad, our only repairer, was still upstate doing his Master's and I went immediately downstairs because we went the whole summer without a TV and I pulled out the knob, sitting extremely close on the floor, as close as possible to the screen, and the picture flowed out filling the box and *POW* the whole gray green screen cracked into tiny bits like a held together web, a window shot, and behind the people kept on moving in black and white not even knowing what on the outside was wrong and I shut it right off in case of radiation.

Marianne Gilhooley's mother said she was forbidden from the sandpit because there might be an avalanche.

—Oh, cripes, Ma said. Give me a break.

I laughed. Ma had her arm inside our toilet bowl scrubbing all around. It was the morning after The Emperor. I said, Well, what if I was in an avalanche? And standing in the bathroom I could still hear the roars of laughter rolling through the red seat hill after my line.

—Please, Ma said. She pulled the seat for girls down, bang.

—Ma, could I please scrub the bathtub today?

—I'd really rather you didn't.

When Ma was growing up she was going full time to college, working part time at Macy's, cleaning their whole house plus cooking their supper every night, like I always saw Ma down scrubbing the floor in Queens.

—I have to scrub the tub to get a housekeeping badge. It's the only job you don't have a choice.

—Oh, Jesus, Ma said. Can't I just fake it? I'll just sign a note.

—Then I won't have really earned the badge. Please please with sugar on top and a cherry. I put my hand on her shoulder.

(—You are such a comedian, young lady, Mrs. Gilhooley said.)

Ma rising, done. I'll be your best friend, I said.

—I just scrubbed the tub!

—Good. I quick grabbed her Comet off the vanity. I swear, Ma, you won't even know I did anything. Just let me pretend, all right? I sat on her little decorative round orange rug hung on our bathtub edge and scattered pale green. Actually I was thinking of quitting Girl Scouts because they were all Republicans for the war. One thing great, Comet changed into a beautiful color with work. I pounded out our water with the control arrow down. Those people were laughing so hard at my line. The good thing about an avalanche was we could have a great 1840s Gold Rush rescue drama at night of all the townspeople rushing frantic with lit torches wildly shovelling (uhh, flesh!) to save our lives. My best report was in fourth about the Bay of Fundy in Nova Scotia where Grandpa who died was born because it had the most extreme tides in the world and you would just be walking along a beach and suddenly a giant green wall of water was rushing in and I'm standing on our fireplace slate hearth looking at that great hinged together black and white of Michael and me in geometric sunsuits, the front exactly covering my scar and my hair in two ponytails made by you would know who, and turning from the wall of bricks feel that wall of water rushing across the room at me and I'm clawing up the rock cliff trying to escape.

I lay like undersea being the girl first, the dust ruffle around the bottom of Marianne Gilhooley's double canopy bed obviously store not mother made judging from all the extreme Southern Civil War belle layers of eyelet white. Eyelet I thought of as a beautiful word at least. I lay at the bottom on her rose pink wall to wall since Mrs. Gilhooley said Marianne was forbidden from her bedspread. Floated legs of furniture, floated bottoms of drawers, like on Diver Dan, fake filmed through an aquarium. Marianne bent licking. Oh, darling, she said, I want to feel you up. The vacuum wailed in another room. I was hung upside down in her full length mirror, making me, watching, also into the camera filming it. Once outside my window Ma and Mrs. Gilhooley almost collided in our driveway. Naughty naughty, Mrs. Gilhooley waved her finger behind the windshield. I was hoping they would accidentally meet again and Mrs. would tell Ma what I did great last night in The Emperor.

—You are some comedian, young lady. Mrs. Gilhooley rushed at me backstage, her hands skull width. My whole stomach heaved. You don't know what they're going to do to you next. She said, Wait till I tell your mother what you did. She said, Why didn't your mother come? and kissed me on my hair. I shrugged. I was wondering how long I could keep this make up on, like make it to Monday or would it go all over my pillow? I could still feel her kiss on my skull. Mark Rogers was laughing it up with Misty Nixon near the ropes. She had on this sexy laced bodice with underneath all lumps and bruises poor thing from that pea.

Actually Dad drove me to the play. I didn't want to ask Mrs. Gilhooley to drive both ways because that would be too much. You try to figure the level, how much you could ask, Dad driving one way, quarter to seven and home by seven compared on the other hand to how bad at school they think your parents are for not even showing up.

—The blue line, the blue line. We had the Ranger game on driving in the dark. I said, What is the blue line anyway?

Dad burped. Sheila! He said, That's icing. You can't hit the puck all the way down the rink.

Dad had on his glasses, barrelling us up Two Mile Hollow, his face lit green from the dashboard. Once coming home late from the relatives in Queens we passed a whole house in flames but usually we only drove in the day. During the day you could see everything but at night it was hard to drive. It was totally dark and we had to aim through the train trestle with rock slabs both sides and barrelling along that curvy road at forty-five or fifty mph.

—Why not? I said.

—Well, they want to give the defense a chance.

Dad smiled. Dad watched those hockey games on Channel 9 even when the whole screen was snow, sitting on the edge of his seat watching snow with his glasses on maybe because Grandpa was a great great ice skater up in Canada when he was young.

—Thanks, Dad. I leaned back in the open door.

—Good luck, babe.

—Well, it's only one line. I slammed the door and Dad drove away. That was amazing Mrs. Gilhooley would go to a whole school play, four fairy tales, just to see her daughter's scenery in one. She said, Of course I want to see you in your play, Sheila. The taillights, no lights, headlights, Dad's brake lights, RED!, gone.

Aunt Dee said Patsy who was three months younger threw herself down on the floor and had a tantrum when we were two years old and I was being taken to the hospital. All the relatives had this dramatic goodbye for me in Queens in case I died. When I told Aunt Dee I remembered my hospital room she said, Oh, honey, I'm not a bit surprised. Aunt Dee said, What do you remember? I felt this shock anyone would want to listen to that. I remembered the crib and the cot and the long empty hall to the elevator, waiting there, and I remembered on the other wall was a beautiful window that showed the city tops of all the roofs and the sky was so blue and I went out through the window and flew.

Two girls weren't supposed to do this. Marianne Gilhooley bent licking around my nipple, her brown hair curtaining. Upstairs Mrs. Gilhooley was groaning banging the vacuum cleaner while downstairs Mr. sat in a La-Z-Boy watching Blondie or East Side Comedy with his jaw dropped, no expression. Marianne moved circling one wettened fingertip around and around. Every Saturday he had his feet up and sometimes walking past Mr. Gilhooley I wished Ma was with me so we could say together, Christ, hold a mirror to his mouth, like you wonder is this guy a mongoloid or does he really have a job?

—Open your mouth, Marianne Gilhooley put her mouth over mine and I pulled my head aside shocked. She had put part of herself inside of me. Using deduction my dear Watson I realized tongue since gums could not move and teeth would be extreme.

—What are you doing? I laughed.

—That's what boys do. It's called French kissing.

I said, They like that? I was trying to think about Eskimos rubbing noses and eating blubber and some combination with how you would do it lying on the cold tile bathroom floor and what he puts inside you. Marianne bent toward the other nipple with her mouth, circling with her tongue while in another room the groaning banging, stretching into a rope, thin white, thickening, and it's like the sailor in the Old Spice commercial whistling from house to house and the knots those sailors had to tie and then you could have two kinds of ropes in gym with knots or some the boys could climb all the way up without knots using their legs wrapped around it climbing all the way. I shot up my head.

—Marianne, you want to switch?

Marianne looked up, surprised. It's okay, she said and bent back licking and I lay undersea with the roseflung bedspread and her special white with roses ivory Kleenex with puff of gauzy pink through the slit and matching roseflung wallpaper with those tiny repeated red roses exactly, little did her mother know, like nipples.

BAM BAM

Marianne Gilhooley's head shot up. We looked at each other like you think if you look at each other it will go away. The vacuum cleaner had stopped. I realized it went off a long time ago down the hall, hurrying down the hall to time now.

—Open this door, Marianne.

BAM BAM

I laughed. It felt like the Gestapo, like a movie about doors. All my life I was waiting for a mother and now here she was banging to get in.

—Quick. Get dressed, Marianne said.

I put on Michael's yellow man tailored shirt buttoning as fast as possible remembering that old buttoning technique Ma taught me long ago of starting from the bottom so as not to end up with a telltale extra at top.

—Ready?

I nodded. It felt like Marianne Gilhooley and I were up on someone's screen. Mrs. Gilhooley stood in the hallway very fierce, The Little Engine That Could, grab you by the throat and shake.

—I know what you girls are doing in here.

So she must have done it herself some time.

—We were doing our homework, Marianne said.

No books out. Mrs. Gilhooley stood fiercely steaming from each nostril. There went all my chances of her ever telling Ma what I did good in the play.

—Don't lie to me. Mrs. Gilhooley hauled off and slammed Marianne across the face.

—Bitch, Marianne said.

—I'm telling your father, young lady.

—Bitch, Marianne yelled down the hall. She slammed the door and flung herself on her roseflung bedspread. The guy would probably just fall back asleep. Marianne sobbed. My bedspread I could fling upon any time because it was machine washable warm tumble dry from Sears but it had ribbing which left indents in your face so you had to fold it down to cry, fold it back when done. Marianne, sobbing, plucked a tissue from her special Kleenex box. They lived a riskier life in the developments. I was wondering about my role, hand her the tissues like the butler on Batman. Marianne's shoulders heaved. Now was when her window banged open and the prince climbed in.

—Well, I got to go, Marianne.

Ma and I would never have a slapping scene, and Marianne had four pillows but in our family you got one and upstairs during a commercial Dad came creeping barefooted in his boxers and undershirt and glasses for watching TV, carrying pillows from the boys' room into their room then later carrying them back, and that summer upstate we had one pillow for six heads so we passed it around but every night Ma waited until the lucky person fell asleep and she snuck in and stole it right out from under your head, one time sneaking, reaching at my head. I said, really loud, What do you want, Ma?

Ma had her hand on her heart, staggering upstate. Jesus, you scared the hell out of me.

—Good.

—Oh, crap. Give me the pillow. You don't want it.

—I do too want it. What do you think I took it for?

But when I awoke, darn darn foiled again. So actually using deduction Ma must have taken me to the allergist's after upstate or otherwise I would have had my own special plastic crackling brand.

—Bye, Marianne.

Marianne did not look up. I looked left and right and sped. Goodbye, Mr. Gilhooley. Thank you for having me over. He lifted his hand a bit.

Thin white trace lines were blown caught into the brown ground like beautiful scars. Woo! I ran. Marianne had white short cuts on her fingernails like ice skate blades which she said were stress marks. What stress if you had one brother, you got all the great clothes and furniture, and a princess phone extension next year. Woo. I had a beautiful white curved moon scar on my hand from that rock wall jump on glass upstate. I pulled the glass out and put it in a garbage can so as not to cut someone else and I was running across that speckled floor with the evergreen ping pong table one side, ice cream machine other, drip drop. I washed it in the sink then that great moment of coagulation when the blood goes like the white back and forth woven threads of gauze. The janitor was very mad downstairs wiping up my blood on the speckled floor. I was running with traffic. Always walk against, Ma would say, but I was running way high on the ground where the cars would not climb, Ma! The trees swayed empty beautiful and the sky so winter blue. White air puffed out of my mouth.

In The Emperor and the Nightingale my problem was I had no microphone and my only line was a soft giggle to reach five hundred people in a whole vast auditorium painted both sides with beautiful history murals of winding water and people of Nissequott in the past. Problem two was the ridiculousness of being in a sixth grade class play when all the parents are bored and the kids are nervous wrecks.

—Third Imperial Lackey, the Emperor called to me. Does the singing of the Jeweled Artificial Nightingale please you?

Hundreds of thousands of faces were looking up at me like it must have been for Ma in the PTA variety show and I was sitting in the audience watching her on the stage dancing the cancan dressed up as either a diamond or heart.

—Tee hee. (Pause.) Tee hee. (Pause.) Tee hee. (Pause.) I stepped back woodenly.

Ma loved in The Producers that moment of the audience's shock when the frauleins are waltzing happily singing Springtime for Hitler. Ma would have been the first to get my joke if she was there.

I went from Marianne Gilhooley's straight in with my reversible jacket still on.

—Oh. Hiyah. Ma had my favorite sky blue ashtray on the ironing board. Everyone's clothes were spread unwrinkled on their bed. A lion was running very fast at the camera in black and white then cut to Tarzan looking good practically naked grabbing a vine.

—Tarzan, Ma? I laughed. She was pretty cute sneaking that in on a Saturday ironing.

—Nothing else is on, Ma said and I sat in her desk chair and together we watched.

Chapter 8

—That was a big thing! Grandma said. Everyone was upset.
That was a big operation you had!

I batted my eyelashes like a cartoon close up of a giraffe's demure look. I loved it when they got dramatic. I was obeying Ma's orders to keep Grandma out of the kitchen as long as possible and also investigating the past. What did they do exactly? I said.

—Well, as far as I know, you had some cartilage that was connecting your front and back and they had to cut that.

I dropped my jaw, also ready to run and upchuck. I said, I had cartilage connecting my back and front? Yuck. What do you mean?

—Well, that was my understanding. There was cartilage grown between your chest bone and your spine and they had to cut that.

—Yuck. I pressed my arms, like when you see something disgusting only quite another story when the disgusting is part of you, inside you, carrying it around for years.

—You should ask your mother or father. They know more.

—Well, they just said it was indented and they pulled it out so I could play volleyball. My grandfather said they put a piece of metal in for ten days to re-form it.

—That could have been. Grandma sat next to our modern art lamp twisted rusty metal and Grandma's hair exact iron gray repeating rounds left from those black spike tunnel curlers and fat jowls on her arms, her blouse autumn leaves growing out of slacks medium brown. Grandma gained a lot of weight since Grandpa died. Christ, Ma said, she's not going to be able to move soon, and Dad just moved through like he did not hear.

—You know what I remember, Grandma said, is your mother staying with you up in the hospital.

—My mother stayed with me in the hospital! I jumped up on my knees like eureka. I said, I thought she stayed with me because I remember her nightgown on the other bed! Finally my life was making sense. Behind us, hidden, Dad shuffled back in the kitchen with his new slippers we all got him for Christmas. He burped and opened the refrig.

—Oh, yeah, she stayed right in the room with you. I remember it was New Year's Eve and I felt sorry for her so I brought her a plate of boiled shrimp. Remember that, Jack, I brought Mary some boiled shrimp in the hospital?

—The hospital? Dad held his Black Label and a little dish.

—From my operation.

—I don't remember that. Dad set the little dish and popped his beer. Dad got very upset if you said hospital.

—You know what they were almost afraid once I was allergic to shrimp.

—Get out of here. Dad smiled.

—I didn't know what else to do! Grandma said. I felt sorry for her. I wanted to bring her something!

—The allergist tested me for it, Dad.

—Ma, have a nut. Dad held out the dish. It was copper shaped like an autumn leaf. Now Dad would say I never went to an allergist.

—No, thank you, Jack. I'll ruin my appetite.

Dad scooped a small amount, popping them in his mouth like at a poker game with the other players Grandma in the Naugahyde, me on the floor, Dad standing, ready to leave.

—Dad, did Ma stay with me in the hospital? I narrowed my eyes. I had a witness here.

—I think she did. Dad's deep brown eyes looked at me then glanced off, ricochet, do I exist or what?

—I remember her cot. I said, That's my first memory is my hospital room.

—Get out of here. Dad picked up another handful, smiling, any second about to leave. Annie rose up the stairs behind the banister bars. Get out of here, Dad said. You don't remember that. Dad kept throwing peanuts in, smiling.

I had my legs out straight, leaned back, my elbows locked. I said, I do too remember that.

—What doesn't she remember? Annie stood at the top of the stairs.

—My hospital room from my operation.

—Oh. Annie walked off into the kitchen.

—Dad, I do too remember it.

Dad chuckled, holding his beer.

—I remember it. It had a window on the right and the hallway to the left with an elevator and Ma's cot was white and it was lower down and I was leaning against this white railing and there was like an apricot frilly nightgown on the cot so I thought Ma was coming and I just remember the sound of that elevator opening and closing down the hall and I didn't know if Ma would come.

—You're making that up. Dad smiled, picking more peanuts up.

—When are we eating? Annie appeared again outside the kitchen doorway. I'm starving to death.

—Six-fifteen. Dad popped a bunch of peanuts in.

It felt like I did not exist. I could see all this living room furniture and walls.

—I got to make my turnips, guys! Annie, you going to help?

Annie and Dad had an argument about supper and then they all went into the kitchen. I sat on the rug looking at the accordion door hifi Dad made. I was going to go distancing if I didn't have someone near me.

The boys were silent blanked, whitish flickering over

them. Hi, Sheila, Robert said. He was downstairs through the banister rungs. I had this small friendly brother who accepted being talked into things.

My knees were raised, Robert's little handcuffs around my ankle bones, my top half flying up and down, moving across the room doing sit-ups. Robert and I were the hoboes on a railroad handcar with the hifi and fake musical instruments hung on panelling for our landscape. Watching TV Robert would gladly sit on my behind and during commercials he bounced like a plastic horse ride outside of Grant's and I went ahhhhhh broken by bumps and you could feel your ribs and great skeletal container while on TV in black and white the single pearl fell twisting breathing fast in, out, your brother watching very concerned, ahhhhhh, dropping slowly through the liquid Prell heart going so hard.

—Hear ye hear ye. I had my hands town crier. Dad startled turned. I said, I just did two hundred sit ups for all those interested. Dad turned back to his flour cannister.

—You better be careful, Sheila, Grandma said. You'll hurt your back.

Dad walked across balancing the little silver shovel. He sprinkled white across the roasting pan. Here, Dad said, do something. Stir this.

—One sec. I stepped out, breathing, on the back stoop. The sky was still orange with all the dark crisscrosses of March trees and air dark wet. Yesterday that sand was so cold, the top rim trees still bare and all around vast tan emptiness. Green is good for the eyes, the mother says in The Ugly Duckling. You wonder about inside and outside, how the green could infiltrate. The wind blew. The sandpit guard dogs barked. I stood and my shadow stood at the bottom of the pit. Yeah, sure, sitting in Queens watching The Invisible Man, sitting extremely close to the black and white and how he sat opposite me unwinding around and around his white bandages, making himself disappear. I waved and the shadow girl waved. I sat back down and she disappeared, the sand very cold, only my pants and under-pants, two thin cloths between. I set my hands in mittens underneath. You can feel the skin web and bones. Then without hands just on the cushion of yarn. Better. Joyce's mother's hands had river run blues of veins that day she made us tuna fish on Pepperidge Farm with Fritos and how she sat downstairs in black and white through their banister watching Days of Our Lives, as sands through the hourglass so go The Days of Our Lives, which I could not remember was that before or after the assassination of JFK, both though at one o'clock.

—Hello, crocus. Soft purple with inside shock orange red.

—I didn't come in here to work, Dad. I took the wooden spoon and stirred his white powder: that worktable scene in Frankenstein of the monster left lying lifeless, lightning hits. It's not just a monster movie, Dad said, it's really about wanting a friend. Why would someone say I'll meet you at the sandpit at one o'clock and not show up?

—Get that good stuff up, now.

—You worry about your red cabbage, Dad. I looked up and our orange clock said fifteen after five, Sunday, March, 1969.

—You making red cabbage, Jack?

—From a jar, Ma. Dad held up the Lohmann's. I thought: my cartilage got cut between my front and back.

—Sheila, you look tired, Grandma said.

I looked down fast at the burners and pan. When she said tired aching shot through my throat up under my face. It beat out like this hydrant hose bulging under my eyes and like a tree trunk rounding choked my throat. I moved the wooden spoon in the flour and meat remains. When people said tired I just automatically looked away, like down the hall, the green cement blocks and the speckled floor, and you know they are going to attack your face next.

—Jack, doesn't Sheila look tired?

Dad bent crashing silver pots around my shins, our

stovelight on my hands and the roasting pan paste of brown but my face up away, out of the light. Dad straightened and emptied the jar as one more brown liquidy area of mine bubbled and I stirred through, calming it. Bags under your eyes could be equal opportunity that anyone could suffer one day from not enough sleep or not equal opportunity, only old age, or in my case being deformed. I read about this boy who started speeding up his aging as soon as he was born and by the time he was seven he looked eighty-two and his parents just left food outside his door on a tray, like I looked partially like all those Russian old men Kremlin guys banging the table for communism, a little like Nixon which was interesting of God. Dad put the small silver pot on medium.

—I'm not tired. I just did two hundred sit ups.

—She's got circles under her eyes! Grandma said and Ma emerged in her soft blue afternoon caftan holding her green cup with pink sponge curlers for Sunday and at that rate of speed a ninety per cent chance she heard.

—How you doing, guys? Ma's voice was soft. You could never tell which way it would go.

Oop boop bitta batta watta chew
Oop boop bitta batta watta chew
And they swam and they swam right over the dam

and singing that softly Ma poked your stomach, but you could never tell which way it would go, like any second you could get screamed at for being deformed.

Ma crossed toward the oven. Circles under your eyes was more polite than bags, lines that could be erased, drawn on from the outside but bags was inside, disgusting bulging from inside of you. You develop like this whole facial specialty system, like once a year you're waiting tensed during The Wizard of Oz for that forest scene. Look at the circles under my eyes, the Lion sobs. And Dorothy dabs with her handkerchief at his face.

(—How's Marianne Gilhooley? Ma said yesterday.

—Fine, I lied. Outside the train shot by gray metal black. Our orange clock said ten after three. I said, I'm cold. Can I make cocoa?)

—Get that good stuff in back, Dad said, our gray metal pliers to turn on the stovelight in back lying next to our brown instant coffee in glass and two orange ashtrays filled with gray and white, and Dad hovered with another silver shovelful of white.

—No more flour, Dad. You always make too much.

—A little bit.

—Dad, I screamed. Now I have to work harder. Jesus. Boo boopie doo he looked at me with those woebegone stupid baggy eyes. Dad picked up his Black Label and drank.

—Oi vay. Ma moved from the freezer, a cigarette in one hand, ice in the other, her hand claw cupped, and her eyes part closed as Dad lit a cigarette.

—Mary, Grandma said, don't you think Sheila looks tired?

Ma dropped her ice and turned and Dad dropped his match. You could hear the TV below. Dad blew smoke. Ma said, I really don't view that as your concern, Lorraine. I view that as my concern. So let's drop it.

Dad stared at Ma with his jaw dropped. Ma bent and slid the garbage, the TV going downstairs, Dad still with his jaw dropped for drama but Ma's back to him reaching the vodka, Dad still jaw dropped, and Grandma sitting confused near our yellow hanging light and I had this sudden feeling like it did not matter if I existed at all to them but I could just pass right through the glass out our window and fly far far away. Dad was shaking his head, putting his cigarette in the orange ashtray slit, still shaking his head. You figure a normal problem the mother would say, Oh, no, she doesn't look tired to me. Maybe she's a little tired, she'll get some rest. I had a fist turned choking inside my throat.

—All I said is she looks tired! Grandma cracked up on the high notes. I'm concerned is she getting enough sleep!

—Excuse me, babe. Dad reached for our kettle and held it under the tap drumming in, our kettle classy copper now. I moved my spoon around.

—Sheila is healthy, Ma said. So let's drop the whole thing. She bent and put her vodka away. Ma slid the garbage back in place.

My head pounded and it ached all up under my face. I felt like shooting myself in the head to stop the pain. Dad shut the faucet and poured a thin stream.

—DAD!

—Give me that. Dad took my spoon and glared at me.

—When are you going to face it you make too much gravy, Dad. I stared at Dad and Dad stared back. Tuu, he said with his tongue and looked away, then burped.

—Good. You make it, I said. I'm taking your watch.

I violently pulled Dad's second drawer which I could stand and see in now no gun. Safety pins, shoelaces, watch with a second hand, total miracle for a family like ours. Crystal of a watch, crystal of a watch. Over and over they had this word talking about the crystal of a watch never once telling you what it is then they only talk about it when it is broken and you're like: JUST SAY WHAT IT IS, WOULD YOU. CRIPES, ALMIGHTY. They never explain fully the truth to you like why would someone say meet you at the sandpit at one then not show up? And I had this stupid lady wristwatch wherever I go she falls off the tightrope. I slammed the drawer.

—GO!

And the white white wrap up white and the crack up crystal screen of our television once.

—GO! Annie said. You're like WOULD SOMEBODY PLEASE TELL ME WHAT IS GOING ON.

—GO! Robert dropped his arm, and I tore off Wide World of Sports up our dark March road, Annie bouncing around the asphalt.

—Nine, Annie said.

—Nine! You read it wrong. I said, Crap crap crap.

—Begin. Miss Whirp clicked her stopwatch on. Anita Garibaldi's feet swung slightly through the air, held up, gripping the silver rail bar, like a girl hung on a clothesline to dry, like Ma and me November 22, 1963. Anita Garibaldi had slight puffs under her eyes. They were not anywhere in my category but were like baby sandsharks compared to a whale. Still, seeing them brought a slight feeling of painy weight under my eyes from me to her, like for Dad, like we were all these moping bloodhounds sniff scrape lumbering across the earth, Hounds of the Baskervilles, solving what? That rail reminded me of my steel bar inside my chest which I didn't remember anyway. I remembered the silver handlebar though and it had those white rubber grip ends so no pain if you poke in your chest riding your red tricycle very fast along. I leaned against the padded evergreen wall, padded cells for us in gym, and unfortunately for the Presidential Physical Fitness Test classes combined so I had to see Marianne Gilhooley twice a week. You would rather not see someone so disgusted she stayed away.

—Ten, Miss Whirp said.

So far I had the bent arm hang record, gripping for dear life, thirty seconds, closest Debbie Diamond four, and Marianne Gilhooley, oooph, less than one, oooph, drop right off, Marianne much more efficient at being a helpless girl and also what with Nixon and the Vietnam War you also don't know the morality of trying hard at the Presidential Physical Fitness Test. Peace, man. Marianne sat on a nipple colored bombardment ball, rolling it, pressured under her behind. Why would someone say I'll meet you at the sandpit at one o'clock and not show up?

—How's Marianne Gilhooley?

—Fine. I hung my reversible jacket and looked out at the gray death lilac bush holding my warm cocoa cup To My

Favorite Teacher actually owned by Ma. After a while you just figure no one will ever come. The bad thing is hope. Pretend you don't exist and fly out the window. I got my biography of Gandhi. What a lucky world we were to at least have had him once. I faked it fine with Ma because once waiting all day for Marianne Gilhooley to go ice skating and she never called Ma stood over me with her dustrag: This is for the birds, Sheila, come on. Staring at me. What? I said. You could hear the TV that slight steady noise of programs coming from deep downstairs.

—I think you get overly dependent on one person.

I slammed the hassock spinning around. I said, Leave me alone.

She said, You did the same goddamn thing with Joyce Sanneefrannee. Christ, with the mooning around.

I said, You know her last name.

—I would not sit around waiting for anyone. Goodbye! Goodbye! Ma sang. I'm having my jollies, man!

—Twenty, Miss Whirp said, Anita Garibaldi hanging silent, a gold cross hung down her chest without a scar I'm sure. At least unlike me Anita Garibaldi had the courage to grow out her bangs and hanging up there she had arm muscles the size of potatoes, not what a girl should have, like little repeats of her baggy eyes, her gold cross though with a little sculpture Jesus, like a question mark, which we would never have but ours just plain, classier, because she was just out from Queens and the gold of her cross clashing with the silver of the bar and her skin off a shade, yellowy tan, more dirtyish immigrant than Marianne Gilhooley and me, one reason Marianne Gilhooley was better off being friends with me, also Anita's hair dirty blond like Annie's yuck.

—Sheila, Marianne Gilhooley said rolling that red ball back and forth below her behind. You want to come to a party Friday night at Kathy O'Rourke's?

—Twenty-five, Miss Whirp said.

I said, Anita's going to break my record.

Anita hung quietly by the neck from the silver rail staring ahead.

I said, She's not even shaking.

When Marianne said that about the party the tanned gym floorboards spun around. It was three days since she did not show up at the sandpit and I learned the meaning of stood me up, an expression I was hoping to keep only on TV.

I said, I thought your mother didn't want us to be friends.

Miss Whirp said, Thirty.

There went my physical fitness record down the drain. Anita crossed her ankles, hanging in the air and people, especially hoodlums, clapped.

—She can go to hell, Marianne said.

I said, Well, is it okay if my father drives there?

Miss Whirp said forty and Anita crossed her ankles the other way, Marianne Gilhooley still sitting pressured on that dulled red rubber bombardment ball rolling it back and forth under her rear. My burst of sweat was only just drying from her saying she can go to hell. My stomach was only just back from the invitation helium jump. Over us hung all these ropes and rings, strung up attached to the ceiling. I knew exactly how Anita felt. She was hung up there shaking, twisting her ankles like a washcloth through which you try to drip the pain. You're gripping staring straight where the evergreen mat edge meets pale green cement block wall. Those tanned gym floorboards are like the Allstate commercial of hands holding little dolls and toy houses which are supposed to be us.

—Forty-five.

Anita convulsed gripping back and forth on that silver bar, her ankles twisting. Everyone screamed, Anita's fists slipping gripping on that silver rail, switched her ankles, then her whole self convulsed, hitting back and forth.

—Fifty, fifty-two, fifty-four. Everyone jumped screaming, Anita's fists slipping her ankles gripping going wham wham hitting her silver rail.

—Sixty.

Anita dropped to the mat in a heap. Everyone was screaming jumping, the hoodlums wolf whistling and across the gym the boys were turned from their silver chin up bar, confused.

—I heard some junior high boys might be there.

I turned backwards and glared at Marianne Gilhooley in the on off oncoming headlights' light as Dad screeched us out of Tanglewood left toward the even more cheapo developments then shifted over his steering wheel reaching for his Kents pretending not to hear.

—South of Poquonsett, Dad. I said it warning. South of Poquonsett was the really hoodlum cheapo part. I said, Dad, did we ever go south of Poquonsett to get rocks?

I had this feeling Dad didn't like Marianne Gilhooley that much. Quite the tension with her in the backseat and us.

—I don't think so, babe.

—How about the barbecue?

—Nope.

—Mr. Convoy lives south of Poquonsett, doesn't he?

—He does.

Mr. Convoy also taught social studies. You try to calm a link. We passed the farmstand, cornfield, bulldozed land where Dad's new high school was going to be.

We slammed the doors. Dad screeched off, little knowing the juvenile delinquency he had driven me to. It was plain cement walk, all the houses painted four sides, unlike Tanglewood, classier, the front cedar shingle three sides paint, unlike us, classiest, four sides cedar shingle, and here all the fences metal chain link, unlike Tanglewood, redwood stockade or chain link painted in large brown and white waves, and unlike us, split rail or if you had to green chain link for a pool. But these people would always have the cheapest metal chain link, mothers working in the cafeteria, killer german shepherds throwing themselves vicious, rattling fence, and no trees, no hemlocks, no junipers, just let the whole cement length of their foundations show. It felt like a movie turning point: would I become a hoodlum or not? I had on my brown hiphugger bellbottoms, Michael's brown, yellow, and white striped polo shirt, summer undershirt to give the underline bra effect more than a winter one. I had my hair in two ponytails, yellow yarn ribbon from Genovese one side, white other. I looked pretty cool. Not cool, but the best possible for someone in my condition. We stood on the stoop, plain cement.

—Marianne, did Kathy O'Rourke's father really die building the Verrazano?

—I don't know. She never talks—

A fat boy about third grade led us down the basement steps. I did not tell Dad they had a basement. You get kind of nervous, pell mell rushing teenagers and many murder movies of falling downstairs. There was a long table of snacks and a bar with stained glass lamps, a Schaeffer clock, and all these hoodlums. There was a record on, Crystal Blue Persuasion possibly about drugs. The basement had maroon poles. The last time I was in a basement was before we moved to Nissequott with maroon poles and I went swing yer partner, crooking my elbow roller skating round and round while down below rolling metal wheels over cement Michael moved his new truck back and forth and against the wall our washing machine with the wringer where I once dashed my Misty Nixon doll.

It looked like a movie set for a teenager party. That snack table had everything: M&Ms, plain potato chips, Ruffles, Mr. Salty pretzels, Doritos, Fritos. That was a hanging Schaeffer beer stained glass lamp over the bar and like five piles with seventy-five coasters each.

—Oh, Sheila, Kathy O'Rourke said, I'm so glad you could come.

I wondered if she was giving me a different polite line since she knew I was not a hoodlum, ease her in. You wonder why someone becomes a hoodlum, like was it because her father fell off the bridge.

—I like your stained glass lamp, I said. In our area of Nissequott we would never have a stained glass lamp but you could argue it had the church effect of reds and blues.

—Oh, she said, my uncle works for Schaeffer.

—Jeannie's here! Marianne Gilhooley kind of squealed and Kathy O'Rourke, who was slightly chubby but perfect straight hair, perfect freckles, also left.

I stood near the snack table corner near the stairs where the fat brother said toll bridge, toll bridge, lowering his arm for M&Ms. The bags under my eyes really bulged. I had this sudden feeling I was the only one with no bra and still bangs. Hoodlums were all around the red record player like doing a scene from Patty Duke, teenagers. Anita Garibaldi was near the food too. Anita was also a chicken wing flat as a board problem face but she had more guts in life. I put an M&M inside a Bugle and ate. Everyone had on really great clothes. A Bugle was the newest snack, like a little cornucopia with a semi-Frito taste, and woven basket look. The reason I put the M&M in the Bugle was then if Anita asked what I was doing I could talk about inventing an even newer snack sensation. They were really cool looking at a record album with a gun. I knew cornucopia because we had one on the coffee table with plastic fruit. When Ma was a girl the only time they had fruit was someone was sick.

—HI, ANITA! Anita was pretty close. I waved so she would know the direction.

—Hi, Sheila.

—Congratulations on your bent arm hang.

I kind of moved down the table.

—Thanks. Congratulations on your shuttle run, Anita said.

—Thanks. How'd you do on the shuttle?

—Fourteen-seven. You got thirteen-six, right?

—Yeah. How come you're so good at the bent arm hang? You do chin ups?

Anita shook her head.

—You're really great at that, I said. Anita looked kind of cute with her dirty blond sideburns and immigrantish skin. I said, You've got arm muscles, don't you?

Anita turned sideways and flexed. I shook my head. I turned sideways and flat. Anita was eating Mr. Salties and in a way she looked like that skinny thin sailor on the dark blue box.

I said, What'd you do in the standing broad?

—Six-six.

—Six-eight.

—That's good, Anita said. Because you're short.

—I know. I don't understand why I'm good at it. Do you know why you're good at the bent arm?

—Nope.

—Did you set a national record?

Anita shook her head. She said, Miss Whirp called Washington D.C. and some girl did seventy-five.

—Crud, I said.

Anita looked off, like bored. I was pretty fast at boring her.

—Anita, who's this record by?

—The Beatles. She kind of stared at me. She said, You never heard this before? She said, I'm getting a soda. Want one?

—Yes. Thank you.

—What kind?

A normal person would say Coke or 7-Up.

—Black cherry.

She looked at me. I figured black cherry I could blend more with the maroon poles. I put another M&M inside a Bugle, also horn of plenty, as Ma put it. I stood alone. I looked up fate in our dictionary. Things you were born into you could not control. My face. The trouble was people thought you had control and they blamed you for living inside it. My favorite thing was when Ma changed the water color in her glass swan swimming on a mirror near our dictionary. Dump it out gush and roll the white bar of Ivory round and round the washrag cleaning it. Actually it was through soap they found out I needed my operation. One day Pop and Uncle Tommy were giving me a bath and he must have got some soap in your eye or something because you commenced to cry. So Tommy says to me, Dad, there's something wrong with this kid. I says what are you talking about? He says look it how her chest heaves when she cries. The kid can't breathe! Now of course by this time you had stopped crying. So I says wait a second and I rubbed a little more soap in your eye and of course you begun to cry again and sure enough I could see what he meant. Your whole chest was heaving in and out. Gasping, don't you know. So I says to Tommy we got to get this kid to a doctor, pronto.

—Thanks. I laughed because they had black cherry and also it was the older fashioned you had to cut the triangles in, which she had gone to the trouble of, and I had an inspiration I could talk to her, streaming back through all our changes we saw in life from pop tops to can opener kind and in cars streaming back from seat belts everywhere to remembering when a seatbelt was a shock. What's that? Joyce said, A seatbelt. It looked like a snake lying there. They backed down the driveway, Joyce's family and me driving down to the beach with that great red plaid fringe blanket.

—I'm going to get my soda, Anita said. See you.

Oh. I got the picture of her soda strategy. All these boys were the ones that got in fights. I drank some black cherry. Who would care about seat belts anyway? Then Ma filled the swan with water and dropped in food color dots coloring it. Those M&Ms were like belly buttons. Once in Queens Ma gave a wild basement party and they had 1950s pictures, black and white, including one with a black man, their friend, and they were all sitting at a checkered table not leaving him alone, possibly the same party Pop came home and found Mr. Convoy standing in the refrigerator light eating raw bacon.

—Sheila, why are you standing near that pole? Marianne Gilhooley said.

A lot of the hoodlum girls were dancing with each other.

—I'm a pole flower, I said.

—What? she yelled. People kept moving in front of her.

I shook my head. Marianne was sitting on this oldest hoodlum's lap, seventh grade though I heard he got left back at least once and his skin was even dirtier colored than Anita Garibaldi's, take a bath, buddy, and he had a cast on one hand I heard from fighting, and this flesh thumb sticking up out of the white, the two sitting on a metal folding chair without arms but his arms around her, like a version of Aunt Rita and Mr. Hanrahan when young.

—Come here, Marianne said. Sheila is an expert at the Jerk.

You could interpret that two ways. Actually I was an expert at the Jerk. But you think why would someone become an expert at a dance with that name? Because our house had two and a half baths and downstairs when Wonderama-a-go-go came on the only dance you could secretly fit in the downstairs bathroom with the door slightly opened to let music in was jerking your top half over the vanity. Also, next thing you find yourself at the bus stop when no cars are coming doing the Jerk to stay warm and to keep those german shepherds entertained.

Artie Vitteretti tossed back his lock of dirty blond, sitting with that white cast and flesh thumb stuck out on Marianne Gilhooley's lap. Sheila, let's see the Jerk, he said.

You feel semi like a performing dog but on the other hand at our Christmas party dancing in the school halls this guy told Marianne Gilhooley my behind looked cute doing the

Jerk. Basically you take the level you can get, and I remembered Ma doing the Twist on the patio when her favorite song came on, all the rest back screaming laughing by the blue jewel night light pool, and I stood on the edge of the slate watching Ma twist to Meet the Beatles, that album we barrelled up to Grant's so fast to get when it came out, and the store manager said is that for her or you? Ma said, Me! and I was swinging on those silver rails to guide the shopping carts on our good trip to Grants, before the allergist's, and then I stood on the patio edge watching Ma pointing out one toe, grinding her hips, her eyes closed, and her head thrown back.

> Little child, little child
> Little child, won't you dance with me?
> I'm so sad and lonely
> Baby take a chance with me!

Maybelline had drawings of eye close ups using a Cover Up Stick to hide crow's feet. I did not have crow's feet. Still, you work up a fake hope what with once maybe I was allergic to birds. In mythology my closest deformity was Cyclops and I had a good joke to tell someone: my eyes were my Achilles' heel.

—Can I help you?

—Oh, no thank you. I dropped the Erase Cover Up Stick and hurried away. For me to appear in the Genovese make up aisle was like for Frankenstein to pucker and ask for lipstick in say Sweetheart Red. I walked through conditioners toward aftershaves. At the ceiling top was a rounded mirror to catch shoplifters and in it, bulging, Marianne Gilhooley and Anita Garibaldi appeared. I shot right toward prescriptions.

It was the end of April. I hadn't talked to Marianne Gilhooley in about a month. Actually our last contact wasn't talk but push. We're sitting in the back with Mrs. at the wheel, those strange purple curlers bulging every oncoming headlights.

—Did they have snacks, girls?

—Oh, yes, I said. Even Bugles.

—Bugles! What are Bugles?

Mrs. and I were really getting along. I said, Basically a corn chip in the shape of a trumpet. I said, They look like a cross between shredded wheat and a Frito, I said, but more corn on the cob taste than Frito.

—Oh. I never heard of them before.

—They're the latest, I said.

—I'll have to try them.

—They come in a box, I said. I guess for more protection. They're supposed to look like a bugle but they look like a horn of plenty, I said.

We drove past the dug foundation for the new high school and we all looked. Telephone pole telephone pole. Marianne Gilhooley leaned toward me. I think I have a hickey, she said. Ugh, I said. I pushed her away. Goodbye, Mrs. Gilhooley. Thank you for driving me. Mrs. Gilhooley was pulled that halfway uphill driveway position. It's like climbing out of an Apollo liftoff. I suddenly felt like kissing Mrs. goodbye.

We both bounced back near the Heaven Scent pyramid without touching. Hi, I said.

—Sheila. Hi.

I nodded and started by. She touched my arm and my stomach felt punched. Her fingernails still had those white skate blades cut across.

—How are you?

—Fine. I felt like bending over and pressing my stomach. She dropped her arm. She said, Are you shopping?

—Yes. My stomach hurt.

She said, What do you need? I'll get it for free.

I thought does she have some deal with the manager?

—I don't need anything, thanks.

Anita Garibaldi rounded the light blue angel display and stopped. Hi, Sheila.

—Hi, I said and I realized they were here shoplifting.

—Sheila, let me get you something. It's free.

There were all these pale blue boxes stacked up.

—What do you want? Marianne Gilhooley said.

I had this instant vision of a plane coming along but instead of pulling a sign pulling navy blue fishnets.

It was almost six and the sun still way up over our chain linked sump. Anita stood at the smaller end of the silver shopping cart jails thinking perhaps of being behind bars. They were going off to be juvenile delinquents and I was going off to be a goody good. I remembered that Candid Camera parakeet caught in its cage. The sun hung over tree brown blur like a fringe of bangs about to turn green. I loved it past the equinox. My stomach was walking along okay now. I loved it when every day no matter what you got more light. I could say I thought she was buying them for me.

—There you are. Marianne Gilhooley smiled, that moon round, white milk bowl face. She pulled a flat package from under her jacket. I checked height, weight, navy not black. Navy was my level sexiness for sixth grade spring.

—Thanks.

—Sure. Marianne Gilhooley smiled.

—See you. I waved and I waved to Anita Garibaldi and I walked away alone.

Chapter 9

—I t's the front page. I passed the paper in to Dad and got our buns.

Woman Passenger Killed
Kennedy Escapes in Crash

Dad headed out from the fire lane past the maroon shopping center poles, Hills, through our parking lot dip too deep to drive through when it rained. Inside had three pictures: a guy in a rowboat poking the car top with a pole, second, front door open and a scuba diver inside, third, Kennedy, blurry, walking away from the camera. He looked like Dad walking away.

Diver Dan used to be one of my favorite shows but only because nothing else was on. They filmed through an aquarium with puppets, very fake, and Diver Dan had on so much underwater astronaut equipment you couldn't see his face to see should you fall in love. I kept trying to figure out what I was watching on TV when Mary Joe Kopechne was upside down underwater in his car searching for that bubble of air they told you to find to survive. Bubble of air, bubble of air. They never said the truth that that bubble of air runs out. In June Pop stopped to visit on his way back from Ireland where it rained on him for forty days and he told me when I had my operation I was in an oxygen tent!

—I hit you?

—Yes, you hit me! Here I come running all the way up to Roosevelt Hospital on my lunch hour to see my darling grandaughter, I reached my hand inside your oxygen tent and you slapped me!

Finally, some evidence to earn sympathy. What a god damn shame, Ma always said about that second cousin blinded from oxygen.

Annie was on the coping holding Dad's watch. My underwater record so far was fifty-two seconds. One of the nicest things was sitting on the bottom and the train goes by. You're weightless, light limbed, feeling the vibrations from the outer world but muffled from it all. I thought fifty-two would be enough to find the bubble of air and survive but Annie just emphasized my flaw.

—I can't believe you still can't open your eyes underwater, Sheila. What's wrong with you?

—It doesn't say in the newspaper story he could open his eyes underwater and she could not. What if your car crashes at night anyway?

Annie stood on our rock wall like a crow's nest peering toward the Hanrahans'. It's Aunt Rita and Irene hitting pots, she said.

—The lunar module just separated from the mother ship. I flopped on my back to rest.

—Aunt Rita, wouldn't it be great if we saw a UFO tonight of all nights?

Aunt Rita had her brown quart Reingold bottle, her glass interestingly frosted with falling autumn leaves, her hair amber, her brown red of tortoiseshell comb, sitting in her yellow back stoop anti-bug light.

—Well, you know, Sheila, not every UFO is a flying saucer.

I did a double take. I said, What do you mean? To Ma Aunt Rita was off the wall with the astrology stuff.

—Some are just meteors.

I could hear the TV inside, their color console with I'm

sure him asleep holding Rheingold about to tip on his lap. Also on the kitchen counter they had an orange Daniel J. Hanrahan prescription bottle for Thorazine.

I said, Well, you know that was how Superman got to earth was holding onto a meteor.

To me Aunt Rita was partially off the wall believing since both of them were Virgos born in August they would be together forever. However, someone totally off the wall would not be so logical about types of UFO. We were sitting on her back stoop with that evening sky washed slight light so his individual tomato stakes stuck out three dimensional and floating off the swingset came those red and white stripes, the TV droning every channel every minute getting everyone down here on earth ready for men to walk on the moon, and if I was lucky Aunt Rita was going to brush my hair one hundred strokes that night.

I looked up Thorazine at Charlotte M. Brewster Memorial Library. I skipped Dennis the Menace, Donna Reed, Lucy, Beverly Hillbillies for neighbor research. It felt like everyone in the reference room was giving me looks for gathering psychological info on my next door neighbor.

Ma was in her red, white, and blue two piece barefooted holding orange clippers, cutting dead irises. I had the folded library notes in my fringed cutoffs' pocket. I said, Ma, you remember that neighbor of ours from before Nissequott who snuck in on his wife with a knife while she was taking a shower?

—That goddamn fool!

This was June, right after elementary school ended forever for me, when the sixth grade tore up all notebooks and threw white pieces out yellow bus windows onto our village green.

—Why did he do that anyway?

—Psycho! Ma yelled.

I was blank.

—Norman Bates, man, Ma said. Get with it. She threw dead stalks down on the grass.

I said, Norman Bates?

Ma looked at me. She said, You mean you've never seen Psycho?

I was kind of shocked Ma didn't know something like that about me. I said, No. It's really scary, isn't it?

—You better believe it. Ma crouched along, cutting dead flowers above slates around their bedroom.

—Oh, I said, I guess psycho is from psychology.

Ma tossed out the dead. She slowly straightened and moved down.

—Ma, remember when you went to Pilgrim State with your psychology class?

—Ooo, what a great trip that was. Ma pushed her sunglasses up.

—Did you see any schizophrenics?

—Oh, yeah. Ma straightened slowly with her hands on her back. Crazy with the schizophrenics, man. And you know finally I said I got to cool out a little. I went and sat on the curb to have a cigarette and this man came over to me. Ma still had her hands on her back. He seemed like a very nice man and he was so knowledgeable about all the patients. We must have been talking for about a half hour and then my prof came out and I introduced them. Doctor so and so this is my professor and then we got on the bus to go and my prof says Jesus Louise, Mary, that guy was a patient.

—Ma!

—He was schizophrenic. Oh yeah. Ma crossed slowly to our planter near the Hanrahans'.

—Did you take your arthritis pills?

—You better believe it!

—They don't look like they're working so good.

—I'll live. Ma bent and cut again.

I said, Janet Irons from the tennis club?

Ma said, Oh, Jesus. She's schizophrenic! I'll never forget

the time she got on the court without any shorts on. What a scene. I mean, Sheila, you know her mother had to lead her off the court? Daddy was shocked.

—Yeah, I said, I never understood why that was a big deal. She had on a dress, right, and underpants.

—Give me a break. You don't do that, Sheila. Do not. Ma threw out more stalks and chopped along.

—You want me to get the wheelbarrow and go pick up the dead stuff?

—I really wouldn't bother, Ma said. If I were you I'd go for a swim.

I heard the screen door open next door at the Hanrahans'. Irene ran out with an entire blue bag of Chips Ahoy. In the mornings sometimes Dad looked out his bathroom window and saw Irene stealing our strawberries and he yelled, Hey!, faking it that he was tough. I could tell Ma wanted to wrap this talking up. I said, Ma, how much compensation is Mr. Hanrahan out on again?

—Danny? I would say seventy. Ma threw stalks and moved away.

—Why is he out on compensation?

—The ulcer! The ulcer! He has got a severe ulcer, Sheila. Ma pushed her sunglasses. That is a stress job, man. You know that? Air traffic controller is the number one stress job you can have? They had it in Newsday. Numero uno with the stress, man. I feel so sorry for him.

Pop loved to tell about the Alice Crimmins double kid slaying, most especially how the neighbor who can't sleep is sitting by her window drinking *iced tea* and how Alice's suitcases when she walks under the streetlight are *peculiarly heavy.*

—This is one for the books, my dear girl.

First of course Pop asked to see my scar. I actually had a two-piece going into junior high. In April I dared to order it from Sears breaking out of my one piece nun habit which I wore to spare the audience. My two piece was Annie Oakley style with a dungaree bottom and bandanna effect top. Pop said, Boy, he did some job on you, like under the sink looking at a good plumbing job. Pop ran his finger down the length starting above my heart along the fine cut scalpel top, thin sliced white of where the knife began, downhill over my bandanna top out the bottom thicker scarred like the stub tail of a doe.

Ma walked by in the sunshine broken by the green diamond chain links pushing our red wheelbarrow past irises, Ma now attacking tiger lilies by the roots. Ma's arthritis looked fine that day.

—All the newspapers had it. Two children kidnapped! Mothers wouldn't leave their babies out in the carriage. Well, you remember my cousin Georgie Hopkins.

—The State Liquor Authority guy?

—That's him! That's the one. Pop ducked. Jesus, Mary, and Nellie. He said, What the hell's that, firecrackers?

—Gun, I said.

—Very funny.

—It is a gun! My neighbor's doing target practice next door.

—Christmas. Pop ducked again. This is like being back in the Seventh Regiment.

—Fear not, I said. Usually he shoots at the railroad tracks. I said, Stop! Stop! You're breaking my arm.

—Making fun of an old man. Pop let go. He said, I don't know my own strength, and ducked again.

I said, Yeah, you should try living here all the time. I said, Did Georgie Hopkins investigate Alice Crimmins back when he was a cop in Queens?

—Indeed he did, indeed he did. When the case broke Georgie called me up. He says Tommy, this broad did it and we're going to send her to the Big House meaning Sing Sing, don't you know. I says Georgie, her own children. It's hard to fathom how a mother could do such a thing. Well, be that as it may. You see, darling, Georgie knew Alice. All the cops knew her. Alice used to go to the nightclubs, to the bars. He said, Well, darling, you know what the cops say? There's no such thing as a perfect crime, you see, because no matter how careful you are, someone's always seen something. Especially in New York.

—Aunt Rita, why do you think this thing happened with Kennedy the same weekend they're landing on the moon?

She straightened the glass and poured a bit of foam, coloring in those autumn leaves.

—The forces in the universe must be completely thrown into chaos, Aunt Rita said. Who knows what this does to the alignment of things.

—You think us landing on the moon could affect people's horoscopes?

—I would say there's a good possibility.

—You think the life in outer space is mad at us for landing on the moon?

—Oh, no, Sheila. Her crow's feet and freckles gathering. I think those beings in outer space are way beyond us. They think of us as children down here. I think they're far more moral than us. They don't even know war. All they know is love.

—Like the Tasadays. Remember that tribe that lived in caves in LIFE? But do you think they would punish us for going to the moon by drowning Mary Jo Kopechne?

—No. She smiled.

—Do you think they would punish us for Vietnam and Biafra and Ireland and the Middle East?

—No, she said.

—But why does he get to escape and she drowns? Every time it's always the girl that gets killed. I said, The nurses in Chicago, the Boston Strangler, Marilyn Monroe, you name it.

We could hear the TV and down the road the other kids playing Capture the Flag.

I said, Do you think he can still run for President?

—Oh, sure, Aunt Rita said.

Even I knew he could never run for President. I always had this bridge dream I would fall in love in Paris and he would give me an amber pendant while we were standing on the span, quite a different picture from on the news the car in Chappaquiddik dripping from a chain and her dead inside. The train came by toward Port Sands with the nighttime windows like an emerald chain. That was when I went inside for the brush.

His glass was on the coffee table, rising bubbles within. He had the TV on but the couch was blank.

It was interesting that Pop knew a million cops and many a crime and even he thought it a bit dangerous to have a next door neighbor constantly shooting his gun, even Pop ducked, whereas by now I just sat unflinching listening to Alice Crimmins again.

—They dumped the boy in a sandlot somewhere in Queens.

—What about the daughter?

—You know, darling, I don't believe they found her body to this day. They just assumed she was dead if her brother was dead.

I said, They only needed one body to bring the murder charge?

—That was enough.

Ma passed by in her pink and white gingham one piece pushing our red wheelbarrow filled with torn out orange blossoms. I gave up trying to argue they were not weeds.

—You know, darling, it's strange what you remember. I remember that time when it happened how hot it was, and I could picture the whole thing. I could picture the glass of iced tea. How she pulled a chair and sat by the window to catch a breeze (pow, the gun). There she was sitting in the dark drinking her tea about two o'clock in the morning (pow) and who does she see down the street (pow) crossing under the light but Alice Crimmins.

—Dad.

I jumped. Ma had parked her empty wheelbarrow at the gate. Next door Mr. Hanrahan shot again. She held the bright green metal but did not step in. I loved Ma's pink and white gingham because it reminded me of her as a 1930s little girl like on The Little Rascals, like the geometric sun suit she put on me covering my scar. Ma said, How about a little lunch?

—None for me. Pop kept looking at me. He said, That was it. They had the goods on that broad.

Ma looked at me and from the middle of town our noon whistle began. Ma turned and picked her red wheelbarrow up.

—That's some story, darling, isn't it?

—Yeah.

Ma walked down the side slope to get another load.

—Peaceful. He must be reloading. Pop patted my arm. It's lovely to sit here with you, darling.

We watched the water filtering.

—You got some stuff on your face there, sweetie.

—No I don't. I pulled back.

—Yes you do. Hold still a minute. He moved at me with the towel. It's right there on your face, some brown.

—Leave it, I said. It's make up, all right?

—Oh, excuse me, darling. Excuse me. He was quiet. I forget you're growing up. What's that, something new, make-up under your eyes?

—Yes.

Pop nodded. He said, You look just like your grand-mother when you get mad. You get fire in your eyes. You look so pretty, darling. Pop patted my arm. I miss her something awful, he said. You know sometimes I'm walking down the beach and I see something, a bird or something, and I'm reaching for her hand.

He reached out in the air.

I stood pretty long looking at that half glass of beer and the television flashes of Mission Control. It's on my vanity, Aunt Rita told me. She had her vanity cattycorner in her bedroom down at the end of the hall. I said just act like you're babysitting going down to check on Irene. I could see the bathroom door was opened and the thermostat was on the right and when I got to the thermostat I heard someone clear his throat on my left. He was standing up going men's style, aiming it from on high. I kept on, straight down the hall. I got into their bedroom. I saw a hand mirror lying face down and I grasped its brush. The toilet flushed. I never got to read all of The Boston Strangler because I was too young but one part that haunted me was they found her soiled sanitary napkin thrown behind the armchair, like the iced tea for Pop. Maybe now he was back on his couch. I got to the doorway.

—Hello there.

I said, Hi. I'm just getting Aunt Rita's brush. I was gripping it.

He said, Oh, you're getting the brush, are you?

I said, Yeah.

—What are you going to do with the brush?

—I think we're going to comb our hair.

—Oh, you're going to comb your hair.

Behind they had two twin beds pushed together held with a queen sized contour sheet. I was in the bedroom. He had the hall exit. His eyes looked like cat eye marbles, hard enough to throw against the wall.

—Excuse me, I said and I plunged by him in the door and I just kept on going down the hall, like any second you're expecting to get grabbed.

—Thank you, sweetie.

She opened her legs, lime green pedal pushers opening on the stoop step and I sat down between on the lower one. Over the dark tree tops was a half moon.

At home Dad was still up with his hand in the cookie jar. It was a half moon that night for us down on earth. I said, Oh, Dad, what a pleasant surprise. Are you staying up for the moon?

—What the heck.

At supper Ma said walking on the moon was horseshit and gunsmoke. Michael said, What is it, Ma? Ma said, Horseshit and gunsmoke. Michael said, You're not going to stay up and watch them walk on the moon?

I said, What are you drinking, Dad, iced tea?

Dad pulled his cup. He said, You checking up on me? I said, No.

Dad had a stack of Lorna Doone cookies and his cup and he went down the stairs first. I wasn't checking on him. I was looking for drink ideas.

Everyone shuffled around fighting in chairs for hassocks and pillows and views. You could feel the excitement in the air of having Dad stay up late with us.

—Sit up straight now, boobala, Michael said because Robert's spine was perfect up and down sitting on the floor. When I walked in he very politely gave me my green chair.

The moonlight came off the TV and lit the bump braids of our Colonial rag rug. Neil Armstrong was slowly backing down, reaching, feeling for the next rung, like Aunt Dee on Weight Watchers backing into our pool.

—They have to get ten rocks each, I said but no one laughed.

—That's one small step for man, one giant leap for mankind, the announcer said.

—What does that mean? we all yelled and looked at Dad.

Dad sat on the black Naugahyde with little TVs in his glasses. Beats me, he said.

Chapter 10

— Sweetheart, sweetheart. Aunt Rita bent over talking to her new monkey. I can't get my work done if you hang on me like this. The monkey had pond sized eyes, hunched, sitting quietly on the linoleum. Aunt Rita got her giant pot and turned the water on.

I sucked up cherry Kool-aid. Finally broke it to Aunt Rita I hated lime. I said, I'm returning your book by the way. I held it up: Flying Saucers—Serious Business. It had a nighttime sighting in South Africa, a UFO landed on railroad tracks. Aunt Rita shut the water, ugh, lifting the heavy pot onto the right front. I said, Aunt Rita, you know what, we believe in the same thing, only opposite.

She smiled, opening a Rheingold. She said, Do we? No. Honeybun, go in the dining room and play. She carried him into the dining room where they had the glass shelves of ceramic elephants turned to the door for luck.

On Saturday night Sharon Tate got murdered in California. Naturally I was alone babysitting for the Hanrahans when it came on the eleven o'clock news. The monkey was locked underneath me in the basement pounding his Tonka on the cement, crying among the maroon poles. They had it like the weather, just a guy in a chair with a map of California: stabbed in her pregnant stomach, rope around her neck attached to another dead guy's neck, two more killed on the lawn, fifth dead behind the wheel of a car, PIG written in blood on the door.

Aunt Rita pushed the far left button to turn the water on high. She put the cover on and poured some beer.

I said, You know why we're the same because we believe in life in other levels but we're the opposite because you believe in life in outer space and I believe in life underground.

—Life underground? Aunt Rita set down her brown bottle and drank.

The monkey looked out from dining room chair legs. It looked like Grandma's mink stole hanging in the closet near the good black telephone in Queens. Ma already told me the announcement Aunt Rita was going to make to me today.

—Did you ever see that two-parter on Superman, I said. Aunt Rita bent in the refrigerator. About the creatures who come up from the center of the earth? I said, You know our sandpit by the railroad tracks? It always reminds me of that.

Actually it didn't anymore. Now I had to go through a Marianne Gilhooley detour to try to get back to that memory.

—You use radishes in macaroni salad? We just use peppers and tomatoes.

Aunt Rita ripped the bag and got her knife.

—The Superman is about these townspeople who dig the deepest mine in the world and they dig so deep they run into creatures who live underground. They're like midgets and bald and totally white from the radium. Aunt Rita, you remember your riddle with the midget?

Sssss, the pot went.

Aunt Rita said, I do.

Every morning a man rides the elevator down from the sixteenth floor, gets out at the lobby, goes to work. Every night he comes in the lobby, rides the elevator up to four, gets out, walks up the rest. Why?

—One night these creatures crawl up from underground and one of the townspeople sees them. I said, Aunt Rita, you remember in Frankenstein he's near the river making friends with a girl and she doesn't know he's deformed but then when the townspeople see him they know so they attack?

The same thing happens with the underground creatures.

Aunt Rita was turned, her knife held mid slice. I had the elevator in Aunt Rita's riddle, the elevator in the hospital long ago, the elevator in the question I got wrong in second on what they called the California test. Aunt Rita lifted her glass and drank. I told her about Superman's love for the creatures. I said, So it's at night and his cape is flapping and he's bending down shaking their little hands goodbye. Meanwhile the townspeople are lighting torches, forming an angry mob.

Aunt Rita was turned, staring at me.

—It goes the mob, the creatures, the mob, the creatures, and just at the last minute the creatures pull their manhole cover back over and Superman sets off a bomb.

Aunt Rita gasped.

—Part of the plan to protect them, so the townspeople can't go digging in their hole.

The water hissed on the stove.

—The end.

—What a sad, sad story. Aunt Rita drained her glass. She said, It's about friendship, isn't it?

More deformity to me but I said yes. Aunt Rita was about to sob. I looked up at her diamond Roman numeral clock. Quarter to ten and already she was a wreck. They had a picture of Sharon Tate in the paper. They had all these women getting killed. I just tried to block how much Sharon Tate and Mary Jo Kopechne reminded me of Aunt Rita. It seemed like you could choose one of two ways to be. We had this big fight in our kitchen between Aunt Rita and Ma. I just wanted to go downstairs and watch Ironside but they wanted to fight.

Ma said, I view astrology as a lot of crap.

Aunt Rita said, You don't believe the universe has a soul?

Ma said, Give me a break.

Aunt Rita said, We're all just pieces of a larger force.

Ma said, Give me a goddamn break.

Downstairs the Ironside music was starting. It was a Thursday night at eight-thirty on Channel 4. How they introduced all the characters was having them climb out of his wheelchair equipped van.

Aunt Rita said, Let me ask you this, Mary, what's your sign?

Ma said, I don't give a rat's ass what my sign is. Do not. Ma lifted her plastic cup and drank. Basically just ice left now.

Aunt Rita said, Sheila, when was your mother born?

Ma set her cup slowly, not looking at me.

—Pisces the fish, I said.

Ma kept her eyes away from me, still holding onto her cup.

—Isn't that interesting. Aunt Rita's eyes shone. She was drinking Dad's Black Label cans.

—I don't find that interesting. I view it all as a lot of crap.

I said, Well, Shakespeare used astrology.

Silence.

I said, In Julius Caesar there's a line the fault dear Brutus lies in the stars.

—Well. Aunt Rita grinned from ear to ear. Ma just gripped her cup. Aunt Rita said, I haven't had such an intellectual conversation in years.

—Intellectual, Ma said. You call this crap intellectual? Give me a break. Forget this crap, forget it.

—Sheila's quoting Shakespeare.

Ma said, Give me a break. I'm going to bed.

Ma pushed back her chair. She walked off to her bedroom. She had her back hunched, moving like eighty-five years old. She rounded the stove counter aiming for the door. Ma was moving like a giant weighted ship.

Aunt Rita smiled at me. The table had their full ashtrays, cigarette packs, matches, silver lighter, cans of beer, Ma's green cup, and her coffee cup. It had wet circles and ashes. If she left right away I could get fifty-five minutes of Ironside. I was trying not to be mean and look up at our orange clock. The orange clock had only the minute and the hour but our old red plaid had seconds. I liked clocks better with the seconds so you could hold your breath and time it. I didn't know how to put it so she would go.

—Your mother doesn't mean to be critical.

I felt this shock hearing someone use a mean word like that, critical, about Ma. I was trying to hear what the music was down on TV. Tonight was a repeat. I liked the system of summer repeats, giving you a chance to think about every minute of the whole season again. I knew the schedule on every channel every time of the day. When it was a certain time of the day and week you could always find your certain person there, like Lucy. Lucy was the best person on TV because she was very cheerful no matter what she tried. Sometimes I wished Lucy could be real, or she could take up more time. My throat felt like a tree growing in there and at the same time my throat was made of glass. I was looking at our yellow hanging kitchen light and the red bricks Dad put up long ago on the wall, Aunt Rita smiling, four beer cans. I said, I think I'm going to watch Ironside. I kept concentrating on this vision of her moving away through our back light. I just had to get her to the door.

Steam billowed softly out of the pot for macaroni, Aunt Rita's stove light on. She said, You want to hear my news?

I said, Okay.

She said, We're moving to California.

I said, Wow.

They were buying a trailer, buying Irene math and reading workbooks to do driving cross country. Life was going to be great skiing in the morning swimming in the afternoon. Aunt Rita was going to open her window in the morning and pluck an orange off the tree. She got out a blue and white Mueller's box. I'm thinking what about mass murder, RFK, the Santa Barbara oil spill. Boil eight to ten

133

minutes, Aunt Rita was singing as Irene ran up the stoop and the monkey trailed, draping back in across the linoleum, as Aunt Rita opened the macaroni box and Irene dashed in and reaching for the monkey, Giuseppe Giuseppe, my long lost Giuseppe, and the monkey raced toward Aunt Rita who picked him up, Irene jumping, grabbing at the monkey as the steam rose out of the pot and the roaring of the train from Stony Point like from the oven, that confused feeling of shooting right through the wall as Irene was jumping, grabbing, and the monkey gave one leap and landed right in the pot of boiling water screaming once in shock.

Everything was quiet. The train gone. Irene's arms dropped. Aunt Rita still held the tilted box. The water had stopped boiling, like it always does when you add something. Only the monkey's one paw stretched up out of the water hooked very politely for rescue. You could see how white its skin was under the fur.

Without even a trace of excitement but like her whole life Aunt Rita had been training for the time she would be a housewife whose monkey jumped in a pot of boiling water Aunt Rita reached in and lifted the monkey by the hook of his arm. She plopped him in the sink and turned the cold water on.

Ma dipped her brush in the can, squeezed, spread it on the bare wood, red. It was that standard red of picnic tables I saw in all the backyards when I rode the train to Aunt Dee's. There were reds of tables and the aqua circles and aqua rectangles of pools, first above ground then built in when your family got classier. Dad just built us a pool cabana for putting on bathing suits so we wouldn't drip inside. Dad bought plain stockade at the lumberyard then designed a blueprint maze on the back of Ma's leftover addition and subtraction dittos. This cabana had no roof so when Dad stood in it he looked like a naked man in a barrel. Neighbors and relatives said, Oh, Jack, what do the people on the train see passing by? Not much. I looked. I requested to board at Port Sands so as to ride through Nissequott right behind our house.

—Ma, want me to paint for a while?

—No thanks.

I laughed. I said, Ma, you're supposed to try to trick me into me paying you to paint.

Ma shifted crabbily, sliding the can set on newspaper with several coagulated rings. What's black and white and red all over? Ma had on her tennis hat, strangely reshaped by machine wash warm, and her oldest two piece, black and white polka dots.

Next door a car started. The monkey was being returned alive to his pet store in a last convertible ride. Wind blowing through his fur. Ma was afraid if she let me paint I would cause an accident, a big permanent red concrete spill.

—Ma, you like the first or second coat better?

—It really doesn't matter. Ma pushed her sunglasses up.

—I think I would like the first coat because it's so dramatic. I laughed since that was a stupid thing to say and better to criticize yourself first than give the other person a chance. I said, Ma, remember when you brought home that painting The Tree?

—I love that painting! Ma dipped her brush.

—I love that painting too. Do you remember I didn't get the title?

Ma dipped her brush and stroked up, doing from the soil to about waist. Ma came home from the framer tearing brown wrapper paper all excited. I was under our dining room table to read and got this sudden close-up of Ma's bare legs with regular ladder rung scars from Ma's operation for varicose veins caused by the four of us. The picture looked like seaweed underwater in a giant whirl and with a single human toe sticking out at the bottom. A toe! Ma yelled. That's a house!

Ma dipped her brush and dripped red off. Sweat ran down

under her arms where it was dark from partly shaved hair, a look one day I was going to have. Today Ma seemed pretty peaceful, thanks be to God about three weeks without the back pain. She had a cup of iced tea, working in the shade.

I said, Ma, I was never in an incubator was I?

—No! Please! You were never in an incubator. You were completely normal when you were born.

I wished I had a tape recorder for that one. I said, I was?

—Oh, yeah. Ma was still calm, smoothing along the paint.

—So when did you notice my chest wasn't too good?

—I forget. Ma pulled the can, still calm.

—Was it always indented?

—I assume. That was so long ago, Jesus. You can't remember these things.

Ma calmly stroked up the red. She looked quite pretty in the black and white two piece, red growing around her, in back blue, completely cloudless sky. Ma said, You were a good weight.

—I was? I laughed.

—Six-eight.

—What were the other guys?

—Annie was seven-two, Michael was eight-three, and Robert was ten-two.

—Ten-two! Ma! Poor you!

Ma dipped and kept on painting.

—The boys were the good babies, right? Annie and me were the pains?

—You were the worst, Ma said. Jesus, you were bad.

I laughed. I still liked driving her crazy.

—I swear to God, Ma said, at one point I couldn't take it anymore. Christ with the crying and the throwing up. Finally I said to Daddy, Here! You take her!

I laughed.

From somewhere I heard men's voices, like murmuring. I said, Who is that?

Silence.

—Ma, someone's trying to give us the Gaslight treatment. Did you hear those voices?

—Yes.

—Good. I laughed. I stood out in the sun listening. Ma worked in the shadow, a scalloped stockade shape that fell on the cement and fell blurrier in the pool.

—They're working on the railroad, Ma. I thought something was fishy. We haven't had a train go by all day.

You really had to zigzag driving your car to the train station in Port Sands. You went once over tracks with no gate, once past tracks on a trestle, once on top of tracks on a bridge, and last of all four sets of tracks with bells and lights at the beginning of the line. That was the route Dad and I took every Sunday in the beginning when Nissequott didn't even have a traffic light and we had to go to Port Sands to get buns. Past the sandpit, past the trestle which had my first Fuck You in spray paint, past where black people lived, their back doors way closer to the railroad tracks than us, with no lawns, no storm doors. Dad brought me to the station in July. I said, Dad, are you going to rush home so you can see my train go by? Dad said, I hadn't thought of it, babe. The sun was climbing, the cabana shadow shrinking with time. Soon Ma would be working in the outright blaze. I wondered if Ma realized one day I was going to leave Nissequott forever. Really only six years left, when I was eighteen. The train started out of the station. It moved past the Purina checkerboard building, past where an old maid music teacher lived. Trees. The backs of houses with clotheslines. Trees. Under the bridge. The woods and the houses of the black people. Fuck You trestle. Woods. Woods. Woods. Sandpit. Woods. The house I dropped the baby. The pediatrician's. Callahans'. Joyce's patio. The Hanrahans' patio. Our house. Our patio, our pool, our picnic table. Gone. I was sitting behind a moving window, all of it disappearing so fast in a line. One day I really was going to leave them. I was glad that monkey was off our block. It reminded me too much of me. I always had this birthday fear there would be cream cheese pie with graham cracker crust lit in flames, all their five faces floating without necks, and they would have all gotten together before and planned singing

> You look like a monkey
> And you act like one too

and that would be their way of telling me to leave the family because of my face. But instead what always happened was they quick turned on our light and as the smoke hung over the white pie with blue and pink and yellow baby color candles Ma would grip my hand in a vise and leaning say only into my ear, I hope you get your white horse, squeezing my hand so hard.

I said, Ma, I think the Hanrahans are bringing their monkey back to the pet store.

—Good. Give us all a break.

—Ma, you know what that monkey reminds me of? You remember when we went to the Buffalo zoo that summer upstate?

—Yes! Ma lifted her brush off the wood, her eyes blazing.

—You remember that? My heart pounded. What do you remember?

And we heard men talking working on the railroad again.

—I remember that god awful snake pit.

I laughed.

—Jesus, that was bad, Ma said. What a smell. That was such a disappointment. We heard such good things about that zoo, how well they take care of the animals.

There was total complete pain across Ma's face.

—That was awful, Ma said. Finally I said to Daddy let's get the kids and get out of here.

Ma stood, painting waist up now.

I said, You know what I remember is the monkey pit. You remember that?

—No.

—They had this giant monkey pit that was all white and below ground and it had these smooth white walls and you looked down in it from the top and whenever a monkey tried to climb out they had this guard with a silver pole and he jabbed the monkey back down and I remember there was blood and fur on the wall.

—Oh, cripes. Ma made a look of disgust. I don't remember that.

Ma dipped her brush and painted up the stockade. Maybe we separated and wandered off to different parts of the zoo. Still, that was the first time we were ever in the same location at the same time in a mutual memory. That was a start.

—Hello.

—Ice, Ma said. I need ice.

I had just come out of their darkened bedroom spying out the window on all of them inside the fence with the umbrella opened at night, all their strange dark human lumps in redwood chairs and borrowed neighbor chairs before the blue rectangle lit pool and quiet small citronellas flickering, Mr. Hanrahan yelling, Okay, let me put it this way. What if Canada was invaded? and Dad hooting, Canada! Canada! Give me a break with Canada! I moved out of their darkened bedroom and at the back door met Ma. She walked slightly tipped.

—Here, I'll do it. I took her little vinyl bucket, ours not the kind of family that got its wedding presents engraved.

—Madness. Ma leaned resting against the stove, like this casual feeling Ma actually wanted to shoot the breeze with me.

—You arguing about politics?

—Forget it. Forget that number. Looney Tunes, man.

I popped the aqua frozen ones out into her bucket. We had two tray types, modern or the older fashioned aluminum with the central handle scar. The back door opened.

—It's all the girls, Aunt Rita said. All the girls meet!

—What can I do for you, Rita? Ma said. You need a beer?

I said, She has a beer. You want the bathroom?

Aunt Rita smiled at me. What a sweet daughter you have, Mary, she said. Aunt Rita shook her head and started crying.

—Oh, Christ, Ma said.

Aunt Rita sobbed, I'm really going to miss this family.

—Here. I gave Aunt Rita two yellow napkins.

—Thank you. She blew her nose. You know, you're my best friend. Aunt Rita wiped her face. Aunt Rita was talking to me.

—Sanneefrannee time, Ma sang. Christ, let's get Rita a beer.

—She has a beer.

Ma went to the refrigerator and got a beer.

—She really is my best friend. You know that, Mary?

—No, I said. I took the beer from Ma and put it back in the refrigerator and Ma shrugged. I said, She already has one.

Aunt Rita was crying into her napkin.

—Oi vay, Ma said and picked up her ice bucket, then hesitated. Ma looked really cute in her two piece in the middle of the night, barefooted, holding a little bucket. I felt like patting her on the back and setting her up in the sand with shovels and a mold.

—I'm bailing. Ma turned.

I picked up the empty ice tray and held it under the faucet as Ma passed through my window, that strange kitchen window close up at night with the yellow bug light on. I set the tray and took the other and filled that, filling each little square evenly while Aunt Rita talked about what a great friend I was. It was already ten after nine and Hogan's Heroes was really what I lived for on Saturday night. Aunt Rita was smiling at me. She looked rather strange holding one of Dad's black and red Black Label cans, not her brown Rheingold and glass. She was all dressed up. She had on a midriff blouse tied around her stomach and mustard gold pedal pushers and gold slippers, her I Dream of Jeannie's, and her hair down. This afternoon carrying her macaroni salad she had on pink lipstick in the sun.

—Well, I think I'm going to go down and watch Hogan's Heroes.

She smiled, standing there.

I said, Aunt Rita, you want to go back out by the pool? I think they're all still out there.

—Yes. She smiled.

—Okay. I walked to the back door and opened it. I said, It's nice out tonight, and Aunt Rita patted my hair, smiling. I smiled back. I stepped out on the stoop, holding the door, quick getting on the outside so she wouldn't fall off into the bush. She walked down the steps, past the picnic table, up the walk, doing okay.

At eleven I was lying in bed having a Mark Rogers pretend dream. We fall in love being prisoners of war. Everyone else was in bed except Dad at the bottom of our driveway yelling, Straighten it! Good! Good! The headlights swung through boxing around my walls across the mirror and ceiling, down. On the wall next to me were glowing fluorescent drips, Glow Juice left from when Marianne Gilhooley and I were friends. Every day they got recharged and came out again at night. Strains of rock music came in my window from a concert at the university. It felt like real life was edging in. The headlights stopped on my closet. Straight, straight! Dad yelled.

Smash. Metal hit against rock.

I lay still. It felt like I should get up and look out the window at the accident but I really didn't want to.

In the morning sunshine Dad came out our back door, bouncing it off his hip, holding a plate and cup. I was standing in our yellow bathtub looking out the window, brushing my teeth. Once I got up early, looked out the window, and saw a goat. Today I got up, looked out, there's

Mr. Hanrahan sitting at our picnic table and it's not even nine o'clock.

After Aunt Rita said I was her best friend in the kitchen she walked up our walk, through the gate, and sat on the pediatrician's lap. Ma said, Uh, oh, and I moved the gauzy curtain back, stepping back so no one would see me. Next thing Dad was leading Aunt Rita out the gate. Dad said, What do you mean, no one's your friend. That's not true, Rita.

—Here you go, Danny, boy. Dad set a plate on our picnic table. Mr. Hanrahan was bent with his head in his hands. Those were Dad's great scrambled eggs, that he scraped and scraped over forever on low heat and came out the brightest cheerful yellow.

—You got to eat something there, buddy.

But Mr. Hanrahan only sat with his shoulders hunched looking down. They looked like Ralph and Norton on The Honeymooners.

Dad lit a cigarette and blew into the blue air. The sky was bright, everything green shimmering. A bird flew straight out from our crabapple, straight across, gone.

—Well, Dad said, I think at least we got rid of that humidity.

Chapter 11

Mark Rogers stood all in black holding his black saxophone case upend with blue metal lockers all around, our two minutes of bell reverberating, like he was the gong. Once in sixth he crossed all along the room in black carrying his Iberian Peninsula like a black moving exclamation point. What are you looking at, Sheila? Mr. Addison said and the whole class cracked up, poor Mark the bewildered blond sex symbol. He pulled the locker handle up, jam, started the combination again.

I had on my olive green wide wale corduroy scoop neck jumper that Ma made, that felt like armor you pull over your head. I had on popular strap shoes and my head pretty good, long bangs and two ponytails. My right hand was held strangely, its bandaged thumb posed like in the old days in Queens when Ma used to go BMT, By My Thumb, to the beach. I said, Hi, Mark, having trouble with your combination?

He laughed. He pulled up and jam. Started again. He turned that combination, like working just below the waist. The bell stopped. His breathing. It was like those horror movies when the victim makes one little mistake: dallying amid the blue metal lockers too long.

No one else was out. The blue lockers were quiet, closed above the speckled school floor. I was making him nervous. I should just leave the poor guy alone, but on the other hand I had my hopes and dreams too. I had gone to Charlotte M. Brewster to look Sadie Hawkins up before approaching him. I had out World Book, Americana, Briticana, Canadacana. I was filling out index cards left and right.

—Tell, tell, what'd he say? Heidi Wolman said at lunch. Heidi wore a wig. Heidi was leaned forward in that fluorescent lit cafeteria wearing a wig the tan corpse color of cafeteria meatloaf, with the movable look of a small bathroom rug, in the housewife style of Ma's wig she kept in her handkerchief drawer, Heidi wanting to hear about my supposed romance.

That fluorescent lit cafeteria was one of my worst areas for spotlighting my baggy eyed face. The portable movable walls had four giant fruits painted on them that felt like those large weights on my face. In my atom bomb pretend dream the camera looks out from the beach and sees a mushroom cloud. Everyone in the world got killed but somehow I wash up like on a Gilligan's Island. I'm slowly dying of radiation until one day I see different sized footprints. Next scene Mark Rogers lifts me fainted in the sand and he carries me to a central water fountain which turns out is the only water fountain in the world that can cure radiation sickness. It's like Notorious when he carries her down the sweeping stairs. Then we get married and begin to repopulate the earth.

Dad took us to the national lab's atomic energy display which had glass encased eyeglasses melted together by the heat of the Hiroshima bomb and also a black and white of a Japanese hunched crying in a city of broken cement. I always liked Oriental people because of the shape of their eyes and I always liked that secret bond baggy eyed Dad and I had when he, smiling secretly, said to us, That's an old trick I learned in the Orient. Oriental people were born in a country where it was normal to look like us, like the underground creatures were normal underground. The display had all the stages of radiation sickness. No appetite. More and more hairs cling in your comb. You're bald. You cannot swallow water. Three days later you die. Annie came back in the exhibit to get me. She said, Dad can't take it anymore. Dad was pacing, smoking in all the blinding sun chrome of a beautiful orange tree surrounded parking lot. My generation could take it more. My generation was practicing for the Bomb since first, crawling under our rose pink desks covering our eyes in case of flying glass, watching that LBJ commercial that showed a little girl our age humming picking daisies until the Bomb, until the screen goes black, humming stops, they tell you think about the end of the world.

I said, I think I terrified the poor guy. He made the fatal mistake of going back before homeroom to put his saxophone in his locker and his combination got stuck.

I had two girls to eat lunch with at a six person table, Heidi Wolman in a wig and Kathy Riordan in acne, both Republicans for the war. Their fathers worked for Grumman building the F-14 to bomb Vietnam, thus richer, thus they could buy lunch everyday. I was eating liverwurst with ketchup on rye that Dad made me. In our family we got to buy once a week. I was saving mine for Thursday, roast beef, mashed potatoes with gravy, succotash, and apple crisp. I loved those perfect white mashed potatoes scooped in an ice cream scoop and the cafeteria lady's hand in a plastic glove, pressing the back of the mound, then switching tools to the long handled ladle to pour gravy in a little kaleidoscope whirl. Today was a temptation because there were Tater Tots, but sometimes I got some of Kathy Riordan's before she threw them out.

—So I see him trying to do his locker so I go, Hi. He couldn't even talk he was so shocked. I said, Kathy, could you open my milk?

I didn't really ask Heidi for food help now that I was bandaged or ask for her leftovers because she was bald, or maybe by now slight fine hairs like those first lime green tufts of grass the first fall the fathers have moved into a new development and surrounded their property with string tied with white rags. I figured she looked underneath like a radium creature. I figured she was from Nassau County, richer, and there was a lice outbreak in her old town and in a rage Mr. Wolman moved his daughter to Small Field to protect her and every day at lunch at Grumman he pushed his blueprints for bombers aside and worked on developing a painless wig glue so Heidi could walk around safely all day without worry of it flying off and at night she could gently sudse it off with No More Tears shampoo.

Heidi said, Tell, tell, Sheila, you're driving us crazy with suspense.

I said, He just started doing his combination again. Thank you, I said to Kathy. I could open the straw left handed but not the milk flap. Heidi thought I actually had a chance to escape our little three person deformity table to the Mark Rogers band cheerleader popularity three tables all joined in a chain, like they were on an ocean liner clinking champagne glasses, meanwhile I'm in a little lifeboat dory with the two of them.

Dad had packed me four Vienna fingers and a tangerine. I held the tangerine with my right hand fingers and peeled southpaw. Bloom of tangerine whiffed. It helped to overcome Kathy Riordan's very chemical aroma of flesh-color Clearasil. Kathy said my parents should have taken me to the emergency room to have my thumb x-rayed. I said, Our family never goes to the doctor for those things. This summer Robert turned back to look for cars and turned his handlebars so extreme he flew over and scraped riding his face along the road. Red was smeared all across his face and shirt. His two front teeth hung by strings. If I tilted his head back to stop the bleeding then he could choke. I had him sitting in Dad's chair using paper towels to be more sanitary, trying to press his teeth back in. Every night when he was little Robert, out of fear, used to appear in his yellow pajamas with feet next to my bed. Get in. Then I remembered running my big toe on his plastic tractioned sole. His shoulders and chest and abdomen heaved. I said, Press this. I ran for ice. He said, She wouldn't even stop the lesson. I was like scalpel, sponge, trying to figure out where to press the ice. I said, Robert, press your teeth up. I was trying to combine direct pressure to stop the bleeding and direct pressure to reconnect his teeth. He said, She wouldn't even stop teaching him. If the teeth were pressed up maybe new gum connections could form. Almost black now splattered his polo shirt, pressing white bone ice in a yellow washcloth on his red mouth. He said, She just kept teaching him. I said, Hold this ice. Ma was teaching swimming lessons to try to get a tax write off for our pool. I ran and got another washcloth and wet it with warm. He was sobbing: She wouldn't even. I wiped the dark maroon off his face, the blood still coming up from his gum a brighter younger red, the baby teeth hanging like little pieces of corn and I wiped the clear under his eyes. I said, I think the gum can reconnect if we press the teeth up.

Robert caused my thumb injury. I reached to the back car door to help him pull it closed and Robert slammed at the exactly wrong time. I got a good look at that hinge before. I knew why there was very little room within those metal pieces for me. It was like a comedy. I was within, completely enclosed in metal and glass with communication difficult. Robert was outside saying, What? What? I said, My hand is caught. Open the door. He opened the wrong door. He opened the front door. I was still on the car's leash. I said, Back door. Back. He shut the front door. He was doing it like the lizard liveryman. When I went in the house Annie said, Did you get the rest of the packages? I was carrying my thumb with my other hand up the stairs. I said, No. I should have gone to the bathroom but I went to the kitchen sink so I would get more attention for my injury.

—Oh my God, Annie said. She's bleeding.

Elevate your wound, I knew from Ma's Red Cross Life-saving book. Apply direct pressure. Press on a pressure point. Apply a tourniquet. I said, Robert, go get me a washcloth from the hall.

Ma rounded the kitchen doorway. Oh, Christ, she said. What happened now?

I said, Don't worry, I'll take care of it. My thumb got slammed in the car door. Thank you, Robert. I took the orange washcloth, better than yellow for blending the blood.

—I'm sorry, Sheila, Robert said.

—It's all right. I still like you but I just don't want to see you right now, okay?

—It never ends, Ma said. Who's getting the rest of the packages?

Blood spurted but the main thing was my nail. Then if I ran water I might just wash my nail protection off. I looked at Annie and Annie looked at me. Annie shook her head. I really did not want to lose my nail. I said, Could you put three ice cubes in the washcloth? Robert, you go get the rest of the packages. Annie looked at me. I said, This ice is going to hurt. Annie said, You don't have a choice.

I looked out the window and blew out air.

—Bad? she said.

I nodded. Uh, I said, and I shook my head so I wouldn't cry. Ma was taking spaghetti out.

Annie said, How did this happen?

—Uh. I shook my head again.

Dad came in the back door in his good clothes from working a half day in the summertime. He stopped in his tracks dramatically and I heard the screen door gently close.

—Sanneefranneetime, Ma sang.

Dad looked from Ma to me. Ma walked to the pantry carrying applesauce. I looked away from him, my eyes filling up. I blinked.

—Jesus, Dad said. What the hell happened?

Ma was picking up Jell-O boxes. We had our screens in, summertime, so blurry and I looked at the black outlet where the radio was plugged.

—She accidentally slammed her thumb in the car door, Annie said.

Dad came over and I lifted the washcloth. Oh, Christ, he said and walked away. He walked to the top of the stairs and stood there, looking out. Ma was walking to the pantry again.

—She'll live, Ma said.

I looked at Annie and Annie looked at me. Annie said, Would you shut up, Ma. Can't you see Sheila's in pain? Christ.

I puffed out air. I was looking out our window at our beautiful blurry crabapple. Ma was hurrying putting things away, always so terrified we would all get botulism but the thing to me was everything she put away so far was non-perishable.

—Maybe he didn't mean to laugh, Heidi said.

—Oh, God, I don't care about him. He thinks he has the greatest hair.

I threw pits in the bag. I put the Glad bag, milk container, and peels in. I said, I'm leaving halfway through inter-murals. I have to get glasses today.

Kathy Riordan said, You might not need glasses.

Glasses might exactly cover the frames of my baggy eyes. Glasses might totally improve my life. I said, How do you know?

—The school nurse can't tell. Only the doctor can tell.

—The nurse said I definitely needed glasses for distance.

—Well, ladies. Heidi stood up in her wig. Sheila, he didn't say no.

I rolled my waxed paper. I said, Heidi, you should have seen that guy tear away. It was like Chiller Theater.

There was a roar in the cafeteria as people got to dessert.

—He just laughed, Heidi said.

—Kathy, what do you say? Does the guy want to go to the dance with me or not?

The end of the meal sounded like the Roman gladiators: quiet opening and drinking our milks, then the room roar growing as we ran out of food.

—I don't think he does, Kathy said. Her Clearasil was especially thick today, wafts moving out.

I said, See? I said, Uh, oh, the teacher aides are separated.

The tall thin dyed blonde with black roots was grabbing Mark Davis's hand. She had one forearm, dragging, and he kept his other hand up in the air too, both his hands palms out with the fingers splayed, like in a hold up, and his mouth dropped in case anyone missed the point. His was an all boy spitball table still giving each other antibiotics against girls. The people around the arrest site were rousing and the other aide didn't know whether to stay apart and be able to run for help or go in and help her friend. That other aide was fat. She was Spanish with that straight jet black hair, that skin tone between Negro and white. A Jehovah Witness family moved into the painted shingle rental house on our block this fall. Half the family was white, half the Spanish Mexican look. The white brother was in seventh, but the same age Spanish brother got left back. The Spanish sent me a note at the bus stop last month. He was cute but it was like having a bullfighter in Nissequott. He just didn't belong. He spelled my name wrong, he spelled friend wrong. But he was fair. He had a check off at the bottom, I like you or I don't.

The popularity table were all the richer Protestants. Heidi Wolman was a Protestant you could tell from living in Small Field and how polite she was, like using her napkin. She got dragged down to our level by her wig. The Spanish aide put her whistle in and blew and the white one dropped Mark Davis's arm. That whistle always worked on us. It was like a face slap to a hundred seventh graders at once. People looked like they were coming out of something, getting their bearings again.

I said, Heidi, I think Czyzewka might throw fruit today.

I had this fear Czyzewka would bomb the portable wall

and snatch the wig, pinning it to the inside of the pear or giant orange slice and Heidi would go on returning her tray bald like Mr. Magoo stepping off building ledges onto steel girders happening to move through the sheer luck air. You could tell it was a wig a mile away. The first day of school when she stepped off that richer Small Field bus I figured she was treating it like a fur. But day after day. What were the odds you would end up in the seventh grade in the United States eating with a girl in a wig? I said to Kathy, Does Heidi still have to get treated with kerosene?

Kathy said, What?

Ma stood high on the hill, the trees around of orange, yellow, the grass bright green and the sun setting behind so all her interior was dark with her hood up and her shoulders hunched, wearing her winter jacket with the old button ropes and her plaid pants flapping around her ankles, so Ma had gone home first to change. I lifted my hockey stick and waved. Ahead Isobel Dickinson dribbled blond head down, a simple kind that forgets she will be attacked and wearing that day around her arm a black band for the nationwide moratorium against the war. I smashed in, smashing at the ball and smashing her wooden stick, the wood wood stick smash extra Mafia violence for discouragement.

—Great balls of fire, Isobel said.

As I ran on, smacking it off right, laughing at her joke, and running I smacked flat the white and ran, smacked flat and ran, the grass greenly thickening to slower clover travelling, smash and smash as my right wing Kathy Riordan ran ahead half turned and I smashed off hard driving the white ball hard straight down out of the clover across balder thinner picking up speed smashing it slightly ahead of Kathy Riordan who running picked it up, hitting down the sideline as panicked their whole defense scurried right and Kathy Riordan smashed again along the sideline drawing their left fullback panicked out, their whole defense sliding panicked lemmings as Kathy Riordan waiting, drew them, then smashed it flat straight exactly horizontal across the twenty-five yard line, past them all without one inch of extra angle in the pass but flat straight exactly interceptionless inside the top of the striking circle, the shortest distance, threaded hard flat straight past the shocked defense which assumed she would do what they would do, head down mindless move as a group, Kathy Riordan instead smashing it flat straight cleanly past our right inner to our center forward, moving straight out of nowhere in and tapping it right, nonstick side of the goalie, turtle weighted in white with pads and helmet and mask.

Score.

—Nice pass. I loped past Kathy Riordan, pulling my red pinnie over.

—Nice pass from you. You set it up. Good luck at the doctor's, Sheila.

The hilltop was empty. I hung my gymsuit by the neck to dry with its chain stitching of my name that I got a C on. The boys just got to write theirs in Magic Marker but we had to waste hours sewing a little chain. I ran past the dumpster around the red school brick corner and blinked, letting black sunset shapes form, looking for Ma. Between you, me, and the lamppost, Ma always said. Down on the soccer field the black and white ball turned in the air and the net a beautiful gossamer red as Mark Rogers jumped, catching it with his hands. I ran back again past the Dempsey Dumpster along the red bricks. I used to love when the boys had chalk talks and came out later than us and I got to watch him walking across the ridge carrying the red net like a fisherman. I still had that I like you I don't like you letter with nothing checked off. It was on looseleaf with the light blue lines, folded in thirds, then folded over and over in triangles to make a little packet with my name Shela.

I looked down the long speckled hall floor for Ma. Passing in front of the distant windows was Ernie Thomas in his

Afro pushing sawdust through the halls with a two handle broom. Kathy Riordan told anti-Negro jokes all the time. She said, What's that black stuff between elephants' toes? Slow natives, she said. I reversed running again along the red bricks. Tiny girls walked along the edge of the fields, cutting from the woods near where our black people in Nissequott lived with their own American Legion and own A.M.E. Zion Church, the girls cutting to shoplift at Genovese. I ran around the brick corner and still no Ma. Black dots formed like a kaleidoscope. I wanted the tortoiseshell rims that would perfectly outline the bags around my eyes and the inner prescription glass would magnify my skin so a person on the outside wouldn't be able to see anything in there was wrong. Why would Kathy Riordan be so against me getting glasses? Kathy said the hot and cold faucets in our upstairs bathroom were on wrong, our family was weird for using waxed paper not always Glad bags, we weren't really Catholic because we didn't go to church, and there was something wrong with Dad because he cooked our food. I walked along the bus circle, walking up so that the setting sun began to rise out of the woods, and then topping the hill the sun began to descend again. The blue asphalt bus oblong was like the yarn held in two hands and the sun like the red ball being wound.

Ma had the newspaper on her steering wheel, the doors locked, the Dodge parked as far from the school as possible, facing the woods. She said, Oh, Christ. She clutched her heart. I was outside, hitting the window.

I said, What the heck did you park so far away for?

Ma said, You scared the hell out of me.

I said, What'd you park so far away for?

Ma folded the paper and I opened it back. She was reading about a secretary's body found in the dumpster of a train station near Aunt Dee.

Ma said, I've never been here before. I didn't know where the hell I was going.

I said, Ma, every school in the district is designed the

same. I said, Oh, what's this? It was four Vienna fingers.

Ma braked backing us. She stared at the cookies like they were from another culture. She said, Daddy thought you might be hungry.

I said, Thank you Dad, and dug in. I asked about the comparative price of tortoiseshells, completely cheerful about this deformity.

I said, Ma, what age were you when you got glasses?

Ma said, Oh, geez, I forget.

I said, You ever think of getting new shapes?

—No. Ma barrelled us out, screeching left. Ma still had her cat eye shapes from the 1950s. Ma did not believe in seat belts but when we made a sudden stop she always threw her arm out in front of me.

I folded my empty waxed paper. I said, Ma, you know what? Kathy Riordan told me today this girl who's a friend of ours has cancer.

—Jesus, Ma said.

—She's our age. She has to wear a wig.

—Jesus. That must be from the chemo. That is sad.

We were passing the giant water tower and chain link fenced sump near Kathy Riordan's house. Kathy Riordan's wasn't really that much of a richer neighborhood than ours. We passed a house preserved from the Revolutionary War and the field where orange lumps of pumpkin lay in the brown, like a farm scene in the fall. The pumpkins reminded me of Ma's giant stomach that time she was standing near a curb in a red and white maternity shirt.

—Pumpkins, Ma, I said.

—How's Kathy Riordan's acne? Ma said.

—Fine.

Now people had their headlights on. We passed the Catholic Church cemetery with plastic bouquets.

—That's such a shame, Ma said. I hope that doesn't leave pock marks on her face.

Ma put on our right red blinker. My throat hurt. There was getting to be more and more traffic now from the university. We passed along the other side of the pumpkin field. The sun was dropped now and the water tower loomed like a giant spider sitting on woods for a web.

Chapter 12

—*H*ello there, darling. This is your favorite grandfather. I pulled the cord out of the kitchen. His voice sounded very hearty and excited. He only said that favorite grandfather joke since the other one died, and I never laughed at it. I said, Nothing, except I got glasses for distance.

—Did you, darling! Can you see better?

—When I have them on.

He gasped and wheezed, hacking for breath, laughing in an uproar.

—When she has them on she says. Oh, darling. You're a funny girl. Now listen, my funny girl. I have a proposition to make.

I said, What?

—What, she says. Now darling, I have before me, at this very moment a brochure—

It was a ten day trip at Easter to the Holy Land with the Telephone Pioneers and on Good Friday everything culminated with participants reenacting the very path He took on His way to be crucified with those who wanted carrying the cross. I had no idea what he was talking about. I had no idea if the Pioneers were like a stagecoach group and the Holy Land was like an Ocean World or a Pirate's World for religion in Florida.

Pop said, Are you with me? He said, Well breathe loud or something so I know you're there. Now I've asked your mother and she says it's completely up to you. The old man will pay for everything, your plane, your room, board, the whole kit and caboodle, all expenses paid. How's that sound?

I thought it would be like one of those religious movies with Charlton Heston where they re-enacted the scenery of the desert and they gave you a robe at the gate. It was Christmastime. We had our plastic ivy thumbtacked in loops around the living room ceiling with tinsel regularly spaced by Dad on a stepladder while Ma directed from below. We had our artificial tree ordered from Sears with big blue green orange red bulbs and a star on top. I was reading about the My Lai massacre when the phone rang.

I said, That's nice of you.

—I don't think you'll miss any school, darling, from what your mother tells me.

Downstairs through the banister bars they had on The Munsters in black and white. Herman was doing a go go dance near file cabinets with a secretary who had big bosoms. He had his flat head, bloodlined eyes, forehead scar. In the kitchen our freezer opened and I jumped. Billowing frost rolled out around Dad, holding my little white dessert bowl with four used teabags, chilling for my eyes. Robert and I had tea with milk and sugar two nights in a row watching Lucy, me coming down the stairs singing, Here comes the tea.

Dad said, What the hell is this?

—It's mine. I grabbed. Do you mind?

Pop said, Are you still there?

I put the teabags in the shadow of the hifi. I said, How much does it cost? I had no idea if the Holy Land was a whole trip or just a day. Pirate's World was fourteen dollars for all the rides you wanted for the day. I was trying to figure out was the place in Florida, was it the involvement of Disneyland or more the Swimming Hall of Fame?

—What the hell difference does it make? That's a hell of a question. I said I'd pay the freight. What's it to you?

Pop said, Well, now, try to restrain your enthusiasm a little there.

I couldn't really talk my throat hurt so much.

He said, I tell you what, darling, you give me a call when you decide what you want.

I could see downstairs it was a commercial for the greatest hits of 1969.

Pop said, How's our nutty friend next door?

I said, Moved.

—You don't say. He go west?

I said, No one knows. She's still there with Irene.

It was a kitchen scene on The Munsters, Herman, Lily, Eddie, Grandpa, and the normal niece eating breakfast as bats flew by.

—Well, darling, you know what they say about California? When they shook the country all the nuts rolled west.

I laughed. Herman was rushing down the haunted house path with his lunchbox and slamming the iron spike gate, flinging himself in the back of an undertaker's car.

They both looked at me.

—What is the Holy Land? I said.

—Jerusalem, Dad said.

—Horseshit and gunsmoke, Ma said.

—Is it a real place?

—Crapola. Ma had her arms crossed in her blue caftan leaning against the counter holding today a gold cup and Dad had the Progresso, dribbling oil in steady circles over our frozen pizza to jazz it up. It was pitch black everywhere outside our house at only five o'clock.

—It's crap, Ma said.

—Is it real? Is it a real place?

—Crapola, man, Ma said. It's a farce.

I said, Dad, is the Holy Land a real place or not?

Dad smiled at me, lifting his can. He had two red frozen pizzas on silver cookie sheets on the kitchen table which would give us about two and a half pieces each. Dad drank and setting it he looked at me, smiling. Dad said, It's real. It's Jerusalem.

I said, The Middle East? The Middle East as in the Middle East war?

—So are you going? Ma glanced away, like glancing at our decorative black hot plates on the wall, and I could hear the TV on downstairs, our orange preheat oven light on, Ma still looking off like she had something really important to look off at and she couldn't look at me, Dad picking up his lighted cigarette and still a silence in the kitchen, the orange light on, Ma still looking off while I waited for her to look at me with this pitch paint black outside our kitchen window, nowhere out there to go, and Dad had turned, questioning because I held the silence so long, holding it to force her to look at me if she really wanted me to answer her question, while Dad had turned holding the silver cookie sheet with our frozen pizza, trying to break down the silence between us I had made.

—I don't know, I said.

—Sanneefranneetime, Ma sang and she twirled, turning her back, her caftan fluttering out, Ma moving to the dish drainer corner, behind our full garbage, and crossing her arms.

—Would you go? I asked Dad.

—That depends. Dad picked up his can. The question is can you get along with Pop? Dad's face was a question, no prejudice.

—Forget him. He's impossible. Im-poss-ib-ley, Ma said, like in French. I would not go. My advice is don't. Why put yourself in that position? Oi vay. Ma put her hand on the counter near the cookie jar.

I said, Dad, do you think it'll all be religious?

Dad was leaned back, draining his beer, then sweeping threw it in the garbage, putting his hand on Ma's back going around her toward the refrigerator as she was bent, reaching under the oven. Dad said, I'm sure a lot will be. Dad got another beer and smiled at me. Do you want to go, babe?

Dad was the one who always brought me to the train station and said goodbye. I shrugged.

—Oi vay. Ma plopped ice cubes in. Time to set. She turned to open our utensil drawer.

—It's Robert's week to set, I said. Why do you always set for the boys but not for Annie and me? Robert! I yelled. Time to set! I fast grabbed my bowl of teabags and headed for privacy.

Across the back of my closet were the steady little navy blue crayon marks left by someone in kindergarten pretending to write and her initials (as Dad would say) were Annie Gray. Last week at supper in front of everyone Annie said, I know what Sheila wrote in yellow ink in her address book. I gasped. I had just pulled hidden my little cold white dessert bowl against my stomach skin. I had my reversible jacket on, the elastic wrist indents moving higher and higher on my arm every year. I had this hope Mark Rogers would be at Teen Center tonight, doing the Iron Cross on the black rings in his great athletic shorts. He spread his arms, shaking, lowering, shaking, staring straight ahead, and from my place in the shadow of the boys' gym door every once in a while I got a split second dark vision down his T-shirt sleeve of where he was getting armpit hair. Before supper read Ann Landers again to figure out sodomy, during supper chill teabags in the great outdoors, after supper rest for Teen Center with my chilled teabags on.

—Dad?

He looked up. He had the ketchup upside down, hitting it into a small white bowl with mayo, making Russian. Dad gave me that address book after his teachers' union trip to California for a week.

I said, You think I would have to get a passport to go to the Holy Land?

—I think so, babe.

We looked at each other. Let Your Fingers Do the Walking, the address book Dad gave me said, with yellow pages inside, plus Dad gave me a pen that wrote in every rainbow shade, including Cowardly Lion yellow to write and not write under R an ugly girl's boyfriend's name. I realized Dad didn't really know would I need a passport or not. Our family was not the kind that went through customs, but at most we went over the border once to Canada. Dad hit the bottle bottom again with his flat palm.

Stars were strewn all over, tiny chipped hard white on ink. My heart thumped at the passport idea. White air puffed from me. The freezing border, thirty-two degrees I bet. Our hemlock was circled with blue lights by Dad and a light blue floodlight from Billy Blake's set in the dead winter ground shone on the entire face front of our house. I'm sure they would all be experts over there. I'm sure they would all be looking at me like, You never made your First Communion?

Our black telephone and electricity wires bounced in the wind. I set my white bowl between two evergreens which I did not know the type name of. I stepped back. It showed. I carried it toward the Hanrahans'. The Hanrahans had their every year chain of multicolored across the eyebrow eave. I did not exactly know the timing of when he left and how she put them up moving a ladder along alone. The lights went yellow orange blue red green straight across like glowing wet little paintbrushes or a doctor's lollipop for good boys and girls. Mark Rogers in sixth always got his maps hung on the wall because he outlined his borders in extremely hard-edged black. Then inside he colored each country different in even always moving together strokes, exactly like he always wore his shirt tucked in. I set my white bowl hidden under our blue-wrapped hemlock and stepped away. To me those Mark Rogers maps were beautiful but untrue. To me the borders were never hard-edged because every nation had low tide when the sandbars rose like bags under the eyes. When Annie said that at supper, I know what you wrote in yellow, I said, Well, at least I don't put my dirty underwear back in my drawer, causing Dad to have to hold her down in her chair. But really Annie was wasting her time. My Mark Rogers' hope was gone. This was long after my sad Sadie Hawkins' attempt, and hearing about that yellow on yellow was like someone showed me an old picture of myself from before I was taught my place in the world.

The Hanrahans' garage door roared open, Aunt Rita inside. This was my first year I wasn't seeing her set in New England snow scenes over and over on Christmas cards strung in her living room. She bent and lifted by the handles one of their garbage cans. They were probably only using one each collection now with only the two of them. The ridges in the can shone in the extra Christmas lights. She moved it down the blacktop, then set it to rest. It looked like she was heaving a pregnancy.

She said, Sheila, is that you?

—Yes. I stepped out in my jacket that now made elastic marks way above the wrist. Too young for boys, too old for dolls, Aunt Rita once said. I was up on the cliff their rock wall made. Below was their silver trailer parked for their trip to California with two cement blocks behind the wheels. There was one two-hour Lucy movie where, again, they're going to California. Lucy's in back alone making sandwiches in the tin can trailer when the hitch to Ricky driving comes undone. Aunt Rita and Ma had a really bad fight this fall right before they took out the screens and put our storm windows in. I was hovering in the hallway near the thermostat listening to Ma push Aunt Rita out our door. Same old crap, nothing ever changes, months and months, how long will this go on, I've had it up to here. Aunt Rita said, Mary, I thought you were my friend. Ma said, I'm not your friend. I am not your friend. I thought Aunt Rita should take control of the trailer without him and drive off from Nissequott alone.

—I haven't seen you in so long. Aunt Rita's voice floated upwards through the dark. Where have you been hiding yourself?

—At volleyball, I called down. I have intermurals and extramurals every day, I called.

—Do you, sweetie. She bent and lifted the can again. They were very neat, or rather he was very neat before he left, leaving tight spring locks adhering lid to can so no animals could get in. I was supposed to go down there and help her lift it. Every lady on our block Ma had a fight with. She had a really bad one with Joyce's mother, she didn't talk to Mrs. Callahan. It's like this driveway feeling of the valley between those Appalachian families having a feud. Ma had no sympathy Aunt Rita couldn't get rid of her love for him. I did. I was still in love with Mark Rogers even though he laughed at the thought of us together at a dance. On Fridays at Teen Center I loved to hover in the gym door and watch him hanging over me in his evergreen shorts.

—Why don't you come over one afternoon and see our tree? Aunt Rita called.

—Oh, I said.

She picked up and staggered the can again. I could picture everything inside their house. She had gold block letters that said Season's Greetings and silver block letters for Happy New Year. She did her window corners with fake snow and she always had a real Christmas tree. We hadn't had a real Christmas tree in years. Ma said the needles were a pain in the ass. A real Christmas tree changed year to year, thus making time stand out. This was the year of our bluish Nordic one. This was the year of our green with spaces between the branches like a soldier. Aunt Rita was Catholic and also did not go to church. I wondered what would she tell me to do about the Holy Land. She was heaving down the steeper, easier part now. If it was the old days I would have gone over and asked her advice. Only someone who was Catholic and did not go to church could understand what to do. However Aunt Rita did not hate the church with the venom of Ma. Aunt Rita was more mild, like she was about my face. My face never bothered her. Aunt Rita I could see still wearing a veil. She had that air now with him gone of Jackie Kennedy in November on television. When she got past my line of vision I slipped away.

My white bowl was hidden under our outdoor Christmas tree. The colors outside our house at Christmas were holy stained glass reds and blues. Ma trained the blue spotlight on our front door which was wrapped in silver paper and tied with a giant fake blue bow, then the blue lights around our hemlock (like up in Cinderella's attic when the birds are wrapping her in ribbons for the ball), the blue along the house top, and in the two front windows owned by Annie and me were glowing red bells so that Ma every evening at four-thirty, hardly able to contain herself, came singing through our house, Plug in your bells, girls!

—Gorgeous, Ma said. I mean.

The first night they went down our road looking up at our house like strangers.

Dad said, It really does look good.

They had on their jackets, leaning together, like in an eager 1950s picture when they were young.

Dad had the two red pizzas on the table ready to cut like hearts. He used our thin C-shape serrated knife for vegetables.

—William Calley is a goddamn scapegoat, Ma said. Done and done. Case closed.

The principle of the teabags, I figured, was calm and relaxation to remove the swollen, over heavy eyes, but little chance of that at our supper table.

I said, William Calley is guilty. He murdered a hundred and nine people. He laid them in a trench and shot them with a machine gun up and down.

—Could we please, Dad said. I'm trying to eat.

—He didn't use a machine gun, Michael said.

—Scapegoat, Ma said. He's a scapegoat.

I said, What are you saying, Ma, a kid in kindergarten in

Vietnam deserves to get shot? Babies should be shot up and down with a machine gun?

—Scapegoat, Ma said.

I said, What's a scapegoat?

—That's ridiculous, Annie said.

—They shot kids? Robert said.

—Guys, Dad said. Could I please eat? Dad burped.

—Yeah, those kids are the ones throwing hand grenades, Michael said. You can't tell who's a Viet Cong, man.

Dad looked at Michael, then at his plate.

Michael said, We ought to just go in there and drop the Bomb.

Dad cleared his throat, breaking his meatloaf with his fork.

—You people are missing the point. Ma showly shook her head. Ma had her eyes closed. It was that time when she took forever to blink. She would set her cup back on the table with her eyes closed taking forever. Ma said, You people are completely missing the point. Ma picked up her cup and drank. It was that time of the cup being empty, when the ice cubes smashed around her mouth, and she had her eyes closed again, everything moving in slow motion.

—The point is you don't know who's a Viet Cong, Michael said. That's the point the liberals don't get.

I stared at Annie and Annie stared back, shaking her head. I said, Yeah, tell me, Michael, a six-month-old baby is really a Viet Cong.

Dad said, Pass those lima beans, bub, and Annie knocked Robert to move.

—You people are completely missing the point. Missing it. I'm telling you Calley is not the big gun. No way. No way is Calley the big gun. He's a scapegoat.

—He murdered a hundred and nine people, Ma, I said. He ordered five hundred sixty-seven unarmed Vietnamese people killed. What are you talking about?

—You don't know if they're unarmed, Michael said.

I looked across at Annie and she stared back at me.

—Scapegoat, Ma said. Case closed. Ma had her eyes closed.

I said, Why don't you talk with your eyes open? Why don't you tell us what a scapegoat is if you're going to say it thirty times.

—You don't know what a scapegoat is? Ma looked at me with disgust, picking up her drink.

—No. I must confess I do not. That is why I asked. Dad, could you tell us what a scapegoat is?

Dad cleared his throat. We all looked at him. Dad said, A scapegoat is someone who might or might not have done something wrong, but basically is being blamed to protect others who are higher up. I think what your mother is saying. Dad was leaned over his plate, holding his fork. Dad had a deep, hurt look in his eyes. Mary, correct me if I'm wrong. What your mother is saying is the point isn't what Calley or Medina did. The point is our whole policy in Vietnam is in trouble, right? And, as Michael pointed out, hey, we don't even know who the enemy is. We don't know who we're dealing with. We don't know who is Viet Cong. Basically, the whole situation is out of control and by focusing on Calley, Medina, whoever, they're creating a false sense that something is in control. Dad speared a piece of meatloaf, everyone calm.

I turned on my regular light in addition to my red bells. Standing down there in the road and they're saying gorgeous gorgeous you wonder do they realize what a red light in a girl's window means or not. I laid back and put my teabags on. It would have been too much a boudoir with only my red bells on. Now I had a whole half hour to relax. They felt like tiny wet weights. I went back through American history from My Lai to really the last teabag scene: that famous textbook picture of the white men dressed like Indians dumping tea in Boston Harbor. I heard there was something like tannin in tea and maybe that was what I was pinning my hopes on. Maybe there was something in the tannin chemical that sopped up flesh weight. I wondered what kind of families these people in magazines had that they could just store their used teabags outright in the refrigerator without anyone saying anything. I was lying there resting thinking about in older TV shows and movies how people sometimes laid down wearing black masks across their eyes when suddenly Ma said, Knock, knock, and burst in my room.

—What are you doing? I sat up fast, swiping, all my teabags falling like little animals around.

Ma looked at me. Ma was standing in my doorway with her arms crossed and her back hunched, walking on her tiptoes like she always did after supper, kind of apologetic, sliding around inside our house.

—What are you doing? I didn't say come in.

Ma stood in the doorway. I instantly felt bad. Ma looked like she had come in to say something mild and I just screamed at her.

—Daddy will be ready in five to take you.

Ma shut my door.

Chapter 13

*D*ad leaned in listening in his kitchen radio position for assassination news. It was spring, our kitchen window crabapple beautiful in white. We're still getting conflicting reports on whether there was a sniper shooting at the National Guard, the radio said. It's a very confusing scene here. I said, Dad, was somebody assassinated? Dad had his head laid sideways watching me while listening. He said, Four students got shot protesting the war in Ohio. I said, Ohio?

I got out our four little juice cups like once I got a delivery of Breck's shampoo to drink in. I was making mad scientist mixtures of detergent and water, biodegradable detergent and water, Ivory soap and water, and water to pour on philodendrons Ma gave me, keeping exact records of how these plants lived or died slowly for the science fair. I remembered upstate long ago my first experience with pollution: Lake Ontario sea to shining sea with floating dead fish.

I said, Why is a shooting in Ohio of only students being said on the radio in New York?

Dad said, They can't just shoot you for protesting the war.

I said, They can't?

—No! Dad was emotional.

I loved it when Dad got outraged. Get him on the Bill of Rights.

—Were chanting PIGS OFF CAMPUS, the radio said, and throwing rocks. We have also received conflicting reports on whether there was student initiated gunfire.

Dad had out the small frying pan, the big spaghetti pot,

the cutting board, and over by the radio in our big roasting pan a paper wrapped butcher lump defrosting with meat blood under it. He had two giant gold onions like coins. He sliced one with our thin serrated, talking about the First Amendment. Dad had bacon draining on paper towels, steam shooting out of the big spaghetti pot, cigarette smoke curling grayish out of an orange ashtray, in back our kitchen window slightly opened at the bottom for beginning spring.

—Man. Dad's eyes were red and watery. He put down his knife and backed away.

—Bad? I whittled Ivory soap shards into a little cup. I said, Ma said put white bread in your mouth.

Ma was in the living room moaning her new vacuum back and forth.

Tears ran down Dad's cheeks. Dad drained his beer, threw it sweeping into the garbage topped with (a clue) potato peels, opened the refrigerator and got another, popping it. Went back to his onion. I clattered my spoon. I was such a picayune scientist I used separate spoons for each. I was glad Dad thought even under Nixon the Bill of Rights applied. All hope went out my window when they elected him. I had my four plant mixtures ready. Now for my face. Dad backed away again. He wiped a striped dish towel across his sad baggy eyes.

—Four-day-old American and South Vietnamese sweep into the Fishook area of Cambodia had reportedly found most of those Communist sanctuaries empty.

I got out a small white dessert bowl, mayo, and one egg.

—You're using more of my mayo! Dad stared at me, his eyes welling, acting too upset to chop. Cripes, I'm buying mayo twice a week here.

—Take a deduction from my allowance. I was going to say it's for a good cause but I did not. I said, What is that?

—Knockwurst! Knockwurst! Dad exclaimed. There were six and he sliced them longways. He said, You're using my eggs!

—You're rich, Dad. I siphoned the yolk broke shell to broke shell, separating. Ma's only recipe for that I could remember was angel food cake, which always collapsed the way people moved violently for food in our house.

—Is growing uneasiness over U.S. involvement in Cambodia. The New York Stock Exchange plunged nineteen point oh seven points, its worst decline since falling twenty-one point one six points November 22, 1963, the day President Kennedy was assassinated.

I felt a shock hearing that date spoken out loud on the radio into a million homes. Then I thought oh good, it's not just me that remembers Kennedy being assassinated.

—You're taking my beer!

—You can spare it, Dad. I poured a little in my bowl. I said, What are you making anyway?

—Hot, hot. Dad carried the big pot with steam rising. Knockwurst and German potato salad, Dad said.

—Woo woo, different, I said.

Dad dumped steam and white into our sink, a great gray-white vat rising billowing before our early May window with white curtains on either side and outside our distant spray white tree, the sink steam swirling. It was The Invisible Man sitting opposite me in a wooden chair, like the electric chair in New York State or the kind the kidnappers would tie you to, gagged, and he was entirely wrapped in white bandages from head to toe and slowly from the top of his head he unwrapped, unwinding in a long long white circle, disappearing everywhere he exposed: his forehead, his brain, his face, chin, neck, shoulders, chest. His shirt and jacket and tie crumpled into the chair because now he was gone, invisible, which he did for some reason to help his friends.

I stopped off holding two little white cups like a waitress in each hand. Ma swiped the hifi lifting Robert's birthday cards. How you doing? Ma said.

—Good. I said, Ma, your philodendron doing best is the

one getting Ivory soap. Maybe you ought to fertilize every-thing with that.

No reply.

—So how's your new Electrolux?

—Wonderful, Ma said. I love it.

I leaned in, pressing against my windowsill, but also trying to keep my face tilted back behind my philodendrons so David Weitzen wouldn't see me from below. Romeo, Romeo. Glamour said wear the masque for five minutes but I tried always at least for ten. I figured the protein in the egg white seeped in, maybe improving my skin. I could make that masque mixture in public in the kitchen because it was for my entire face, not just my eye skin, like the withered stump of an amputation hanging out a sleeve. Many teenage girls put masques upon their face. The Patty Duke Show, in fact, began with that. Down in the driveway they were playing one on one, beating that orange ball into our asphalt, tremoring up through our foundation and two by fours into me, pressing perpendicular to my scar into my wooden sill. I had this pressuring in there lately bothering me. It rose, larger and larger, orange spinning round toward my face, enlargening. Drop.

I stood before my mirror and began to peel the white skin. The nice part about the masque was like my Oriental Third Imperial Lackey face it blended my bags away. I pulled off little white bits. I had a moral dilemma about my science experiment coming out in favor of pollution. I could see now and then as I worked at my face, peeling, the orange round risen basketball in the window in my mirror, like a boy who won't give up. There was a lot of pressure to be against pollution. I was dropping little white skin tabs in my bowl, watching my face emerge. It was interesting they never showed the werewolf change close up in reverse, the face becoming human again. I heard another girl was soaking her baby teeth in Pepsi for the science fair, watching the enamel strip. My philodendron fed with Ivory soap was growing leaps and bounds, next best plain water, third place biodegradable and last, hunched and yellowed like a widow in a wheelchair, was my regular detergent, like I wished I could be the grandfather in Heidi who fed Heidi's invalid friend good Swiss milk and cheese and carried her every day to sit in the clean Swiss mountain air until the roses came into her cheeks. Then I was going to stand before my four plants set on the O'Rourkes' borrowed card table, more strange eyed than usual in my tortoiseshell lady scientist glasses, and my time and symptom soap chart explaining to fairgoers who came too close that this experiment was like when I was a baby and Pop rubbed soap in my eyes, his little family experiment to prove I needed an operation on my chest.

I went back to my window. Spring air seeped in the bottom. I still had this pressuring inside my chest. The brown that held our rock wall together was rich rain wet. Our lilac was tight hard purple buds about to explode. For some reason I was happy.

—My chest hurts, I said at supper. I was leaned on the wooden table ledge trying to ease this extreme internal pressuring. I heard of appendix operations where the surgeon dropped a sponge. Maybe they left a little scalpel in me. The more I grew the closer I pushed that rusting blade to my heart. I was killing my own self slowly just by growing up.

—What hurts? Ma said.

—Here. I motioned back and forth across my heart, perpendicular to my scar. I said, It feels like this pressuring.

They're all stopped in mid chew, like once my staring patio goat, maybe even a little concerned.

—You're growing, Ma said.

—I am? I giggled. They were all looking at me like I just turned on my own country. It felt like that Little Rascals when Alfalfa, all skinny white indent chested, beats the bully in the ring and Spanky quick lifts Alfalfa's two fists over his head. I plowed up some of Dad's sliced potatoes with onion, bacon, and oil, speared knockwurst dipped in mustard. They all seemed moping, but I was sailing on. This had implications for my social life: a meaningful I Dream of Jeannie pink Baghdad top. I appreciated Ma's honesty. She could have lied.

—This was about April 1954, Pop said. Now every morning the whole gang of us telephone men would gather for coffee and doughnuts at Horn and Hardart's on 42nd Street and Third Avenue. That was an automat. You put your quarter in, you open the little window, take your cup of coffee, tea, whatever you like. Every morning the whole gang of us would gather and tell each other lies and then I as foreman, Pop leaned back, his eyes very impressed with himself, would give out the day's assignments, don't you know? Nosey, I'd say, you go over to 54th and Lexington, we got a complaint about a switchboard there. Mulligan, you drive over to Broadway and 71st. Well one morning I come in, we have our coffee, I give out the work, and I'm going off to my car when Jimmy O'Boyle calls to me.

Pop looked around our backyard like he just heard a voice.

Pop laid his hand on my arm. He said, Now, darling, I must digress and give you a little information about Jimmy O'Boyle. He said, Jimmy was a nice fella. Quiet. Irish, of course, all Irish in them days. Jimmy lived over in Brooklyn with his widow mother, and he was her sole support.

Pop's eyes bore at me saying sole support. I had a large white carved ivory Holy Land cross around my neck. I was no longer in my red bandanna bandage chest top and denim two piece. My new two piece was like pineapple orange frozen juice concentrate that you needed to mix three cans of water with. It had top and bottom ruffles like oo la la. In French we learned Toulouse-Lautrec painting the cancan.

Pop said, Jimmy was about thirty-eight, thirty-nine at the time. Never married. Why I don't know. Now, Jimmy had one fault.

I said, What?

—He was vain.

Pop said, Sheila, I never seen nothing like it in all my born days. That guy could not walk by a glass without looking at himself. He'd walk by a shop window, he's looking to see his reflection in the glass.

I made no movement.

Pop said, He was like a girl!

I had my hands on the arms of the redwood, flat on the wood. I could feel all across in my shoulder blades, tense, like you know exactly where is the gate to get out.

—He was not a bad looking man. He was better looking than your grandfather, that I will say.

I smiled.

—So, as I said, Jimmy called me over. I says, Hello, Jimmy, what's up. I had things to do, don't you know. So Jimmy says, Tommy, would you do me a favor and look at my nose.

Pop shrugged in our backyard, both his palms up. I didn't know how much of a family plot this was. Pop was always good about my scar, but as for my face, you never know.

—What am I looking for, I says. Look again, Jimmy says. Don't you see the hair growing out of my nose?

Pop raised his right hand Boy Scout. He said, Honest to God, Sheila, I'm not making a word of this up. So I look again and I seen there was a hair there. To me, it wasn't anything at tall. But I seen it bothered Jimmy. So I says, Jim, now that you mention it, I see it, but it's hardly visible at all. Well, Jimmy says, it bothers me. When I go home tonight I'm going to pull it out. Suit yourself, I says. What are you going to say?

—I don't know, I said.

—I didn't know either, Pop said. A person gets an idea in his head and it's no use trying to reason with him.

Pop looked at me. I had no idea if this was like that Playboy time with Dad where Ma tells the man to have a talk with me.

174

Pop said, It was like with your mother.

—My mother?

—She was a young girl, a year or two older than you and she got it into her head she was stout. Pop made two fists at his shoulders, like a football player with pads. Pop said, She wasn't stout.

I said, Wasn't that when they took that picture of her? She looks like a movie star?

—That's it, darling. That's the time exactly.

—She wasn't fat. She looked like a movie star.

—She did indeed, didn't she. She was so pretty. She had the long curls hanging down her back. Pop demonstrated with his hand. He said, You know who she looked like?

I said, Ava Gardner? I had no idea who Ava Gardner was.

—Ava Gardner is right, Pop said. But she was convinced she needed to lose some weight. Well, she put herself on some fool diet. You know I finally had to bring her to a doctor. Do you know she gave herself anemia?

—Mom, I said, shaking my head.

Next door the screen door slammed and the new dogs barked.

I said, That's Mr. Hanrahan's new dogs. When he moved back he brought dogs. I said, Guess the kind.

—I give up.

—Doberman pinschers.

Pop said, Those are brutal animals.

I said, Tell me about it. He's training them to do things in German. They whine all day because they're getting their ears trained. Have you ever heard of that?

—What's that, darling?

—Ear training? You know what that is?

Pop stared with old green turtle eyes. He said, I'm waiting with bated breath.

—Don't be sarcastic. I said, Did you ever know anyone with dobermans? They wrap the ears in really tight bandages like you know Oriental girls when they wrap their feet

so they don't grow? I said, They cut off the circulation?
They bandage up the dobermans' ears when the ears are still
floppy and then the cartilage restructures so they stand up.

I put my hands on my skull and grew two stalks out.

(It's cartilage, Mr. Hanrahan said leaning in at me and
touching my nose. It's pliable. Aunt Rita was standing there
smiling. The jerk was back. He moved my nose cartilage
back and forth, demonstrating.)

—Is that so? Pop said.

Babysitting I looked up ear training in the Hanrahans'
Doberman Pinscher book on their coffee table, a change
from my Playboy days. Zero, zip, in the index under ears.
They were in constant pain trying to pull their bandages off.
He just whacked them on the behind with a rolled newspaper to shut them up. I had no idea if this guy was a dog
torturer or this was a real process. I was going to try some
dog books at Charlotte M. Brewster.

—Dad?

Ma stood outside the green repeating diamonds in her new
two-piece, black with thin white piping. Off in the middle of
Nissequott our noon whistle began. Poor Ma was trying to
give him a regular feeding. Ma never learned.

—How about some lunch?

Poor Ma.

—None for me. Pop turned abruptly back to me in his
chair. He said, Well now to continue my story.

I said, Ma, he never eats lunch.

I meant that info kindly, but Ma cast me a dark look and
walked away. Ma was mad at me in general for looking too
long in my mirror.

Pop was looking around our yard like he just walked into
Horn and Hardart's.

—I says, Where's Jimmy O'Boyle? So Nosey says,
Jimmy's out in the truck. He asked could you come out and
speak to him there. I says, Well, Jimmy will have to wait. I
have my coffee, I give out the assignments. Gather my

belongings. Out I go. There I seen Jimmy leaning his head against the window of his truck. At least, I deduced it was Jimmy because it was his truck. All I could see as I approached was his profile. I tap on the window.

Pop tapped in the air.

—Jimmy turns his head.

Pop reared back, both his hands in the air, his face aghast.

—Mother of God! I says. Sheila, I never seen nothing like it in all my born days. Jimmy's head was all blown up, all swollen.

Pop held his hands around two feet apart.

—It was all blown up like that disease, what's that disease, darling, they get in Africa?

Next door Mr. Hanrahan yelled and you could hear the chains rattling.

—Sleeping sickness? I said.

—No.

The pool filter pushed out.

—Elephantitis?

—Elephantitis, darling! That's it! That's it! That's the disease I mean. How did you know that?

—We saw a filmstrip on it in science. It comes from a parasite that gets into your skin.

Pop's eyes all lit up.

—Well, that's exactly what Jimmy O'Boyle's head looked like is right. When he turned his head I couldn't help but cry out. I says Jesus, Mary, and Nellie, Jimmy, who did this to you? I assumed he was in a fight, don't you know. No one did this to me, Jimmy says. I done it to myself.

I said, He did it to himself? How?

—My words exactly, darling. You know what he said?

—The hair?

—He went home that night and he pulled out that hair with a tweezer. The next morning he woke up and his whole head was swollen. It must have gotten infected.

—He should have sterilized or something.

—Something is right. Well, nevertheless, this was the situation. Well Jimmy, I says, I'm sorry but I can't let you go out like that, you'll scare the customers. I know it, Jimmy says. You wait here in the truck, I says. Over I go and call Jake, Lord have mercy on his soul. You remember Jake?

—The guy you took him to Harlem when he said you were working too slow and someone dumped a chamberpot out the window on his head?

—That's the one! That's the one, darling! Bald as a billiard ball he was. Not from that, of course. What a good man he was. Well, I call old Jake up. I says Jake, Tommy. Are you sitting down? You're not going to believe this one. Tommy, he says, nothing you say could surprise me. And I proceed to tell him the whole story. Well, he says, you outdid yourself Thomas. I says, never mind that, what are we going to do for Jimmy? We didn't want him to lose a day's pay, don't you know. Jake says send him up to headquarters we'll put him to work shuffling papers around.

—Wait, I said. The train.

What happened with Ma was I had my head tilted back, trying camera angles in front of my mirror. The best way to view me was from below because my bags gracefully merged into my cheeks. My best hope for a boyfriend would be a midget like in that old circus riddle Aunt Rita gave to me. Now suddenly Aunt Rita wasn't going to get a divorce. In the spring she was best friends with Mrs. Callahan and I had hope for her escape. On Earth Day in April they were outside my window picking up garbage off our road, grown ups with more Pollyanna hope than me. I had this whole Lucy and Ethel scene of like two neighbors going for a ride on the Staten Island Ferry with the wind blowing their hair. It's still in New York, before California, and Lucy tells Ethel she's getting a divorce, thus she is able to save the black and white I Love Lucy series by continuing on alone. Whap! It felt like a gun just went off. I clutched my heart which almost hit the ceiling. It was Ma in the hallway with our still lifes of

1800 steam engine trains. She had her hands full of dirty clothes pulled out of our hamper and that must have been the lid she slammed. She said, Would you quit mooning around the goddamn mirror. She said, Christ almighty, enough. She looked like she was going to kill me.

The train passed going toward Port Sands. Cars were mostly empty in the middle of the day.

—Fifty-thirty Broadway. Five oh three oh Broadway, Pop said. This was where New York Telephone headquarters was.

The train whistled, passing our sandpit now.

Pop's hand was plunging to the concrete, demonstrating the change in temperature. He said, So instead of sitting outside to eat their lunch the workers were forced to eat inside, in the cafeteria. Now. Pop leaned back, eyeing me. All women worked in this joint, all babes doing the paperwork, sending out the bills. Very important work. Keep those pension checks coming in!

Pop squeezed my leg until I screamed.

—Well, twelve o'clock comes. All through the building a bell goes off. All the dolls drop what they're doing. They all get on the elevator. The elevator descends, straight down to the cafeteria, which is in the basement.

Pops stared at me with wild green eyes.

—What an awful life, isn't it, darling? A bell to begin in the morning, a bell for your coffee break, a bell when your break is over, a bell for lunch. I'd be wacky! They'd have to call the boys in white coats.

—Yeah. We have bells at school.

—Not for me, sister! Not for me. Well, I will say this though, that cafeteria had some excellent food. I ate there a couple of times and that's the best macaroni and cheese I ever had.

—Just tell the story.

Pop wheezed, leaning forward, shaking in his redwood chair.

—Aye aye. Aye aye. Pop saluted.

I saluted back, which I should not have because it caused another laugh delay.

—So, as I say, twelve o'clock, all the dolls go down to the cafeteria to eat their lunch. All women, the whole room is women except for Jimmy O'Boyle. Now, this cafeteria, as I say, was in the basement and also in the basement was the boiler. This boiler was horizontally mounted. Hori—moving his forearm stiffly level back and forth—zontally mounted. Now when the temperature rose the previous week, naturally they shut the boiler off, and when it dropped that morning they had to turn it back on. Well, something must have happened to that boiler. What it was I don't believe they know to this day, and all morning the pressure had been building and building. At twelve-twenty-five, five minutes later and the joint'd've been empty, at twelve-twenty-five, that boiler exploded, shot straight across the room.

Pop's arm shot straight by my nose.

—Straight at Jimmy O'Boyle and decapitated him.

Pop dropped his arm. I wanted to ask did he die.

—Well right away the telephone company sent a couple of lawyers out to Brooklyn, pronto pronto. Had Jimmy's mother sign a paper agreeing not to sue in return for a lump sum. How much it was I don't recall. Not enough to make up for the loss of her son, you can be certain of that! No amount could make up for that.

—No, I said.

—That's some story, darling, isn't it?

The leaves rattled in our sumacs with tiny repeating leaves, fun to run your hand along and cruelly strip off. Pop put his old bent and rebent hand on top of mine.

—It's so nice to sit with you, darling. I wish you could have come with me to the Holy Land. I know you'd have enjoyed it. Some of the places, darling, to think I was standing in the very same spot where two thousand years ago our Lord walked. I said to Brother Michael, he was the Franciscan monk, pinch me, I said, so I know I'm not dreaming. What a trip that was. I know you'd have enjoyed it.

Pop's hand stayed on top of mine. He stared off sadly with his giant round turtle eyes.

—Patsy saw you on TV carrying the cross.

—So I heard.

—It was on Channel 5. The pressuring beat again inside my throat.

—Why wouldn't you go? Pop said.

I looked down at our coping. My whole face was in pain and this pressuring beat inside my throat.

—All your expenses paid. Why would anyone turn down an offer like that is beyond me. You'd have to be a nut case to turn down an offer like that.

He glared at me.

The water in the deep end was pretty calm but in the low turbulent with the two silver ladder rung hoops to climb up out and behind our fence in the bright straight sun our daisy thin whites wavering, this pressuring hitting inside my throat and face.

—Well, Pop said, I suppose a young girl like you, you didn't want to leave your mother and dad. Is that why, darling?

I nodded. I looked off quick toward our cabana which had water running down its red since I was starting to cry.

—I can't blame you for that, Pop said. I know you love your mother and dad, don't you, darling?

I nodded and the pain welled again up through my throat, up inside my face, climbing toward my eyes. It really hurt under there. Our Father who art in heaven hallowed and I breathed out and it went back down and I said the rest because I loved God so much and at the end I rubbed my forehead and touched my stomach, then, scratching, touched my left shoulder and dragged across and rubbed my right.

Later Dad was in the kitchen making spareribs.

—How you doing, babe?

—Good.

Dad threw yellow slices on top of the raw bones.

—Dad, is this your favorite summer meal to make?

Dad looked at me and picked up his beer and drank. It's a good one, he said.

—I like it.

—Good, Dad said. That's what I like to hear. He set his beer and scraped his metal tablespoon around his metal silver pot making the sauce.

—Could I please make cucumber salad? I put my hand on his shoulder, feeling inside under his muscles the movement of his bones.

—Again!

—Small.

—All right. Then Dad left with his two potholders, spear fork, and his beer. I sliced the cucumber with decorative scalloping around the edge and filled the white small bowl with red wine vinegar, but keeping four slices out. I moved my bureau against my door. I lay down with two on each eye. The sprinkler pattered across my window screen. It was true I had a mirror problem. I looked in mirrors every single chance I got. Coming home from school I looked at myself walking by broken paned in our garage windows with luckily green curtains behind so I could see. Riding in the car I looked at myself in that great rearview band which cut off below my bad part. If I was the front right passenger I tilted my head and watched our sideview circle at my face and the blue retreating road. Going downstairs to watch TV I hoped and prayed the bathroom door would be opened all the way so that descending my whole self appeared more and more.

In my own room I had a small mirror Grandma gave me that was one side magnified, one not, and I did many views, dollying. Below, above. Magnified was my best because it blurred my bags right out of the frame.

At sparerib supper that night Ma and Pop had a really bad Catholic Church fight. All day I was like steering him from our driveway top to avoid our wind vents which did not have a Reader's Digest pro-Vietnam War flag decal, though he knew I got two in April and May to adhere.

—Dip that bread in, Dad said. Come on, guys, get the good stuff up.

—I can't believe you still go to church. Ma picked up her green cup and drank, covering her mouth.

Here I was all day thinking the fight would be Vietnam War with Ma screaming Michael was going immediately to Canada at age eighteen, Michael and Pop arguing Michael should go to Vietnam and become a P.O.W.-M.I.A.

—What's it to you? Pop said. I merely asked directions to the church. What's it to you if I go to Mass?

—Nothing! Ma yelled. I don't give a crap what you do.

Annie stared at me across the table. She had the wild flaring bangs from getting out of the pool and not combing and her white Peter Pan collar blouse with the slobby sleeves down and Robert sat with his brown dark eyes very bright, his spine straight, looking what to eat next like a robin, while Michael had the slight fish-like protrusion around his mouth and his face very white, lumpish with those puffs of hurt underneath his eyes and a steady jaw ache since this spring from having his braces tightened every Friday at four and Dad reached holding his roasting pan, rocking it, scooping with Italian bread to get all the gunked sweet onions, the pressuring constant flesh weight below his eyes. Ma set her cup, all the food exactly untouched on her plate. Ma had on her really battered tennis hat, wearing it everywhere since that day in June I found her wearing like a plastic rain hat in our kitchen with Kitchen Bouquet-colored drips running down her neck and Clairol Medium Brown on our stove, Ma next a perfect chocolate head without any gray until, unfortunately, the next day when she dove in our deep end brown and rose out our low end orange. I should count my blessings, Ma said, it could be green.

—I just view it as a complete waste of time, Ma said. I view the Catholic Church as strictly a money making operation.

Pop stared with drips of mayo and white green cabbage caught in his grizzled crevices, also reddened from the barbecue, Pop famished from not eating since seven that morning.

—I merely asked directions to the church.

—Pop, I said, I'll draw you a map after supper.

—What crap, Ma said.

—Am I hurting you? Pop went on hunched low, forking food in.

—No. You're not. And Ma picked up her cup and drank.

—Dip that bread in, guys! Annie, eat!

And Pop bent chewing with white cabbage pieces around his face as Ma sat, arms crossed in her two piece and battered hat.

The next morning I was coming down the hall.

—The least you could do, Ma said, swinging back her foot, both in Annie's room, Pop in his gold suit from church and Ma in her white tennis dress, is make your bed, and Ma kicked his suitcase hard.

I went on fast down the hall into my room and shut my door. Next thing we're all four out in the driveway waving watching our Dodge descend, Pop sinking backwards toward the next plane out of La Guardia.

Chapter 14

Nissequott looked like in a View Master. All bulging three-dimensional. I was looking out the Charlotte M. Brewster window Saturday, two days before I got drowned in junior lifesaving. You always got drowned by the Red Cross. They drowned me in first for swimming lessons. I can already swim with my whole body underwater, you want to see? No, put your face in the water and blow bubbles. But what's the use if—. Put your face in the water and blow bubbles. We were on the rocky North Shore as usual. Once Joyce had great white rubber shoes perfect for the North Shore. Walk on rocks walk on crabs walk on mussels never feel a thing. Walk on and on until Connecticut. Connecticut looked like Gulliver tied down. Ma told me once she tied me to a tree. Lowering, the distant horizon sleeping giant, then the rocks below, all clear and separate whites and browns and floating seaweed green and suddenly that Red Cross lady shoved my head under and held. Possibly that tied down chapter was as far as I ever got because in second that book was too hard.

I was looking out the Charlotte M. Brewster window Saturday. I had no idea what to read next. Now the Nissequott School field had pop up aqua portables, very psychedelic for such a red brick colonial town. I remembered when that field was blank and only one school in our town. I got sent to so many schools I felt like writing to Reader's Digest Humor in Uniform which had sympathy once for military kids always moving around. I never had sympathy for the other kids like both Annie and Michael had operations, tonsils, but I could care less. Last night I tried to comfort Annie about getting shot in archery.

—Don't feel bad because I know I'm going to get drowned in junior lifesaving.

Annie lay corpse-like under her pink pig shaped bulletin board. Annie got sentenced by Ma to four weeks at day camp while I got only two at Red Cross. The sprinkler went by her window. Every Sunday magazine I looked at those small black and white ads for rubber white beach shoes, checking were they still there, also obesity camps for girls—all your problems solved—and I was always too polite to mention Annie could have gotten that. I said, How come you were the only one that got shot if he ordered everyone to pick up their arrows though?

Last winter Annie allegedly got hit by a rock wrapped in a snowball and that meteor was still flying at her face.

Annie said, They all planned it ahead to get me. They could have shot my eyes out, man.

I was sideview in her great Newmark and Lewis vertical mirror holding her silver P.O.W. bracelet, the mirror only on her legs and her pig, like why if your mother was always putting cottage cheese on the list for you would you order a pig bulletin board from Sears? The sprinkler passed fanning no color lines. Three days of day camp they already knew to pick on her. We always picked on her. This spring we went sneaking up during Ironside. We burst her door opened. She's on her toes in a black leotard. Bravo! Bravo! Michael, Robert, Dad, and I all clapped.

—Day camp is bad, Annie, but they're going to drown me in lifesaving. I said, Annie, don't you remember when Ma took senior and she got that moose for her test and she put him in the cross chest carry and he tried to drown her and she put him in the hair carry and he had a crewcut? Sprinkler. I said, And you know I'm not as good a swimmer as you.

I ate Cap'n Crunch and two Dutch Apple Pop Tarts

without frosting this morning two days before lifesaving and about half an hour later everything got strange. Maybe someone put LSD on my Pop Tart. I remembered that Nissequott School field blank without flower power pop up portables, just grass, then they set up card tables for a scene when the whole town flocks for the polio vaccine on a sugar cube. No shot! I was balancing that precious yellow liquid drop. Reader's Digest had about a hippie that took LSD and suddenly on a divided highway he has a flashback, walks into traffic and dies. I wouldn't mind having a nice clearcut flashback to clear everything up. That blue asphalt library parking lot was either part of my stomach or not. I felt very strange today. Hallucination, man. Hundreds and hundreds of books. Through steady reading and exercise she becomes President of the United States. A movie or biography, a kindly librarian would give me advice.

—Ooo, Sheila, I'm telling you, I read the greatest story today.

Twilight at our picnic table, when the rabbits jump jump across the grass then pause, listening.

—About a father and son playing a tennis match. Ooo, it was so good. I mean! Ma picked up her green cup and drank, Ma telling me about a book. Ma had on her red sweater from Macy's and her checked headband made from caftan scraps.

—Why was the story so good?

—LOVE IT, Ma yelled. I'm telling you, Sheila, you would love this story.

I held our big white bowl with empty aluminum foil balls leftover from potatoes, further leftover from the dear dead days beyond recall in Brooklyn and Queens when Ma and Dad ate baked mickies cooked on the street. Ma liked to talk to people after supper but everyone else fled. I said, How come it was so good?

—Tuu. How shall I put this? Ma leaned back with her

arms crossed. Ma looked at me like I was counterfeit gold.
Why was it good? You're asking me that?

—Yes. Why was the story that you read today so good?

—Because it was true. Ma lifted her shoulders. What more
can I say? Truth, man, truth.

Birds flew out of the crabapple tree.

—What was the story about? I picked up our platter with a
steak bone Dad had totally gnawed. Clearing, you can
always exit, stage left, fast. Ma stared at me. Ma had totally
sharp, totally smart eyes. You never knew what was going to
happen next, really funny or really bad. Be ready.

—If I had to put it into one word? Ma slid out a cigarette.

—Well, you don't, but what word?

Ma struck, struck. Oh, shee-et, she said. Ma threw the
unlit match onto the patio probably meaning the pachysandra. She struck another and it flamed. I put all our
utensils in the bowl, put the bowl on the meat platter with
bone, poured all the leftover milk into one.

Ma waved her match out.

—Rivalry. Ma's eyes went off to either the pachysandra or
the stacked slate. Rivalry, she said again. It was amazing. All
it was, very simple, a father and son playing tennis, but you
could tell, man, a lot more, huh huh, Ma laughed, was
wound up in this tennis match.

—Huh, I said.

—You know what Freud said. Ma stared at me.

I had one foot up on the red bench balancing the platter
bowl and a four cup stack, letting in a little pause.

—NO BOY'S A MAN UNTIL HIS FATHER IS DEAD, Ma
and I chanted together.

I laughed. Ma eyed me. You got it, man, Ma said, put her
cigarette to her mouth and sucked. I had this urge to remind
Ma when we played tennis I lost bad, though actually that
more enraged her than if I won because I smashed them out
so hard. Wham, the fence. Wham, the fence. Christ, Ma
said, does every one have to be a winner with you, and softly

she pattered it back. WHAM. Alas, impossible for Ma and me to ever appear on that mother daughter Grapenuts tennis commercial, the two running with their rackets at the camera to show how mutual cold cereal made them look alike.

—You want more instant, Ma? I piled the coleslaw container on my load. I'm going in and watch Lucy.

—Thank you, no.

—Oh, you still have some. I was telling Ma this. I moved away.

—Sheila, I'm telling you.

I turned back.

—You would enjoy that story no end.

—So I'll read it.

—You can't, Ma said. I returned it to the library.

—So I won't read it. I laughed. This was Friday, three days before lifesaving.

Ma said, This writer was so good.

I turned back again.

—You know with the building the tension. The tension is building and building all through the match and finally this son is ready to strangle and I mean strangle his father over a line call, OUT!

Ma's voice died and the birds began again.

—Do you ever know who's right about the line?

—No. Ma stared at me, like suddenly deeply depressed.

I slammed shut Little Women. I had no idea what book to read next. Those aqua portables popped up outside the Charlotte M. Brewster window were like a hippie flower power day glo version of the Nissequott earth with bags under its eyes. It was very strange how Annie had to be fat with normal eyes and I had to be skinny with baggy eyes, like a girlhood Richard Nixon-J. Edgar Hoover face, and both the boys got to be normal, like why wouldn't God combine the two sisters to make one normal, good. I figured read every book alphabetically by author but forget it with the sisters sweetie sweet. Forget it any book with World War II fighter planes on the jacket, everyone always refusing to admit the Vietnam War was war too. In fifth getting a P.O.W. bracelet was the latest fashion but in seventh no. I was leaving some guy hunched and starved alone bent in a Viet Cong bamboo cage because I was vain. At the tennis club the richer ones got copper bracelets for arthritis making a green wrist ringworm in their skin, Republicans I'm sure. The P.O.W. was silver with his name, birthday, city, and rank engraved, blackening in those indents where it never got touched.

I said to Annie, I thought you were supposed to wear this until your guy got released.

She rolled over under her fat pink animal. She said, I couldn't take it. I woke up screaming from a nightmare with him, man.

The sprinkler. Annie was the kind who got a nightmare from the first Ironside. All you had to say was it's dark and he's walking onto a wooden porch and she screamed.

—Once I had a nightmare, I said, I was walking in the woods next to the Hanrahans' swingset and this bloody Indian ran by me.

The sprinkler. Annie narrowed her eyes. She said, You would do anything to have a worse dream than me, wouldn't you, Sheila?

Once for no reason Annie tore up my gum wrapper chain. It was over six foot with color bands, white spearmint, purple grape, red wild cherry, lighter red strawberry, yellow Juicy Fruit. One spring day I opened my lime green flower power storage candy box to weave on it again. My whole legs dissolved. It felt like on a rainy nighttime street coming on the white chalk outline of a murder victim. That chain was all torn apart. Then secretly it's a relief. How long are you supposed to go on lengthening it? I smashed Annie so hard for that. Lizzie Borden took an axe. All the flesh and ribs and that central empty core of where we breathe and beat. It felt like my arm floated off I smashed her so hard. I was like, matricide, patricide, fratricide, no sister word— maybe this was not a crime?

Basically I wanted to read about love. Either love or morality. In all the biographies the kid gets reading advice from a kindly librarian but those Charlotte M. Brewster ladies were all living in another age in cardigans. I could just see a First Amendment battle scene when I was at the check-out desk trying to use my new thirteen and over adult card for The Sensuous Woman or The Love Machine.

—Ant, I said, you want me to wrap your birthday present for Dad? She hated it and loved it when I called her Ant. The sprinkler passed. I said, I don't mind since I'm getting out the wrapping paper for Robert's and mine.

Annie rolled over. That hanging pink pig was instead of for our family a crucifix.

Water.

—Robert and I both got him tube socks, I said.

Annie said, Get out of my life. I hate your guts.

Then after I tried to kill her I almost had to give her mouth to mouth. She's lying motionless in the hall. I read parts of Ma's Red Cross Lifesaving. Lift the jaw, put a rolled jacket under the neck. Annie had halitosis bad. That wouldn't go over too good with the jury. Annie, I said. The word possum keeps running through your mind. Annie? Annie opened her eyes and laughed.

A, Ba, Be, C, I was rounding past that very large library window where slowly, like the CIA, a panelled station wagon trolled. When I saw people today they all looked coming at me with those glasses and fake nose. That library sign NO BARE FEET looked imported from France. I came to Fa to Faulkner a famous guy I heard of, but with almost three shelves. I figured start at the lowest level, A Fable, two words, or Sanctuary, one. Sanctuary would be nice. Marble floors, pews, no attack, except they could ask you: name all the apostles. Fables used to be my best hope to learn morality because they were with animals who could care less about Christ. This is good. This is bad. I opened this Fable and the first page was a giant black cross. I looked from the page out the window again where water rose up the glass.

I started A Fable again. I jumped over that cross. I said get the first word. Now the second. Join the two. Get a third. Join the third. I looked up: watery glass again. I could get one word, I could get two words, but I could not join three words, let alone a sentence, let alone a paragraph, let alone a chapter, let alone a book.

Down the library aisle came a bald man like Fred Mertz. Everything felt strange today, like holding A Fable as Fred Mertz walks down your library aisle you expect any second your town noon whistle to blow. I was wavering between dimensions today. Fred! Fred was always so calm! I felt like clinging to his pant legs, Fred! Once in Connecticut Fred was in the PTA show carrying a constantly growing plant across the closed curtain stage between each act, every time the plant growing and Fred marching along like his sole reason to exist was to carry this plant, finally he's staggering and it's a tree.

Fred disappeared around G-H. G-H in the library was Hai Karate in Genovese, and I was in eyeshadow, eyelash, Erase Cover Up Stick. I put back A Fable. I saw another F guy I heard of.

> In my younger and more vulnerable years
>   my father gave me some advice that I've
>   been turning over in my mind ever since.

Uhrrrrt. I stopped at our red Nissequott traffic light. I paced on our sidewalk trying to get to my cherry tree to read. I had that book wrapped in my arms beating against my heart. I opened it, pacing, reading that sentence again. I felt like that pacing spotted leopard in one cartoon about touring the zoo and suddenly that leopard grabs his bars and shocks you talking English about his fate. Uhrrrrt. I just raced by the wooden heroes, Our Lady of Alaska, our American Legion for whites, our deli with fireballs for a childhood hallucination drug. I did not need that today. Everything was strange enough, two days before lifesaving, thank you. This Nissequott corner looked like a diorama for social studies. The Methodist Church. You know that siren is pressured waiting inside our red brick firehouse, any second about to explode. I stopped. My jaw dropped. Cars moved back and forth dimly across. I could not believe my own eyes. All the woods next to the Indian's shack were gone! All the woods were bulldozed, flattened, knocked down, smashed, and they put up a sign which was a total mystery to me.

JACK IN THE BOX COMING SOON

—Ma. I walked past her thin straight lovely middle July purple flower bells, along our straight gray slate, through our green open gate, past our cherry tree dotted with red.

Ma looked up. It was Monday, two hours before junior lifesaving. Everything was clear. Ma had on her sunglasses, holding my Great Gatsby from the library, which she grabbed every time I set it down. The never mentioned most exciting part for us was that book was set on Long Island. We had a black and white picture showing Ma and me earlier with a book, Ma in her sunglasses looking in that giant heavy brown collection of fairy tales, and I had on my brown second grade cardigan and my great white elastic head band which somehow helped my face, and Ma was in her red and white striped maternity shirt, though her stomach flat and Robert born long before, all of us resting on the sunny slate spring stoop from building another wall, and I was pointing, when Dad snapped, asking Ma the meaning of a word.

—Ma, I said again, though she was already turned, full attention, like I guess you carry more meanings, Ma, in your voice than you know. I walked through the gate under our cherry tree. I held light blue toilet paper, light blue from their bathroom. When Joyce and I went together, one on the toilet and one on the tub, uhh, uhh, waiting for you, and Joyce always used rolls and rolls but I always used exactly three. I cupped it, walking, from the sun, like I remembered all those special 1969 eclipse precautions to keep from going blind of paper, pinhole, backwards, shadow, moving moon and sun. I did not want the sun to burn away today my evidence. Ma looked up, stopped in the middle of my book, which actually she already read once, but forgot. I thrust my paper into the sun.

Then say it's like a comedy. A man is bringing flowers to the lady he loves, holding them behind his back, not even realizing a goat has stolen up behind and nibbled off all the blooms. What if that whole time moving from the bathroom, out into the sun, up the walk and through the gate, that whole time my color evidence was blanching away. I would be like that poor slob holding out a bouquet of chewed stems and Ma would throw her head back and laugh at me. I once picked daisies for Ma on the ground where Joyce and I buried our shoebox of mementos, like in that cartoon where daisies pop up on a grave, only when I knocked on our back door and presented them to Ma, yellow and white, unfortunately they were crawling with black dots moving everywhere. Oh, Christ, Ma said, these things are crawling with ants.

—Ma. Behind the pool was a deep clean blue faintly filtered rippling, our trees full middle July stopped green, our cabana stilled a deepening red. I said, Is this blood?

The strange reversal was: blood was good. Actually that dot was watercoloring away. But suddenly standing there while Ma sat below in sunglasses holding my book, suddenly I was not afraid to let that blood disappear. I knew I could always get more.

—Where did this come from? Ma looked up at me. I smiled. Ma looked cute befuddled.

—I think I got my period. I laughed. You would think the combination toilet paper and red would clarify possible juxtaposition with age, like you know this wasn't like Dad with those reddened toilet paper dots stuck on his face. Ma looked at me completely confused. Ma needed to see Growing Up and Liking It more than me.

—I guess so, Ma said. But she was still stopped, like halted back in time, while I laughed again, moving on. For a second I thought she was going to try to say something was wrong with me.

Everything was clear. The pool, the green, the daisy petals white wavering. The sun was high. I said, Well, I guess it had to happen some time.

Ma looked at me. I liked Ma a lot.

—Come on, she said. She stood. I'll take you to Genovese.

I laughed. Genovese seemed like a strange place to celebrate, not like Grant's, out of business now, which once had a countertop with spinning stools to get some ice cream, but then once Ma and I had a great time in Grant's just buying Meet the Beatles, when I was swinging from that guiding aluminum bar.

> There were bells on a hill
> But I never heard them ringing
> No, I never heard them at all
> Till there was you.

—MA! Ma and I were barrelling through Nissequott in the red VW convertible bug, top down.

—To have killed at least three hundred eighty-four North Vietnamese soldiers and to have wounded many more. American—

—MA! I turned the radio down. I'LL READ YOUR LIFE-SAVING BOOK, I yelled, as we barrelled cutting left—whoah!—on two wheels screeching under Nissequott's first traffic light—errrrrrt—blinking to red, and I looked back for cops.

—What? The wind whipped Ma's orangish curls, passing Esso, with fading orange traces of that Tiger in Your Tank on the wall.

—SINCE I CAN'T GO TO LIFESAVING, I yelled, I'LL MAKE UP FOR IT BY READING YOUR RED CROSS LIFE-SAVING BOOK.

Ma made a face, basically the face that I was weird. Reach, row, throw, and go, I already memorized from that book, and now by exactly timing my first period right I saved myself from lifesaving.

—The United States has sped up shipments of F-4 Phantom fighter bombers to Israel, the radio said, low. I looked along that thin dirt path for our Indian. It seemed like he should be walking madly along for this big scene.

—MA, ANNIE'S GOING TO KILL ME FOR GETTING OUT OF LIFESAVING.

—I'LL TAKE CARE OF ANNIE.

—Court-ordered busing to achieve racial desegregation.

Ma whipped left—ehhhhrt—right, left, into a spot, creak, fast pulled out our emergency.

—A B-52 raid, the radio said. Off.

I felt kind of dazed, like I just won an Academy Award. I rescued my own self from Red Cross Junior Lifesaving on Dad's birthday. Ma was racing past all the Hallmark cards, the beach balls in a thin black rod jail, past Hane's and Fruit of the Loom men's briefs. Ehrrrrt, facing the other way. I never even knew there was a third hole down there. I just assumed two. Like, I never knew where he was going to fit in. Yuck, yuck, where you pee, yuck. Now the future had more hope.

Ma was bent grabbing a giant box.

—The booklet they gave us was Moddess, I said.

—They're all the same. Ma lifted a pale blue box of Kotex not pink and white marbled Moddess, choosing the same kind for me as always for her even though she said they were all the same. You could hardly see Ma peeping over that box was so big. I passed her at beach balls and she said, Wait!

—You need this. Straining her chin over the box, reaching, Ma slid a package off a rack. I took it from her. I laughed.

—Ma, this looks like a torture machine.

—Let me see that. Ma grabbed it fast, like possibly she gave me the wrong thing.

—Look at the teeth, I said.

Ma looked at me, shocked. I said it to give her a Genovese thrill.

—What's it have teeth for?

—That's to hold the sanitary pad in place.

And Ma looked at me again, like still startled.

—Well, they're pretty extreme, I said and laughed.

At the front Genovese had huge plate glass windows and huge paper signs for sales and words fell in shadows backwards on the dirty white floor, BOUNTY PAPER TOWELS. Ma put the gigantic light blue Kotex box and the white elastic belt on the black conveyor belt. I put out a teenie box of pink blue yellow and white birthday candles.

—For Dad, I said.

Ma fumbled for her wallet and threw out crumpled bills which I took up and straightened flat. The lady put the Kotex in a bag but it stuck out.

—I'll take that. Ma quick jabbed her wallet away, her pocketbook swinging wildly at her knees. She picked up the brown bag with way obvious light blue Kotex sticking out and headed past the gum machines, including some selling small rubber insects inside a clear capsule shape, though earlier, in my gum machine days, those capsules had day glow go go rings and once, before Joyce moved, we were in her blow up pool when a boy visited and gave me an orange pink ring, so once my face could not have been that bad.

Ma and I walked out into the overhang shade, then out beyond the maroon shopping center poles, blinking, into the sun, shining way high over the sump, dulling the parking lot asphalt to a whitish sheen, Ma proceeding first bearing the huge huge obvious light Kotex blue in case anyone we knew from Nissequott drove by, Ma taking all the embarrassment on herself.

—Here. Ma handed me an empty brown bag, like you got with your initial written on for lunch. She said, You put your dirty Kotex in this. Come here, I want to show you where to store it. Here. She bent, Ma bending in our bathroom, giving me another bathroom lesson to proceed on in life, like actually great times for Joyce and me were going to the bathroom together, the one sitting on the toilet in control, the one sitting on the bathtub edge having to guess which wallpaper figure the one going was thinking of. The guy behind the curtain taking a shower singing? No. The lady who just got out of the bathtub and the poodle is pulling off her towel? No. The fat opera lady taking a bath and she lost her soap? No. And all the men were taking showers, but the ladies could be either way, shower or bath, and the artist made them out of blue lines which was one line to tell you they were made of skin and wet, though now the O'Rourkes covered that wallpaper over and more and more my watery memory figures were drifting away, though I remembered another time before Nissequott when we had plaid living room drapes and I went to the bathroom, number two, aiming it exactly on the wood next to the rug, which was that important difference between a rug and wall to wall, where I knew it would be easier for Ma to clean.

Ma rattled the empty bag, gesturing it toward our dark empty cabinet. She said, I store it in here.

—Roger.

Ma looked at me then swung, low, the cabinet closed. She straightened, the multi-orange shower curtain folds behind. She looked at me.

—I don't feel anything, I said.

—Good!

—What about cramps?

—You'll know it if you have them, believe me.

I followed her out. I had a sense cramp would be the same interior feeling-shape as claw like crab since both spelled alike and both were important in Red Cross Junior and Senior Lifesaving, one dangerous at low tide and one at high.

—Ma, do you get cramps?

The Moddess booklet said you could predict things from your mother.

—Once in a blue moon. It's not a biggie. Ma picked up her pack of cigarettes and leaned against the kitchen counter with our window and white curtains behind. Ma said, Jesus, I'll never forget I knew a girl in high school she used to get cramps and stay in bed all day. Ma waved her flame out.

—What happened to her?

—She died.

Ma threw her match off.

—She died from her period?

—Oh, cripes, no. I forget what she died from. Ma blew her smoke off.

—Well. I said, Well, they said in Growing Up and Liking It you should still get exercise, just not swim.

Ma shifted her weight, eyeing me. Ma had her striped orange yellow blue and white bermuda outfit on, not just putting on one of her caftan dresses over her two piece, but dressing up for Genovese.

—Maybe I should go out and do some sprints.

—Whatever, Ma said. Come here. I want to show you something on the calendar. This is very important.

It was a Girl Scout calendar with, unfortunately, for July a color picture of two Brownies feeding a bottle to a goat. Across the squares of days was all Ma's handwriting, with relatives and arrival time, Sgles or Mxed Dbls, and Dad had written Dbls for himself once or twice, and two Tuesdays F wax, who was our floor waxer, who was black and always came in the middle of Hollywood Squares, and every Friday

Ortho 4 p.m. for Michael's jaw tightening, and on Dad's birthday, DAD, in my handwriting, because Ma wrote all our names on our days but she never wrote hers or Dad's so I always did.

—You always mark down when you got your period, Ma said.

—Okay.

—It's very important. You have to mark it down. Ma looked at me with deep strain.

—What day?

Total confusion passed on Ma's face.

—What do you mean what day?

—The last day, the first day, the average day?

—The first! Ma yelled. The first!

—Oh. Okay. I'm just asking.

—Always the first, Ma said, a little calmer. Look, here's what I do. I put down my initial. Ma hesitated with her pencil.

—S, I said.

Very fast Ma wrote S, capital, in script. She said, Then I count forward twenty-eight days and I write my initial then. Ma counted four Mondays and wrote an S on August 12. August 5 already said M.

—Okay, I said. I dropped it back to July. It said S on the same square with DAD. That was pretty weird. I changed the subject. I said, Ma, Growing Up and Liking It said some cycles could be twenty-one or it could be like thirty-five.

—Truth, Ma said. But I would go with twenty-eight, to begin.

—Like taking out a library book. I smiled.

Ma blinked. She said, Do not forget to do that. It's very important. Ma stared at me. I thought, yeah, so you don't get a stain.

I sat lump-centered in the black living room Naugahyde like on a throne, the Princess and the Pea. It was three-thirty, just when I would have been dragging myself up on the sand, gasping at lifesaving for Ma to drive me home. But no. I was home, feet up, drinking Nestea, having a ball reading Sports Ill, Faces in the Crowd. Not many girls made it into Faces in the Crowd and they all did the point type sports, like gymnastics where you had a judge and pointed your toes, not my type, right halfback on field hockey defense or rather low batting average softball, second base. Sheila is slow but short, Dad always said, kindly, about me. Dad's tube socks were wrapped. I figured rest until four-fifteen then make the Bisquick for strawberry shortcake with real whipped cream. Everything was perfect and nothing was wrong. Anytime I wanted I could go in the bathroom and pull down my pants and look at this great red collection I had totally made. You're sitting around normal on the outside meanwhile all this machinery is moving and spinning, rolling levers and spinning dials deep inside. This is your womb!

Ma rose behind the banister bearing a chained up tower of plastic cups, left downstairs by the slobby boys. Ma halted looking at me over her dried flower vase.

—How you doing?

—Good. I let a little silence build. It feels like a diaper, I said.

Ma's jaw dropped. She threw her head back and laughed and laughed and I turned the page, The 19th Hole, The Readers Take Over, acting cool.

I smoothed a spot underneath our cherry tree. American, you think naturally of telling lies. It was two weeks later, two weeks until my next period. The ground below was dark and rough with pits. Once, before Nissequott, Ma was going wacko with kids so she tied me to a tree. I always hoped it was a dogwood, more company. Ma, I said to her once, remember how you once tied me to a tree?

No reply.

I said, How?

—What do you mean, how? With a rope!

—I know a rope, but how? The ankle? The neck?

—The neck! Jesus! You think I'm Attila the Hun? I'm bad but I'm not that bad. I tied you by the waist.

—Oh, thank you. I laughed. Did it work?

—No!

I laughed.

—You wrapped yourself around and around that god-damn thing. I said I got to let this kid go or she'll choke herself.

—Well.

Ma looked at me, waiting.

—That's one way to get free.

Ma's jaw dropped.

I wiped those cherries smooth. In Little Black Sambo the tigers chase him around the tree so much the ground turns to pancake batter, saving him. Those cherries fell with dark maroon flesh and after time they wore to pits, wood dots left on the ground reversing my old horoscope days with Aunt Rita when we gazed up, now my life permanently changed. My ground below was dark and rough, the cherry bark dark and rough, the circle of leaf shade cool, but everywhere else beyond extremely bright, like a constant flash.

Ma rose beyond our pine in white with apricot braid scalloping hem, crossing in sudden white across the extreme of green, almost ended July. I remembered the shock I had Ma also learned photosynthesis and chlorophyll when she was a girl in Queens. Ma held her racket, medium weight with huge, five-eighths grip.

—Listen. Ma rounded the gate. I had this immediate instinct to run. Ma stood over me in her white and trace apricot holding her racket, like the Statue of Liberty. Ma said, I found a book for you at Charlotte Brewster.

The last time Ma got me a book was about the swimming of sperm. I said, I already have a book. I held up The Implosion Conspiracy, which was about Julius and Ethel

Rosenberg and the atom bomb, finally a woman getting into history, though in her case, better left out.

Ma said, I was talking to Judy Lazarus at the club. She recommended this book for you.

Ma held the book out. Judy Lazarus was Ma's doubles partner, who Dad called La Boca Grande.

—Yoga? I laughed. I thought, yogurt, yoga, like what was Ma suddenly with the hippies and Woodstock, woo, love the one you're with?

—Judy says there's something in there called the Lion that'd be good for you.

—The Lion? I laughed. I thought Africa? My lion on The Wizard of Oz?

—Maybe there's a table of contents, Ma said.

—Oh. I turned to the front. The index in back would be quickest, most efficient, but I did not want to injure Ma's feelings so I went frontward, slower, her way.

—Sixty-seven, Ma said.

Then I kept staring at the Table of Contents like I wished it was a table and say it had some grapes and you would just sit around and eat. That hollowing dripping acid stomach sense began. I turned some pages, turning not that fast, thirty mph. Thirty mph was the speed limit everywhere almost in Nissequott way way until the LIE. Then you could go fast, fifty-four, fifty-five. I turned and turned. Sixty-three, sixty-five.

—Sixty-seven! Ma said.

It had three black and white pictures on the left, close up of a woman's face, more and more opening her mouth, then finally the largest full color right page close up with her mouth opened to scream.

An exercise for getting rid of baggy eyes, it said.

Ma had moved away from me toward the gate. It was like a jumped juncture, one sec close, the next Ma really far away. Ma had on those same hospital colors I had in my first memory.

—How about some Nestea?

I thought why is she offering me Nestea? I thought of those tasters for poisoning some royalty had. I was kind of in shock. Everything was around, our rock wall, our fence, but it felt almost like I disappeared. It's like you look down and see limbs attached, growing out. Oh. Part of me. I shook my head: no.

—Well, use that if you're interested. It's worth a try, right?

I nodded. It hurt all up under my face and pounding throat like a very big tree growing there. It felt like I was sitting underneath this tree and someone came along and beat me up and left.

—Oi vay, Ma said. We should dive in the pool, right?

Chapter 15

—You're cutting through my wall!

   —Ich bein Berliner, Dad, whatever that means. It's a stupid wall, Dad, face it.

I walked with my arms spread, the card table a good shield anyway in case those maniac slobbering fang toothed dobermans broke free. I heaved the O'Rourke's card table over the juniper and little rock wall, probably our last and only three to four rocks high. Only the adults obeyed it, possibly the point anyway though they told us it was to keep the kids from wearing out our lawn. Dad was snaking our vacuum hose off the fence and Mr. Hanrahan wrapping styrofoam around his arms so he could train his doberman pinschers to attack when he said attack in German, those dogs steadily whining because now they had a new variety of anatomy pain: Tuesday the vet chopped their curly pig tails off and wrapped on stiff stub white bandages to improve their looks.

I said, You think I'm going to lug this thing all the way down the O'Rourke's driveway, down the road, up our driveway, up those steps? You're lucky I'm helping you this much.

Dad raised his eyebrows, sucked in his cheeks, puckered out his lips like boo boopie doo, that aqua white snake hose tumbling. They got totally excited about these stupid pool parties but to me all it meant was after eight, Adam-12, stay downstairs and watch TV. Plan everything. Get your whole food supply for the night. Bring your toothbrush and toothpaste downstairs so no one walks in on you in the upstairs. If someone's legs come near the top of the stairs, quick hide in the bathroom so you do not have to talk.

(handwritten: Calmes better ~ electronics ...)

—IT'S SHEILA. HERE'S SHEILA. They're screaming their heads off. SHEILA WANTS SOME POTATO CHIPS. WHAT ARE YOU STARVING YOUR CHILDREN, MARY? SHEILA, IS IT TRUE THE RUMOR WE HEAR ABOUT YOU AND MR. CALLAHAN?

Dead silence. There's the pool lit blue and the yard all surrounding dark and the table yellow low citronellas flickering and in the middle of the night they're all in bathing suits with the flowered umbrella still up. They're all looking at me.

—What rumor? I said.

—Yeah, let me in on it, Mr. Callahan said.

—What's the rumor? Ma said. Please. Tell us.

Ma was drinking beer.

—Don't you know? Mr. Hanrahan said.

And I looked at Dad, like help, but he was leaned throwing his matches back on the table.

—What rumor? And Ma leaned putting her beer can back on the table, that time when she puts the drink back on the table and holds onto it a long time.

Everyone was silent, waiting. Our yard was dark.

—He taught your daughter to do a backflip.

They screamed and screamed. Did you do that? Ma yelled.

I was standing in the sunshine. Our backyard looked all trimmed and everything neat. They got everything into good order and then when night fell everything was wrecked.

—Dad, I'm leery of these card table legs.

—I'll do it, babe. Dad had the hose end by the filter, sliding off the plywood top he painted green to blend with the plants.

I said, If you set them up right you could puncture your

skin and if you don't set them up right the whole thing could collapse. Dad bent on his hands and knees reaching underground to attach the hose. Actually in May for the science fair I set this card table up alone. That was a good experience. I had to tie my hands with ropes to keep from cleaning those tell tale pieces of Ivory soap off my best plant's soil. Dad unhooked the silver pole. I tried to think about the old I Love Lucy card table episode, holding the seance around the table, but more in my mind lately was after that, in the 1960s, when Lucy was divorced. Ethel is called Viv. Lucy has a different last name, living in a different place with a different job and all new friends. It was Labor Day weekend, I'm sure a more special pool party in Dad's union heart. I'm sure Dad was really looking forward to the pool party today, but me not at all. I went inside.

Ma shifted our gray yellow and white plaid tablecloth on her ironing board, her cigarette smoke rising at the end in a line. I loved when she ironed that thing.

—That's my favorite tablecloth.

Ma shifted it, then used the heat. I didn't think she would ask me why. Why was because of all my plaids steadily through my life, second because the colors were gray, our name, and yellow, once a good color between Aunt Rita and me, and third because it had so many complications of shades and widths, moving from solid white to pale fog to gray Long Island Sound to bright hard-pressed crayon yellow of crocuses.

—Here. Ma had gently folded the tablecloth and she walked toward me with her arms spread and I spread mine, walking toward her.

—Ooo, still warm. I'm going to want to wrinkle it Ma, it feels so good.

—Please!

I walked with my arms out, holding in front the cloth. I moved sideways through the gate and laid the plaid. Red scotch of kitchen clock LBJ. Red scotch with fringe of blanket at supper picnic Joyce. Aqua plaid of second grade reversible raincoat with elasticized old maid-style hat—the time of the allergist—and outside along our roadsides the water was running brown, the rainwater carrying dirt, the brown water swelling and running down over rocks and branches and fallen caught leaves and I could feel those bulging weights below my eyes.

—This is all I'm going to help, I yelled across the pool. Ma won't let me carry her precious liquor bottles anyway.

Dad looked sharply up, then away. Dad glided the pole inside our deep end, moving it deeply with his deep sad bagged eyes. I felt really bad. Ma would let me carry out the mixers, and I knew that. The pole went straight but refracted wildly where it submerged.

—Dirt really collects around that drain, doesn't it, Dad?

Dad lifted the pole straight and holding it upright stepped up on our diving board, holding the pole up, and stepped down on the other side, again angling the pole. He moved it rubbing over the deep end seam, pushing toward three leaves. It's like moving things inside a mirror because it's all so indirect. One leaf popped, floating, the other two caught. Next door Mr. Hanrahan yelled in German. I always figured Dad knew Mr. Hanrahan was crazy and Dad was just being nice, but one day I had to get Dad for a phone call, looking everywhere, finally knocking on Mr. Hanrahan's trailer and Dad's parked in the driveway with him in that silver and red 1950s sleazy Las Vegas type kitchenette, Dad even switched to Rheingold. We both just looked at each other, like shocked. It was like reverse of when Dad straightened me out about Playboy. Dad's looking at me with his big brown sad bagged eyes what is it babe?

I said, Dad, what was your batting average that year again?

Dad got a trophy from the real Babe Ruth for having the highest batting average ever in New York City.

Dad smiled and raised his eyebrows, maneuvering along the deep end. Dad never even told us this. Mr. Callahan told us.

—Six-sixty-seven.

—SIX-SIXTY-SEVEN. Jesus, Dad. How many times were you up?

Ten I thought Dad would say.

—Well, we had about twenty, twenty-five games. It was a full season.

—You played twenty-five games and got up probably about three times a game and you had a six-sixty-seven batting average! That's unbelievable. I sat down on our diving board. It was quiet now. Mr. Hanrahan stopped training. Sun coming over the trees. All the kids in the road. No lawn mowers. Just every once in a while some blue jays fighting as Dad moved our vacuum silently around.

—Getting to be the time of more leaves.

—Pain in the ass. Dad made a face and I laughed. Dad's head burst into the sunny half, his hair shining blond. Dad looked behind and gauged the deep end corner to backwards negotiate.

—Dad, did you ever fall in vacuuming?

—Once. Dad pursed his lips, his eyes smiling.

I hooted.

—Luckily it was the shallow end.

—Yeah, luckily, I said. The silver pole crept out, top half in the sun. Dad was not a good swimmer. He always jumped in by the ladder where anyone could stand, holding his nose, yelling woo-aoooo-eey, no matter what the water temperature. Dad stepped over the footbath, barefooted, feeling along backwards, bursting between sun and shade. That footbath was murder to stub your toe on.

Dad slammed his brakes and I ran around the front of the Dodge fitting between the grill and our first rock wall. I never trusted anyone's brakes on our driveway.

—What are you driving with your window up in the summer for? I slammed my door. It had taken him forever to hear me yell.

Our rock wall rose, travelling rising backwards, our strange regular family way of backing into the world. Ahead was the maple tree where last pool party Dad threw up. The day after that we built our probably last rock wall. Dad and I slid backwards then curving, flattened. Yellow oblong leaves were fallen on the widow's lawn for Labor Day. It was a strange part of the day: not morning, Dad's coffee, not afternoon, Dad's beer for me to hold. First they went over to the Hanrahans' like some U.N. delegation to explain the wall, next they invite the Hanrahans to a pool party, next the wall turns out ankle high.

It was very bright, sunny, the day after Dad vomited. We were going to get rocks. Annie and Robert sat in the back seat not speaking because of Dad throwing up in the dark underneath our tree the night before. Dad had his sunglass flaps down, very dark. They were saving the front seat for me to handle it.

—I bet this is the last rock wall we build, Dad. My voice was cheerful.

I had no idea rising that morning how it would be. Would Dad still want to go get rocks or not. Annie and Robert kept looking at me. I was trying to be on the cheerful side, a beautiful sunny day. I couldn't tell was Dad's skin blanched or not. To blanch, babe, normally Dad would say, looking up the cooking term in his Fannie Farmer. Our summer sumacs blurred green. We all had our windows open for the breeze. Dad stepped on it, flinging us left trying to beat that dangerous sight trestle distance. During about our first two years in Nissequott you could turn right to find rocks but now always left, south, the middle of the island for developments.

—Is this our first time in summer getting rocks? I said. I looked back and Annie stared at me, then out at the blurring green. No one was going to help me think of anything to say. I looked at Robert and at least he looked back. It gets to you trying to constantly pep everyone up. I put my hand back palm up until Robert put his littler hand on and we shook hands and I could see on his face how lost he felt. I squeezed his hand and I faced forward again. I said, Don't all answer at once, Dad, and Dad made a slight face. Dad turned CBS down.

Forest Glen went by. Forest Glen had fancy schmanzy bricks painted white for a development entrance, pretending to be a rich mansion. Those kids would probably be on my bus this fall. That would be fun. I would like to meet new people, maybe get a friend. It seemed like you should have to pass a certain amount of time alone and then God would say okay, that's enough time, now let her have a friend. Dad hunched over the dash and got a cigarette. I had no idea if Dad knew all four of us saw him throwing up under the tree. The only thing I knew about a hangover was the name, which I thought of a black hanger, combined with that song How Dry I Am. And suddenly it hit me after all those years of watching Alka-Seltzer commercials maybe hangover was the basis of those type bad times.

We drove past the farm stand, cornfield, new high school where Dad was going in the fall, which was good for him to have something new, and I noticed they were ridiculously trying to plant grass seed there in August. Everyone in the world knew when you should and should not plant grass seed. We turned right onto Poquonsett Highway, past that awful Tanglewood golf course with a rusted chain fence with blown garbage which someone could clean up in one morning with a bag and pointer stick if they just tried. We stopped, clicka clicka, in the divided highway median. Cars and trucks tore by our front and rear, shuddering us completely each time. Dad stepped on it, our Dodge sputtering, shooting us across. It felt vaguely like the direction of the dump.

—What road is this? I said. Dad, is this a new road? Is this another new development?

—Mr. Finn told me about this, Dad said.

Flat here, trees not too green. Suddenly we veered off onto some cleared dirt and Dad shut our engine off. Dust rose. Across was a red brick building with a gathering of people dressed up like for Easter, all staring at us. I realized it was Sunday. We all got out and of course those people didn't know it but two of us were missing. Ma stayed home to work and Michael stayed home probably because Dad threw up.

—How many? Annie said.

—Seven or eight, Dad said.

—Only seven or eight and there are only four of us? I said. You're kidding me! I was trying to be enthusiastic and pep them all up.

—That's it. Dad smiled. He had his dark sunglass flaps down, Dad always using the Genovese plastic flaps because he wouldn't treat himself to prescription. Dad threw his cigarette off like he was in the movies and plunged out in his maroon plaid bermudas.

Across the road the girls wore a lot of frills. The sign said Kingdom Hall for those of the Jehovah Witness Faith. I didn't really know what faith meant. This was probably the church our white and Spanish neighbors went to before they moved on. I saw all the little boys had on suits, something Michael and Robert did not own since we did not go to church. We did other things.

—Dad, did you notice there's no mountain laurel here?

Dad walked fast, knees splayed, lugging, dumped into our trunk. Our family was coming out of the rock wall building stage: no station wagon anymore. Now we threw them in our classy trunk with black wall to wall. A stomach area of dirt showed on Dad's white T-shirt. Once driving along toward the tracks Dad told me it was against the law to dig up mountain laurel. I said, Why, because it's so pretty? Dad said yes.

Dad said, The soil's too sandy here, babe.

I was trying to see if Dad had a head or stomach ache.

—You mean the soil changes where you go on Long Island?

—Yup, Dad said.

—I didn't know that.

Dad raised his eyebrows like Groucho Marx and walked off to search.

The front two doors of the church were closed. That was too bad they finally got that church built and our neighbors moved. They were singing in there, Sunday, I'm sure about God. I wondered if they would be strange, Southern, falling on their knees with the powers shaking in them, which would be their way of reaching Him.

Dad pulled an illegal U, turning all of us, each one's view of the bulldozed dirt and blue road and red church breaking and changing as we spun, Dad driving up a little on the Jehovah Witness' unplanted soil. Then Dad built our probably last family rock wall all alone in one day.

GRAND OPENING, red white and blue bunting said across the half glass building named Jack in the Box, though you could be sure that bunting was not socialist, for Labor Day. Socialism meant from each according to his ability to each according to his needs, Dad said, but in our country people hated socialism and really they hated people like Dad, because Dad believed in that.

Esso.

—Whoa, I said, I just passed here three days ago and there were still trees.

The bulldozers were stopped for Labor Day, a whole other area of woods in Nissequott smashed.

—I heard that's going to be another supermarket. And leaning, wide backed hunched, Dad took his cigarettes off the dash.

—How intelligent, I said, three supermarkets in a row.

213

In a way I said that because I knew Dad loved to buy food.

We pulled into the distributor's and parked diagonal. Everyone always parked diagonal there. I laid my head on the window, where the glass rolls away, my face half in the sun. I didn't feel that great. Sometimes when I was younger at the ocean Ma let me wear her sunglasses and you could lay staring at everyone, then cupping your hand make a close-up camera reflection of all the blond side hairs and freckles and skin near your eye.

—You coming, babe?

What happened was we were all four downstairs watching Mannix and we agreed one shouldn't have to go out alone to get food, but we would all risk it together. We all four came around single file the extension in the dark. The pool light was on, exact flat turquoise jewel. They were all screaming under the umbrella and Dad was walking toward the gate, meanwhile all of them screaming laughing behind. Dad was misaligned. I said, Dad? And Dad kept on walking straight into the fence and he bounced off. Dad straightened and aimed again and walked through the gate.

I said, Dad, where are you going?

Dad kept walking. He seemed like walking in his sleep. He walked past us toward the pine, toward those very steep stairs he built out of concrete. Annie said, Stop him. And Dad veered walking instead into the circle of light he installed because those stairs always scared our relatives when they left at night. Dad walked onto where the green grass was strangely pale. He fell on his knees, crawling toward our maple tree, then he stopped, and his whole self shook backwards and Dad was throwing up, the stuff flowing up out of his mouth.

I kept my head down on the opened window shaking my head no but in a moody actress way to get attention, which Dad did not fall for, but only walked away, first turning the key in our trunk and bouncing that. I sat up. Dad walked away fast holding his car keys stepping with his lovely delicate athletic knees in his red white and blue bermudas for Labor Day. Dad walked very springy, full of action, planning I'm sure his whole pool party and the excitement of say four-fifteen when he brought out the cherrystones or big necks, little necks, all Dad's many excited exact names for clams, and serving either cooked on the grill or raw, Dad sitting on that rock wall he built of cement saying on the half shell, on the half shell, the wet gray salt juice running over his hands as he split them open for everyone with his knife.

NISSEQUOTT BEVERAGE CENTER, it said in red script. I hated it when they pretended it was real handmade script but really it was made perfectly by a factory machine. Dad went in. I laid my head again on the window sill where the sun reached. A worker passed inside the sideview, like in a movie, pushing an empty red dolly with a muscle man shirt showing armpit hair. I tried to have an immediate pretend fantasy of falling in love fast and Mark Rogers flies into a jealous rage and there is a fist fight near the Dempsey Dumpster, but I couldn't figure out how Mark Rogers would be passing by this vicinity, let alone the minor problem to begin with neither guy liked me.

ECI, it said in blue in the mirror, each letter sculpted out of melting ice blocks like AIR CONDITIONING at that Ho Jo's upstate. I tried for a quick nice memory of Mr. Popper's Penguins, the father brings ice home to maintain the family animals. In the mirror I saw another worker, lost. I jumped out yelling, Here! The red tilted dolly was loaded with Budweiser. Dad was treating himself to fancier tonight.

—Yoohoo! I yelled. Irene! Irene was stopped in the middle of our blue road, both sides with green and tiger lilies and in front of our slope the asphalt blotched with smashed blackberry blood. I invited Irene on a pond picnic before our pool party. Yabbadabbadoo, she yelled, we'll have a gay-old time! I figured Irene didn't have that much longer on our block and I wanted her to remember some of its good things, like our woods. I made us tunafish on white, cut diagonal, like for an overhead camera on The Galloping Gourmet. I took one of our old mayo jars and peeled the label leaving trace white mistakes which, to me, made it more beautiful. It reminded me of lace and lace curtain Irish, as Ma said, and the white lace I hoped to own one day. I made us frozen lemonade with red food dye. I got down my red and white Brownie sit-upon and I looked across my room.

I returned that yoga book to the library before the due date and I told Ma. I don't think it would help, I said. Ma sat below in her sunglasses reading some murder thing. She looked at me, like appraising my worth. Ma said, I don't think so either. She was looking up through her sunglasses. I felt weak. I felt like the world flipped up over and there was only air for land. I thought why did you give it to me if you didn't think it would help? You start to get a little paranoid about torture. You think did I just make this whole yoga drama thing up? Is this the facial Gaslight treatment? I felt like grabbing her throat. I glanced off at the water and then I walked away.

—I'm taking Irene for a picnic near the ponds, Ma. I set up the card table as much as I could.

—Thank you. That's a help.

I felt like asking Ma to wear her cute pink and white gingham one piece but she would think I was nuts. Ma crossed stealthily barefooted, balancing with great concentration her aqua ice cube trays, filled. I had an urge to knock them all up in the air.

— Ma, why do you make ice for three days for a party when you can just buy it at the distributor's for fifty cents a bag?

—Get off my case.

A terrible pain shot through my throat, up under my face, straining into my bone structure, where my baggy eyes bulged.

—Quiet, please, Ma clapped her hands. People!

They all sat under the opened umbrella in the dark, behind the flat glow blue pool. I was sitting out during Petticoat Junction because that show was like torture it was such a railroad lie.

—You ready for this one, Jack? Mr. Hanrahan said. All the men laughed at how Dad blew his smoke out hard and shook his head.

—Why do you laugh at me? Ma said. You don't even give me a chance to open my mouth and you're all ridiculing.

—Ask your question, Mr. Callahan said.

—I will. Ma sat there.

—That's a hell of a question, Mr. Hanrahan said.

—Would you please, Ma said. How shall I put this? I'm trying to term this in the least offensive way.

All the men groaned.

—Give Mary a chance, Aunt Rita said.

Ma ignored her.

—This is directed toward you, Bob, Ma said.

—Uh oh, Mr. Callahan said.

—Do you still find the fact that Danny has a gun intimidating?

Silence.

—I am not intimidated, Ma said.

—You should be, Mr. Hanrahan said.

—Oh, Danny, stop, Aunt Rita said.

—I'm not intimidated by you at all, Ma said. I view you as a pussycat.

Dad stood. He pointed at Aunt Rita. Rita, another?

—Thank you, Jack.

—Christ, if you ever came over here with that gun, I would have the goddamn cops here so fast, you wouldn't know what hit you.

—Danny? Dad pointed at Mr. Hanrahan.

—Fuck the cops, Mr. Hanrahan said.

I felt like this shock. I couldn't believe he said that on our property.

Dad went to the cooler. I was sitting under our cherry tree and they were up on the patio nearer the pool, the cooler by our rock wall, so not certain Dad could see me.

—I'd have the goddamn cops here so fast, you wouldn't know what hit you. I view you as a pussycat.

Dad laughed, hoo hoo hoo, handing out the beers.

—Now isn't this a great example, Aunt Rita said.

Dad sat down in his chair and popped open his beer.

—Here we all are living on the same street. We're neighbors.

—We're what? Mr. Callahan said.

—Neighbors, Dad said.

—I can't hear her. Speak up, Rita.

I was sitting under the cherry tree and I could hear fine.

—We're neighbors and look at this tension, Aunt Rita said.

No one spoke.

—What tension? Ma said. I'm telling you there is no tension. None. Zero. Zip. Zip with the tension. Ma lit a cigarette, concentrating, holding the match.

Dad burped.

—Excuse me, Dad said.

—If there's a problem, I call the goddamn cops, Ma said.

Everyone was shouting and I stepped up on the patio and approached. I said, Can I have this? Can I have this? Ma, can I have this?

— —Take it.

They were all shouting. I carried the citronella candle back and sat again under my cherry tree.

—Why can't we all live in peace? Aunt Rita said.

—Give me a break, Ma said.

—He's the one who first got the gun, Mr. Callahan said. I did not buy that gun first.

—Cut the crap, Rita, Ma said.

—Living in peace is crap, Mary? To wish mankind to live in peace?

I held the candle in my lap. At the end Tom Sawyer's crawling along in the cave feeling along by the bits of fallen warm wax hoping against hope it's not that murderous Indian he's moving toward.

—You know, Martin Luther King had a dream. Do you believe in his dream? Aunt Rita said. Bob?

—Quick another beer, Mr. Callahan said.

All the men laughed. I rolled the candle around, the liquid yellow melted wax rolling in tidal circles around the central flame. I had on my off white cutoffs and my yellow black and white plaid shirt, the closest to our family tablecloth coat of arms I could get.

—Hey, I'm a nice guy, Mr. Hanrahan said. Why would you call the cops on me?

Dad lifted his hands like he didn't know, laughing. Behind him was the cabana, very still and dark. It looked like a monster to me.

—Four one one, Ma said.

—Four one one? Dad said.

—Four one one, Ma said. I'm telling you. So fast.

Dad said, What the hell is she talking about four one one?

I understood Ma. Ma meant emergency.

—Four one one is the fire department, Mr. Callahan said. Nine one one is the cops.

—Whatever the hell, Ma said.

I didn't know if they used nine one one on Adam-12.

—I don't give a crap. I view you as a pussycat.

—I'm really interested, Aunt Rita said.

I lifted the orange bumpy glass still rolling the wax around in circles, watching it roll around the deformities of glass. It looked like the skyscraper lights opening the Million Dollar Movie, tonight The Hunchback of Notre Dame.

—I'd like to go around the table, Aunt Rita said, and see what people think of Martin Luther King's ideas.

The orange bumpy glass citronella was over my head, rolling it around and around, above that the dark maroon cherry claw branch, rolling the burning wax more and more.

—And do you know what I'd like to do? Ma said. I'd like to go around the table and play patty cake.

I tipped the candle and the hot wax poured on my face. It hit and I screamed and I could see it glowing blob over my face stuck up falling through the air and then it hit and everything went dark and I screamed. I had not meant to scream. Probably they were all turned, curious, in their patio chairs.

—I poured wax on my eyes, I yelled. They were probably all turned in their chairs watching me. The reason I said that was so they knew what happened. It didn't matter if they knew what happened because nothing could be done, but you should be polite. I was in one world and they were in another world. I was inside my capsule where I just poured on wax and I couldn't see. I was blind. I couldn't see because hot wax poured on my eyes. For the rest of my life I would be walking with my arms out, feeling along. Okay. Accept your life. Okay. Okay. I was sitting under a very good tree and not everything was bad, it was just that from now on I had to be blind.

Suddenly I was lifted off the ground without using my legs. Dad? I said. It was his smell of beer and then the crinkling in his shirt pocket of his cigarette cellophane. Dad had me lifted in his arms. I felt bad I was crushing his cigarettes. Dad was running, carrying me. It was like in a cartoon when someone is very confused or has just gotten hurt or burned and he runs around and around in circles expressing himself. Poor Dad was running us in circles because he felt involved. Then Dad stepped up. Dad was running in a definite direction. To me, everything was dark. I was lowering. Splash. I was dunked. Dad had carried me to the pool. In New England that was how they tested for a witch. Instantly the wax stopped burning my eyes. That was so smart of Dad. What a father. What a father.

Dad lifted me, dripping. Dad had held me under the perfect amount, unlike Mary Jo Kopechne who got drowned. I was sopped, all my water thundering off. I laughed. I just went in the pool with all my clothes on.

—It's hardened, I said to Dad. I did not know if I was held now over the cement or water, all my water pounding off, really sopped because much more material in clothes than a bathing suit. That was why they made bathing suits. Any other questions? Maybe Dad thought I should be dunked again. I pulled my eyelid muscles hard.

—Take it easy.

I was trying to hurry open them and stop being such a pain. Dad set me on my feet. I was trying to feel from the exact cement flatness was I wobbling or not. I said, My eyes feel glued. I laughed. I was getting embarrassed because I knew they would all think I poured wax on my face to get attention.

—Come on, Dad said. Let's go inside.

Through skinny bottom slit I could see blurry forms, the hazy wall and house, the fence. I felt bad I was going soaking into the house when not doing that was so important to Ma.

—What's wrong with her?

—Hi, Annie.

—Wait here, babe, Dad said.

The bathroom was strange, yellow gloom with dark and gray black swallow patches and above the mirror the light burned searing bright. I said, I got citronella wax on my eyes.

—Is Sheila okay?

—Hi, Robert!

—Watch it, guys. Dad broke through the gathering crowd. Here you go.

It was a blurry shotglass.

—Fill that with water and we'll try to soak the pieces out.

—Oh, God, Dad, I can't open my eyes underwater.

—You have to, Sheila, Annie said. Michael.

Dad had the water running. Tepid, please, I said.

—Sheila got wax in her eyes, Annie said.

—She did? Michael said.

—Keep your eyes open, Annie said. Sheila.

—I'm trying, I'm trying. I can't tell if I'm crying or it's the water dripping out.

I kept blinking. It was like looking straight into the sun that bathroom light was so bright.

I said, These pieces feel like rough concrete on my eyeball.

—How's it going, guys?

I said, Hi, Ma.

—How's Sheila? It was Mr. Hanrahan, and suddenly he seemed like the Scarecrow and Aunt Rita also crowding in. It felt like the end of The Wizard when they're all gathered, really worried about her.

Chapter 16

—Hold still, and I leaned in drawing with a charcoal briquet on Isobel Dickinson's really beautiful face, blond hair blue eyes, drawing with that briquet I toted all the way from Nissequott. I noticed her family had no barbecue. The bathroom light was a thousand watts for confessions. White cracking walls, white plastic not cloth shower curtain, white cracking tiles, the silver curtain rod, silver mirror with our two heads, one blond one brown. I had never had a blond friend before. All the white and silver it looked like I was having a dream that could float away. I was kind of shell shocked to have a friend. I leaned in drawing on her face. I smudged along her cheek, Isobel with already natural blue black color in the corners of her eyes.

I said, This reminds me of Suddenly Last Summer when they do the lobotomy. I meant all the hospital silver and white.

Isobel said, They already tried that on me. No effect.

I said, It's got to be the perfect smudges of walking on the railroad tracks for years.

I said, I live next to the tracks, Isobel, so I should know. Now, turn the other cheek.

—Yuck yuck, Isobel said, so funny I forgot to laugh.

I said, This Scotch Magic tape is crackling in my ears. I feel like a radio.

I rubbed along her forehead, Ash Wednesday. What's a WASP? Dad said the definition. I said, Do they usually vote Republican? As a rule, Dad said, I would say yes.

I said, Isobel, the weird thing is when I was in kindergarten I was a pumpkin made out of curtain rods and now I'm in eighth grade and I'm a gypsy made of curtain rings.

Isobel said, That's the wonderful thing about America. Ahh say to you my fellow 'Mericans Ahh, will not lie, Ahh will not cheat—

The trees blew branches over us and beyond the empty branches was smooth glinting which I realized with a shock was water. We lived on an island. I always forgot. Then I saw the water again and I got that excited shock. Slightly on the asphalt our three moon shadows smoothed, fainted, the moonlight draining the road of color through its distant sieve. It felt like Texas here in Stony Point, like wide open, do whatever you want, attack. I said, I can't believe I'm out in public without ponytails you guys and I can't believe it's Halloween and I'm not in Nissequott. I said, They sure do give way more Mounds and Almond Joy here.

Joanne said, They do?

Isobel opened the mailbox, bent, and peered.

—This her house? I said.

—Pristine, Isobel said in the moonlight. Nothing like a virgin. Let's wreak some havoc, gals.

—Not too much whatever you call it, Joanne said. Joanne looked at me. They wanted to knock on this lady's house who was a Jehovah Witness.

Only one yellow light glowed muffled, faraway, as in a fairy tale, the witches outside in this case. I said, You guys, my main thing tonight is I want to attack some boys.

Isobel hulked across the moon sheened lawn. She hulked everywhere. I stopped. She walked like Planet of the Apes. Joanne stopped. Isobel turned. She said, What are you men or mice?

They were both Protestants.

Joanne said, Anybody got any cheese?

—What are you commies? Isobel said, Come on, gals, she looks forward to this every year. She'll be in there crying her eyes out.

—Oh, God, Isobel. Joanne moved toward the house. I'm sick of you always getting your way. This is the last year, I swear.

They moved away and I followed down across the lawn, only the yellow right living room light on. Her stoop was central concrete but edged with bricks and no pumpkin. Isobel bent and knocked, that barrelling sound. Our storm windows were all back in, dark, back in eastern standard time. I stepped behind and Joanne stepped behind me and I stepped behind her and Joanne—

—Children. Isobel snapped her fingers twice.

We three stood side by side. The emptying branches of the topmost blew together above in waves. I had on a costume, plus it was dark, plus not even my town. The inside wooden door opened, throwing in and out light. A woman with mousey hair and a drab pioneer farm dress stood behind the white storm door framed with scalloping like Kodaks from '61 or 2.

—Trick or treat, we said.

Earlier this fall I was selling candy. Plain or almond, giant, a dollar a bar. They were like the giant Chunkys Marianne Gilhooley and I purchased once at Genovese that almost made me sick. In September I was earning money to go to France. These candy bars were wrapped in aluminum with a paper outer sleeve in a brown box with flaps on top, CANDY in red on the box outside. I had on my red and yellow patchwork jumper, my colors ahead of the September trees. I had five outfits for five weekdays and my red and yellow patchwork was my best. Red was for energy and yellow for a home. Wearing patchwork quilt I could while moving upright around our junior high still have pretend dreams based on the 1800 frontier show Here Come the Brides.

The drab woman opened her outer storm door a bit, her face partly hidden by the scalloped frame. She said, I'm sorry, girls, we're Jehovah Witnesses and we don't celebrate Halloween.

We three stood there.

This day I had my candy I had no hockey, taking the regular bus home with a half Tanglewood hoodlum population, risking seeing Marianne Gilhooley if she did not have a shoplifting appointment. We had about thirty throbbing buses, lined up in corrugated yellow in our blue asphalt bus oval. Same thing as when Kennedy died. I got on the bus. I was talking to Joyce. Joyce was behind me. I was climbing up the steps. Everyone said, Be quiet, the President just got shot. Cap the bus driver had a radio. He had the radio in front of the steering wheel, holding it near the window with the antennae up. It was about one or two o'clock in the afternoon.

—But we want some candy, Isobel said, and she sadly held out her opened bag.

Our bags were loaded with Mounds and Almond Joy.

—I'm sorry, the drab woman said. If you'd like to come back tomorrow I can give you some cookies then. I'm very sorry to disappoint you. Good night now. She let the storm door go and stepping in swung the inner wooden closed.

We three turned and walked across the white sheened lawn. The moon was up the hill. You could see some stars and the black shadow form of a witch riding a broom taped in the window of the house across. In junior high the buses parked in this blue oval. Their engines idled and the drivers stood in partners conversing. They had the big regular black painted numbers, but you couldn't go by that. Go up close and read the little paper sign in the window with the bus driver's handwriting. Then you knew to get on.

—It's cold out. I said, It's always cold out on Halloween and you have to be cold or ruin your costume.

—It's freezing out here, Joanne said. The trees blew over her tall head and turning the moon glazed her spectacles. Joanne said, I should have listened to the old bitch. Joanne screeched up her voice, Now you put on that wool sweater Nanny brought you from Europe.

226

I said, You mean your mother?

We stepped off the softer bodily give of her lawn over the curb onto the road. We started up the blue drained road with our bags, walking toward the moon. This day in September with my candy I had homework in all my five subjects, read The Red Pony, plus an extra book about American violence this WASP blond I hardly knew had loaned to me. How violent is violent? our English teacher said. Hildebrand was backed up against the blackboard which said symbolism, his hands up like the fat lady the Marx Brothers pursued in Freedonia.

—He murders this white woman by throwing her down an elevator shaft and burns her body in a furnace piece by piece. Isobel said, It's really great. She said, Sheila, what do you think of The Dead Pony?

My stomach hit up. I was this wormy person who tried to slide through the halls of life. Spent most of her days in off-white knee socks not colors. Tried to cause little commotion by matching her hair ribbons exactly to her outfits. I gathered my books in the English classroom. On The 4:30 Movie, Splendor in the Grass, Natalie Wood had this English class scene. Everyone in school knows Natalie's boyfriend just went all the way with a girl underneath the town waterfall. The English teacher makes Natalie stand up and read this poem, Nothing can bring back the glory of the past. You can see the springtime trees outside Natalie's movie classroom windows. It's rising chlorophyll. This day in Nissequott was fall. I said, I think we're old enough now for more than the love between a pony and a boy.

This day with the candy I had my spiral notebooks on the bottom, larger textbooks, The Red Pony, Native Son from Isobel, and on top my box marked in red on the outside, CANDY. I already made the sales. This day I was making deliveries. I got about halfway down the aisle. This boy stood up and blocked it. It was your standard black rubber ribbed aisle with traction lines, the green repeating seats close set either side, aluminum frame repeating windows. He had brown hair like the Gillette commercial The Dry Look Is In.

—Dogface.

Dead silence in the yellow school bus. I just stood there. All the kids were in their seats and we two were standing in the aisle.

—What do you have there?

I was blank. I just had myself basically. I had no idea what he meant.

He reached his hand at me toward my chest. Since I had the scooped neck jumper on it felt like the operation. It felt like he was reaching inside my chest. He was going to pull out my bones. I was reminded of that word extract. In baking there was vanilla extract. I had this feeling since I had a scooped neck jumper on he could reach his hand in my body. He reached his hand in my brown candy box and pulled a chocolate bar out. When he saw the bar his eyes looked delighted. He looked like a brown grizzly bear who successfully scooped a fish. His eyes were glittered, really happy. He took the candy bar and smashed it on the floor.

He reached his hand in again and pulled out another. Seeing candy he looked like an ape puzzling over something from civilization. I had this sense of myself standing in the bus aisle, black ribbed rubber so that children would not tumble. The evergreen color seats were lined like pews and halfway down the windows was one that said Emergency and Emergency at the back. He smashed that bar on the floor too.

He reached his hand in and pulled out another candy bar. When his hand was inside my box I could feel it rumbling like moving around inside my anatomy. He dashed that bar down. It was okay that the candy was breaking but I couldn't take it when his hand was inside my box rumbling around. It's like your heart could get accidentaly injured. He reached his hand in again and pulled out another candy bar and he smashed that. Four.

I was just standing there. They had the ribbed rubber for traction and roughened aluminum made up each seatback so if a kid was flung forward while driving your face flesh would adhere in the grooves and hold. This kid had nice brown hair and nice brown eyes and maybe it was slightly tough being in seventh grade shorter than me a girl and being from the cheaper development of Tanglewood. I never really even said hello to him before.

—Now try to sell your candy. He returned to a seat.

Actually I had one candy bar left. I wondered should I confess. Everyone on the bus was looking at me. Outside the bus the trees were still uniform summer green, but inside I was wearing the red and yellow colors of autumn, and when Kennedy died, zero zip no leaves at all. The candy bars lay held together in their aluminum but inside they looked broken. My cousin jumped out of a tree once and broke her arm on the patio, the flesh holding her pieces together. I thought I should clean up my garbage. Everyone on the bus was watching and I didn't know what to do. I had all my books balanced, crouched down picking up the candy trying to keep my jumper covering my behind.

I sat down and looked out the closest window. People had started talking again. Red bricks that made up our school building. I had my books stacked and my brown box on top with broken candy. I was trying to think of what to do about my sales, thinking wholesale, retail, whole sale, well when you digest anyway you break the pieces up. I remembered when I got on the bus with Joyce it was quite a shock that the President had been shot. The bus was a deep dark low pew evergreen, above that the repeating aluminum windows creating lighter air. I was talking normally, climbing up the bus steps, and they said, Quiet, the President got shot, and I turned backwards and I could see the whole wide bus windshield and then right next to me was Joyce. In the movie Dorothy is on her bed sleeping and as the house turns through the tornado scenes of her past fly by. The Little Rascals once did a show about Butch the Bully taking candy from a baby. A lollipop, I believed. Then Spanky teaches Alfalfa boxing and it all ends clearly in a ring with rope and robes and a ref and a bell. Alfalfa wins.

They got richer candy and more of it in Stony Point and you could tell the people were not Catholic. I said to Dad, what's a WASP, when Isobel first acted like she wanted to be friends. You figure they were mostly for Nixon and mostly for the war. Isobel and Joanne had real Halloween bags from the store with orange and black scenes and white loop handles whereas mine was a brown bag from Hills.

—Heavens to Betsy and holy shit. Isobel snapped her fingers and we stopped.

For a second I thought Isobel was going to say we had done the wrong Halloween thing and we should go back to the Jehovah Witness and apologize.

—Her punishment, Isobel said and turned.

Joanne looked at me and shook her head, her glasses glinting like someone blind. Isobel had stopped, the white curb concrete along beside her and her faint shadow falling down the hill, peering in the ugly woman's opened mailbox. I remembered Ma pregnant near the curb.

—Wasn't she a dog? Joanne said to me.

—Ugly as sin, Isobel said. Egg, please. Isobel upturned her palm.

—Use your own eggs, Joanne said.

I had never heard ugly as sin before.

—Here, I said and gave her one of mine. I remembered once making pound cake with Joyce. We had to stand up on kitchen chairs to reach and I forced her to use a knife to break an egg not tapping on the bowl because it was my house. Isobel spread the egg inside like frying it. She put the broken shells inside and shut the box. I remembered a terrible joke Heidi Wolman told me. What's black and white and red all over? A nun sliding down a banister and it turns into a razor blade. I figured she told that joke because she was a Protestant. The KKK was against Negroes, Jews, Catholics, Jehovah Witnesses I didn't know. We all three turned climbing toward the moon again, the asphalt lit ghostly pearl. In my candy emergency I told all the neighbors awaiting deliveries the union went on strike in Pennsylvania and I gave them back a dollar each drawn from my inchworm-shaped bank.

I said, All I care about is attacking some boys tonight.

Joanne said, All I care about is not going bald.

Isobel said, All I care about is getting more candy than anyone else.

Once upstate Ma took us to a candy factory, Nestle's. At the end you got a whole giant see through bag of delights. I was really hoping for lots of Nestle's Crunch. We were walking through all the turning wheels and factory machinery repeating and repeating with many black and white scenes for me of Lucy working faster and faster to swirl those chocolate bonbons. SPEED IT UP. I stopped upstate in real life near a black conveyor belt with a nun. All the rest of our group had moved on. Silently the nun and I stood watching rows and rows of kisses unwrapped proceeding down the black rubber belt when suddenly that nun swept her hand and stole two quick.

I said, What does that water connect to anyway?

—The crick? Isobel said. The Sound.

—Wow. And I turned and we all walked, the map of the world increasing for me. I said, Joanne you're too tall to go bald.

She said, Yeah, what if they hold you down and rub it in. They're so sick.

We meant Nair. The moon moved on our right partly dipped in the leafless trees. We walked down around past

231

Isobel's, wildly lit and pumpkinless, and to the bottom, their bus stop, where I had made it alive through another treacherous bus ride, this one in October. I said, You guys, is Billy Baersmith going to be out tonight?

Joanne said, I doubt it. He was too hot shit last year in eighth so I doubt it in ninth.

I said, Tant pis so much the worse.

—Wait a minute, you guys, Joanne said. Safety check. She set her Halloween bag on the road and bent in it.

You do think why would the same thing, just slightly different dialogue, happen in the same school bus setting three times, in September (Dogface, he says), in October (You're too ugly to ride this bus, he says), and in November (Quiet, the President—).

Joanne reached in her bag, extracting, and threw off, branches snapping, thud. She picked up her Trick or Treat bag, a rising peace sign on one cheek though her family, richer, Republican, for the war, and underneath her hippie headband hidden in Magic Marker written in her skin said 69. We walked again. She said, I don't know why those bitches think they can get away with giving us apples in this day and age.

—I happen to like the taste of razor blades, Isobel said.

I said, I prefer the taste of glass.

Isobel said, I find glass shards and rat's hairs are supreme.

—Gross, Joanne said, moving smoothly along blond, straight haired with wire rim glasses like Julie on The Mod Squad.

We walked around the half-circled split rail where that old lady's single red rose still grew, almost November, growing now in moonlight.

I said, Well, you guys, ideally I would like to attack Billy Baersmith for what he did to me Wednesday on the bus but I would accept attacking any boys.

—What'd he do to you on the bus, Sheila? Joanne said.

I said, Extra! Extra! Read all about it. I said, You didn't

hear? Last Wednesday I was getting on your guys' bus with Isobel and I gave the bus driver my note? I was like a total wreck getting my mother to put the right date October 21 on my note so nothing could go wrong about me taking a different bus? So I give the bus driver my note? And I was following Isobel down the aisle? And suddenly Billy Baersmith who I never talked to in my whole life, only drooled about, suddenly Billy Baersmith stands up blocking the aisle and you know what he says?

—What?

—You're too ugly to ride this bus.

Joanne burst out laughing.

I looked up at the telephone lines. There were white fluttering broken pieces of toilet paper caught in the trees and caught in the black phone lines. They looked like snagged pieces of soul. The one comfort would be someone is giving direction, for example giving your life a secret repeating pattern. We were coming along the old lady's split rail fence with inside a human figure draping on a cross. However this old lady was a Protestant. On a Saturday morning when I rode my bicycle to Isobel's I passed her working in good clothes in her garden, specifically a turtleneck. People in Nissequott did not dress like that. This cross figure was straw coming out of the sleeves, pumpkin head, plaid old man's shirt, a scarecrow not Jesus. Isobel was moving smoothly along with smudges I made on her hobo face. It felt like a miracle to be found by her, just to be in Stony Point for one night. Her hair was parted down the middle, usually looped behind her ears, and when she passed me that book Native Son in the speckled school hallway she then quickly moved her one hand and tucked her hair behind showing a little white complicated shell, listening to me.

On the nighttime Halloween road you could see wonderful clear shadows. I said, Well, I'm always going to be nice to Isobel because she saved my life on that bus. I bent to the asphalt, dipped my hand in white cream and sniffed. I smiled up at Isobel who started the stripper close shave song.

—Let me smell that, Joanne said. I quick stabbed some at her nose and she screamed, wiping fast.

Isobel said, Your nose—it's disappearing. Isobel walked on. When people looked at her they said, oh, yes, Isobel is beautiful.

I said, The whole bus was looking at me. I was like ready to resign and get back on my bus to Nissequott. I thought oh crap, they have a facial border requirement in Stony Point.

Joanne was laughing.

I said, With my looks you get prepared for anything, believe me.

Joanne shook her head, laughing.

I said, So you know what Isobel did?

—Able to leap tall anthills in a single bound, Isobel said.

—He's standing there, right? You know those magazine things with the skinny guy getting beaten up? It was like ping. Isobel just touches him on the shoulder and ping. He totally collapsed in his seat.

—Ditch it, Isobel said and we all three jumped away from the car.

After the book loan I didn't try anything, but Isobel asked to be my gubernatorial election survey partner in social studies. On a Saturday morning I had my blue bicycle leaned against the maroon shopping center pole since I owned no kickstand. I sat on a white curb listening to the repeating car doors and watching the sun move through the sky. Three orange trees held mid-flame next to the pure white steeple of the Catholic Church and behind my old Nazi bakery lady probably looking out over her dusty creviced wedding cakes with the groom in black, the bride in white and temporary cakes shaped like a witch and a pump-kin. YREKAB TTOUQESSIN. I suggested meeting on the Nissequott-Stony Point border. I kept getting up to check, peering with my hands cupped around my eyes, through the Nissequott Camera Shoppe glass where an Oriental man worked over the glass display of lenses, more and more Orientals moving into our town as science grew at the university, slowly changing our town's face. Ten-thirty-four.

It felt like that Greek chariot went round and round the sky.

I kept checking the time.

I was just pepping myself up I could sit against the rock wall in our backyard where the sun came hard even in October and eat hard salami wrapped around some raisins, one of my best foods for feeling alone. I had the asphalt church steeple three tree horizon, then this figure enlargening. In English Hildebrand made fun of the end of Shane when the boy calls longing toward the figure disappearing on horseback on the horizon. Come back, Shane! In that case Hildebrand was being a bit mature for me. That horizon longing still made me sob, though here in my case the figure growing, as in moving toward. She swung her leg over, standing two feet on one pedal. She had blond carefree hair parted down the middle blowing back, wearing this really great sweater. It was maroon crew neck with knitted in white snowflakes and two white mooses standing face to face. She jumped off at the level of the Smart Set beauty parlor, rearing back, using handbrakes. It must have been ten after eleven. I stood up kind of shook. I had never met anyone late before.

She said, Whoa, Beauty.

I got this panic I was about to be sarcastically attacked. It would have been more fair to arrive on time for that. Then I realized she had an English Racer, WASP, Protestant. Those girls got to ride horses, like I heard the terms English or Western, and she was therefore extending horse treatment to her bicycle, not me. I should do some research and see National Velvet, helping us communicate.

—Hullo. Sorry I'm late. Does your alarm clock behave?

I thought is this some secret other level she already understands me about my lady wristwatch cartoon? I said, I don't have an alarm clock. Only my parents do.

She kicked her silver kickstand down, thus drawing my attention to what she owned. Her sweater matched the poles. She had the kickstand, more fenders, reflectors, handbrakes, three gears, looked like a real leather saddlebag. That looked like the black bicycle I once had that got stolen from me!

I said, It's okay. I don't think they really start shopping until eleven.

She said, Here. I brought a bunch of pens.

My heart beat up. She had prepared. My heart was like pounding. I said, Your family has that many Bics?

—They might not all write.

I giggled. I never heard of having pens that might not write. In my house either they wrote or you threw them out. I said, Test. I held out Mr. Callahan's clipboard. She looked at me. I said, Don't worry, we got like eighty dittos my mother ran off. I held the clipboard and she pressured, writing on the little plain I held. It felt like she was cutting a cake.

—Here. You take half. She divided them all in various states of caps off, stoppers there, not, amount of chawed white rough plastic, all clacking, and all with different amounts of central vein ink. Quite the bouquet.

—Ahhhttt, she said like the bell on Jeopardy when you are wrong. She put that pen in her empty hand.

—Let's assied toi. I pointed. I said, In the sun.

The sun was already so distant from us on earth in middle October and slanting lit hard only part of the sidewalk under the overhang, part triangled warm lit and part abrupt dark cold. We sat in front of the Smart Set. I was dying to mention how her sweater matched the poles, but I realized control your output if you want to make a friend. Isobel lifted her hair completely off her neck and dropped it, bunch blond again. My whole stomach roiled. I had never seen anyone do this before and I was waiting for it to mean something and then I realized that was it. It just was.

We leaned, pressing, the clipboard shared on each's knee, the distant rolling calming wheels and shaking bars of travelling silver carts over the roughened ground. We leaned, pressing, the pressure of start stop, some invisible ropes, some blue lines, a very clear happy blue, like the blue drawn lines of wallpaper figures long ago with Joyce and every time I saw there was another hand also drawing my stomach lifted, like when you, playing, keep hitting up a balloon.

On Halloween the headlights smoothed along the road. We were squatted in the cold October woods. You could see our breaths. I whispered, Isobel says shut your face, Baersmith, then she grabs my arm and pulls me back to the back of the bus. I whispered on to Joanne, I was in a total sweat. Isobel just goes on talking about the chariot race in Ben Hur like nothing happened.

—He's an asshole, Isobel said. Ovary check, gals.

The slow moving undoubtedly parent controlled car was past. I felt each lumped side of Michael's jacket.

—Four, Joanne said.

—Four, Isobel said.

—Three, I said and upturned my palm to her.

—There, Isobel said. Let's go.

The red heart taillights glowed and I could feel the egg weights and my wealthy Stony Point candy weight in my bag. Isobel's Scotch Magic tape crackled in my ears. Ahead was their giant old oak.

—That guy Baersmith, Joanne said. He thinks he's so great just because he's gorgeous and has the perfect bod.

—You guys, I said, victims ahoy.

—Ditch 'em, Isobel said and we all jumped off into the woods.

The giant old oak was fenced off with a tiny eyelet grass

area in the middle of the road. It had no leaves and giant wood limbs, like a single antler and above shining stars. It was a beautiful night, Halloween. We watched our victims approach.

—They're seventh graders, I think, Joanne said.

—I'll attack anything, I said. I'm desperate.

Ma was leaping in our living room with a snapping rag against cobwebs. It was the Saturday I was to meet Isobel in front of the bakery for our election survey. I remembered the Aesop's Fable about the fox jumping for the vine, but as often was my case, the moral escaped me.

—What? Ma turned. I held emptied gray plastic between thumb and forefinger. Ma said, What's that?

I felt this shock. Here I was sleeping on this plastic pillowcase snapping and crackling underneath my head into my dreams for years and Ma did not even recognize it. I said, This is my plastic pillowcase that the allergist said to buy.

—Jesus, you still have that crappy thing. Ma turned to smooth her rag over the rough metalled lamp Ma told me the moving man told her looked like an accident.

—It's been on my pillow since second and I don't think it's doing any good.

Ma dusted under her various ashtray contraptions, lifting them.

—I'm sick of it crackling in my ear every night.

—So fling it. Ma went to our mustard chair. She dusted on its wooden arms. I figure now Ma could say something, final, bad, about my face, then get it all done. Enough. No more. My face was my face and just forget about it. Ma dusted over her autumn pumpkin painting made with roughened paste and palette knife not brushed smooth, made by the mother of the little boy Ma had taught to read. I wanted to be fair and give Ma a complete adequate space to say something critical, then I go. Ma dusted the frame. I realized Ma was upset. I turned, walking slowly, holding it, gray plastic. I passed our hifi, our magazines, our banister. It's like any moment you expect to get shot in the back. I passed through our kitchen doorway, proceeded under our clock. I dropped that blurry gray plastic pillowcase atop all our ashes and butts.

—Well, farewell, Ma. I threw that pillowcase out.

Suddenly I felt really happy. I felt like clicking my heels. Ma bent dusting our beautiful accordioned wood slide door on the hifi cabinet which Dad had made.

—Well, I'm off to meet this girl Isobel Dickinson in front of Hills to do a survey for the election for social studies.

—Have fun. Ma swiped our hifi where you always put your birthday cards.

I didn't think Ma got it where I put my election rendezvous. I purposely put it near Hills where Ma once wrote out a check to Eugene McCarthy for President, for peace. I said, Ma, did you ever have a friend with blond hair?

Ma rolled her eyes and I laughed. It was a stupid question. What do appearances matter anyway? Goodbye, Ma, I said.

Outside was gray leaden November 1 and almost noon though we had all the living room lamps on, a record, ended, bumping around and around, hard to tell the time in Stony Point because I had this eerie Nissequott absence feeling of no noon whistle in this town. And I had a feeling this couch was not Naugahyde but something more original.

—There's the little bugger. Isobel pulled my wrist round moon bone into the lamplight, warm. Now just hold still, she said.

And that rug might be Oriental because it had all these unstructured patterns in it not like standard geometric like Ma's bedroom rug looked like Hollywood Squares. I said, Isobel, is it true at your post office the eagle flaps his wings at noon?

—Shocking but true. Don't move. And she bent, aiming the tweezers at my wrist mole and plucked. Tears welled in my eyes at the little improvement sting. They were only seventh graders nevertheless on Halloween I gladly attacked. He said, My eye, my eye! I couldn't even tell what costume the kid had on because he was bent over in someone's driveway with his hand cupped around his eye where I hit him exactly with my egg.

—One more, Isobel said, bending again, her blond hairs curtaining.

Then I turned running away down the driveway leaving him with his hand cupped, screaming my eye my eye. I could imagine him in the bathroom trying to pluck the white shell pieces out. It just takes a little time.

—Hold on now, Isobel said, plucking. She leaned back. She said, What a relief.

I looked at my improved bared wrist bone hollow. I said, Goodbye Fu Manchu.

On Halloween I pulled up Isobel's sister's flowered gypsy skirt entirely forward in a lump in my left hand and I crouched, pulling the hot pink tights crotch as far north as possible to pee. Leave them laughing. Yeah, I had said, I'll just be thinking of all that toilet paper in the sky. I pulled that borrowed skirt as far north as possible since it crooked off surprisingly now sometimes with my bottom hair. I hunched, the air cold. Woowee. I was in the woods. I did not wish him a scratched cornea but neither did I wish him peace. One hour to November. My breath blew white. I set my feet wider. The moon had a giant face and I finally had a friend. I said, Hello, moon, in a low voice. It started streaming. I wondered if they were talking about me. I crouched, whizzing, the last hours of October, whizzing into the planet earth. The stream arched slightly, clear, tinged yellowy in the white moonlight and my behind full white behind. The arc dropped. I shook back and forth, ooo la la, airing it, and pulled up, covered again.

Chapter 17

The crick was winding green, high tide an hour later every day, deep enough four hours a day to swan dive off the dock, belly flop at other times, and sometimes do the ostrich. A guy in our grade dove off the wrong time and broke his neck. At dead low tide the sandbars rose like white whales. You could walk places where before you swam. Absolute best was dead high tide at two o'clock, plentiful water all afternoon. Usually we cleaned houses in the morning starting nine-thirty, The Donna Reed Show, ending at noon, Jeopardy, shows that now I never watched.

—Sheila, I'd like to talk to you.

The Supreme Court just ruled July 3 Nixon had to let the Pentagon Papers out. That was a good sign, anti-Nixon, for our country. Interesting timing with eve of Independence Day. Already at nine a.m. the first firecrackers shot off distant in Tanglewood like black clots.

Ma sat on the rock wall so I rose up to sit also on that level holding Gone With the Wind. Ma said, I have a suggestion. Why don't you consider plastic surgery for your face?

Ma lit a cigarette, the match sound ripping. Her smoke blew off.

It felt like I'd just been killed.

—It's a very simple procedure. She said, All that in there is fat. Excess fat.

I looked at our rocks built up in a low wall.

—It's called a herniation. All they do is remove the excess fat. Ma threw the match off into our pachysandra.

—You're in the hospital one night.

I felt this panic coming on. All the rocks and pool and trees rushed up.

—In and out like the E train. I think it'd be great. You could have it during the summer when school's out.

Summer was my only good time in life.

—I called around a couple of places and got some info. They say two weeks you're out bopping around again. No one even knows you had it. Ma smoked her cigarette.

I was crushing my finger in Gone With the Wind.

—It'll cost a thou. Daddy and I will pay for it. It'd be worth it, believe me. Done and done, man. Done and done. I say do it. What do you think?

It hurt all up through my throat and beating out my face bones, paining under the bags really bad.

Ma inhaled and blew off. My finger hurt inside the book.

—Well. Ma stood. It's something to think about, right? Hey, listen.

I looked up at her. Ma looked very practical.

—Why should you suffer with this? You should not. Think about it.

Ma left.

Some birds chirped and our cherry tree branches shook around, then the branch bouncing, gravely. It was a pretty summer day. The branch bounced and the water pushed out of our filter, our cabana red and still. I sat back down, leaned against the wall and reopened Gone With the Wind. I didn't totally like Scarlet, but I still cared about her. I still had about fifteen minutes before I had to go clean a house. I started reading again. Then suddenly I saw hospital printed down there and I looked up at the full trees.

—Hiyah, babe. Dad sat in Ma's chair writing on bud green paper with a pencil, also listening to CBS. Bears a quote heavy burden of presumption against its constitutionality, CBS said.

Nine-twenty-five, our clock said.

—You want anything from the store?

I shook my head. Dad looked at me and cleared his throat. Dad was writing a list on the back of June's menu. He reached for his cigarettes on the table and took one out. Dad scraped back his chair and went into the pantry. The radio talked about Vietnam. Dad came back in the kitchen and looked at me. Five mayos, he said with his eyes lit.

I said, I'm going to Isobel's Fourth of July barbecue at the crick so I won't be here for supper.

Dad stopped, his jaw dropped. He said, What! I'm making spare ribs!

Ma came out around holding her sneaks and pink pom pom Peds. She looked at us. I said, Well, I'm not going to be here. Ma dropped her sneaks and dropped into my chair. Oi vay, Ma said. I looked at Dad. Dad nodded his head twice in Ma's direction, smiling. Big match, he said.

Ma bent slipping her Peds on and looked at Dad, Dad looking back at me. Dad had the biggest, most wonderful deep cow brown eyes. I walked out. I put Gone With the Wind down on my bureau and looked at my face. It was bad. It was definitely deformed. I bent my head and drew down my scalp with that sharp pointed barber's comb that to me was 1950s, Ma's time. The train whistle blew. I tried to rest my hair and not put it in tight pulled ponytails all the time. I pulled one side and wrapped on a red band and pulled the other and my silver mirror tapped against the wall as the train went by and I wrapped a white band three times. Silence. I had no more bangs because Isobel said I should grow them out. I took that as a sign my face wasn't that bad. Should I grow out my bangs? It was getting a little ridiculous with my age. She said, Sure, why not? When I went over there Isobel's mother thought I was the cutest girl on earth. I tied one side with a red and a white yarn and the other blue and red. If you were against the war people thought you were a communist. I was against the war, but deep inside I was really a patriot.

Isablue sponged the dripped flesh colored liquid off our employer's Maybelline bottle. When we divided it she got the tiny pickyune jobs that you had to scrape over forever and I got the major swipes. The reason we had this job was the woman just had an operation. The husband worked for Grumman so they could afford to hire us to clean. We figured hysterectomy since she never said. My face felt like a mask working here. I took out the slimy yellow soap and sprinkled Comet, wet with hot, the center silver control down, behind me the steady tap tapping of Isablue swabbing each little bottle bottom. The Comet darkened to seaweed with wet. Isobel had the medicine cabinet door open swinging the mirror around, working inside. She had no idea what just happened to me with my mother. I washed out the yellow slime and single long dark hairs until the three simple white straight soap traction ridges showed, Isobel tap-tapping along like in my old watch cartoon before she falls and they operate. The only time I ever in my life heard of plastic surgery was criminals going to Switzerland on those detective shows at ten p.m., getting a new identity. It sounded like they melted your face. It seemed like you must have to be out of your mind to suggest your daughter get plastic surgery.

I said, The way that gravel shot out, she's definitely having an affair, Isobel. I bet they meet at the Holiday Inn.

I heated the sponge again and rubbed the tub line of grime particles left minuscule by minuscule by each of the family's bodies through time, the day by day dirt of where they had been. The medicine cabinet mirror was swung out putting yellow tiles atop Isobel's neck. I used to have this pretend dream based on a deodorant commercial my medicine cabinet opened into the apartment of this really cute guy and gradually every morning he got used to me, brushing our teeth, and we fell in love. I felt like putting my arm around Isobel. I was very lucky to have her for a friend. On

Memorial Day she had pulled her band strings and got me a position marching in the parade holding one end of the banner wearing white bellbottoms, a white shirt, and white T-strap sandals that everyone had, marching from our town memorial soldier triangle green with central rock near the Presbyterian Church past the blue portables and red brick Nissequott School. I didn't know in eighth should I march through Nissequott since my face was so bad. Jo said, Definitely, Sheiley. Isobel wants you to. I thundered the water down swabbing round the tub. Watering the cement again, I see, Mr. Gray, Isobel said for Dad's misaligned sprinkler, or she walked right in and threw her arm about Dad saying what's for dinner, Dad, and Dad dropped his jaw and looked at me and I looked at him and we were both smiling at each other because we liked Isobel so much. Then everyone came running from all the different ends of the house when Isobel came. Is that Isobel? Ma ran out from ironing, holding her drink. Robert came in dribbling an imaginary basketball, stutter stepping like the Knicks and Annie slipped fast into her chair to hear all the jokes and even Michael sometimes stood a second and grinned. Everyone liked Isobel so much.

I said, Isn't my bathtub beautiful?

It was perfect white, three white wavering traction ridges, no dirt, no hairs, the white of the dish with straight uplifts, and the simple single slim lemon yellow oblong slime up to dry: clean.

—Magnificent, Isobel said in French and swung out wider her flying tiles for inner display.

I said, They all look like little medicine bottle kids dressed up for church.

Ma came in through the gate on the Fourth of July. I looked up. I didn't feel anything. It was a nice day and after your mother has told you your face needs to be cut up and resewn, remolded, plastic melt wax drip, slashed with a knife not much else can go wrong in that department.

—Hi, I said.

Ma said, How about we bomb off to Aunt Dee's and have a few laughs?

—Who?

—You and me. Ma looked at me. I thought why would Ma want to go somewhere with me if I'm deformed? She said, Let's go! A little action, man.

Ma looked pretty on the morning of the Fourth. She had on orange lipstick and her orange yellow white blue striped traditional summer bermudas and top outfit that she sewed from Simplicity.

—I can't. I'm going to Isobel's for the Fourth of July.

Ma blinked. I saw a slight facial stun. I thought of Uncle Tommy slamming Ma across the face and Ma with no expression walked into her room and shut the door. A kind of throat clearing look passed over Ma's face and she said, What time?

I looked at her. That was brave. I said, I don't know, I'm waiting for her to call.

—Call her. Maybe you can do both.

I was shocked. This was my mother suggesting this. I said, What time is it now? I said, Let's wait fifteen minutes and if she doesn't call then I'll go.

I knew Ma was totally depending on me in order to make this trip.

Ma and I jumped in the red VW Bug with the top down. I turned off CBS, turned on ABC top twenty including some songs mutual, some for Ma too extreme. The Bug had light speckled gray separated seats with in between a pull up emergency handle and seatbelts for both which I used but Ma did not. We bombed along with the top down, the music loud, our brown hair blowing through our town. We turned right on Poquonsett, past a foundation being dug for a real live mall in our town. A&S, Macy's, Sears, Lord & Taylor, just like further in toward the city. When a commercial came on I popped it to 66, Imus in the Morning, who Ma and I both loved for his sicko religious song

I can go a hundred miles an hour
Long as I got the Almighty Power
Glued up there on the dashboard of my car.

We were riding on this divided highway, going about fifty, miles and miles rolling under us and the Long Island countryside. I had this wish Ma would say it was all a joke or somehow she would make it clear that plastic surgery rock wall scene never happened, I imagined it. We drove under traffic lights, past farm stands, gradually more stores, less woods and the pink house where once that time we drove upstate the four of us thought that was the pink cottage we were driving to because then we didn't know what distance was.

—Ready Freddy?

I stood and said yes, meanwhile still pat pat patting the head of her fang toothed dog. Isobel led outside and separate to our bikes. I was ready for her to suggest I ride off permanently in another direction. We rode up the hill past the house with the pink shutters and pink garbage cans, past the Jehovah Witness lady's road. It was a bad time. July Third Ma suggested operating on my face and July Fourth my friend did not call. I said, I'll do the upstairs bathroom. Isobel said, Okay, I'll do the downstairs. Outside gravel shot, making her escape. I said, You don't have to do the whole downstairs, I'll help. She said, That's okay. I thought does she want to be around me or not? I did the sink, the mirror, all the little make ups, the tub, white grooves. I put Comet in the toilet and washed the rims and wiped the bottom marble pedestal. I walked back down and Isobel was using Lemon Pledge. The Lemon Pledge song was actually a make over of a much better more original song about a garden which we learned in third grade, but now I forgot.

Isobel wiped a little table. Eleven-thirty, said a Roman numeral clock. Hollywood Squares was on. I did not like Hollywood Squares but I always had this wish somehow the level questions would be transformed higher into the challenge of Jeopardy. The vacuum cleaner was out. Our mothers were very different but they had both bought an Electrolux from possibly the same travelling salesman.

—What do you want me to do?

—This room is almost done.

—Okay, I said, I'll do the stairs.

The stairs was one of the worst because of tramping the machine to levels and using two attachments for rug and bare.

Isobel said, You don't have to do the stairs.

I'm like either she cares about me or this vacuum protection is for show. I said, Don't worry, it's better for both of us to finish fast anyway. I'm like why would she want me not to do the stairs but talk for a month about how great her Fourth of July picnic party is and what a great time I would have then not invite me to it? Next, out on the lawn. We're right across from the path to the crick. Isobel says, You want to come over for lunch? I say, Well, I was going to go home and go swimming. I said swimming to emphasize swimming, out, expand, the afternoon, larger invitation. Isobel says, Why don't you stay here and we can just go to the crick? Oh, I say, but I don't have my suit. Oh, Isobel says, you can borrow one of mine. Oh, I say, like surprised.

—Take that, Isobel every single summer day said, throwing at me, and with my other hand I kept on pat pat patting the small bone white skull plate of her maniac dog, fang toothed slobbering and with really a lot of tartar if you asked me. Then I caught whatever bikini Isobel threw, which were like her Red Cross donations to my deformity case. Hot pink red fuschia orange or simple blue and white or flower power pink and green, pat pat patting the dog one hand, catch with the other, meanwhile Isobel's mother sat sobbing next to me in her faded movie star negligee, Isobel screaming at her mother Quit blubbering, quit chewing off Sheila's ear, and Isobel every day remembering always to throw, Take that, at me, never once letting me leave her house without a more normal bathing suit compared to that faggy heavily ruffled Hawaiian diaper affair from last year which my only hope would be to sit a long long time on our pool coping slightly moving back and forth wearing a hole in the bottom before Ma would ever let me get a new one.

—It looks good, Isobel said that first time.

I laughed. People usually did not tell me that I looked good. Usually opposite. I said, I used to think I would always have to wear a one piece because of my scar. I never thought I could wear a bikini. I laughed again.

—What scar?

I zipped down my frontal length. We were in her sister's room with twin beds and one window, a screen, outside June summertime fulled green sunshine and steadily moving bugs, but meanwhile inside dark, like that two bed, dark light contrast of my hospital room. Of course that hospital time for me was winter. June, twin separated beds, one window behind and Isobel stared at my skin shocked. You wish you had an eraser and you could tear that scar right off your flesh.

I smiled. The thing is to keep the other person calm. You think I'll just hold onto my railing. Out the window, it's so pretty out there. From down the hallway came the slidings and gaspings of Mr. Dickinson sucking his pipe and moving his coin collection around. I said, I had an operation when I was two and a half because my chest was bent in too far. I think my scar is shrinking. I smiled. I sat down on one bed and bent to tie my shoelaces. Actually also I bent to cover my cut. I said, What color are you wearing today?

She lifted it. It was a pretty extreme scar.

—The tropical paradise, I said. C'est beau.

—Isobel, where are you storing your steak knife?

—In my hot little hand.

—You're not going to sleep with it all night like that?

—I'm not getting killed, no sirree bob.

—Watch we roll over and stab ourselves. I said, Thank God Shell switched from giving away glasses to giving away steak knives.

It was July 6, Isobel and I in our sleeping bags in the dark under my famous cherry tree, the gate closed, combination lock locked, each holding a steak knife and a baseball bat between us, which I remembered once on Abbott and Costello Meet Frankenstein they disagreed so long on use of the bat, successively piling their hands, gripping to the top, taking so long the monster attacked. The crickets came beating and in Ma's white window her fan blades turned.

On Memorial Day when we cleaned Mr. Hanrahan's convertible we still had on our all white from the parade which was stupid but we were young. Windshields were hard to clean because you kept dashing your hand triangled into the dashboard trying to clean out the years of tobacco and match grit. Isobel and I sent out flyers run off secretly on the school machine by Ma advertising we would clean anything for two dollars an hour each. Luckily Isobel also wanted to go to France. I twisted the rear view, filming her.

—Isobel, you don't have to clean the back ashtrays.

—They're disgusting.

—Yeah, but try to control yourself. I want time to play tennis too.

I squirted Windex at my face, a good thinned rear mirror view with the bags cut out, though of course on Memorial Day I did not know the bad surgery suggestion time ahead.

—Isobel, I'm leaving you the radio and speedometer since you're better at the picky stuff.

His garage door roared open. He stood in the mouth in his white alleged James Dean T-shirt and slipping pants.

—Hubba hubba, Isobel said Memorial Day, all the gunshots fired on our town green to celebrate war, all our azaleas in bloom orange red, his driveway just freshened black with sheening sealant in the sun. He opened the driver's side door and got in next to me. The car sunk.

—I want to get this out, Mr. Hanrahan said. See this? He pulled something out from underneath between his legs. He said, You know what this is?

—A billy club, I said. This was my neighbor and I should take the protective responsibility and save Isobel's life.

—Notice the point. Mr. Hanrahan ran his finger along it and tippy touched the end. He said, I sharpened it. Anyone gives me trouble. Mr. Hanrahan stabbed the air.

I nodded. He smacked the billy club on his palm. It's a fine line. You don't want to say it's too good and you would like to get stabbed and you don't want to say it's bad enraging him into a gouge. The Boston Strangler threw that dirtied sanitary napkin behind the La-Z-Boy. Smack. The car doorway, the pressed flat aluminum, a threshold, escape?, and beyond the driveway sheening black and I would quick grasp my seat side and throw it forward so that simultaneously as he stabbed into the cushion Isobel could escape.

—Okay, I'll leave you. The car rising. Ladies to your task.

Off he went across his painted black. One very early book a boy paints his floor green the wrong way painting himself into a corner like the rising tide. I got out of the car. You set your own traps. I would like to get out of all my traps. I walked behind and sopped the rag and bent bumped over the red taillight and outbent chrome, NEW YORK THE EMPIRE STATE, and in the bumper sopping was my disgusting face, though earlier on Memorial Day things not quite so bad as Third of July. Isobel still sat duty confined in the back, cleaning filthy crevices for him. I felt like smacking her. I thought you're supposed to be the leader. She was still sitting inside that car doing everything she was told. I sopped the rag over outbent chromium facial magnified like that rounded Christmas ornament view they give of the arrival of all the relatives on one Alka-Seltzer commercial, my face like a sea lamprey living in the dark deformed.

I really didn't know after the Fourth whether Isobel wanted to be friends or not. Logically it had to be that Isobel knew nothing about what Ma said to me. It would be like shows on separate channels and yet what if one on one channel reached across the airwaves and characters began to intersect. I could see the white line shining of our gravel under our chain link fence as Isobel breathed next to me July 6. I turned on my side, Isobel blocking my back, like once my two stuffed bunny rabbits. The white moat of gravel shone where the fence met the ground and in the window Ma's fan turned. I had a normal up and down life and then I remembered my mother wanted them to operate on my face and I got this deep shock. You think: I must have made this up to have a drama. I really did not want to see someone climbing over the fencing coming in to attack. We had the black dark claw cherry tree over us and above that stars and Isobel breathed regularly next to me, my heart going thump thump. I was scared.

Jo fast plunged the straps and pulled back taut: nothing exposed. I stood holding her paddle and my paddle business ends up in case her father was looking out the window for canoe mistakes. I said, You know she just didn't even call me on the Fourth of July.

Jo said, I said to her didn't you invite Sheiley for the Fourth of July?

—What'd she say?

—Oh, you know Isobel. You can never get a straight answer out of her. Jo shook her head, her spectacles glinting in the sun.

—Yeah, well, you know my position. I'm like on the fringe hanging out with you guys. I'm like the desperate one.

—We really like you, Jo said. Isobel's always talking about how much she likes you.

—Oh. I handed her her paddle. I looked out at the water. It felt like I was going to cry. That crick was the most beautiful thing I ever saw in my life. I said, Yeah, well, I guess Isobel doesn't always have the greatest life.

—Oh, God, Jo said. That's the most maniac family I ever saw in my life. Her mother is so sick she would rather have her teeth rot out of her head because she's so afraid of the dentist.

—My mother loves the dentist, I said. That's her favorite thing. Let's get in, Jo.

—Yeah, well, Sheiley, we're flat as boards and everything but at least we have a chance to grow up normal. At least we have normal mothers.

—You only met mine twice.

—Yeah, but you can tell she's normal.

—I guess she's normal, I said. I'd rather just be the no brain paddling in front if you don't mind.

—Okay, Jo said. I'm used to it.

A seagull climbed. Jo was the steerer in back. I said, Jo, do you think I have horse teeth? I bent my head backwards on the aluminum gunnels, smiling.

—Yeah, they do look a little like horse teeth.

—Crap. Isobel said that. Crap crap crap. My one normal thing because I never had to get braces.

—Yeah, well, she calls me a pinhead so don't worry.

All the green water stood full, still, the canoe stopped, unrocking. Dead high, I said.

—Yup.

Way far out a car moved down the beach road, a station wagon with metal rack glinting, some mother loaded down with kids.

—Yeah, Sheiley, Jo said, I think we have to be really nice to Isobel now. You know what I heard about Mr. D?

—How is Isobel? Ma said. She is such a nice kid. How's she hacking it with her father gone?

I said, Fine.

Dad threw raw gray pink meatbones in our rocky bottomed aluminum roasting pan. For his birthday I gave Dad a blue and white pin striped chef's apron I made and I wrote SPARERIBS across in black Magic Marker which was a three way joke about Dad putting on weight, his favorite meal, and something in the Bible. But every present I gave Dad he put in a drawer and never took out again.

—I really like Isobel, Ma said. I think she's a great kid. Don't you like Isobel, Jack?

—I like Isobel. Dad turned and smiled at me and drank.

—Isobel is a nice kid. Don't you think Isobel is a nice kid? Sheila? No? Am I wrong? Isn't Isobel a nice kid?

I didn't say anything.

—Well. Ma set her cup down. Color me naive, Ma said, but I really think Isobel is a nice kid. And she is pretty. Gorgeous. I mean. She is a gorgeous girl. Sheila. Isn't she?

I looked at Ma. Ma picked up her cup and drank. Dad tilted back and finished the can.

—Lem oh! Dad said. Lem oh! Got to have my lem oh! Dad was imitating Ma's imitation of a French accent. He held up a lemon and showed it to me.

—How's Isobel coping with the pressure? Ma said. Can she cope? Ma struck a match and looked away from me, flailing it out.

—I don't know, I said. The family can't get any food because he's the only one that drives and Joanne just told me today they don't know how long he'll be gone because he ran away with a younger woman.

Dad looked at me then turned his back. Ma picked up her cup and drank. Dad walked over to our spice cabinet and looked in it.

—Well, that's ridic, Ma said. I can't believe Isobel's mother does not drive. Are you telling me Isobel's mother does not drive?

—Yes. Isobel's mother does not drive.

—Oh, cripes. Give me a break. No way I would let myself get in a position like that. No way Jose.

Dad turned and held the Worcestershire bottle toward me, showing me what he was using. I nodded. It was like two weeks since Ma suggested plastic surgery on my face.

—You've got to be able to move, man. I hope to hell you wouldn't let yourself get in a position like that. Ma's voice was fierce.

—No. I'm getting my learner's permit the first day.

—Good! Ma said. Christ, that's ridic. And now Isobel has to suffer. That's not right. Why should Isobel have to suffer? Can we bring some food to her?

Dad turned with his jaw dropped.

—I would really like to bring some food to Isobel. Would that be too intrusive?

I shook my head.

—I don't want to be intrusive. I don't want to embarrass the kid, Ma said. I like Isobel. I think Isobel is a great great kid. Don't you? Don't you think Isobel is a great kid?

I nodded and I started to cry.

—She's crying, Ma said.

Dad turned and looked. I couldn't stop.

—Come here, boobie. Ma had her arms out. I walked around the table from Annie's chair and I bent and Ma put her arms around me and she rocked and I was bent over with her hugging me, crying. Cry it out, Ma said. Just cry it out.

I thought what does she mean, it, and I kept crying.

—What's the matter with Sheila? Robert said.

—Out! And Ma's hand lifted off jerking dramatically.

—Here you go, babe. Dad gave me one of his folded, ironed handkerchiefs. He looked at me.

I wiped my eyes and blew my nose, standing up away from Ma. They both looked at me. I'll be right back, I said. I went in the bathroom and put cold water on my face. My face always looked the worst when I cried. I went back in the kitchen.

—So. Ma came over and put her arm around my shoulder. We were standing under our orange clock. She rocked me, gripping around my far arm, the two of us standing parallel, her rocking me. So, she said, how about we take a ride over to Isobel's after supper? Would that be good?

I nodded.

—Cripes, chase the blues away. Ma rocked me, standing up, the two of us standing, rocking, Ma gripping me very tight.

—Ma. I laughed. You're going to knock me over. And Dad lifted his eyebrows like Groucho Marx.

Ma got out spareribs, coleslaw, Italian bread, apple crisp. We said, You're giving away a whole apple crisp! Ma had it all packed in a cooler with ice and we had to fight her off to prevent donations of all our cold cuts including ham. I said, Ma, it's a five minute ride to Stony Point. I swear no one will get botulism if you don't use ice.

—I don't want to take any chances, Ma said. Done and done with the ice.

Ma turned the rearview mirror totally her way.

—Jesus, Mary, Dad said.

This was one of their favorite fights they had on all the roads, Two Mile Hollow, Expressway, Northern State. Ma combed her hair fast and vicious, Dad meanwhile veering all over like he could not possibly drive forward if Ma had the rearview in her control, Ma pulling vicious at those knots. Fast she swiped with lipstick.

—Done. She twisted the mirror violently away, showing the ceiling seams.

—Jesus Christ. And Dad's face flashed worried, trying to get a stable backward view.

—Is that coral? I leaned near Ma's jugular from behind.

—This? Ma threw it in her pock.

—Let me see it. Coral, the bottom said. I said, Coral is a really good color for you, Ma.

—I don't even look. I don't have the time.

Forward all the green came rushing and in the rearview Nissequott, disappearing backwards, tilted strangely, then our wooden war heroes gone and forward the Presbyterian Church, curving, and Dad's hand lifted off the settled rear-view angle and the triangle Memorial Day soldier rock centered in our town green, rushing backwards.

—Goddamn it. Ma's whole face was twisted, looking in our trunk. I knew it, she said.

—Oh, Ma. I patted her and lifted the earthquaked apple crisp. Appearances aren't everything, I said. I had it in my right hand, wrist bent back. Those pie throwings on Soupy Sales were never that funny to me because they skipped the face smashed by the aluminum pan. I said, Ma, I have to tell you two shocking things. First, the Dickinsons keep their Christmas lights up all year.

Ma made a face.

—And second they have a somewhat wild dog.

—She-eet, Ma said.

I held up our family's Hills bag inside Isobel's kitchen. I said, This is not garbage, it's Italian bread.

I was trying to make a private joke between Isobel and me about last Halloween when I mortified her by traipsing with a Hills bag. I didn't want Isobel to feel like we were the grand welfare workers coming in.

—This is really nice of your parents. She bent in the refrigerator, its light still out, out since at least October when we met, and above the kitchen fluorescent tube trembled, half dark.

—Well, Isobel said, I better go in there.

I was shocked. Her mother already had extra people to comfort her. Then they all piled into the living room for her soap opera. I sat down on that outer couch and petted the dog. I thought what about me? I was pat patting Rex-osaurus's cranium for dear life, watching that dog's very sharp eyeteeth. In the next room Mrs. D. was having her soap opera with Ma and Dad and Isobel gathered around. This black leather outer room couch was like the doctor's table with rolling white paper. I thought what about me? Outside their dog smeared storm window the day still had some light, entirely July filled green, everything out there beautiful full stop dead high green, while inside they went on sobbing and murmuring comforting her in the next room, and I patted the little head, their console off but with gray green strangely flattened dog reflection inside. Outside was a beautiful summer night.

—I think that was a nice thing to do, Ma said. I think we really helped her.

—Light me one. Dad turned us onto the dark road back to Nissequott, our headlights barely lighting into the black and their two dark figures in the front seat ahead.

—Here. Ma passed it.

I watched out my window.

—I really think she appreciated that, Ma said.

Their small orange glows lifted and dropped and the green white of the dashboard, my window opened, and as we drove the bugs accordioned, all the dark bushes and trees moving beside us, and it came over me that Ma and Dad were married, and I had my window opened all the way. I wanted to get out.

Next morning Ma came through the green gate in her gingham pink and white. I had on my shorts. I never went in our pool anymore. I liked the crick with seaweed not chlorine and I liked the seagulls and I liked the distant winding water and how the sandbars rose and fell.

—So, have you thought anymore about the plastic surgery?

I kept reading A Bend in the River. Ma had a brownish dirty dishrag. She wiped our round white table, slightly puddled from night rain. The train roared through toward Stony Point. Gone.

—Why don't you think about it? Done and done. Ma straightened like her back hurt. She said, If you can solve the problem, solve it. Why suffer? I don't believe in suffering.

—I'm reading. Do you mind?

She walked out the gate and around the extension. You get this feeling you are trapped on an island with one other person, each trying to kill the other, which was a story we read in English. After a few minutes Ma came back out with her sunglasses, cigarettes, iced tea, and a book. She sat in a redwood.

—I had to wipe mine off, I said.

Ma lit a cigarette and stared at me.

I said, Is that a new Truman Capote?

—Why don't you think about the bag job? Two weeks, man. In and out like the E train. You put a little Cover Girl on. No one even knows.

—If no one would even know why should I have it done?

Ma threw her match in an ashtray. I felt brilliant. I said, You act like it's nothing, Ma, but they cut into your face. I know what surgery is. They cut into you, right? They use a knife.

Ma blew smoke off. She said, I view that as a complete overreaction. Complete.

I looked at the pool.

—I really think you're overreacting.

I kicked a little red bench over.

—Sanneefrannee, Ma sang. I'm telling you, Sheila, it's a minor number. Minor. I think you would be shocked at what a minor number it is and it would make a big difference in your life. Tremendous difference.

Everything was going weak and melting.

—You wouldn't have the bags under your eyes. Wouldn't that be great? I think that would be great. You don't even get a general.

I set the red bench back up. I was halfway thinking then I could knock it down again.

—What do you mean a general? Why can't you talk English?

—A general anesthetic, a general anesthetic, Christ. You knew what I meant.

—How am I supposed to know what general means, Jesus. Why can't you just talk English?

—You knew.

—I did not know. Don't tell me what I know and what I don't know. God, you are such a pain in the ass, I swear to God. Why don't you just leave me alone? Just forget I exist. Just let me read my book in peace, okay? Okay? Would that be so hard for you?

Ma lifted her iced tea and drank.

—Do you have to swallow so loud?

—I'm telling you, Sheila, you would be shocked at what a nothing the whole procedure is. Nothing! Daddy and I will pay for it, believe me.

The dogs next door started howling and running on their chains.

—How about I make an appointment with this guy Howie Weinstein?

—Who the hell is Howie Weinstein?

—He's such a nice guy. He's the plastic surgeon. I got his name from the AMA. He sounds like such a nice guy. How about I make an appointment? What could it hurt? You just get the info.

Dad came up the walk and through the gate to where we sat. He took one of Ma's cigarettes and her matches, lit it, and he threw the matches down on the table like that was a speech.

—Sanneefranneetime, Ma sang. Have you figured out the lumber?

—I figured out the lumber. Dad smiled at me and I looked away.

—I tell you, Ma said, it'll be such a relief to get that tool shed up, won't it?

Dad smiled at me. He nodded his head twice in Ma's direction. I said, Goodbye, I'm going to Isobel's.

—Hello, ladies, Mr. Hanrahan said, and held his back screen door opened, rather a tight fit to pass in. You gals ready for some work?

—Yes, we chorused. I said, Where's Aunt Rita?

—She's at the store. He drained his glass of beer. Just let me use the facilities.

—And please close the door, Isobel whispered because I told her about the past.

I fast swung closed his inner wooden. Uncle Fester I presume, I said pointing at the line of nails hammered in the door to train his dogs not to jump. I used to have this Playboy pretend dream the perfect thing would be to wear a little white apron covering the front and the white tail bow down the crack. Then Mr. Hanrahan would be sitting in his La-Z-Boy and say I'm up on one of those sliding ladders that attach to the wall dusting off the shelves with only the apron on and he was ordering me around.

—This way, ladies. He looked sharp eyed and bushy tailed. He opened the basement door. EMERGENCY, a red switch said. The furnace, I thought. Once babysitting at the Callahans' I called Dad because of noises and he rushed over with a flashlight, which I never even knew our family had. Dad came up and said it must have been the furnace, babe.

—This light just went out. I apologize, ladies.

I figured the basement mess would be a lot of old newspapers stacked. He went first, me second down the dark stairs. If he turned at the bottom with an axe the blade would first hit me, thus giving Isablue the chance to escape.

Ma completely did not believe me when I told her how bad Mr. Hanrahan was. When we got the call to be hired she just held out the black phone to me, said, It's Mr. Hanrahan for you.

—Me? I looked at Isobel and Isobel looked back. It was the

middle of August, about two months since his billy club. I said, I have to ask my friend.

—Oh, you have to ask your friend, he said like there was something undercurrent funny in this.

Isobel was looking at me when I hung up. I really did not want to do this alone. I said, Isobel, you want to clean his basement for three dollars an hour each?

We were looking at each other.

Ma poured Nestea over ice, crackling. I really did not want to do that job alone, but on the other hand I really wanted to earn enough money to go to France.

Isobel shrugged. Isobel was richer. At birth some relative gave her a trust fund. She really already had a thousand to go to France and in a way she was doing this cleaning business just to be friends with me. She said, Do you want to?

I said, Well, I need the money, but if you don't want to then don't.

—I'll do it, Isobel said. Live dangerously.

—Jesus, Isobel, Ma said, you call cleaning out a basement living dangerously? You live a quiet life.

Isobel smiled. I saw when she smiled that what Ma said was funny but I also felt like bursting out in tears. I could feel all this broken pain inside my throat. I said, Ma, last time we cleaned out his car he showed us his stupid billy club that he keeps sharpened for a weapon.

—Oh, shit, give me a break. Ma turned and opened her cabinet. Ma shut the cabinet and turned with her sunglasses and iced tea. Her hands were coated with dirt from weeding, scratches on her bare legs, dirt around her ankles. In Nissequott the noon whistle went off.

—You don't believe me about the billy club, do you, Ma?

—Hey, if you don't feel comfortable, don't work for him. I have enough problems in life, believe me.

Ma walked out.

—She didn't believe me. She thinks I'm a total hysterical exaggerator and I would do anything for attention. She didn't believe me, did she? Isobel just shrugged. Isobel didn't know anything about what Ma suggested for my face.

He said, I really apologize for this light being out.

Isobel's voice came from behind me in the almost dark. She said, Where was Moses when the light went out?

I said, To get to the other side.

—What's that? He said, Why don't you gals just wait here? I'll get the other light.

Why don't you gals just stand right here in these footprints I've painted especially on the floor and practiced swinging an axe on in the dark for a week? Okay, great. I had this sudden wish to hold Isobel's hand and we could die together, like sliding down in those beer boxes holding Marianne Gilhooley's little paw.

—Just let me get this light, he said.

In May as usual Psycho came on Channel 3, total interference, and we formed a brother and sister calling chain from Michael on the roof turning our silver antennae trying to get Connecticut, to Annie on the stoop, to Robert at the top of the stairs, to me below, trying and trying to get that famous blood swirling down the drain. He pulled the light on. He was standing next to the string like Thomas Edison proud. Across against the wall was the washing machine and dryer, white, and I had this immediate flash of the lonely Maytag repairman waiting for the phone to ring. You'd like to call for help. Other light bulbs hung from the rafters and other small bits of torn hanging string and the many standard maroon basement poles like you wish it could be the happy past swinging your pole partner on roller skates, no. I saw at regular spaced distances over the white concrete little tufts of brown.

He said, I keep the dogs down here sometimes.

I realized it was shit, halfway twisting into his shit, rushing down, dropping his pants, dropping little tufts.

—I got a couple of shovels here. Probably this flat one will work better.

I took the flat shovel and I took the round. Isobel was in shock.

—And here's some Hefty trash bags. He pulled one out of the box and shook it, unfurling. Then this could just be a very strange Hefty commercial. He said, It's got the ties. Here's a bucket and some ammonia.

I nodded.

—Anything else you can think of?

—No, I said.

The water lapped around the wooden dark stork dock legs: night. I could see the shape and reshape of the crick curving which was the Sound pushing into the land, and in the woods the crickets beat. Water lapped. I said, Did you tell him we'd be near the dock?

—He'll figure it out if he's got any brains at all. Isobel lay with her head on her rolled sleeping bag, but I sat up so at least he would see a form. If it was me I would have sent the guy mapped out instructions mailed two weeks ahead with camping equipment and a rented station wagon including fresh water in a canteen to make sure he got to me. I said, There he is! Isobel sat up. The flashlight joggled crotch high down the path then flat across the sand.

—What are you the Gestapo? Isobel said.

—Sorry. He turned off the light. He was going into eleventh. That blinking aurora came. Isobel stood. She said, I'll be back soon.

I extended the antenna all the way up. Actually I remembered when transistor radios were a shock. They were little black private miracle things you held to your ear and people in your surroundings didn't know what you were listening to. Maybe I was facing a lifetime of sitting by a stream alone. If I thought about my life and my face I got this panic. I never read a book or saw a movie where a girl's mother wanted her to cut up and restitch her skin. It came on to static and in the woods the flashlight went off.

Isobel reached for the rounded shovel and she walked out to a brown pile. She shovelled under it, scraping, and lifted. I held open a plastic bag with my face turned away, trying not to breathe.

—Is it in? I said.

—Yes. She walked to the next. She shovelled under it, scraping metal over cement.

I walked to a pile and shovelled under it and it moved, like brown liquidy. I dropped the shovel and ran for the door. I gasped in huge garage air. I really wanted to go to France. The trouble was without oxygen it would be hard to work. Isobel's shovel scraped along. She said, Are you all right?

—I'm going to throw up.

—Go sit outside.

—Maybe if I hold my breath.

—Go sit outside.

All these rocks and rocks and rocks were piled into his wall and inside Isobel's shovel scraped along. Once in Ma's psychology the guy said if you dream about money that's feces and Ma raised her hand and said what if you dream about feces? I remembered before Nissequott when I went to the bathroom behind the plaid living room drapes, a gift for Ma.

The tide was coming in: by the strength of the lap. A voice said, Our current temperature at downtown Chicago's Wrigley Building is a pleasant seventy-eight degrees.

—Chicago, I said, alone, out loud.

—Winds tonight are light and variable. Tomorrow will be hot, high in the nineties.

Chicago, I thought. I felt this excitement through all my skin and veins. I felt this whole huge sense of the continent so near. I felt this faith Isobel would perhaps return. The stars were hard bright white and the crick lapping in. Far far away little white lights were Connecticut and two closer reds were the Lilco smokestacks at Port Sands. The water lapped. You never know how it will go. Across a car slowly drove its headlights like moving against a wall. I looked up. I said, God? I could see all these stars so beautiful.

Our little group crossed the gangplank onto Connecticut. Now there were no trees. From a distance over the railing it had looked like rural countryside but when we landed we were in this city with only glass and rock cement and upwards miraging waves of heat while the sun glared off blinded windows. It looked like a Godzilla movie, the city abandoned.

—Get away from that broken glass, Mrs. Dickinson said.

—What do you think I'm retarded, Isobel said.

—Get away from that glass, would you, Mr. Dickinson said. Christ, Isobel.

—Please, can I jump up and down on the glass?

—Shut up, Mrs. Dickinson said. Can't we for once have a nice family outing? Is that too much to ask?

—Keep your goddamn mouth shut, Isobel, Mr. Dickinson said.

—You think they like you criticizing their city? Mrs. Dickinson said.

A black woman came down the abandoned concrete street in purple curlers and her skin purplish dressed in striped pants cut at the knees, too long, and a huge-flowered blouse. We passed silently. We went into a McDonald's filled with all black people eating and only black people making the food.

McDonald's is your kind of place.
(Clap clap.)
It's such a happy place.

(Clap clap.)
A clean and snappy place.

It felt like we were the radium white underground creatures. This was my first other state beside Florida. After we
left Long Island you could see the continent ahead almost
right away. Isobel and I were leaned forward looking over
the railing. There were life preservers and actual little rescue
dorys. My favorite Time Tunnel the two brown haired guys
are thrown onto the Titanic yet manage to escape to their
delivery tunnel before the iceberg. The last shot they're
standing relaxed near the railing, safe they think, while the
camera pans to behind them the life preserver that says
Andrea Doria.

—Isobel, I had said on the ferry, I have a question for
you.

Isobel said, Shoot.

This was kind of a strange August honeymoon invitation,
Mr. Dickinson returned, but they wanted the two of us
along.

—You want another fries?

I could remember when it was like only about two million
served, now in the double digits.

—No, thank you. I smiled at her.

On the ferry we had leaned together on the railing. I was
about to shock her. For our trip to Bridgeport she wore her
glen plaid pants, woven blue belt, white T-strap sandals,
and her sister's navy blue short sleeve shirt with a round
neck. The plaid was like Dad's bermudas. I felt kind of bad
for her standing there with what was going to hit her next. I
had this half a guilt I should stay silent maybe and protect
her.

I said, This summer, like in July.

Isobel looked at me, leaning on the railing.

I said, My mother.

I had this sense around of blue water, sand cliffs of departing Long Island. There were seagulls.

I said again, My mother.

I looked down at the water. I looked back up at Isobel. I said, My mother suggested I have plastic surgery.

All my bangs were grown out, my hair totally down with tortoiseshell French barrettes on each side, thanks to Isobel. In McDonald's we all slipped our trays inside the garbages that said Thank You.

—No one in there knows where the goddamn P.T. Barnum Museum is, Mrs. Dickinson said. What are you crazy, Isobel? You want to cause a goddamn riot?

—Why not? Isobel said. Black people don't go to museums?

—You want to get us killed? Mr. Dickinson said.

Slowly we moved through the streets empty and sparkling with broken glass, the windows yellow staring eyes, and proceeding grouped four like in a horror movie when the four move their backs to the center, ready at any moment to be attacked. ADMISSION, the sign said, and Mr. Dickinson paid for me. Inside was dark, air conditioned, totally filled with white people with all mahogany, and maroon looping velvet or velour guidance ropes kept Isobel and me back from Tom Thumb and his midget wife's bed, in a way my life not a total loss: I found a tribute to once that happy circus midget in the elevator riddle Aunt Rita told me when we were friends.

I said on the ship, On my face. On the bags under my eyes.

—I think you should do what you want, Isobel said.

I could feel all the water around. People look at you and it's really humiliating, like you have turds hanging on your face and you just would like to wipe. I could feel the rock of the ferry. There was the roar of the turbines moving us forward and everywhere on the ship were stencilled little sayings that told you what to do, where was safety. I felt like I got knocked over onto the wood planking. The sun was high, the sky azure, dizzy. I could feel her standing quietly next to me but you know the other person would rather veer off and not be near you like at low tide we had a mud fight with three boys, perfect, our grade. She picked up more and threw and Jo picked up some and threw and I threw. We were running dead low in the crick throwing the spots of dark brown and they picked up throwing and running throwing, perfect three boys and three girls slap on your flesh and sliding down on your leg or stomach or arm, the land all flat and sun high dead low tide and he came chasing throwing the dark brown and hit and I picked up the muck and threw and hit and he came throwing and I moved then moved the other way and moved and moved the other way and moved and moved like once I saw on the Baltimore Colts on TV or came close the way he moved I moved out the other way and he threw down his mud and said, You're too ugly to chase, over half his face a red brown like mudspread but redder birthmark, and you wonder how deep that birthmark went into him, and he walked away, refusing to chase me. He's an asshole, Isobel said.

I balanced gripping the telephone pole, my heels hanging off the edge of the dock. Otherwise I never would have asked her advice but she saved me on the bus and she got me in the parade and saved me in the basement and she said he was an asshole. It was almost September, school. Do a backflip, Isobel said. I gripped with my sweating toes the fine hewed grain timber of that dark telephone pole wood. The water fast swirled in. I brought my arms up level to my chest. Sky almost black. I waited for the thunder to clear, the water swirling below. The bowling ball rolled and crashed. I settled my spirit, Isobel watching up at me. I threw back flipping everything. The land was the sky and the sky was where we walked. I hit, went under, surfaced. We cast out and the current carried us, Isablue's head bobbing in the green. Stay under, I yelled. Isobel, stay under. One Mississippi, two Mississippi. It's getting closer, I yelled and we rushed along inside the warm green tide rushing out and the rain came across and Isobel's pale face bobbed.

Ma stood looking out the storm door at the hard cold spring rain. It was April 1972. Run like bunnies, I said so close to her she jumped. I ran out first, the earth a deep brown and only the yellowish forsythia in all the brown and gray. I slammed the passenger door. Ma backed us, our rocks rising, going to get material for my new curtains at Sew What's New.

—All clear, I said.

—It's amazing they don't put real gates here, I said and we both flung back against the seat as Ma stepped on it trying to get us both across alive.

We drove past the sandpit, all the machinery stopped.

—Well. Ma threw her match out fast into the rain. I called Howie and made an appointment.

I felt this total complete rage at her taking control of my life. I said, I never told you to make an appointment.

—For me! Ma said. I called Howie for me!

Chapter 18

ary, Indiana, lay spread, stretched out all below, thousands and thousands of houses and cars and factory smokestacks, United States, driveways, and the whole sky oozy polluted brown over it, the sun sunken sliding sideways out of its form. It was August 1972, our furthest point west. I sat atop a two storey tall Goodrich, Goodyear tire with treads so deep you could slide your hand in. Instead of a horse and a man on a pedestal, Gary, Indiana, had this. Ma was a thousand miles behind playing tennis in public again, dotting flesh-colored Cover Girl on her eye scars, then the sweat ran down mixing it all with the make-up chemicals and she cried. I said to her, You don't need plastic surgery, your face is fine. I said to myself would she totally do it as a sacrificial victim to get me to do the same?

Ma's face was beaten welts with black stitches like black ants sewed into her black and purple skin where Howie pulled the silver needle through, sewing up where he had cut. Ma sat at supper with sunglasses on, the bruising out beyond the frames. Dad slammed shut our kitchen window, sudden cold in June 1972. He poured the rest of his beer down the drain and sat. He said, Pass me those lima beans, babe.

—Gladly. Annie screwed up her face.

—Tuu. And Dad looked hurt, Ma lifting her orange plastic cup.

—Wait. I grabbed the white bowl. I spooned some, tiny green fetus positions on Ma's nearly empty plate. You need your vegetables, I said. Ma lifted her cup and the ice hit against her face that distant potholder way, like when the person is bare flesh holding a pan from the oven and the feeling has not registered. Ma looked like Ray Charles rocking singing blindly sunglassed at his piano, Hallelujah, I love her so. No one eating much. The three of them looked at their plates. Dad, I said, they're very good with the bacon added. Thank you, Dad said. He added the bacon for Ma's first supper after the hospital. Keep your head down and watch your plate.

—I can't see a thing, Ma said. I got to take these sunglasses off.

—NO, the four of us screamed.

I could see Wyoming, Idaho, yippie oh, mountains and buttes. We might have crossed the continental divide. Aunt Rita was in California now. We heard he stopped three times to go to the bathroom before the George Washington Bridge.

—Howdy, Sheila. Isobel stood below holding hands with Alexander Helmintoller.

She switched boyfriends somewhere either Jersey or Pennsylvania, either The Garden State impressed on dessicated beige or You've Got a Friend in Pennsylvania, which was the Quakers, like Nixon as Dad always pointed out. Her first was perfect all American Bud on Father Knows Best but then she switched making out in the bus seats with this guy, fattish, acned, sashay faggy swaggering all around. I was trying to interpret this image switch in terms of her facial advice for me.

—You've got yourself the ideal position, Isobel called up to me on my tire. Basically I just wanted to climb up to a place where no one could reach.

—I hear the car, Annie said.

I turned down the volume a bit: whistling on Andy

Griffith. But you can never tell who's doing it. There's never a body attached.

—Shit, man, Annie said, I hope she's not bad.

One car door slammed. Our front door opened. Ma was back from the hospital. You could see on TV that commercial starting, the screen door sound like something torn. My stomach hurt. A baby is crawling across empty white. Ma was bent with sunglasses and Dad had one hand under her arm, shoving her in on Codeine. The screen door hit back in, hitting Dad's back, the TV on, Dad trying to push fly the door opened outward behind him at the same time shoving Ma in across our slate, the TV still on. Ma veered smashing our wooden banister and banging veered off against the panelling and behind me Annie stood up off the couch, the TV still going waxing back and forth across someone's floor.

Dad had his hand under Ma's one fleshy part of her arm, shoving her up the stairs. She smashed again off the banister and we were both moving forward toward the lower rails, our house a split level. Is she okay? Annie said.

—How in heaven's name did you get up there? Alexander Helmintoller exclaimed.

—I climbed up the fissures, I said saying fissures eccentrically to keep the two of them as far away as possible. I looked ahead again. I wondered where Aunt Rita was. I had never been so many days without television. I was missing Lucy, the 1972 Summer Olympics in Munich, any more news about the break in at Democratic headquarters which I really hoped Nixon caused.

—Have a good time, Isobel said.

I had nothing to say to Isobel anymore. When I looked at her I felt dead, floating in a completely separated world and she was gone.

—Enjoy your view, Alexander said.

They walked off hand in hand. My hand was on the black

rubber. I was trying to figure out my life. Why would you go on a cross country trip and get as far west as you could and for a demarcation was a giant black rubber tire poised above a totally polluted city allowed to have the only black mayor in the United States?

—Sheiley! Jo, small, waved near the yellow bus. I had my palms flat on the black rubber looking out as far as I could across the United States, below scrape brown crossed with steel and concrete smoldering in heat. I could hardly even remember that great breezy aired moment of crossing westward over the George Washington, that black and white moment in the convertible of all four singing moving toward the best show on the series, when they sleep next to railroad tracks and Lucy and Ricky's bunkbeds slide across the room, then west to California.

—Sheiley, what's the matter, don't you want to go back?

—Hi. I looked out again across the country.

—Don't you want to go back, Sheiley? We can go swimming in the crick. You can get your ears pierced at the mall. Jo said, Are you worried about being in high school?

—No. I smiled at her. Jo had on cutoffs and her gold rim lovely Joanne spectacles. I said, I'm sorry you had to say goodbye to Sam.

—Oh, I don't care so much. It was just a good adventure. You better come down now, okay? He's going to start blowing the horn and everyone'll be looking at us.

—They're too stoned. Was it sad saying goodbye to him?

I was saying this from the outside. I never had said goodbye to anyone and I never had fallen in love.

—He's nice and everything but it wasn't permanent. Come on, Sheiley. Jo wove her hands into a ladder step for me below.

—I'm going to jump. I jumped and dust rose. I slapped my hands. I said, Well, it was fun being taller than you for five minutes of my life.

We started to walk. You seem kind of sad, Jo said.

I felt the throat pain. I didn't really want someone else to tell me I needed plastic surgery on my face. I said, Well, I don't want to start school.

—Ladies, the reverend said, his hand on the swinging silver door bus handle. We climbed up the steps. He said, The Gary Indiana Chamber of Commerce would be thrilled beyond belief, Sheila, if they could have a picture of you enjoying their city so. Are you sure you don't want to stay here?

—No.

He swung shut the bus door. He was this hippie reverend at the Nissequott Presbyterian Church and everyone was getting stoned the whole way west. He said, No you want to stay or no you want to go?

I moved up the bus aisle.

—Women, he said. She ignores me.

Ma hit off the panelling and hit the banister again, Dad behind, pushing her up the stairs, Ma with her face totally bruised and deformed with stitches flying out and the banister boinging back and forth, trying to guide her so as not to hit against the banister again but also not to hit the wall and smash her head on our planter for plastic plants.

—Ma, this is so funny, I called out. I can't stop laughing. It was July, Ma's eye bruising eased from dark to oleomargarine colored. Ma came through the gate in her sunglasses and her new black and white two piece holding Newsday. I held up Catch-22, which began with Yossarian lying in a hospital during a war. From across the road came hammering.

—Oh, Christ, I love that book, Ma said. Sicko, isn't it?

—I'm crying laughing, I said.

—Listen, Ma said and I heard the hammers pounding across our road. You want to barrel up to Fabric Bonanza with me?

—Ma, you're going out in public? You still have your stitches in.

—The hell with it, Ma said. I'll go Looney Tunes sitting around here. Come on, let's move, man.

—Wait, wait! Give me the paper, s'il vous plait.

They went on invisible hammering across the road amid the thin stick splints of new house frames, the pause of one finding a new nail, the others hammering, then the silence of two or one and sometimes the beating of all three, then one, two, the third, then three, abrupt one, then silence, then all three beginning again. Before Mr. Hanrahan moved out this spring the builder installed a new improved brighter streetlight for his new houses where once we had had woods and ponds. Three times in the middle of the night Mr. Hanrahan got up and shot the new streetlight out and next day you could see the kids on their banana seaters circling around the glass and when the builder came knocking on each of our doors asking who could it be everyone including Dad said they had no idea. So he quit with the light.

I said, Thanks be to God they're hammering over there, otherwise the silence would really get to me.

—What silence? Ma pulled another towel off the line, folding it.

—The silence of Mr. Hanrahan not shooting anymore.

—Dang it all, I said. Ma stopped, holding her folded towel pile and her black stitches flaring out. You had to develop an excited leading way to get her to stop and listen to you. I said, Everyday, day after day I look for more on that break in at Democratic headquarters. I think Nixon did it and I hope he gets impeached.

Ma'e eyes flicked away under the brown pale stain of her sunglasses, like lake water, not sea or pool, like from that summer upstate long ago.

—I'll meet you in the car in five. Ma walked away, bored.

To me the President impeached was exciting. I thought

276

maybe I'm crazy. Maybe I make up things of excitement. I just thought if the President ordered a break in at Democratic headquarters that would be a big deal but Ma just walked away.

—Nothing on the break in at Democratic headquarters. I threw Newsday in front of Annie. She kept reading Sports Ill. She had the fan on low. There were the shelves over her head and our dictionary and Ma's glass swan gliding on a mirror, going nowhere. I thought how come no one else cares about what Nixon did?

—What are you standing there for? Annie said.

—Nothing. Just thinking.

I had no idea what any of them thought about my face.

—Would you mind not standing so close? Annie looked up at me.

I turned and walked out. I went in the bathroom and as usual cried.

—Sheila. Ma was knocking on the bathroom door.

I shut the water off which I turned on to cover my noise. I was leaned, dripping water off my face into the sink.

—What?

—I'm going to the car.

—Okay. I'll be right there.

Then I could sense her waiting outside the door. I turned the cold on again, trying to sense down the bloat.

I walked out our front screen door. All the woods across the road were bulldozed down and our two ponds filled but I heard there was a spring the builder couldn't find that kept flooding up. All clear, I said. I felt very tired.

—Ma, why Fabric Bonanza? Why not Sew What's New?

—Fabric Bonanza is pleasanter, I think.

I laughed, very tired, laughing toward the grooves of our glove compartment, my head shaking and jittering just over the windshield edge as running came those two german shepherds toward their fence. Fabric Bonanza was in Stony

Point, so I guess my friendship with Isobel had at least changed something for Ma. I said, Ma, why do you care if it's pleasanter? You're just going to hide out in the car.

Ma cleared her throat, unrolled her window and rolled it back slightly more. STOP it said in very bright red. I sat staring forward and we turned. Ma put her directional on. We turned up away from the house marked 1700, proceeding up that hill in summertime.

—There's the Indian, I said.

—Oh, cripes, that rat's ass. And swinging wildly, tires screeching, Ma floored it west on 37A, the car coming straight at us blaring its horn, its grill abruptly plummeting, uuuurht, Ma speeding wildly toward our town's rolled Rug Works billboard in red.

—Ma! Behind, retreating forward in the telescoping back window scene, the Indian swung his arms striding hard forward retreating from us along that thin dirt path. I said, Ma, you want to get us killed? I laughed.

—That goddamn balloon, Ma said.

Ma had this wildly bent hat and black stitches flaring out around yellow oleoed eyes, her bruising aged now, Ma moving through time, and I remembered that happy time of Aunt Rita's Maybelline party and the next morning in front of the bathroom mirror Ma demonstrating black eyeliner which she wore everyday forever after. None of the other kids could stand to be near her now looking like this.

Ma said, I didn't tell you about him?

—What?

—Oh, Christ. I was sitting in my classroom one day after school, I think it was in June. I was sitting at my desk marking papers swigging a soda and who walks in but him!

I said, He's a custodian.

—Well, I was startled. I said hello, can I help you? He said hello, Mrs. Gray, I want to warn you I'm with the FBI and the CIA and I've been assigned to follow you.

Ma looked at me, then back at the road.

—Well, Ma said, I'm glad you're getting a laugh. Christ, I swear to God. All I could think was the kids'll walk in tomorrow at ten to eight and they'll find my goddamn body on the floor. SECOND GRADE TEACHER SLAIN IN HER OWN CLASSROOM.

I was bent over, laughing. I said, Ma, you should be flattered, the FBI and the CIA.

—Christ! Beyond Ma's profile passed the ground broken for a new Nissequott Post Office.

—So, what'd you do?

—I didn't know what the hell to do! All I had was a goddamn red pen for a weapon. I just said that's nice and I grabbed my pock and walked straight out the door, straight across the playground, and I zoomed home. I told Daddy and he got on the phone to administration right away. Goodbye! Ma sang. That dingbat's up sweeping the floors at the district office now.

—Ma, I said, that poor guy.

—That poor guy! What about me? Forget it with the poor guy.

—It's sad.

—Yes, Ma said. It is sad.

LID NEL, the empty train trestle passed by. I had this pain of something larger inside my throat. We passed the train station and Ma turned us right and shut our engine off, parked.

—Why are we here? I said.

—I need some navy blue bias tape. Ma was plucking chaotic dollars. Here. She threw at me.

I flattened them. I said, This is too much.

—Take it, Ma said. You never know.

Boom, the farmer's cannon went and outside our classroom windows, wide open, no glass, black specks floated up, scared, and disappeared. You think it could be settled just look straight in the mirror yes or no decide. Your face is deformed or not. I really did not know how bad my face was. Boom, the cannon went, and the birds flew up again out of the field, still vast green out there in September and still good deep red tomatoes and sweet corn which Dad always got for us. I had no idea what Dad thought about my face. Boom, the scarecrow went. Our old friend Pythagoras, Mr. Steinberg said. He wiggled his gray gas station glass and sipped in the quiet gray classroom dim, our fluorescent lights off, boom, easier on my face. Number six, he said, meaning his glasses of water diet. The black specks lifted. He snapped his fingers. He said, Did you hear the news? Delicate finger polite tugged again downward straining his shirt over his flesh. The birds lifted from the field. He said, The war is over.

—What war? I said without raising my hand.

—What war? The Vietnam War. What other war is there? He laughed and sipped again. He said, The government just announced all American troops are being withdrawn. Boom, it went and Mr. Steinberg sipped, hardly taking any at all. I remembered that black and white in LIFE of a sailor bending a girl backwards to kiss and in the background a million hats lofting in the air for peace, before. Of course, Mr. Steinberg said, some find it suspicious that this comes how many weeks until Election Day?

I walked through our gate, the train roaring east to Port Sands, beginning of the line, our crabapple, September, stunned red in spots and our cherry tree was gone. They chopped it down because it dropped cherries which stained our granite. Our Bahamian Sunset rose was still in bloom. I never got to the Sacre Coeur, made of white marble in Montmartre, some arrondissement, the secret of a red heart beating inside all the white. But when the Presbyterian Youth Group drove west we stopped in Wilmette, Illinois, driving past all these houses and driveways and lawns, and we pulled up suddenly to a huge white marble dome which was the

Baha'i Temple of all the world's faiths with nine sides and nine rose gardens and everyone went inside for the tour except me. I didn't think they would ever put all the world's faiths in one place. All the benches were carved of rock. I sat on one alone. Rose was my only flower I could draw and the green thin sticks had such thorns and next to that a white marble church of all the world's faiths and all this such a lovely accident, it felt for a moment as if I'd met God.

Our filter still churned in September, kept on until the last summer moment of tomorrow when our pool would be closed. Ma had on her red Macy's sweater, cooler and cooler after supper when they sat out. The bags sagged below Dad's eyes. The train roared eastward toward the beginning and ending of the line.

Out of nowhere in the dark comes a bellowing roar, Lucy, Ricky, Ethel, and Fred clinging to the folded edges of their sheets, lying wide eyed in the dark as their beds skate across the floor.

—Hiyah, babe.

And Ma stopped talking at this.

—You can make an appointment with Howie for me.

Ma swallowed loudly, the liquid siphoning down through her. She leaned, stiffened to set her cup. If she made one false move I was going to attack her. Dad cleared his throat and lit a cigarette. I had deliberately said this in front of him so he would have to take a stance.

—I'm not saying yes to the operation. All I'm saying is you can make an appointment. Get it?

I glared at her.

Ma reached for the cigarettes and Dad slid them helpfully. Dad cleared his throat again, our filter constantly running on. He said, Is that what you want, babe?

It was not what I wanted. It was not what I wanted at all. I just wanted to grow up and forget about it and move somewhere far away. Dad's deep dark brown eyes looked at me, the bags under his eyes more or less subdued in the waning evening light. The sun was gone. The water steadily lapped. My throat. Ma sat with her arms crossed watching off at something. The weights bulged underneath my eyes. Ma was trying not to move because if she made too large a movement she might teetering affect my balance, splat, I would say NO WAY. The pool filter pushed on. The season was about to change. I turned and walked away without answering him.

Whap-a whap-a, the windshield wipers beat frantic in the November driving rain. We all live in a Yellow Submarine, we all lived in yellow safety slickers when it rained standing at the bus stop. Ma and I rode past the bus stop. Whap-a whap-a, south from Nissequott. A string of blackbirds hunched drenched along a black telephone line.

—I think you'll really like Howie. He's such a doll.

Leaves fell, red and yellow rescue colors, help, splat. One whapped and stuck against our glass, the wiper moving dumbly over and over it. Nixon had beaten McGovern yesterday in every state except one.

—Ma, you remember my second grade teacher, Mrs. White?

—Oh, yeah, with the two different color eyes.

—Yeah.

In the November near dark the pastels of Tanglewood split levels sogged. I heard Marianne Gilhooley let this combination dirtball jock shave her legs.

—What made you think of her?

—Oh, I said, once we were having a lesson on the signs of spring and she said one sign was red-winged blackbirds.

Whap-a whap-a.

—That's it? Ma said. That's the story?

—Yes.

I leaned my head on the window. We passed the cornfield, the boarded farm stand, the high school where Jo was spiking volleyballs without me today. Actually there was way more. Just when that teacher said red-winged black-birds were a sign of spring a whole entire flock of red-winged blackbirds in real life landed on the puddle outside our strangely lit cement block room and running we all went to press against the glass and watch in the pitched dark driving middle March rain at the whole happy flock outside our school, the opposite in meaning of that bird gathering scene in Alfred Hitchcock outside the school.

—You ever hear from Isobel anymore?

—Yeah. Sometimes.

—She is such a pretty girl, isn't she?

—Yeah. Ma, could you please roll your window down? You're choking me to death.

Ma rolled it down a bit and rolled it immediately back up.

—Ma.

—Oh, shit. She rolled it back down a little.

—What do you think I'm stupid? I said.

Whap-a whap-a. We passed dead orange neon GRANT'S with plywood boards FUCK YOU in black spray paint.

—What do you think you're the Witch of the West and you'll melt in water? I said.

Ma cleared her throat and I laughed. She puffed on her cigarette. We passed Billy Blake's, also now boarded because of the mall.

—This reminds me of going to the allergist's.

—Why? Ma shouted.

Whap-a whap-a.

—Why do you think? I'm going to see a doctor about my face. I glared at her.

—Oh, God, Ma said. I can't believe the crap you remember. Give me a break.

—I did not like going to that guy, I said.

I watched again those long strung black telephone lines and I was trying to remember how long ago those red wet flames beat on the birds' arrival spring wings. In plays there used to be deus ex machina, actually a machine wing contraption that lifted the person out of danger on the stage.

—Howie is nothing like that guy, Ma said. That guy was a fool. He didn't know what the hell he was doing, testing you for all those allergies. I could not believe what he did to you.

I stared at her. I said, What do you mean?

—I couldn't believe what your arms looked like after you got out of there.

—What did my arms look like?

—You don't remember? Christ? They were completely red. You were crying!

—I was crying? I don't remember that.

—I swear to God, then he wanted you to come in for the shots once a week. What a load of crap.

—Well, I always wondered why you didn't take me in for those shots. But then what was it with the pillowcase?

—What pillowcase?

—The plastic pillowcase that was crackling under my head for about eight years.

Ma reached and ground her cigarette out. She reached inside her pock and slid another out.

—Who the hell knows, Ma said.

Whap-a whap-a. We passed the mall, just opened. You got to ride in golf carts driven by old men because only the department stores at four ends were opened so far: Father (A&S) Son (Macy's) and Holy (Sears) Ghost (tropical birds in a giant cage).

I said, I think he was just testing my arms for what I was allergic to and he had to break the skin.

—That's crap! Crap, Ma said. You do not do that to a little kid. I mean, Sheila, get real, would you!

Ma glared at me.

I opened my window. Bits of rain hit my face. I said, Could you open your window, please?

Ma unrolled her window and rolled it back up. She said, I tell you though, Howie is completely different. Completely. I think you're really going to like him.

—Could you open your window and really open your window?

Ma clicked her tongue and rolled it down and left it. She said, I have complete faith in Howie. Complete. You know what I like about him?

—No.

—He takes time out to laugh. I really admire that. We all need a break once in a while. Christ. I'd be Looney Tunes if I let the pressure get to me. Looney Tunes, Sheila, I'm telling you. I really admire Howie's attitude. He's got his pool, his gorgeous house. Ma rolled her window back up. She said, His attitude is, hey, I am not going to let these goddamn fools get to me. Numero uno, man.

—Your window.

—Oh, she said and rolled it down a bit. Numero uno. Looking out for number one. He takes good care of himself. His attitude toward the rest of the world is screw you, I'm enjoying myself, and I admire that. I really do. Ma rolled her window back up.

I looked down at our directions in Ma's handwriting on October menu paper supposedly orange but more creamy apricot. LIE west Exit 56. Whap-a.

—I told you about Howie and the gardening, right?

I turned on the radio and switched away Ma's faggy music station.

—I didn't tell you about Howie and the gardening?

—No. You can tell me Howie and the gardening if you roll your window down.

Ma made a face. She said, Howie cannot even rake his own leaves. Do you believe that? She rolled it down a bit.

—Yes, I said. I got it to ABC and stopped.

—His hands swell. He told me! He tried raking one Saturday just to get a little exercise and his hands swol up so bad he couldn't go back into O.R. for three days. He has to hire someone to do all the sanneefrannee around the house! Ma looked at me.

—Well, at least he makes a good salary, I said.

Ma cleared her throat and looked off. The black windshield wipers whapped back and forth.

—I tell you, Ma said, maybe I'm naive, but the more I get to know Howie the more I admire how he's set up his life. Very little stress. Zippo with the stress, man.

The headlights coming at us were split crying soft yellow wet down the glass. The clear streams zagged and stopped down our windows slanting painfully this way and that.

—Ma, I think you should put your lights on.

—Oh. She put her cigarette in her mouth and squinted leaning, concentrating, steering in the dark divided highway, speeding traffic behind and toward us, westbound on the LIE, Ma concentrated steering us in our lane with one hand, pulled the lights on with the other, Ma extremely nervous about driving anywhere outside of Nissequott.

—Now, could you read me those directions? You're going to be my navigator, right? Please!

—We got a ways to go, don't worry, Ma. I read the bottom of her paper and laughed.

—You're laughing? Ma said. What are you laughing at?

—I can't believe his office is on Hospital Road.

—Oh. Well, that's just the service road, Ma said.

I looked at her and laughed, basically laughing at my life. I turned up the radio. It was a woman singing.

Time was old, from September, of them running with their submachine guns along the Munich, West Germany, 1972 Olympics dormitory tiers. You could feel this sense over you everywhere around of before and after color photographs pinned all over his waiting room walls. The central table was circular. I said, Ma, why don't you read a magazine?

Ma sat highly flustered on the edge of her chair, her pocketbook strap crossed very longish over the chair arm. She said, Maybe I will.

Only Family Circle and Better Homes and Gardens were left because I had grabbed the only decent magazine there. The outside door opened. I had this sense of three walking in but you don't want to look in case their deformity problem was really bad.

—Here, Ma, I'm done. I handed her Time. I picked up hers.

—Sheila Gray?

I deliberately stayed seated so as to see Ma's reaction.

—That's you!

—Is it? I said.

—Right here, Ma called. Hiyah, I'm Mary Gray, Sheila's mother. How you doing? Ma rushed toward the nurse.

I figured there would be a dried human skull on his desk.

—Hello, Mary. He rose behind his square wood.

—Hiyah, Dr. Weinstein. Thank you for seeing us.

—You're welcome, you're welcome. You must be Sheila. He reached to shake my hand. Oh yeah, the old pretending she's an adult act. I had a sense don't shake his hand too hard and ruin his surgery. He said, Sit, please.

There was an opposition set up, two one side, one the other, and behind him the white Venetian blinds horizontal, bandaged, across his window.

—You look wonderful, Mary.

—I know it, Ma said. I look fab. I think I look great.

Ma told me before the Hanrahans left separately for California he made Aunt Rita play Russian roulette holding a gun to her head and pulling the trigger, but I never saw that. I felt sick she let him do that to her.

—I never expected such good results, Dr. Weinstein. I'm so pleased.

—Good. If you're pleased, I'm pleased.

To the right of the window diplomas hung on the wall.

—So now, Sheila, what can I do for you?

I looked down at my hands, holding each other for

comfort. I wanted actually to just check those diplomas to make sure this guy was not a fraud. Say it's a movie and the doctor says excuse me a second and leaves the room then quick knock Ma unconscious with a trophy or paperweight and check the diplomas and just as you hear footsteps revive her fast with smelling salts and turn smiling again as he walks back in the room.

—Robert, I said.

Robert sat in July 1973 with the fan on low, tied with twine to hang in our living room window, Robert reading Treasure Island at the couch end where once he knelt moving Batman figures saying pow and whap.

—Robert, it's time for your final daily quiz.

—What quiz?

I sat and gently took his hand. At the head of the stairs was our family's only overnight case with inside my summer no sleeve nightgown Ma made me with collar lace, my toothbrush end wrapped in waxed paper, Breck's shampoo for normal hair in a former aspirin bottle, and nothing for me to read.

—Now, Robert, if one of my friends, say Jo, if Jo calls and asks to talk to me, what are you going to say?

—You're in Connecticut visiting relatives.

—Good. I patted his hand, his fanning finger bones and thin skin flesh. I put Robert's hand between the two of mine, patting the top, actually acting like he was the one going to the hospital for an operation. He picked up his Treasure Island again. I never read it and I never wanted to. I slid, the fan turning on low, and laid my head on my little brother's shoulder bone so I could feel him breathe, more strenuous now with braces on, fighting for the air. At night in total dark you could walk through and hear them all breathing in and out and see them lying each in their beds wrapped in white, their hearts beating quietly as their lungs worked on. The fan spun on, blurring in our window. Behind, the train went by. Our usual vases shook. I was about to go to the hospital. The fan sped and slowed with a breeze and from downstairs the TV voices welled and passed over our banister. Down my ribs sweat trickled and behind the wall, hidden, our kitchen clock moved forward in time.

—You girls better hurry up. Mrs. Harrison stood at the far pink locker funnel end in her baby blue uniform with her deep brown-black skin.

—We got to look like beauty queens, Mrs. H, Jo said.

—Yeah, you girls better just get to the game, never mind beauty queens. She disappeared in the pink.

Jo's hands moved steadily at the small of my back. She said, So tell me your secret already, Sheiley.

I said, I had plastic surgery on my face this summer. I twisted to look at her.

Jo blinked behind her spectacles. She said, You did?

—On my eyes. The bags under my eyes, and on top.

Her hands moved at the small of my back.

—You couldn't tell?

—Not really.

—Look. Can you see? I stared at her.

She shrugged. I twisted facing forward again. I said, You can tell more in the light. Then you can see my scars. Kathy Riordan bugs me every day that I have pinkeye and I should go to the doctor. Can you see any scars? I twisted back.

—A little bit. Not really though. You know my sister said she thought something was different about your face. Okay, Sheiley, that's the best I can do.

I turned completely around toward her. I said, I'm sure it's perfect. You always tie them perfect. I just feel bad you have to have me tie yours. I'm not good at this picky stuff. I sat on the bench and Jo turned her back. We had on our mustard colored hockey tunics that made us look like Roman gladiators and our only hope was to have a good bow in back. I said, Jo, did your sister say if my face was better or worse?

—She didn't say either. She just said something looked different.

—Oh, great, I said, after all that.

—When did you do this?

—Last summer. Remember when I told you I was going to Connecticut for three weeks to see my relatives? I never went to Connecticut, I went to the hospital.

—I was wondering why you kept talking about Connecticut. You were talking about Connecticut all the time.

—Okay. There's your bow. It's only slightly deformed.

—My bow doesn't matter as much. You got to look good for Blue Alert.

I slammed my locker and locked the lock, my stomach in a total state. I forgot about him. Passing out along the pink rows way in back Mrs. Harrison sat in her baby blue uniform and her dark brown skin sitting in a white plastic chair in all the pink crocheting white yarn into some form.

—Yeah, I said, the thing that gets me is how could he really like me if he didn't like me last year before I had plastic surgery?

—Maybe he did.

—I doubt it. He doesn't like me now anyway. I changed the subject. I said, Isobel knows I had it. I asked her advice like two years ago, should I have it or shouldn't I? I totally didn't know what to do. I was a wreck, man.

—What'd Isobel say?

—She said do what you want. That was a lot of help.

Jo nodded, the glasses of her spectacles tinting off so I couldn't really see her opinion—yes surgery or no, no surgery—as we climbed the stairs. Jo said, How did you ever think of it?

—I didn't. My mother did.

Jo stared.

I said, Did you ever think I had bags under my eyes? We were stopped at the top of the stairs with pink surrounding cement walls.

—I don't know, Sheiley. I think I got it too. Maybe I should have that operation.

—Your eyes are beautiful, Jo. I really like your eyes. I opened the door. I said, Don't do it. Believe me, it's not worth it. Just stay regular.

We passed the girls sports bulletin board with a diagram of the hockey team and all our names and the headline over it, The Whole is Greater Than the Sum of Its Parts, put up by our coach. Parts still reminded me of surgery. It took me like two weeks walking by that everyday to figure out she meant that as encouraging.

—Blue Alert, Jo said. Hiyah, Mr. Nesbitt. Jo had snotted her voice like a fat lady from a development in curlers pushing a stroller through the mall.

—Hello, Joanne. Hello, Sheila. He stared at me and I burst into a sweat. He said, You girls got a big game, huh?

—A real biggie, Jo said.

He smiled, staring at me. We were holding our shinguards and cleats and hockey sticks standing in our Roman uniforms, my armpits and hands totally in a sweat.

—Did you hear Agnew resigned? I said.

Jo snorted. I stared at her and she stopped. He looked back and forth, smiling, like maybe this was a code.

—I mean Agnew really resigned, I said.

—I heard. He grinned at me.

—Jo, I said, did you hear that?

—I forget, she said. He resigned?

—Yeah. This afternoon? I looked at him.

—Yeah, as far as I know this afternoon. He was smiling at me.

I really did not know what the hell this guy was so happy about.

—Well, you never know, Jo said. Do you, Sheiley?

I looked at her and she stared at me.

—Well, I wish I could watch you girls play today.

—You have practice? I said.

—You know what they say. He grinned. Practice makes perfect.

I laughed a bit. Jo just stared. He had a whistle around his neck and the clock over the exit said twenty after three.

—Sheiley, we better hit the road. We got to pick up glass off the field.

—You girls are tough, he said.

—Bye, Mr. Nesbitt, Jo said.

—Bye, I said.

—Sheila.

I turned. I walked back to him. We were standing almost in the middle of the gym, the cross country team walking by and also David Weitzen sitting on the bleachers watching us.

—Can I give you a lift home?

You could tell he was older the way he called it lift.

I said, What about your wife following us with the camera?

He said, That wasn't her in that car. I made a mistake.

The football team started to come out in their shoulder pads. I couldn't tell if he was lying she ever followed us or if he was lying now she wasn't.

—Yeah, okay. I'll meet you at the car. I have to think of some lie to tell Jo about the late bus. Goodbye. I looked at him. He was looking at me, smiling. I said, You know what?

—What? He lifted his chin toward me, smiling.

—I got a hundred thirty-five out of a hundred on my chemistry test.

He laughed. I had a pretty good idea what could make him laugh. I said, Really really goodbye.

—Goodbye. He smiled and I turned away. Sheila, he said and my stomach lifted and sank. I turned back. He said, Good luck in your game.

—Thank you. We'll probably get killed. They're from the middle of the island.

Jo sat on the speckled hall floor, wafts of chlorine and invisible splashing rising up the basement stairs. Out the doors the cannon boomed and within the white frame, the frame split by white, the black specks winged up bunched then broke apart. I sat to buckle my shinguards.

—Sheiley, who's Agnew? Her eyes were blanked about us staying together after she left.

—Vice president of the country.

—Oh, yeah, I knew I heard of that guy from somewhere. Here, she said. She held out her hockey stick and I grasped the curve and she pulled me up. She said, I hope we don't get slaughtered to death today.

The cannon boomed and the blackbirds lifted off, unframed, from the browning stalks, straight up into the unending blue sky. Muted came the whacking of hockey balls against the wood and softly in a distant dream less violent girls lofted tennis balls sweetly back and forth.

I set our flowered overnight case on the blue-black slate. Dad came to the top of the stairs to say goodbye to me. I said, Wait, and I went downstairs to kiss Michael goodbye. The Watergate hearings were on TV. I bent and kissed him lightly, sleeping on the couch. He turned and leapt throwing his arms around me. Bye, I said, I'll see you in two days. He didn't say anything but kept his arms hugged around me. On the mantel was that double framed picture of Michael and me in our geometric print sun suits in black and white. It's okay, I said. Michael hugged me harder. I love you, he said. And I laughed a little because I didn't want to cry. Okay, I said, I got to go.

I started up the stairs. Dad came to the top of the banister, throwing his striped towel over his shoulder. Ma came down the stairs. She said, I'll meet you in the car and she picked up my overnight bag, like a bellboy.

—So what is it? Dad said. Dad wanted to know what meal I wanted when I got back from the hospital.

—I don't know, I said. It's with the ham and the swiss cheese in the middle.

—I'll look it up in Fannie Farmer, Dad said.

Annie appeared from the hall. She put her hand on Dad's shoulder. She said, Dad would be lost without his Fannie Farmer. Dad made a face and nodded in Annie's direction.

I really didn't feel that much. I said, Dad, I might not feel like eating right away.

—You'll eat! Dad said.

—Tell Howie drink a lot of orange juice, Annie said.

—Orange juice? Robert said moving across the living room holding Treasure Island.

—Forget it. I'll tell you later, Annie said.

He needed it for energy during my operation.

Robert stopped behind the top banister line and below behind the bottom banister Michael watched me, the TV voice travelling on.

—Well, goodbye everyone, I said. I'll see you guys in two days.

—Bye, Sheila, Robert said and Dad was coming down the stairs with his hands out the width of my head, puckering his lips, and I saw Annie standing up there steadily watching straight in my eyes.

—Well, Dr. Weinstein said, I suppose you already know a little about the procedure since your mother had it done.

I was looking really at the edge of the desk and the white Venetian blinds behind. I was wondering if it was mahogany like the most beautiful boats at Port Sands sometimes when they took us down to run on the docks.

—Maybe, it would help, Ma said, if you could tell her what to expect in terms of appearances if she had the bag job. Ma cleared her throat and totally readjusted her pocketbook strap which snaked the other way on her lap.

He walked around his vast impressive rich mahogany desk and stood, my eyes level at his crotch. He said, Let's see, Sheila. I looked up. I learned Pavlov's dog in Ma's psychology book. He reached down toward me and pat pat, gently he patted below my eyes. I never thought he would touch me so softly.

He pressed lightly under my eyes, like you test a cake to see if it is done. He said, There does appear to be some herniation. He moved off. He said, How do you feel about the surgery?

I lifted my shoulders. My throat hurt too much and I was holding my breath not to cry.

—Well, Howie said, it couldn't hurt to take a picture. This way if she decides to have it, you save yourself a trip, right?

—That's a good idea, doctor, Ma said.

—Sheila, why don't you stand against that wall?

I stood against the wall. Ma was trying not to look at me having a humiliating Before picture taken.

Nesbitt dropped me off at the bus stop and I walked up our driveway with my mouth like rubbed raw red from kissing and I walked up the stairs where Dad was cutting things up. Dad turned right away. He said, Hey, babe, did you win? Across the road now all the houses were built some even already calmed with lawns and a Mayflower moving van was backed up the Hanrahans' driveway, letting a different family out. Sometimes I felt like sending Aunt Rita a postcard in California about my face.

—Is it five o'clock? I said. It was supposed to be five o'clock in the morning when they woke me up and I wanted everything to go right. I was hoping it was a male nurse who would give me my shot in the behind. Roll over, Sheila, they said. Am I getting a shot? I said. Then they rolled me over. Ooo, I said. They rolled me back. I was lying in white sheets in the hospital. We're going to transfer you, Sheila. I said, Okay. I had a lot more to say but I couldn't. I realized this new bed came on wheels. You're very helpful, they said. Then they wheeled me along.

The hallway ceiling swung like a chandelier, also the walls. I was in a hospital. One was in front and one behind like the guards wheeling me along. When Ma brought me to the hospital my roommate had grabbed the window one right away. Mastectomy I figured. She was watching General Hospital, which was very brave.

—I'm going to be blindfolded. I won't be able to see for twenty-four hours, I said to the old lady in solid pink renting TVs though to me I always thought those Candy Stripers were in red and white and young. I said, I'll be blindfolded for twenty-four hours so I don't want a TV. She didn't seem to want to talk about it. I felt reassured to have upbringable guardrails on my bed.

Lugging my face welted and bruised with black stitches flying out, lugging I set Ma's sewing machine on our red picnic table. I went back in for the extension cord. I set it with my back to the tracks and my back to the steady movement of the sun since Howie said stay out of the sun and I tended to obey. I had on Dad's old Tinker National Bank great kelly green baseball hat and sunglasses with wild black monstrous stitches flying out. I pinned my material in repeating rows of flowers, solid, plaid, checks. I was making a quilt for my bed. One good thing I lost a lot of weight from my operation. All your weight's in your legs, Ma always said and now if I could just starve and only eat a yogurt for lunch then I would stay as skinny as need be.

They parked me on the side of the wall, everyone in requisition green, like in a hospital on TV. They had parked my stretcher for the guards to rest. I looked for a no parking sign but none. The most serious category would have been NO STANDING. I got one wrong on the written. What does an orange triangle mean? Slow moving vehicle, dummy. They started me up again, sliding past an angry old man. He was angry because I was young and I still had a chance. He was Mr. Death and he just missed me in O.R.

—You laughing? Sheila?

—Yes. The guard was laughing too and I would go out on a date with him later this afternoon maybe if he wanted if he was the one who gave me the shot in the behind.

He said, What's so funny, Sheila?

He was repeatedly using my name to reassure me I was still alive and this was only surgery. I knew their tricks. I said, Operating room. I was looking at the gold on black words upside down and why I was laughing was after all those years what O.R. really meant.

—Open your eyes, Sheila.

I opened my eyes. The prince kisses her. He had a mask on just like in a movie.

—That's a good girl, Dr. Weinstein said.

—Is that the fat? I said.

—That's it.

The tweezers were silver blurry and a blurry white like wet cotton held between. It seemed kind of sad after all these years.

—Okay, roll your eyes back, Sheila. That's a good girl.

—Everything is blurry. I was alerting him in case things were wrong and we were a team and God was punishing me for being vain.

—That's okay, he said. That's the way it's supposed to be.

All these faces with green masks peered down at me.

—I'm really tired. Can I go to sleep?

—In a few minutes, Sheila. I need your cooperation. Be a good girl and roll your eyes back.

—Okay. But then can I go to sleep?

—Yes.

—I'm very tired.

—Okay, Sheila, you can go to sleep now.

—Goodbye, I said.

I walked in the kitchen where she stood alone, putting her cigarette in her ashtray, about to scrub Dad's meatloaf pan. I said, Ma. Ma turned. She had the pink foam Brillo pad ready to work, looking at me with her head against the window. You just give up. You get backed up and backed up and you'll just do anything to get away. I said, I'll have the operation. Her eyes lit up. I swung up my hand before she could talk. I said, I will have the operation but I don't ever ever want to talk about it again. Ever ever in my life. Got it?

I still had my hand up.

Ma cleared her throat. Okay, she said. I'll give Howie a call.

—I don't want to hear about Howie. I was moving my hand as I talked. I don't want to hear you called him or where he cuts or what kind of scalpel or whether he drinks orange juice or grapefruit juice. I don't want to know anything. I turned and walked out.

My favorite thing to read used to be those Ayds weight reducing ads where you eat candy like a Kraft caramel and all their struggles and most especially the Before and After shots and how the Before she's just really fat sitting near a picnic table little knowing she's a Before specimen for Ayds. Or it's taken near an above ground pool with the corrugated metal around like we had before we got our built in, when the four of you, brothers and sisters, stood north south east west and you moved around the pool, lifting up your thighs, struggling against the water weight, faster and faster around and around then I say, okay, float!, and we all four lie circling in the whirlpool we have made as the Long Island Railroad cuts straight by.

When I was inside my bandages I didn't know keep my eyes opened or closed. I was inside a wall of white bandages. I could tell from elevation I was sitting up in bed. My hands were wet and sweat trickled down my chest onto my sheet.

I twisted my sheet in my hand. I could hear sounds all around.

—Sheila?

I turned my head, listening.

—Sheila?

—Annie? I reached out. Someone took it and it was Annie. She said, Mom's here and Dad said to say hi.

I thought Dad's not here? I said, Ma?

Annie said, She's outside talking to the nurse. And Annie held my hand. She said, How do you feel?

I said, It really hurts.

—Hiyah.

I said, Ma? I reached out.

—Hiyah, babe. Ma gripped my hand. Ma said, How you doing?

I said, it hurts.

—What hurts?

—My face hurts.

—Your face hurts? It's not supposed to hurt.

—It hurts.

—Howie said no pain at all.

—It hurts her. I could hear Annie somewhere behind. Annie said, Where does it hurt, Sheila?

I motioned across underneath my eyes.

—It's not supposed to hurt, Ma said.

—What are you going to argue with her? Annie said.

—Oh, Jesus, Ma said. Nurse! My daughter's in pain here.

—She's not supposed to be in pain, someone said.

—Well she is, Annie said and laughed.

—Look at her, Ma said. She's in pain.

—You can tell I'm in pain? I said.

—You're white as a ghost, Ma said. Look at her, she's crying.

—How can you tell? I said.

—It's coming under your bandages, Ma said.

—I have no authorization to give any medication, some-one said.

—She's in pain, Ma said. I'm calling Howie. This is for the birds.

Ma let go of my hand and I reached. I said, Annie? Annie held my hand. I could describe every skin thing of my sister Annie's hand. She said, Sheila, I brought you the kitchen radio. I figured you can listen to Watergate.

—Oh, thank you, I said.

—Let me plug it in. I got to let go of your hand.

I heard her moving and something was laid on my bed then lifted. I said, There's a plug like two inches to the left of the night table. See it?

The radio came on, off.

—Yes, she said.

—How is Dad going to cook without his radio?

—He'll survive.

I was kind of shocked Dad hadn't come to visit me in the hospital. I said, What's he making for supper for you guys tonight?

—Beef bourguignon.

—Howie was shocked that you're in pain.

Ma was back in the room.

—He's sending a pain killer right away. You'll be in la la land before you know what hit you.

—Where are you? I reached and Ma gripped my hand. Ma had a more thinnish hand from years and years of work.